I AM
SOPHIE TUCKER

3/29/15

HI DIANA,

THANKS FOR COMING!

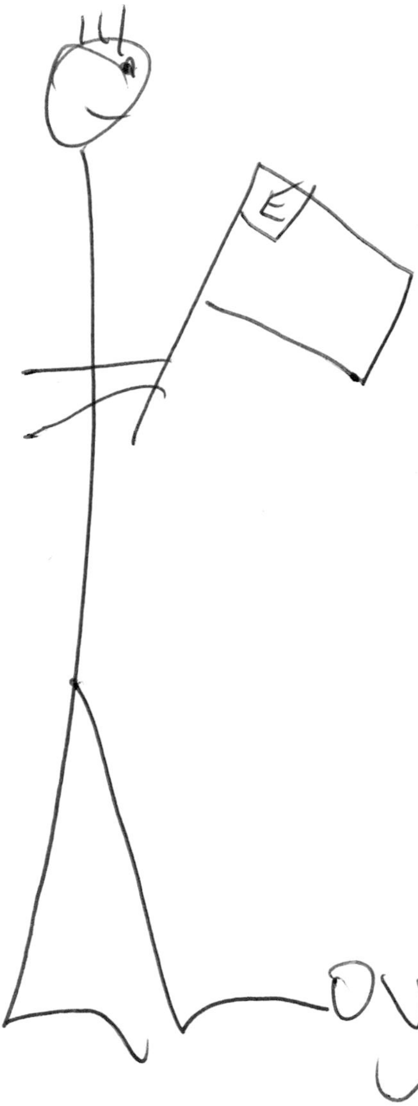

Sue
+
oyd ecker

I AM
SOPHIE TUCKER

A FICTIONAL MEMOIR

FROM THE PRODUCERS OF
The Outrageous
SOPHIE TUCKER

SUSAN & LLOYD
ECKER

PROSPECTA PRESS

Published by Prospecta Press
P.O. Box 3131
Westport, CT 06880
www.prospectapress.com
(203) 571-0781

Hardcover ISBN 978-1-63226-006-2
eBook ISBN 978-1-63226-008-6
Enhanced eBook ISBN 978-1-63226-007-9

Manufactured in the United States of America

First edition published November 2014

10 9 8 7 6 5 4 3 2 1

Sophie Tucker tended to exaggerate . . . a lot. She recounted multiple versions of every event over her sixty-year career and, after six years of research, the authors could not tell the difference between truth and tall tale. As such, this will be considered a work of fiction. Any references to historical events; to real people, living or dead; or to real locales are intended only to give this work of fiction a setting in historical reality. Other names, characters, and incidents either are the product of the authors' imagination or are used fictitiously, and their resemblance, if any, to real-life counterparts is entirely coincidental.

Any people depicted in stock imagery provided by Thinkstock are models, and such images are being used for illustrative purposes only. Certain stock imagery © Thinkstock.

Because of the dynamic nature of the Internet, any web addresses or links contained in this book may have changed since publication and may no longer be valid. The views expressed in this work are solely those of the authors and do not necessarily reflect the views of the publisher, and the publisher hereby disclaims any responsibility for them.

To Phil Ramone
The coolest guy in heaven!

And to Bette Midler
Best first date ever!
November 9, 1973

Contents

If you're interested in the sights and sounds of Sophie Tucker's life, the enhanced online version of this book includes more than sixty audio and video recordings of performances by the stars mentioned throughout the story. To view them, visit www.sophietucker.com and click on Book Extras.

Prologue

November 1, 1965

The last time I died was probably sixty years ago in some no-name theater in Sheboygan. Back then, when I was new to show business, my act still took a nosedive every once in a while. Now? I bet I could read the phonebook and still pack a theater, but I'm dying for real.

My son of a bitch doctor won't tell me how long I've got left, but I'm pretty sure the wear and tear from smoking three packs a day and decades doing fourteen shows a week won't exactly help extend my run here on Earth.

For an old ham like me, even sixty years of performing isn't enough. I am *not* looking forward to the moment when the last red velvet curtain drops and the spotlight fades into the bright white house lights for good. Before I go, though, I think I deserve my final encore! My audiences always want one more song, a crowd-pleaser belted right to the back rows of the balcony. A real bawdy number that'll leave your ears ringing and all your other bits tingling, too. After all, that's my specialty—and that's what I've done with this book.

The cover of Sophie's autobiography, published by Doubleday in 1945.

I'm sure you're wondering what more Sophie Tucker can possibly have to write about herself. Hasn't it all been covered *ad nauseum?* Well, let me tell you, that so-called autobiography they put out back in 1945 was total horseshit.

It was like a Reuben with no corned beef: bland and cheesy. I gave them thousands of pages of show business dirt, intrigue, romance and murder, every word the absolute truth—or even better! Somehow, they managed to edit it into a snore.

As a matter of fact, those publishers can *kiss* my posterity.

It's because of that watered-down volume of *drek*[1] the studios rejected the movie Betty Hutton would have made about my life. They insisted there weren't enough compelling moments to make a whole film. Please. You could make more movies about what I did last Thursday than MGM released in the last ten years!

From left to right: Betty Hutton, Sophie Tucker, and Tallulah Bankhead celebrate Sophie's fiftieth year in show business.

So, here's what I did. I took all the good stuff they left out and added a few more stories about love affairs, gangsters, presidents, kings, and scandals so hot they would've burned a hole through Doubleday's pages. Then, I wrote the whole thing down, sent the manuscript to my lawyer, and asked him to keep it all sealed up until everyone in this book

1   *Drek* – Garbage.

was safely doing our fifth or sixth encores at the big Palace Theater in the sky.

I do wonder who'll want to crack this book open in fifty years. Will anyone even know who the hell I was? To you, the person who saw a picture of some ridiculous lady with a bunch of feathers in her hair and wondered why she and her four chins were on the cover of this book, please allow me to introduce myself with a story.

In 1928, I was a globetrotting member of Vaudeville royalty. I'd been singing to sold-out crowds in England for six months when Jack Warner, head of the Warner Brothers Studios, called me back to the States. Warner was finally making good on an old promise to turn me into a movie star. I was sure I'd be the next big bombshell of the silver screen (emphasis on the *big*) but when my songwriter Jack Yellen met me at the pier in New York, he was a nervous wreck. Turns out, tastes had changed while I was abroad. Even though my old jazz tunes were killing 'em up and down that wet little isle, in America my act was yesterday's brisket—a little too tough to sell. The powers that be wanted me to come up with a whole new image to reignite the crowds at home. Jack was in a tizzy, but me? I was a cool as a cucumber.

"You have nothing to worry about, Jack," I said, throwing an arm around Yellen's shoulders. "I'll always be a red hot mama and there's no keeping me down. You know why? Because fat floats! And I, my dear, will always float to the top."

That night, Jack and his partner Milton Ager were inspired by our conversation and wrote me a killer new tune that I've been performing ever since, called "The Last of the Red Hot Mamas". That's who I am, kiddo, and that's what this is. Welcome to the last red hot stories from the all-time, number one red hot mama of the stage: yours truly, the outrageous Sophie Tucker.

Part I

Leaving Home

Chapter 1

Ain't She Sweet?

It wasn't until prizefighter Jack Dempsey saw me knock a mouthy bastard flat on his ass that I realized my mama, Jennie Abuza, taught me three things: how to cook, how to work hard, and how to land the perfect uppercut.

When I think of my mother, I imagine her stirring a pot of goulash so tall she could hardly see over the lip. Running Abuza's Family Restaurant meant she delivered the majority of her motherly advice while waving a long wooden spoon in my face. When she wanted a vacation from the sweltering kitchen and from her four screaming brats, she'd retreat upstairs to our sewing room to mend an endless pile of socks and ratty cotton dresses that never quite lost the scent of fried onions. She worked from seven in the morning until well after the rest of us had gone to bed, even on Fridays when other kosher[1] restaurants closed for Shabbos[2]. There were too many hungry Jewish theater actors passing through Hartford, Connecticut to shut down the goulash factory, even for a night. Hanging around all those flamboyant

Jennie Abuza in 1901, age 51.

1   *Kosher* – Jewish dietary laws. For example, meat must come from an animal that chews its cud and has been killed humanely in order to be considered kosher.

2   *Shabbos* – Friday night to Saturday night, designated a full day of rest in the Jewish faith.

actors, I guess you could say that I got a taste of show business pretty early.

When we Abuza kids weren't in school, we spent every waking moment working at the restaurant. From the first day we opened in Hartford, my two brothers, my sister and I each had a job to do in order to keep the business running. Phil, the oldest, was the lucky kid in charge of all the heavy lifting. If there were crates to cart down to the root cellar, barrels of pickles to move or garbage to haul, Phil was our man. Moe, my younger brother, was our busboy. He cleared away the empty plates and Mama's potato peelings so quickly, Hoover should've named its first model "The Moe."

Annie, our littlest sister, was only five years old when Abuza's Family Restaurant opened but no one could slice bread, fill water glasses or serve hot coffee quicker than that little imp. You could barely see her darting between the tables, a cloud of steam from her pitcher of hot black Joe surrounding her little face. She looked like a friendly ghost.

And me? I was the waitress and dishwasher. I handled all fifteen tables and I never dropped so much as a poppy seed on a customer. Old friends from Hartford insist I got my powerful pipes by shouting out orders to my mother all those years, but personally I think the secret is a childhood full of massive doses of schmaltz[3], which is what we call pure chicken fat. Ask my old friend Caruso. I got him to try it and for the next ten years he ate a dish of mashed potatoes schmeared[4] with dollops of the stuff before every performance.

One may think it's fitting that a zaftig[5] broad like me grew up inside a restaurant, but I don't remember snagging even a single errant spaetzle[6] throughout my entire childhood. Come within a foot of the strudel[7] meant for paying customers and you'd get the business end of my mother's ladle. Moe once tried to swipe the heel of an old loaf of pumpernickel and nearly lost an eye. Still, I had a sweet tooth that

3   Schmaltz – Chicken fat.

4   Schmear – A spread; often refers to chicken fat, cream cheese, or butter.

5   Zaftig – Chubby, curvaceous.

6   Spaetzle – A soft egg dumpling common to Eastern Europe.

7   Strudel – A layered pastry, often filled with fruit or other sweet ingredients.

begged for babka[8], so I learned early on to take the long way home after school and schmooze[9] with every shopkeeper along the way.

Until I was six or seven, batting my big brown peepers worked for some penny candy or a small piece of coffee cake. By the time I got a little older—and a little rounder—I knew I had to knock their socks off to earn the top-shelf treats I really wanted. I tried to dance for my delicacies, but I'm about as light on my feet as a plow horse in two sets of iron shoes. Then I remembered that old saying about singing for your supper, so I learned a couple of ditties that seemed to pay off in all the snacks I could stomach.

Some days I would stop at Landi's Bakery and sing something sad for glum old Mrs. Landi. It seemed like she'd give me a piping hot doughnut for every tear that rolled down her wrinkled cheek. Other days, if I felt like sharing with my brothers and sister, I'd swing by and visit my schoolmate John Sudarsky at his family's pharmacy. I'd stand at the drug counter, right at the front of the line of people waiting to fill their prescriptions, and sweetly sing John's father his favorite Yiddish lullaby. I'd walk home with a pack of Wrigley's gum and a handful of peppermint sticks. When it got warm, the best stop was at the ice cream parlor. Mrs. Chipanic was a sucker for a love song. I'd sing "I Love You Truly" and she'd go all moony-eyed and waltz around the freezer with her husband. That got me a double scoop of any flavor I wanted.

During hot summer days, when the air in the restaurant was so thick with sweaty bodies and steaming plates that I wanted to lock myself in the icebox, I would try to convince my parents to let me go to Riverside Park. That's where my classmates spent their summer lazing around on the grass and listening to the brass band that sometimes played in the gazebo. If I was lucky, my mother and father would let Annie and me set up a little table in Riverside to sell corn on the cob and bottles of Coca-Cola from a bucket full of ice. I didn't care if I sold one single bottle of pop; I was just glad to be somewhere I could feel a breeze on my face. Many a day, I would leave little Annie in charge and sneak away with my friend John for a ride in the Sudarsky family rowboat.

8   *Babka* – A cake commonly filled with chocolate or cinnamon, then rolled, twisted and baked in a loaf pan.

9   *Schmooze* – To chat, make small talk.

One hot Sunday in July when I was twelve, Annie and I were hawking a few last sweaty bottles of Coke before heading back to the restaurant. The band in the gazebo wrapped up an energetic Sousa march with a flourish of cymbals and the bandleader, looking so dapper in his red jacket with tails, announced that the Hartford Ladies' Auxiliary was going to host a talent show the following Sunday. First prize was five dollars.

I signed Annie up for the competition even faster than she could fill a water glass. It's a little known fact, but Annie was the best singer in my family. I might be able to shatter a glass in the bar across the street from one of my sold out engagements, but Annie had the sweetest little soprano voice you'd ever want to hear. She was painfully shy, but five dollars was a lot of money back then. All I had to do was to teach her one measly song and convince her to sing it.

Every single day that week, I drove my sister nuts. In addition to a drug store and a rowboat, the Sudarskys had an old upright piano and a decent selection of popular sheet music. By Wednesday, John helped us settle on "Mama's Little Baby Loves Shortnin' Bread." I showed Annie

Though Sophie occasionally posed with a piano, she never learned to play any better than she did at 13.

how to bend her knees and bob up and down each time she sang the word "shortnin'," which made her giggle a little. Her curls bounced like springs. The whole picture was so sweet it could rot your teeth.

By Saturday, Annie had shortnin' coming out of her ears. Even though I was no Chico Marx on the piano, I had memorized how to pick out some notes with two fingers and figured that was good enough to be my sister's accompanist. When we got to the park, one of the Ladies' Auxiliary told us we were going to go on after a husband and wife waltz team and before Mr. Schpielvogel and his musical spoons.

I made Moe watch the corn on the cob stand while Annie and I got ready and nervously waited for our turn. When they finally introduced the Abuzas, Annie was as white as a sheet. I sat behind the piano. Annie inched to the front of the small stage like a prisoner walking to the gallows.

I picked out the fifteen note introduction. After an uncomfortable silence, Mama's little baby wet her pants.

I mean, she opened the floodgates and left a puddle on the stage the size of Lake Titicaca, and then promptly bolted. Old Mr. Schpielvogel took that as his cue, slipped in the pish[10] and accidentally flung his spoons out into the by then hysterical crowd.

Sophie, age 13.

Needless to say, the waltzing couple went home five clams richer.

Years and years later, after I'd hit the big time, Annie accompanied me to a society party in London. Lady Haverford asked me to sing a few songs, but I told her I was feeling under the weather.

"I have an even bigger treat for you," I announced. "The real talent of the family, Miss Annie Abuza!"

I'd be lying if I said I wasn't curious what a puddle of *pish* would look like on the Lady's priceless Oriental rug. Annie made it through "Mama's Little Baby" that time, but if looks could kill, I'd have been kaput.

10 *Pish – Pee.*

A couple of years after the disastrous talent show, I got a bee in my bonnet about doing something special for my mother's birthday. Papa let it slip that Mama was turning fifty and the more I thought about it, the more I was convinced I needed to mark the occasion with something monumental.

I feared and idolized Mama in equal parts. She could put your lights out with a red hot spatula if you looked at her cross-eyed, but by the time I was a teenager I could see that same fearsome determination was what held our family together. One of my favorite jobs as a kid was to rub my mother's feet while she did her late-night sewing in the parlor, because once she got to take a load off of her barking dogs, she could almost be sweet. It became sort of a ritual. I would rub and she would lecture.

"Nothing is more important than family," she'd repeat as she stitched up our holey old socks.

"Always look after your brothers and your sister. Especially your sister. God only gave you one."

"If you have extra—food, money, anything—share it with those less fortunate."

"Find yourself a good husband and have lots of children."

"Sophie! Pay attention!" she'd bark if she noticed me nodding off, poking a knitting needle in my arm. "These things I'm telling you are very important. You think I like all this sewing, or cleaning, or cooking? Of course not. But I do it for the family. It's the most important thing."

That's when I got one of my brilliant ideas—the perfect surprise gift for Mama's birthday.

I recruited my brothers and sister to help raise money through odd jobs, which we worked every day before the dinner rush at the restaurant. Phil lugged logs at the lumber yard and Moe swept up at a local hardware shop. I helped wash the dirty pans and trays at Landi's Bakery (and helpfully ate any leftover danishes) and Annie scurried around the neighborhood collecting empty bottles. Still, after a month we only had a couple of bucks in change.

It was a particularly delicious pot roast sandwich that gave me my next idea. Not one restaurant on all of Front Street opened before lunch, yet crowds of men had to pass by Abuza's darkened windows on their way to work. I begged my parents' permission to try selling boxed lunches in the morning before school and they, suspicious of my sudden interest in the family business but unwilling to look a gift horse in the mouth, said yes. Every morning at 4:30, Phil, Moe, Annie and I hopped out of bed and slapped together meals to sell at the front counter. After the news spread, the line was out the door by dawn and we were selling more than a hundred sandwiches a day.

The key to my plan was a big empty mayonnaise jar I plopped on the counter right next to Annie. I stuck a sign on it that said, "If you like Mama Abuza's eats, donate to her birthday fund!" The one-two combination of a hot meatloaf sandwich and Annie's big eyes peering up over the counter made it rain nickels and dimes. Mama never suspected a thing since we were finished and off to school before she came downstairs to start chopping the day's onions.

We were rolling right along toward buying the big gift when a sudden spring thaw caused the Connecticut River to overflow its banks and completely flood Front Street, leaving all our customers on the other side of the road with no way to get to us. Come rain, come hail, come three feet of brown water on our stoop, the Abuza children would not be stopped. Remember the Sudarsky's rowboat? John met Phil at the Riverside Park boathouse and they rowed back down Front Street together. The next morning we made an assortment of sandwiches, crossed the river in John's boat, and sold as many sandwiches to our hungry customers as we could fit in the U.S.S. Lunch Pail. Our tip jar was so heavy on the trip back that John was afraid it would sink us.

Every girl should have a pal like John. Sure, I think he might've been a little sweet on me, but he was the first one to recognize that singing was what really made me happy. Back then, in the Dark Ages before radio and television, I'd go over to John's house and listen to him play the sheet music his parents brought home from the local music shop. We would share the piano bench, John playing a new song again and again until I could sing it without looking at the words. A lot of people think I fell in love with music watching Vaudeville shows at Poli's Theater in Hartford. That's just not true. It was all because of John and the hours we spent sitting at the ivories.

After the river subsided it was back to business as usual, but according to Phil's bookkeeping we were still going to fall a couple of smackers short. Thank God I was humming one of John's newest tunes when I put down a plate in front of one of our regular customers, a widower named Mr. Woodstein. He asked what I was humming.

"It's a new one called 'Sidewalks of New York,' Mr. Woodstein."

"Sounds catchy. How about you sing it for me?"

So began my first ever café appearance. It wasn't a great gig—I was holding a baked potato for another table—but Mr. Woodstein flipped me a fat quarter after I finished. This was the answer to my prayers. For the rest of that night I served every meal with a different ditty and almost everyone left me some extra change, which I deposited right in the mayonnaise jar.

A few days shy of Mama's big day, Phil did an audit and reported we were still short five dollars and little Annie, eager to help, pointed out that there was going to be another talent show in Riverside Park. We were flabbergasted that she wanted to take another crack at the spotlight, but Annie seemed so keen on helping we couldn't turn her down. It seemed that Mama's little baby got shortnin' *brave*.

When the big day came we were all convinced Annie was going to come through this time. She strode right up on the stage, I played the intro and she sang the whole song, knee bends and all. The problem? Nobody could hear her tiny voice. In those years before microphones, Annie sounded great in the parlor but she never stood a chance in the middle of a bustling park. I was dejected. At the end of our number, I got up from the piano and stood next to my sister to bow like we'd practiced.

"Let's hear the fat girl sing!" bellowed a voice at the back of the crowd. I still have no idea whether it was a school chum or a restaurant customer or even a heckler bent on embarrassing me, but I was desperate for that five dollar prize and under no delusion that I was svelte.

"Oh yeah? Whaddaya wanna hear?" I yelled back.

"Whatever your sister just sang!"

I grabbed my sister's hand and together we did an encore of "Shortnin' Bread." I don't know whether the crowd was more impressed with my volume or my *chutzpah*[11], but I went home five dollars richer and in love with the stage.

My mother's birthday was a great success. After the candles were blown out, the cake was gone, and we were all tucked in, I heard Mama singing. I quietly tiptoed down the hall and peeked in from the doorway of the parlor. There she was, humming just like me with a big smile on her face. As I watched my mother that evening, her feet didn't seem to be in any pain as she worked the pedal of her new Singer sewing machine.

Singer sewing machine circa 1900

11 *Chutzpah* – Guts, nerve.

Chapter 2

Oh! Papa, Oh! Papa

From left to right: Jennie Abuza (42), baby Annie, Sophie (5), Charles Abuza (37) and Phillip (7) in Boston, 1892. Not pictured: Moe, age 2.

My father, Charles Zachary Kalish Abuza, was as funny and as complicated as his name. Having arrived in America from the Ukraine by way of Italy, Papa embraced both his unlikely Italian moniker and his knack for getting into trouble. It's a shame he looks like he's attending a funeral in the one family portrait I have from my childhood. Photographs were an extravagance back then, and I will never forget my mother screaming at her husband to stop making funny faces while the photographer rolled his eyes and prepared another plate.

He ended up charging us extra and my father slept in the parlor for a few nights afterward, but Mama got her proof that the Abuza family could be dignified for thirty consecutive seconds.

Papa was like a circus bear; a hairy, squat slab of muscle always doing something a little bit ridiculous. He loved to sing even though he had a tin ear. If he had to unload a truck full of turnips for the restaurant, he would hum a Russian marching song. When he counted out the register, he tapped the coins in time with an old Yiddish melody he whistled off-key. Following him around for a day was like listening to a record of Jewish folk songs that someone left out in the sun.

Mama thought my singing was a waste of time right from the beginning, but Papa had other ideas. When the tips started rolling in from customers who liked my songs, he managed to convince my mother to part with twenty-five hard-earned dollars to buy a secondhand upright piano for the parlor. Papa was convinced that mastering the piano would guarantee me fame and fortune. Sure, that might have worked out for Liberace, but my fingers were so fat and clumsy it was like trying to play a piano with kosher dill pickles. Six months later, the ivories were gone at a five dollar loss. At least Papa had some extra room in the parlor when Mama exiled him that night.

Papa was about as talented a businessman as he was a musician. Whenever I see a rerun of my old friend Jackie Gleason on *The Honeymooners*, I can't help but think of my father's get rich quick schemes that always, and I mean *always*, failed.

He idolized Thomas Edison—he kept his framed portrait on his nightstand—and also fancied himself an inventor. How he settled on doorbells as his ticket to the top I'll never know, but he was convinced he'd make his first million with just the right jingle.

He once spent a month rigging up strings and pulleys that stretched from the three outside doors of our restaurant up to the second floor where we slept. Each would ring a cowbell with a different pitch so you knew which door to answer.

Papa was hell-bent on patenting his invention and installing the "Abuza Announcement Service" in every house in America. He even went so far as to get competing bids from three different cowbell companies around the country, waiting patiently for estimates to arrive in the mail from Amalgamated Bells and Whistles or some other cockamamie company.

My father's plan fell apart when some of the older kids in our neighborhood found out about our special doorbells. After a week of being jolted awake several times a night by clanging cowbells of varying tones, Mama put an end to the Abuza Announcement Service with a pair of sharp sewing scissors.

The thing Papa truly excelled at, though, was getting in trouble around a poker table. We shared a love for gambling of all sorts and, unfortunately, I inherited his piss-poor luck. Over the last sixty years, every time I manage to lose a hand while holding four kings, I look up to the heavens and think of my dearly departed father and fork over my chips with a smile.

My father was so unlucky he must been conceived under a ladder. Even when he won, he lost. He once won a big poker pot that included the deed to a small hotel down the street from our restaurant. Of course, he came to find out that there were back taxes due and the place looked like a two-dollar whorehouse on the inside. But that didn't stop my father! He took the rest of his winnings, squared up with the city of Hartford, and refurbished the old Boston Hotel. Opening day, we put up streamers and flags and it seemed like the whole neighborhood dropped by to celebrate with a cup of punch. Business was good for the first three weeks—right up until the moment he bet the same deed on a longshot hand and lost both the building and his dream of becoming the Jewish Conrad Hilton.

I got hooked on gambling at the age of nine, when I became Papa's lookout. While he bet the take from our lunch service on a card game in a back room above the restaurant, I'd keep an eye out for Mama and belt a chorus of "Someone's in the Kitchen with Dinah" if she was headed his way. If Mama was safely downstairs cooking, Papa would let me sit on his lap while he played.

His poker buddies were a colorful group of ne'er-do-wells who'd earned their crooked noses and limps through a variety of *interesting* occupations, which was why Mama hated the card game so much. Not only did I learn the different kinds of poker while sitting on Papa's lap, I got to be pals with every gangster in Hartford. Turns out, the criminals' code of ethics wasn't all that different from my mother's lessons in the sewing parlor. When it came to right and wrong they both subscribed to the same four sacred commandments: never go back on your word; always return a favor; make lots of money; and never screw your friends.

My three favorite regulars were Tommy "T-bone" Palazzo, Sammy "The Socket" Turcott, and "Deaf Davey" D'Angelo, nicknames courtesy of yours truly. T-bone was Hartford's premier bookie and there was nothing he loved more than a juicy T-bone steak. My dad used to bust his chops by serving steaks to everyone at the card table except for T-bone, who got a plate of gefilte fish[1].

Sammy had a double-jointed arm that he could pop in and out of his shoulder socket. He pretended it hurt and begged us kids to push it back in place, which we did with glee. Sammy, demented as he was, was as close as we came to being entertained by a clown. When he wasn't making us laugh he controlled all of Hartford's dock workers.

Deaf Davey ran all the prostitutes and liquor in town. I gave Davey his nickname because he wriggled out of answering every question the same way:

"Hi, Davey."

"What?"

"I said how are you, Davey."

"What?"

"*How are you doing?*"

"Stop screaming. I can hear you!" Davey would yell.

The only time Deaf Davey's hearing was perfect was when he was getting a liquor order.

"I want two cases of bourbon, three cases of gin and five cases of vodka."

"That's two burb, three gin, five vod," Davey would repeat.

"Can I get that tomorrow?"

"What?"

Once, during an intense hand of five-card stud, Papa sent me downstairs to the fetch some beers from the icebox. Ever the little

---

1 *Gefilte fish* – A Jewish appetizer made from ground poached fish, often whitefish or carp.

waitress, when I returned to the back room I went around the table and popped open a cold bottle for each player. Aside from the regulars, that particular game included Stanley Walski, an old friend of T-bone's who was new to the table. Stanley had just opened a butcher shop on Front Street.

It was Stanley's deal, so I waited to hand him his beer and watched while he gave T-bone three cards, but sneakily pulled his own card from the bottom of the deck. I put down the beer, moseyed over to T-bone and whispered what I'd seen into his ear.

T-bone didn't move a muscle. He and Stanley were the only two players left in the pot and T-bone played out the hand and lost, taking it on the chin with no more than the usual grumbling. However, walking home from school later that week, I found Front Street was blocked off by what seemed like every policeman in Hartford. Turned out the new butcher was discovered on the floor of his shop with a meat cleaver in his chest. When word spread about how Stanley was killed, I was less shocked than my schoolmates. They were the kind of kids who didn't serve beer to gangsters and never heard horrific bedtime stories from a Russian father who grew up under the thumb of the Cossacks.

T-bone returned to the card game as usual that week. When I squeezed past his chair to bring Papa a fresh beer, he grabbed my face in his meaty hand.

"You know the last time I was here you did me a big favor," he said. "I just wanted you to know how much I appreciated it. When someone does Tommy Palazzo a big favor, he always pays it back."

"Wow, kid," said the Socket, whistling through his teeth. "Why don't you ask Tommy to tell us who's gonna win the sixth race at Saratoga this Saturday?"

"Just remember what I said, kiddo," repeated Tommy. "I owe you one, anytime you need it. Capeesh?"

"Capeesh, Mr. Bone," I said, and shook his giant mitt.

Stanley Walski's murder was never solved, but from its brutality the cops knew he wasn't killed by a customer he shorted on a pound of salami. Besides, the butcher's cash register was still full of money and Mr. Walski was still wearing his big diamond pinky ring. Even the shop's inventory was intact, though it appeared that there had been a run on one particular item. The butcher had been completely cleaned out of T-bone steaks.

Papa found other creative ways to get swindled when he wasn't playing cards. At the restaurant, my father was the head buyer, the cashier, and perhaps most importantly, the chief *kibitzer*[2]. He had the gift of gab. Even with his deep Yiddish accent, Papa developed a polished repertoire of American slang. Nothing was funnier than hearing him work "gee villikers" into a conversation. Because he was so friendly, he attracted unsavory characters like flies to Mama's baked apples and cream.

When I was about twelve, a distinguished elderly gentleman came to the restaurant five nights in a row and ate dinner alone. Papa took pity and chatted with the man while he dined, and by the end of the week they were hunched over cups of coffee, intensely talking business. It seemed Papa's new best friend, Mr. Farnsworth, had a very successful restaurant in the Bronx right next to a stop on the Third Avenue elevated line. Mrs. Farnsworth wanted to retire and move to the country and, though they'd saved for years, they were still about five G's short.

Enter the enterprising Charles Abuza, already picturing a chain of successful restaurants in New York City and a house on Park Avenue next to J.P. Morgan. Of course, his better half wanted nothing to do with it. Mama was content to slave away on Front Street instead of getting caught up in a pipe dream, but even her most pointed eye rolls in Papa's direction couldn't stop him from taking me to visit the Farnworths' restaurant. I must admit, I had never seen such a commotion. I thought Saturday goulash nights at our restaurant were pretty busy, but this was mayhem and it was only two o'clock in the afternoon. It seemed like Papa had finally stumbled into some luck.

Mr. and Mrs. Farnsworth agreed to come to Hartford in a few weeks to sign over the deed and close the deal. Papa had even managed to talk them down from the original five thousand dollar asking price to just a grand up front, with yearly payments of a thousand dollars sent on to their country home for the next four years. As good a deal as this was for a booming restaurant in the big city, Papa knew it was gonna take more than a couple of "gee villikers" to get Mrs. Abuza to

2   *Kibitzer* – a meddler, a chatty busybody.

agree. The train ride home to Hartford was very quiet. Even though I was only twelve, I knew my father's wheels were spinning with ways to come up with a thousand dollars in just fourteen days.

I don't know how Papa came up with the money, but he did. You can't sell silver you don't have. I can only guess that Mama believed our over-the-moon descriptions of the restaurant and tapped into her secret savings, the stash she kept away from Papa and his big ideas. The Farnsworths arrived as scheduled, the money was counted, the ink dried and we were on our way to New York. The transfer of ownership would take place in a month.

The following Sunday our whole family headed into the Bronx to check out the restaurant and look for a new place to live. During that train ride, my family was the most excited I had ever seen them, including my mother, who smiled from ear to ear as I pulled her into the magnificent Grand Central Depot.

When we got to our new restaurant, however, there were no tables, no chairs, no counter, or even a kitchen. The windows were dark and the sign above the door was gone. A policeman happened to stroll by and Papa asked what happened to the restaurant. He cocked his head and told us the building had been empty for four years. Mama went pale and silent. It was a rare sight since she was normally such a bulldog, and it scared us kids to the bone.

Once the officer heard our whole story he knew what had happened: we'd been set up by a gang of local con men. Their M.O. was to find an abandoned neighborhood with an empty building and stage a successful business for a few hours to sell it to a wide-eyed patsy like Charles Abuza.

We were back on the train sooner than we had expected, only this time we were dazed by shock. Grand Central didn't look quite as grand once we knew we weren't going to be living on Park Avenue, our pockets fat with cash from our booming new business. But once we were on the train and chugging through Connecticut toward home, the strangest thing happened. Mama started singing one of Papa's silly Yiddish songs. At first I thought she had lost her mind. Papa had just blown Mama's life savings and she was singing about *pipiks*[3] and *pupiks*[4]? Then Papa joined in, then Phil. Before you knew it all of us were singing, even shy little Annie.

With our family there wasn't a lot of time for hugs and kisses. We all worked sixteen hours a day just trying to scrape by. When I think back, it seemed like my mother was always mad or yelling at my father. Living with him must have been exhausting. His harebrained schemes forced Mama to be the one always saying no, while doing all the real work to keep us clothed and fed. Her little Yiddish hootenanny on the train may have started to help us forget we were out a thousand dollars, but it let us know that despite everything, she loved us and she loved Papa, and that made us feel like a million bucks.

---

3   *Pipiks* – An innie bellybutton.
4   *Pupiks* – An outie bellybutton.

Chapter 3

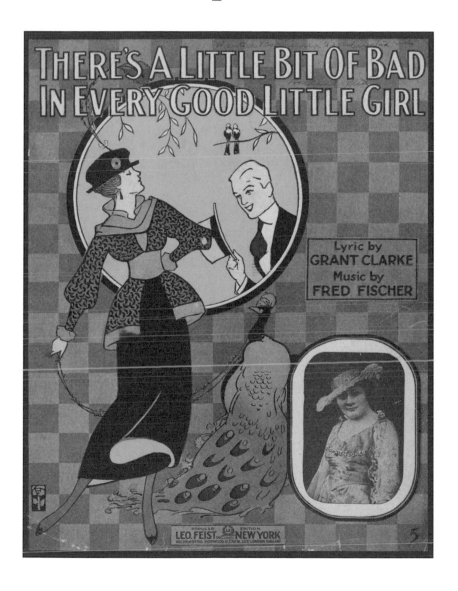

There's a Little Bit of Bad
In Every Good Little Girl

When Milton Berle called me in 1953 and asked if I wanted to be the first woman roasted by the Friars Club, I asked, "What's the matter? Did you run out of schmucks[1]?" Truth was, I couldn't have been more thrilled. No woman was even allowed near the dais until me. After a night of fat jokes and insinuations so blue Elvis would try to wear them as suede shoes, it was my turn to make a little speech.

Sophie with Milton Berle and Frank Sinatra at her Friars Roast in 1953.

1   *Schmuck* – Literally "penis," but a common epithet for a fool.

You guys have given me a good going over tonight, but this old baby can take it. I've been taking it a long time. The only difference is this is the first time you've told me to my face what you've been saying behind my back for years. Don't kid yourselves. I know you've had many a laugh at my expense and I'm glad of it. When you're not playing gin rummy, you're worrying about my age or the size of my tuchus[2]. Yes, I know all those wise cracks. There's been more talk about my bangs than Mamie Eisenhower's. And I know all about you songwriters and your rhymes for Tucker, too.

Then hit those sons of bitches with a dirty poem I'd written just for the occasion:

My first love was an artist
Of the Louvre he could boast
But he was not hung
Where it mattered most

My next was a jockey
Up the creek with a paddle
But my gentleman jockey
Couldn't stay in the saddle

The piece de resistance was when Frank Sinatra, the Chairman of the Board himself, stood up and sang a song he'd written for me to the tune of "Mother."

S is for the sweetness she created.
O means she's the one that we adore.
P is for performers she has aided.
H is for her humbleness and more.
I is for the industry that loves her.
E is for her endless curtain calls.
Put them all together they spell SOPHIE.
The only Friar without balls...but we're not certain!

That was far from the first time in my career that I was accused of having a brass set. I guess you might say I earned my pair at the Brown School Christmas pageant of 1900.

2   *Tuchus* – Rear end.

I was about to turn fourteen when I attended the first day at my new high school in a blue dress with puffed sleeves that Mama made on her Singer. The summer was over and instead of selling corn at the park, I'd be splitting my days between classes and the restaurant. First day of school or not, we Abuza kids were still expected to get up at the crack of dawn to sell sandwiches. Because of that, by eleven I was snoring in the middle of my first mathematics lesson. The next thing I remember was Mrs. Hickey's ruler cracking my skull and demanding I go straight to the principal's office. Not exactly a grand entrance at the Brown School.

Over the summer, I'd heard all kinds of rumors that the principal, Mr. Ames, was a big bully with an even bigger paddle to tan your hide if you dared to disobey your teacher. As I stepped through his door, I was determined to turn on all my charm and explain to this gorilla that I wasn't a bad apple, just a tired one. However, I had to bite my tongue almost in half to keep from laughing when I laid eyes on the terrifying Mr. Ames. The older kids had suckered me. He was tiny mouse of a man. Sitting in the big leather chair behind his desk, his feet barely touched the floor.

I tried to explain that I fell asleep because of my hefty work schedule, but he insisted I should be punished—by joining the school choir. It met every single day at noon.

"No lunch?" I gasped.

"No lunch," Mr. Ames confirmed.

I should've just asked for the paddle.

I sulked all the way to the music classroom and took a seat at the back, sneaking bites of a fat sour dill pickle and my pot roast on rye until the choirmaster arrived. He shuffled a stack of sheet music onto the upright piano and nervously introduced himself as Mr. Elliot. This brand new music teacher had been charged with the task of turning a ragtag bunch of children into an angelic choir in time for a Christmas recital. Trying to imagine my mother's reaction to one of her children singing hymns to the baby Jesus made me snort into my pickle.

"Is there a problem, young lady?" asked Mr. Elliot. "What is your name? Are you eating in my class?"

"I'm Sophie Abuza," I said with a smile, "and I'm eating a sour dill. I've got an extra if you want it."

"Do you intend on eating through all of our songs as well?" he asked.

"Mr. Elliot, my family owns a restaurant. In the time it takes for you to switch your sheet music I could cook a meal, eat it and still have time to clean my teeth with a toothpick."

Frankly, I don't understand why he didn't send me and my smart-ass mouth right back to the principal's office. Maybe he hoped my flair for comedy meant I'd make a good performer. Whatever it was, instead of kicking me out, Mr. Elliot got down to business. He made each of my classmates sing a scale so he could figure out what part they would be good for in the choir. When he got to me, I wanted to impress him so I really let 'er rip.

Mr. Elliot tried not to betray a smile but I knew he liked what he heard. With each note of the scale I got louder and louder and Mr. Elliot's eyes got wider and wider.

"Well," he said when I finished. "Miss Abuza, I think you are the alto section."

At the end of class, Mr. Elliot pulled me aside to tell me that I had quite a voice, and a personality to match. I hadn't a clue what personality meant, but I'm fairly sure Mr. Elliot didn't know what a knish[3] was so I'd like to think we had things to teach each other.

"Have you ever seen a Vaudeville show?" he asked.

"Is that where the Yiddish actors work? Sometimes they eat at our restaurant," I explained.

"No, they work at the Empire Theater. Vaudeville at Poli's is different—I'm sure you'd like it. I fill in for the piano player occasionally. If you'd ever like to see what's going on inside, just let me know."

Unfortunately, I was already scheduled to do two shows a day at the restaurant refilling the jars of chicken fat. Still, I was curious about this Vaudeville. I handed Mr. Elliot my extra sour dill as a thanks for not sending me back to Principal Ames and headed on to history class, my curiosity goosed.

When I got home from school that day my parents were arguing, as usual. This time Papa had won a bet from Yitzhak, the local printer. Instead of cold, hard cash, he accepted 250 printed handbills the restaurant didn't need. Mama was livid. Every Jew within twenty miles already knew about Abuza's. She was coming up with creative places Papa could store the whole thick stack of flyers when I had a brilliant idea.

---

3   *Knish* – A Jewish snack food consisting of dough stuffed with a filling, often potato.

"I could bring some of the handbills to the theater downtown and pass them out to the actors between the two shows," I chimed in. "Everyone at the Yiddish theater already knows about us, but maybe the Vaudeville actors at Poli's might come? My choir teacher told me about it."

"What is this vode-a-ville?" asked Mama. "I'm sending you to school to learn about bum actors?"

Papa liked my idea, however. The next day after school, I headed to Poli's armed with fifty of Papa's flyers. When I arrived I asked a lady in a glass booth in front of the theater where the actors came out of the building. She told me to go down the alley on the left and look for the stage door, which is where I waited. I could hear faint music coming from inside the building.

Finally someone came out holding what appeared to be a bag of tools.

"Here you go, mister. Come to Abuza's Family Restaurant on Front Street. Five courses for fifty cents."

"Fifty cents? I can't afford that. I'm a plumber, not the star of the show."

"We also have a four course plumber's special for twenty-five cents. You get soup, roast beef, potatoes, and bicarbonate to clean your pipes!"

The plumber thought my joke was about as funny as an overflowing crapper. As he left, I managed to grab the door before it closed and tiptoed toward the sound of laughter coming from inside the theater. Backstage, people were running to and fro moving big pieces of furniture and racks of spangled costumes. Two men were trading rapid-fire jokes on stage in front of the curtain. The audience seemed to think they were hysterical. Eventually the orchestra played them off and the performers dashed toward me into the wings. The minute they were out of sight, one smacked the other on the back of the head.

"You stepped on my laugh again, *putz*[4]!"

"What laugh? The way you delivered that line, there was never gonna be any laugh!"

They grabbed each other's hands and ran back out on stage, smiling and bowing as though they were the best of friends, and then ran back to the wings.

"Why don't you take your shitty timing and stick it up your ass?" said the first one. "Let it bake in there for a few minutes and then serve it to yourself for Sunday dinner."

4   *Putz* – Literally "penis," but a common slang term for a jerk or loser.

That was all the opening I needed.

"Or you could try dinner at Abuza's Family Restaurant on Front Street for just fifty cents!" I said with a wink, sticking a flyer under each of their noses. The men stopped talking and looked at each other, confused.

"Are you the new kid act? How old are you?"

"No, I'm not an actor. I'm fourteen. I fill chicken fat jars."

"That must be something to see," said the second man. "Can you do it on stilts? I'm looking for a new partner to replace this steaming pile," he said, gesturing toward the other man.

With that, the two walked away with their flyers, bickering all the way to a little dressing room backstage.

Eugene and Willie Howard, pictured later in their career.

The curtain closed and I thought the show was over, but there was a quick flurry of set pieces rolling on and off stage. Suddenly I heard my name and Mr. Elliot—dodging a little dog in a top hat that'd broken away from his handler—ran across the stage toward me. He explained that it was only intermission and, quickly, before he had to return to the piano, he set me up smack dab in the front row of the balcony to watch the second half of the show.

The curtain went up and a man with ten trained dogs coaxed his pooches to jump through flaming hoops; even the little runaway in the top hat dove admirably through the fire. Next, three brothers with flying feet did a complicated tap dance. Then came the Howard Brothers, the comedians I'd met backstage. I laughed until I nearly pished on the soft velveteen theater seat.

The clincher was the final act. The house lights dimmed almost entirely and out from the wings floated Nora Bayes in a sparkling purple gown. The audience was mesmerized simply by the way she walked to center stage. All she had to do was stand there and sing a ballad, and she had the whole theater in the palm of her hand. I was dumbstruck. I watched the crowd hang on her every tiny movement and, in that instant, I knew Vaudeville was my destiny.

Nora Bayes

I met Mr. Elliot backstage after the show was over. He asked me if I'd enjoyed the acts, and for the first time this loudmouth was at a loss. When I finally found the words to thank him, I blabbered on about how lucky I felt to have seen such a once in a lifetime spectacular. Mr. Elliot chuckled and explained that if I liked the show, I could come back and see a different troupe every week. I almost *plotzed*[5] in my pants.

"How long has this been going on?"

"For the last twenty years, in every city in the country. This is Vaudeville, kid!"

As if on cue for an encore, the Howard brothers came walking by and both slapped me on the shoulders.

"Hey, Chicken Fat Girl! We're going to try this kosher restaurant of yours," one of them shouted.

"This isn't some *farkakte*[6] plot to poison us and steal our wallets, is it?" cracked the other, waggling his eyebrows.

"No, but watch out for my Mama's stuffed cabbage," I said with a wink. "From that you might die and go to heaven."

"How about your *borscht*[7]?" asked the first.

"It's so good, they say it can't be beets!"

The Howard brothers took off chuckling and I asked Mr. Elliot why they seemed so friendly now when they'd been on the verge of killing each other earlier. He explained that they'd been fighting all ten years they'd been headliners, a word I'd never heard before.

"A headliner's the most talented act on a bill, Sophie," Mr. Elliot said as he walked me back to my parents' restaurant.

"A bill? The headliners have to pay to sing?"

"No," he smiled. "The audience pays at the door—we call that the "gate" in show business lingo—and then all of the performers get paid a different share. Me, I make a little for playing the piano. But a star like Nora Bayes? She makes a pretty penny."

5   *Plotzed* – To collapse, faint.

6   *Farkakte* – Lousy, messed-up.

7   *Borscht* – A Ukrainian soup made from chopped and boiled beets and usually served cold.

As we walked through Hartford, I asked question after question about how Vaudeville worked and Mr. Elliot patiently explained each foreign term, like "marquee." Thankfully, that was different than the Marky who sat next to me in grammar school. The only show he could headline was the Breaking Wind Spectacular. I'd never heard of a "chaser" either, which is what Vaudevillians called the act that followed the headliner. They were usually the worst act on the bill, who sang off-key or told rotten jokes to clear the theater so the ushers could clean the aisles before the next show.

"The best guy's not last? So it's the opposite of a baseball lineup?" I asked.

"Sorry, Sophie. I could tell you all about what drives headliners, but I don't know a thing about line-drivers."

As the weeks went by that fall, Mr. Elliot and I developed a close friendship. He taught me all about Vaudeville and in exchange I explained the suicide squeeze. The things I learned from him that year—how to put over a song, how to project—I still use today. Mr. Elliot could've been a real road musician but with a wife and two young babies, he decided to stay put. That's how he ended up my music teacher. To make some extra money and satisfy his sweet tooth for show biz, he would occasionally fill in at Poli's Theater. When he ran into me, he remembered the excitement of developing a new act. Mr. Elliot helped ignite my ambitions with a little of his own gasoline.

"If you really want to have a shot at going to the top," Mr. Elliot told me, "you have to eat, sleep and breathe show business. There's no room for a personal life. It has to be one or the other."

Boy, was he right. I should've embroidered that on a hanky and kept it in my pocket every day as a reminder.

After choir practices, we would spend a few minutes each day working on the latest popular song. By the time winter rolled around, my repertoire had dramatically increased and my tips had doubled at the restaurant. I nagged Mr. Elliot to let me do a solo in the Christmas recital and by Thanksgiving I'd worn him down. When the big night came, the school was packed with parents, family, teachers and Mr. Ames. The entire choir was happy to perform, but no one was more excited than me. It was to be my first headlining slot, with a secret number Mr. Elliot and I had worked out.

My excitement edged into nervousness when I peeked out into the audience and saw my first packed house. That's an awful lot of peepers pointed in your direction. The crowd at Riverside Park had been more interested in their picnics and their wandering children than in me and my shortnin' bread.

Mr. Elliot must have sensed my apprehension as he approached me with a small bag in his hand.

"I don't feel so good. Mr. Elliot," I said. "I think I've got those caterpillars you told me about."

"Not caterpillars. Butterflies! Don't worry about them—I've got a present to help calm your jitters," he said, handing me the bag.

I opened it and found a juicy sour dill pickle. My friends know me, and they know me well.

I don't remember most of the songs we sang that night, but one of them was definitely "Silent Night." In hindsight, having a choir chock full of Jewish kids singing about yon virgin mother and child was a real hoot. The only other time I'd ever heard the name Jesus Christ was when Sammy the Socket folded at the poker table.

Right before we started the last song of the night, Mr. Elliot turned to our audience and said a few words.

"Our final song is going to feature a solo by Miss Sophia Abuza. Truth be told, Sophie would not be in the choir tonight if it wasn't for our principal. He recognized her talent and sent her to our first practice. So Mr. Ames, on behalf of Sophie, me, and the whole choir, we want to wish you and everyone else here a merry Christmas."

Then he sat down at his piano and played the introduction to "Jingle Bells." We sang along like usual until right before the first chorus. That was my cue to step to the edge of the stage.

"Oooooooooooooooooooooooh!"

After belting my note to the back of the room for an ear-splitting five seconds, instead of moving on to the second verse, Mr. Elliot and I broke into one of the most popular songs of the day.

Hello my baby
Hello my honey
Hello my ragtime pal
Send me a kiss by wire
Baby my hearts on fire

If you refuse me
Honey, you'll lose me
Then you'll be left alone
Oh baby, telephone
And tell me I'm your own

Oooooooooooooooh.

As I held my note for the second time, I looked around the room and everyone was smiling with anticipation. Well, almost everyone. Over the back of a chair in the third row, I could just make out the top of tiny Principal Ames's head turning bright red with rage. I made an executive decision to limit my lashings and launched back into "Jingle Bells."

The next day I got called down to the principal's office and ate crow for our little stunt at the recital. I don't know if Mr. Elliot got in trouble but I took credit for the whole idea. True to T-Bone's commandments, I would never screw a friend. As Mr. Ames swatted my behind with his infamous paddle, I hummed a few bars of "Hello My Baby" and hoped my future performances got better reviews.

So, when the Chairman of the Board said I had a set of balls, I took it as a compliment. I earned those fair and square. My tuchus had the bruises to prove it from Christmas all the way until New Year's Day, 1901.

Chapter 4

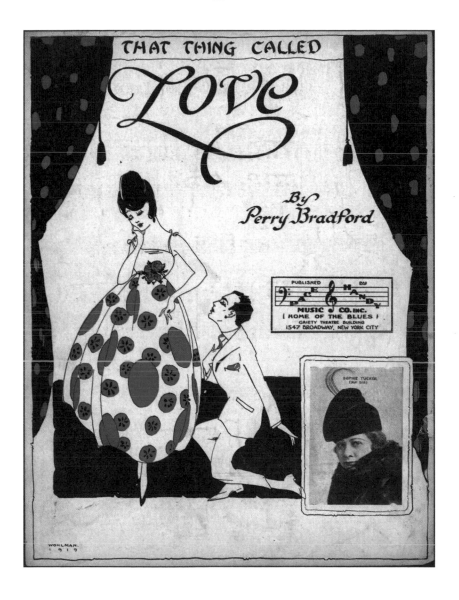

That Thing Called Love

By and large, the fellas in my life have been warm, kind and generous. If I threw a dart at my address book, telephoned the man it landed on, and asked him any outlandish thing that popped into my head, I guarantee you he'd bend over backwards to help out his old pal Soph. And it's not because we fooled around, either. Sex, I've found, is the surest way to kill a perfectly good friendship.

In truth, I've really only ever been with a few men other than my *schmendrick*[1] husbands. That's right, Sophie Tucker, the Last of the Red Hot Mamas, the duchess of the double entendre, has only had a handful of lovers. And let me tell you, my husbands were enough to send any lady running from the entire male population. My first husband in particular left such a sour taste in my mouth it should've been easy to pucker up to someone new, but he nearly put me off men altogether. Sixty years later, I've concluded that a juicy steak is always more satisfying than a lousy love affair.

When the Abuzas arrived in Hartford in 1895, they did what every young Jewish couple does and joined the local synagogue. It was the quickest way to find friends and playmates for us children, and eventually to drum up business for their restaurant. It's a double-edged sword, being in such a tightly knit community. By the time I was a senior in high school there were no secrets left. I knew when the Lipsons got a $500 inheritance from an aunt and that their twelve year old son Milton was still wetting the bed. I knew that Mr. Cherniak, the fish man, sometimes left his thumb on the scale. And the greater Jewish community of Hartford knew that Sophie Tucker was a fat girl with a big mouth whose mama thought she would never find a husband.

---

1   *Schmendrick* – An inept, stupid person.

For months leading up to my high school graduation, my mother had been nagging me to sing less and work harder on finding a man, but I was already single-minded about show business. Boys were last on my list of things to do. I wasn't interested in changing diapers, or putting in the pot roast before my husband got home from work, or staying up until midnight to fix holey socks. I wanted to move out of Mama's house as much as she wanted me gone, but I'd rather have bought my own little dump and lived alone than gotten married to have the Hartford house and family of Mama's dreams.

"I'm going to be in Vaudeville, come hell or high water! I'll move to New York and marry the biggest theater owner there!" I recall screaming at her one evening in April. I grabbed a handful of rugelach[2] and marched out of Mama's kitchen in protest.

"Why stop there?" Annie, then twelve, hollered down the stairs. "Why don't you propose to Teddy Roosevelt and move into the White House?"

"You could hear me up there?"

"They could hear you in Albuquerque!" Annie said as she slammed her bedroom door.

Secretly, I was panicked. I knew that I was no great beauty, but I was beginning to realize that my looks might keep me from both my dream and Mama's, equally. If I didn't look like Nora Bayes, would anyone ever pay to hear me sing? And if no one wanted to hear me sing and I couldn't make it on the Vaudeville circuit, how could a plain old cow like me catch a husband?

After the dinner rush, I sat out on the curb in front of the restaurant and buried my face in my hands. Besides my husband dilemma, the biggest social event of the year was rapidly approaching. The High River Ball was not to be missed, but I hadn't even entertained the idea that anyone would ask me to go. I sat stewing in my sadness like a big round *matzah ball*[3] until someone said my name.

"I know you," I said, looking up at a familiar face.

---

2   *Rugelach* – A small rolled pastry, a Jewish delicacy. Common fillings include cinnamon, chocolate, raisins, walnuts, or fruit.

3   *Matzah ball* – A dumpling made from matzah (unleavened bread).

"Of course you do. I'm Louis Tuck. I've lived down the block for the last seven years."

"They called you Louie the Lummox[4] back in grammar school, didn't they? We both used to be…pleasingly plump back then. At least you grew out of it."

"I don't know what you're talking about. I think you look great, Soph."

I investigated Louis's face, which was so perfect it looked like it belonged on the cover of *The Saturday Evening Post*. He seemed friendly but I couldn't fathom why he was talking to me. The last conversation we had was when I was ten and he and my older brother Phil got in a fight over a game of marbles. I knew—through the Jewish grapevine, of course—that he was working as a deliveryman for a local beer distributor. Tuck was famous for his snazzy duds and his good looks, and charming lots of girls with both. He had quite a reputation.

"Did my brother Phil punch you in the nose again? You want me to tell him to leave you alone?"

"No, I wanted to know if you'd like to go to the High River Ball with me. I think we could have some fun together."

"Fun? I've heard about your idea of fun. Besides, you could have any girl in town. Why me?" I asked suspiciously. Even in the days before I was a comedian, I understood that every joke has a punchline. I wanted to make sure I wasn't going to be his.

"I've already dated every girl in town, Sophie. They're all boring. Maybe you're the one I've been looking for and you've been right under my nose the whole time. Whaddaya say?"

"The girls all say you're fast," I said, after a long pause.

"I've got a lot of plans. I have to be fast. What's your plan? Fast or slow?"

My mother didn't say much when I told her about Louis's invitation, but at least she put a halt to her nagging. I knew she was happy, though, because I caught her humming an old Yiddish tune once or twice as she chopped onions for the goulash. Our parents were friends, of course, and both families were thrilled with the match. Louis always dated the wrong type of girl, so his parents couldn't have been happier that he finally was interested in a hardworking gal who looked like she was built to pump out a whole Jewish baseball team.

4   *Lummox* – Clumsy, stupid person.

Louis Tuck

While Mama may have been pleased, I knew that all the girls in town were whispering behind my back about why Louis Tuck would want to take me to the ball. I found that pastrami sandwiches with extra mustard were a great way to dull nasty rumors.

Mama stayed up late for a week before the dance, pedaling away on the Singer to make me a gorgeous white lace dress. Louis showed up in a neat gray wool suit and a matching hat, a pink rose pinned to his lapel and another for me in his outstretched hand.

I don't remember what made me happier: dancing with Tuck all night or watching my classmates try to puzzle out how Sophie Abuza ended up with Louis Tuck at the biggest social event of our young lives. I think I actually heard a head or two explode when, during the last dance, Louis tilted my head up and planted one right on my kisser.

After that first smooch, Louis became my professor of hi-dee-ho. I was his star pupil all semester, but I refused to take the final exam. No ring, no hanky-panky. He bellyached and moaned, threatened to leave, bargained with me, and repeated over and over that he'd never gone with a girl for longer than three weeks without sealing the deal.

One starry Saturday night in May of 1903, a year after our first date, we found ourselves on a blanket behind the boathouse at Riverside Park. As always, I'd tagged him out at home base and Tuck was sulking.

"I can't afford to get you a diamond right now," he whined. "I want to, but I just don't have enough saved up yet. But, I was thinking..."

I braced myself for his nightly snake oil sales pitch on the healing wonders of Tuck's Erotic Serum.

"Let's just get married. Let's get in my truck, drive up to Massachusetts and get hitched right now."

"You want to elope?" I gasped.

"Exactly. C'mon. Marry me. We'll have lots of fun."

Louis hadn't lied—so far our relationship had been lots of fun. I'd practically forgotten how much I wanted to join a Vaudeville troupe, instead spending most of my time mooning over my dreamboat beau. Besides, whenever I did mention my showbiz dreams, he seemed to turn a blind eye, or chuckle, or pat me on the head. Better that kind of a husband than some plumber who wanted five sons.

I grabbed Tuck in a bear hug and said yes.

It was too late to go that night, so we planned to run away the following weekend. The only person I told was Annie, who helped me come up with a good story for Mama as to why I would be gone all day the next Sunday. Supposedly, Louis was taking me to his annual spring company picnic which included a late night of fireworks.

When the big day came, I snuck out of my house with my little cardboard suitcase and got into the passenger seat of Tuck's Phelps Runabout, breathing in the romantic aroma of motor oil, Tuck's cologne, and the stink of old beer. We chatted at first, like usual, but as we approached the state line we both fell silent. I guess I must've been swept off

The back of this picture is dated May 14, 1902 and reads "Our wedding day." It is likely cut from what was once a shot of Sophie and Louis together.

my feet, because I never bothered to consider why I should pay for the license, judge, bouquet, a cheap bottle of champagne, and our room at the Springfield Lodge. By the time we got there I had fifty-eight cents left. Luckily, the rest of the day's activities were free.

By that evening, any lingering thrill over my elopement and our brief consummation had disappeared so quickly it felt like Moe had cleared the table in my brain. With every mile we drove closer to Hartford, I grew increasingly more scared about facing Mama. We got back to my house a couple of hours later than planned and found Mama still awake and sewing up in the parlor. I knew I wouldn't have the guts to spill the beans, so Louis agreed to do the talking.

"Mrs. Abuza, we have some wonderful news for you. Sophie and I love each other very much, so we went to Massachusetts today and got married," he mumbled.

Mama didn't say a single word. Her needle hovered above one of Annie's dresses, shaking ever so slightly with rage. Her face turned an alarming shade of crimson. She froze like that for a minute, then set down her sewing and slowly left the room. She returned dragging Papa by his arm.

"Tell him," said Mount Vesuvius.

"Louis and I got married today," I whispered.

Papa's face broke into a goofy grin. He moved to give me a hug but Mama, even more infuriated, smacked his arms down.

"You're not married until I say you're married," she hissed.

She began pacing the room, detailing all of the ways I had disappointed her—we weren't truly married, even if it was legal, because we hadn't yet had the big Jewish wedding of Mama's dreams. Eventually it was decided that if Louis valued his heir-producing equipment, we would announce a proper engagement and have a wedding ceremony in the synagogue three months later.

Louis was less than thrilled with all the religious rigmarole, but now that we were officially married I found other ways to keep him occupied. Our second ceremony was beautiful and no one ever knew (well, until now) that we'd eloped. Annie was as good as a jewel safe for my secrets, just like I was for hers. Louis and I moved into a new little apartment after the wedding celebration which had been decorated with extra furniture from both sides of our family.

It should have been an omen for things to come: when we got to our front door, Louis tried to carry me over the threshold and threw out his back. The doctor said he couldn't work for a month.

I guess you could say that's when the fun stopped. As Louis's one month recuperation grew to three, I needed to go back to work at the restaurant for food and rent money. I started to get suspicious when Tuck declared himself healthy enough for extracurricular activities but too weak to drive his route. In bed, he could do a high wire act. Out of bed, I had to chew his food for him. He finally went back to work in November and that extra fifteen dollars a week should have meant I could cut back on a few shifts at the restaurant. Instead, he blew his money on new suits and nights out with his chums before the money ever came home.

By the time we reached our first wedding anniversary, it had become quite clear Louis was in charge of living the high life and I was in charge of paying for everything. Louis had married me to get his family off his back and he had little interest in being a husband or contributing to our small household. I pleaded with him to look for a higher paying job or to ask for a raise and, to his credit, he got another five dollars a week. Unfortunately, all that raise paid for were more hats and more highballs. I never got a dime to help pay the bills.

If it wasn't for Annie, I would have gone batty. The Abuza gift for girth had somehow passed her over and she was growing into a beautiful young woman—and a sympathetic sounding board for all of my marital woes. When we weren't working together at the restaurant, she would come over to my apartment to do her homework and listen to me complain about my hapless husband.

One afternoon in June of 1904, Louis came home early, so we had dinner together before I was due at Abuza's. I was washing the dishes and my genius hubby was reading the funny papers when a heard a knock to the rhythm of "Shortnin' Bread" on our front door.

"Come on in, kid!" I yelled to Annie from the sink. "Why so formal with the knocking?"

"I saw Louis's truck parked out front," she said as she entered. "You two are still newlyweds. Who knows what's going on in here? I was just on my way home from school so I thought I would stop by and say hello. Hi, Mr. Tuck."

Louis grunted from behind his newspaper and Annie and I smirked at each other.

"What smells so good?" asked Annie.

"Me," replied the hidden Tuck.

"It's leftover filet mignon," I told her, rolling my eyes at Tuck. "Louis has a friend on his route who works at a fancy restaurant. You want some?"

Annie was thrilled to try such an expensive cut of meat. I plated the remainder of the filet and plopped it on the table in front of Annie as I made a beeline for my coat.

"Sorry I have to run, Annie. Mama needs me to peel. You better dash over yourself as soon as you're done. You're on *shmutz*[5] patrol tonight. I'll see you later, Louis."

Another grunt rumbled out from behind the *Hartford Courant*.

"Before you go, Soph, do you have a steak knife?" asked Annie.

"Louis, reach in the drawer behind you and get Annie a knife," I asked as I stepped out the door. Louis growled and threw down his paper. At this stage of our marriage, my husband was turning even the most minor task into a full song and dance number.

"Don't dilly-dally, Annie. Your shmutz awaits," I said as I left.

As I hustled down Front Street from one kitchen to another, I thought about how easy it would be to run over to Poli's Theater to catch the end of the Vaudeville matinee. Maybe Mr. Elliot would be on the ivories and he would let me sit in the balcony like old times. That seemed like heaven compared to peeling potatoes for eight hours while Mama relentlessly asked when I was going to have children. Of course, I went directly to the restaurant. The theater may have been just a few blocks in the other direction, but it might as well have been on Venus.

---

5   *Shmutz* – Dirt or grime left on someone's face, clothes, dinner plates or anything else that should otherwise be clean.

If I thought things were bad then, they got worse over the next few months. I was far from skinny, but even Mama noticed that I'd started to look a little swollen around the middle. My worst fears had come true—I was stuck with a little Tuck on the way. By the end of the pregnancy, I looked like I'd stuffed my dress with so many pillows I could give birth to a sofa.

When the big day came, Louis was, of course, in Atlantic City on a gambling trip with his pals. I held Annie's hand through the whole five-hour labor until little Albert made his debut appearance. He had Louis's good looks from day one but I prayed that he'd inherited the Abuza common sense.

Before I realized it, Albert was nine months old and I was approaching my nineteenth birthday. Louis was no more than a boarder in our household. Any love he felt for me at the beginning of our courtship had long since flown the coop and he showed about the same interest in the baby. The only thing that changed was Albert's diaper, eight times a day, seven days a week. I found myself praying the kid would get constipated but he was as regular as Big Ben.

Believe it or not, working in the restaurant was the thing I looked forward to. I'd drop off the baby with Annie and she'd manage the fertilizer factory upstairs while I slung *schmaltz* and sang for tips. Eugene and Willie Howard, the two Vaudeville comedians I'd met backstage with Mr. Elliot, came to the restaurant each time they were in town to get a fix of chopped liver and to harass their favorite singing waitress. They tipped even more generously than they applauded. I'd started to build up some savings and, by August of 1905, I had squirreled away almost a hundred dollars where Louis couldn't get his paws on it.

"Get a load of Chicken Fat Girl!" said Willie after one of my numbers. He never let me live down his nickname, even years later when we were on the MGM lot together. "Your voice is as good as your mama's stuffed cabbage. You should be on the circuit already."

"What are you after, free latkes[6]?" I said, gently punching him on the shoulder.

---

6   *Latkes* – Fried potato pancakes.

"He's right. You're never going to get anywhere singing for their suppers," Eugene said, gesturing to the diners. "Let Mr. Beer Driver watch the kid and head out on the road with us."

"The only thing Tuck is good at watching is skirts," I said, frowning.

"Well if you ever change your mind, look us up and we'll get you in with all the right people." Willie and Eugene looked uncharacteristically serious.

"It's a deal."

Because of that conversation I couldn't sleep for weeks. How could I have fallen for slick suits and hats when the guy wearing them was such a bum? I'd had enough. I came up with an idea to fix my dead end situation and enlisted Annie to help me put my plan into motion.

After yet another silent dinner, Louis retired to his overstuffed armchair in our tiny parlor and hid behind his newspaper. I finished cleaning up, took off my apron, sat in the chair directly opposite Tuck and stared at him. I thought about how I'd wasted two years of my life on that no good *schmuck* and gave him the stink eye until he finally lowered his paper. I'm surprised my glare didn't burn a hole right through it.

"You can go now," I said coldly.

"My poker game doesn't start until nine," he said.

"Listen very carefully. I want you to go to your poker game tonight and never come back. You've done all the damage I'm going to let you do. It's time for you to walk out of my life before I fix it so you can't walk at all."

"You're kidding, right?" he said, a dismissive smirk spreading across his mug.

I jumped out of my seat. I must've looked like an angry bull in a dress, snorting and getting ready to charge. My fists clenched. Louis realized I wasn't kidding. He quickly gathered his coat and hat and made for the door.

"I'll go, but can I ask you one last thing?"

"How much?" I had anticipated his request and reached into my bank through the top of my blouse.

"Five will get me where I'm going."

"Here's ten. Just make sure you stay when you get there."

I slammed the door on my old life and immediately prepared for my new one. I gathered up all the baby's things and put them in a small bag. The next morning, I wrapped Albert in a warm blanket and grabbed my cardboard suitcase, which I'd packed a week earlier in anticipation of this moment. I took one last look at my newlywed apartment and tried to dredge up even a few romantic feelings about my married life, however brief. Instead, I felt like a parolee looking back at a prison.

We arrived at my parent's house a little before six on that chilly September morning. All the lights were out except for the lamp in Annie's second story window. I thought I had whispered her name up toward her room, but my sister threw open her window and hushed me.

"Did you ever consider hiring yourself out as a steam whistle?"

"Come down already so I don't miss the seven o'clock train!"

Annie met me outside on the stoop of the restaurant and gently took the baby from my arms.

"How did he take it?" she asked.

"He took."

"Are you sure about this?"

"I've been sure for six years, minus Tuck's interruption." I paused and looked her in the eye. "I'll send money as soon as I get my first job. Every week, I promise."

"Don't worry about us," she smiled.

Albert grabbed Annie's nose and they both laughed. I couldn't muster anything but guilt for asking my fourteen-year-old sister to take care of a baby while I went out on the road. The fact was, though, I could help Albert and the whole family a lot more by becoming a headliner. Albert would be able to go to the best schools and I could see to it that Mama and Papa could quit the sixteen hour days and retire. But I'd be lying if I didn't admit I was also leaving town because of my overwhelming ambition to become famous and rich, in that order.

"Everyone's going to say you abandoned your family," Annie predicted.

"Everyone can go fuck themselves," I said, drawing myself up tall and straightening my coat. "The same know-it-alls will give me a standing ovation when I'm headlining at Poli's."

Sophie, Albert and Annie 1905

Chapter 5

Broadway Blues

A couple of years ago I was appearing at the Blue Room in New Orleans. I came in a few days early to watch a young up-and-comer with one hit song, but she got eaten up and spit out by the Blue Room's notoriously rough crowd. I have to admit, I get a little kick out of watching a new starlet try to tackle a rowdy audience. The reason we old timers are still going strong is because we've paid our dues, with interest. There's no audience we can't win.

I love the Blue Room. It's one of the last old guard nightclubs left standing since the British invasion changed music forever. At a late night show there not too long ago, I had just finished singing one of my old songs when I spotted a flying object glittering in the spotlight. I couldn't believe my eyes when it landed at my feet. Some drunk had thrown a goddamn quarter at me.

An advertisement for one of Sophie's shows at the Blue Room in 1960, when she was 73.

The last time that happened was fifty-eight years earlier in New York City during my first few months away from home. That fall and winter in Manhattan were just as tough as any Marine boot camp, without the pleasure of the three square meals a day.

When I got off the Hartford train in September of 1906 I found myself back inside Grand Central for the first time since my family sang our way home from the debacle in the Bronx. I had arrived in town with one suitcase and $148.00, the sum of my Abuza Family Restaurant tips from the previous ten months.

I still remember feeling the wind on my face when I stepped outside onto 42nd Street, a gale that whipped off the street from the rush of hustling bodies and speeding carriages. In the era before stoplights, my first challenge was just getting across the street. I happened to spot a stray horseshoe on the cobblestone in front of me, which seemed like a good omen. I had to have it. It was only a yard or two away but the carriages and small delivery trucks were coming fast and furious. When it seemed like there was a lull in the traffic, I flung my hefty bottom into the street and came out on the other side with a filthy horseshoe reading "NYC Sanitation."

That same horseshoe still hangs in a place of honor over my fireplace. Whenever I feel the need for a bit of extra blarney, I've been known to take down my first lucky piece of New York City and kiss it, *shmutz* and all.

Gathering dark clouds and the sound of thunder forced me to find a place to sleep in a hurry, so I stepped into the first hotel I saw. The lobby was huge and extravagant, with blue velvet sofas where delicate women perched like expensive pet birds. It was five dollars a night, a luxury to be sure, but I was convinced I'd land a singing job in a few days and could afford to splurge.

While signing in at the front desk, I heard someone playing the piano in an alcove off the gigantic lobby. I followed the music and came upon a scrawny kid of no more than fifteen wearing a suit two sizes too big. But boy, could he play! I was bowled over. He didn't even need sheet music. He just sat there with his eyes closed, effortlessly playing tune after tune on the piano. It seemed like he might go on forever, so eventually I strode up to the baby grand to break his trance and introduce myself.

"Hi, I'm Sophie Tuck," I boomed, my pipes getting the better of me, as usual. I startled the poor kid right off his stool and onto the floor.

"You're something, you know that? What's your name?"

"My name is Chauncey Oswald," he mumbled in an obviously phony baritone. That name coming from a kid who weighed less than the sandwich I'd packed myself for dinner sent me into one of my patented belly laughs. That seemed to irk him.

"I really am Chauncey Oswald!" he squeaked, this time in his true boyish falsetto.

"Okay, kid. If you say that's your name, that's your name. It's just that I've never met anyone named Chauncey who looked like a kosher salami."

He finally cracked a smile and confided in me that if he'd used his real name, there was no way that hotel would've let him through the doors. I guess the only reason I passed muster was because the name Sophie Tuck didn't give away my Jewish roots.

It was still pouring when I woke up the next day after the best

Chauncey Oswald

night's sleep I'd ever had. No Tuck, no Mama and Papa screaming over where the money went for the fruit and vegetable delivery, no Annie sneaking into my bed to sleep with me when she had a bad dream, and best of all, no crying baby. I got dressed, asked the manager at the front desk to borrow an umbrella, and headed out onto the wet streets. I had a card from Willie Howard with the address of his friend who worked in Tin Pan Alley.

If you were in the business of music publishing back then, this was the center of the universe. Any act, big or small, that needed a new song would have to come to West 28th Street and tour the hundreds of tiny rooms filled with songwriters convinced they had the next "Bicycle Built for Two." There were more pianos in those buildings than on the rest of the entire Eastern seaboard. You could hear it from blocks away, like the din of slot machines on the floor of the Flamingo Hotel casino—the sound of a thousand pianos playing a thousand songs at the same time.

The editors of my 1945 autobiography crossed out my description with the biggest red pen they could find, but to hell with them! The experience was positively *orgasmic*.

Tin Pan Alley circa 1906

Willie's directions took me to Harry Von Tilzer's office where I presented my introduction card to the receptionist and was told to take a seat. The waiting room was filled with six young women, each more stunning than the last. One by one we were called to the back room. After about an hour I was shown in to see Mr. Von Tilzer, who sat behind a big desk chomping an enormous cigar.

"If one of the Howard Brothers thinks I should see you, I'll see you. Where was your last engagement?"

"Abuza's," I answered honestly.

"Is that on the Pantages circuit out west?" he asked, referring to Alexander Pantages, a big Vaudeville producer who Willie and Eugene said owned a slew of theaters.

"No," I admitted. "It's on the chicken soup circuit in Hartford."

"Is this some kind of gag Willie cooked up? I'm looking for an ingénue and he sends me a fat girl?"

"This is no joke Mr. Von Tilzer. Willie wanted you to hear me sing. He thinks I could be the next big thing."

"You're already the biggest thing *I've* seen all day," rang out a woman's voice from behind me. To my astonishment, there stood Nora Bayes, in the flesh. She glided around my chair and arranged herself on the corner of Mr. Von Tilzer's desk, interrupting my conversation without a care in the world. All I managed to do was sit there with my mouth open in awe.

Nora Bayes

"Harry, the girl said you were busy but I just had to see you this very minute. I need my new song for the Hammerstein's opening on Monday."

"Nora, let me finish with...what is your name, girlie?" asked Von Tilzer. "Sophie Tuck."

"Miss Tuck, why don't you come back another day when I'm not so busy and I'll be glad to listen to you sing, okay?" asked Harry.

"The next big thing sings?" giggled Nora, evilly. "Perfect. I'm a little bit hoarse today. Harry, be a dear and let her sing my new song. It'll be a scream."

For the first of a thousand times in my career, I was about to debut a song that would become the trademark of another artist. Did you ever hear Al Jolson sing "When the Red Red Robin Goes Bob Bob Bobbin' Along"? Well, that was mine first, in a musical called *Lemaire's Affairs*. How about "Blue Skies" by Bing Crosby? That was first my showstopper in another musical called *Gay Paree*.

On this particular wet day in late September of 1906, I treated Nora Bayes to an ear-splitting rendition of Harry Von Tilzer's next colossal hit "Shine On, Harvest Moon."

"Well, that was certainly something!" Harry remarked. "What do you think, Nora?"

"A little *too* something if you ask me," winced Nora, rubbing her ears. "The song will be a winner when I sing it, though." With that, she took off out the door in a whirl of fur coat and attitude.

Though Sophie sang this first, Nora Bayes made it famous.

Mr. Von Tilzer was a touch more polite but still sent me packing, saying he had no use for a heavyweight who couldn't box. I thanked him and immediately started knocking on other doors up and down Tin Pan Alley. By the end of two weeks my feet were as sore as my throat. I must've sung in over three hundred of those little cubbyholes without finding a job. I hadn't lost faith, but I was starting to get discouraged.

Thank God for my pal Chauncey Oswald. After the third night I spent sitting by his piano, demoralized and depressed, he suggested I move to a rooming house that would only charge me five dollars a week, provided I washed the breakfast dishes. Oswald also told me about a few cafés on 6th Avenue where we could perform for throw money, which was what they called it when diners tossed a nickel or a quarter at you from their table. Whatever they threw, you got to pick up and keep. We rehearsed a few numbers in the hotel lobby and then hoofed it up and down 6th Avenue. After a week we'd each made $21.48, which wasn't bad for a skinny kid swimming in his father's suit and a female prizefighter.

Not every week was so successful. Chauncey fell ill for a while and I raked in far less on my own. Those days, I'd try to make friends on Tin Pan Alley during the day and at night I'd try to convince a café owner to let me sing for my dinner. That worked out for a while until they got wise to how much food I could pack away in a single meal.

Eventually I got to be a fixture in the neighborhood, just like when I walked home from the Brown School. Billy the fish man would trade me some lox for a song. Down the block, Larry the delicatessen owner would toss me a corned beef on rye for an old standard or two. But there were still plenty of nights I went to bed hungry. A bad snow storm could shut down the city and my meal ticket with it, and I'm not too proud to admit that on those days I'd beg for a slice of bread and a bowl of soup.

You can go on to make $15,000 a week, fifty-two weeks a year but you never forget what it's like to hear your stomach growl louder than the horn on the Staten Island Ferry. I guess that's the reason I always have a soft spot and an open pocketbook for any trouper down on his luck. Who knows what would have happened if I hadn't met Chauncey, or the Howard brothers? Without a little luck and a helping hand, I could've ended up a has-been before I even got started.

So, there I was at the Blue Room with a quarter at my feet. I leaned down and picked it up, which is no small task when you're in your seventies and zaftig to boot. There was a drunk up against the stage on my left who'd been a thorn in my side all night, so I walked over to address him directly. The club owner made a move to have the drunk ejected, but I waved him off.

"You know, friend, there was a time when I needed this to buy supper. I don't anymore, but you should probably use it to get some breath mints," I said, and flipped the coin back to him.

"It wasn't me!" he slurred.

"I did it," boomed a familiar baritone voice a few rows back. "Me, Chauncey Oswald."

We were both a few decades older and he filled out his suit a lot better than he used to, but I'd recognize him anywhere—and you would too! It was Irving Berlin, my first New York accompanist.

Sophie and Irving Berlin in 1940.

Chapter 6

Why Do They Call 'em Wild Women?

According to Harry Von Tilzer, I was an unknown heavyweight. I wasn't about to give up noodle *kugel*[1], but I'd be damned if I was going to stay an unknown. After a month of throw money and daily trips to Tin Pan Alley, it was Jimmy Durante—then an unknown himself, though his nose had quite a reputation—who helped me get my first break.

It's not surprising that most of my closest friends in show business were just like me, a little too funny looking to be a star. You could dress me or my pal Fanny Brice in the fanciest gold lamé gowns on earth, but you know what they say about a silk purse and a sow's ear. Yet give that sow a personality the size of Cleveland and a set of pipes? That's an act people will pay to see.

Sophie with Jimmy Durante and his famous schnozz.

One afternoon in the middle of October of 1906, I went to visit Jimmy in the Alley where he worked part time

1   *Kugel* – A Jewish noodle casserole. This dish can be sweet or savory.

as a demonstrator. All the acts would go from room to room and ask to hear the newest tunes, and young pianists like Durante would play number after number from their publisher's stock. Pianists were a dime a dozen but a pianist like Jimmy, who could charm a penguin out of his tuxedo, had a job for life.

"Hiya Soph," Jimmy greeted me. "I've got some great new songs that just came in."

"Save it for the customers with more than two cents to their name," I said.

"As a matter of fact, I did hear about a job…but I'm not sure if you'd want it," Durante hedged.

"I'm singing for sandwiches, Jimmy! I'll take any gig that pays."

"I heard there's a place up on 41st street looking for some new singers. But…how can I put this delicately? It's an establishment of ill repute."

"A whorehouse?" I yelled.

"Not so loud! You'll get me canned! They have a couple girls who just sing, upright and clothed," hissed Jimmy.

"That I can do," I said.

I may have been a mere nineteen years old but I already knew all about brothels. Papa's short-lived Boston Hotel was a few doors down from one of Deaf Davey's whorehouses, which was managed by a formidable old broad named Madame Jeanette. When I asked Papa why men came and went from her hotel at all hours of the day and night, he explained that it was a club for rich men who could afford certain favors. When I pressed the issue I got a smack in the mouth and was sent to wash every window in the entire hotel. It was finally my friend Dora Pearlman who filled me in at school. I haven't got a clue where Dora ended up, but I'll bet you she's working at the United Nations—at the International Sexual Relations desk.

I went up to 41st Street that evening to check out the joint, which was called the German Village. As I walked up Broadway, I noticed that the higher the street number, the better the women on the street were dressed. It had never occurred to me until that moment that I should feel self-conscious in the clothes my mother made me.

The ground floor of the building where Jimmy had directed me looked like a typical beer hall, except there were pretty girls everywhere.

Some carried trays full of overflowing steins, and some sat on the men's laps laughing loudly at whatever they said. Another was singing on a small stage toward the back of the room. I took a seat at an empty table near the stage to try to get a feel for her job. It wasn't long before a swollen old drunk fell into the chair beside me with a wet thud.

"You are the most beautiful thing I've ever seen," he slurred into my ear.

"Not interested," I replied.

"Then why are you here?"

"To get a singing job."

"I'll give you five smackers if you sing me a song upstairs, somewhere private," he said, his tongue stumbling stupidly over the words.

"I don't sing that kind of song," I said, shoving him off of me.

"Let me teach it to you," he whispered.

Before I could stop myself, my tablemate was on the receiving end of one of Mama's uppercuts and all hell broke loose. A crowd pushed in close to see if there'd be any more action but my admirer was down for the count. One small plump girl stepped out of the crowd and patted me on the shoulder.

"Nice work, honey. The Chief has had that coming for weeks."

"Chief?" I asked.

"Chief of Police," she said with a smile.

A giant man came careening through the crowd, practically throwing girls to the side to get to where the Chief of Police lay motionless. He screamed at no one in particular to explain what was going on.

"He must've slipped on a piece of ice, Tiny. No one ever sweeps up in here. Pretty soon all the girls are gonna need skates!" said the plump girl, unafraid of the mound of muscle seething in front of her.

Despite the girl's excuses, Tiny zeroed in on me.

"Who are you?"

"I'm Sophie Tuck. I came about the singing job."

"You trying to get me closed down? Delilah, take your chunky friend here and get the hell out. You're fired!"

Before I knew it I was out on the chilly sidewalk with Delilah, who was weaving a blanket of profanity thick enough to keep us both warm. When she finally stopped to take a breath, I apologized for getting her fired. She giggled and explained that Tiny, despite his bluster, fired her about twice a week and always took her back since she was one of his highest earners. She even treated me to dinner for knocking her most annoying customer flat on his ass.

We traded life stories over big bowls of goulash. Delilah was an orphaned Jewish girl with no family. With her hair, her beautiful dress and her expensive rouge and powder I would've thought she was thirty, but she was actually a few years younger than me. She had a sailor's sense of humor and we hit it off immediately.

Delilah swore she'd get me a job as a singer at Tiny's brothel. The next night, in fact, she borrowed a dress from one of her fellow working girls and wedged me into it, then coiled my hair up in the latest style and painted my face with buckets of her makeup. When I looked in the mirror I was astounded to see the same kind of girl looking back at me that I first viewed from the balcony at Poli's.

I sauntered into the brothel looking like a million bucks. Just like Delilah taught me, I wiggled my way through the room winking at the men and smiling at the working girls. Delilah had told the ladies that I'd be coming in, so they could make sure the crowd was friendly. Tiny was at the bar and I pretended we'd never met, hoping my makeup would erase the memory of last night's K.O.

"Hey bub, are you the manager? I've come about the singing job."

"You're in luck," he said, after giving me the once-over. "I've got an opening for a girl on the second floor. It pays fifteen dollars a week plus tips. You interested?"

"When can I start?"

"How about tonight?"

I was so excited I nearly skipped over to the stairs, but caught myself and remembered to saunter. Tiny stopped me right before I turned the corner.

"Hey," he hollered, "You can sing, right?"

"You won't be sorry," I assured the big galoot.

"Good. Just do me a favor. Remember that in this establishment, girls *drink* punch. They don't hand them out like Gentleman Jim Corbett. You understand me, Tuck?"

So much for putting one over on old Tiny.

The German Village had three floors. The second floor, where I started, was where gentlemen came to pick their lady for the evening. The men who made a beeline for the second level weren't there to have a drink or hear me sing. The girls had appropriately nicknamed this floor the Shooting Gallery—once a man picked his target, she was flat on her back in a second.

World Heavyweight Champion Gentleman Jim Corbett.

Most of the regular customers preferred to stay on the lively main floor, and it usually took a year or two before a girl got promoted to that stage. But the real place to be was downstairs in the rathskeller, where the drinks were twice the price and so were the tips. I intended to skip the main floor entirely and get right to work in the basement, but I wasn't yet sure how I'd pull that off.

As I learned the ropes at the German Village, I grew close to Delilah and the other ladies. It was easy for me to overlook their profession once I realized how much we had in common. Many of them came to the big city to make money to send back home to their families, and to a woman we all agreed that motherhood was for the birds. Even those of us who had kids winced at the thought of living as a housewife again. We had all decided to take a pass on days full of dirty diapers and nights with shitty husbands who snuck out to visit women like us.

It seemed like a good idea to hitch my wagon to Delilah, because it was clear she wasn't going to be in the German Village forever. She was a born leader. Tiny relied on her to rally the women together when he needed them on his side because she could work her magic on anyone, man or woman. By the end of the month, Delilah even arranged a room for me in her boarding house, where a lot of the girls lived. Although I was the only resident doing any plain old-fashioned sleeping in her bed,

I was welcomed as an equal. Instead of a twenty block walk after work, I was now thirty seconds away from a good night's sleep.

About a week after we became neighbors, Delilah told me another one of the Village's singers, a girl named Ellie Redford, was moving on to Vaudeville. Although Delilah was happy for her, this left her in a real spot. You see, Redford was the bank. Each girl received her fee plus tips from a john, which they were expected to deliver to Tiny after every trick. He'd give them their pay at the end of the night, and they'd take home only a small portion of what they actually earned. In order to beef up their income, they'd each slip a few bucks to the bank before they reported back to the big galoot. That way each girl got her stash back in addition to the pittance she earned from Tiny.

Delilah wanted me to be the new First National Bank of the German Village and I was honored to do it. In return, my new friend worked out a plan to get me down into the rathskeller. We talked it over on our walk to work, which included a customary detour to see Officer McDougal, a beat cop Delilah fancied. Every night we would casually run into the officer so Delilah could flirt with her dreamboat. I wasn't quite sure if he knew where we worked, but for my friend's sake I hoped he did and didn't care.

The night went by normally. I usually sang my last song around one in the morning, just as the rathskeller was starting to come alive. At around two, Delilah motioned to Ellie—who was in on our plan—to bring me up on stage.

"Well boys," cooed Ellie. "Some of you might have heard that after eight years in this stinkin' shithole, I'm off to the big time."

"Where, Leavenworth?" heckled a regular.

"Not the big house, you dumb fuck, I'm talking about Vaudeville! But before I go, I want you to hear a little lady I've been listening to upstairs. I'm looking around this room and I don't think you assholes deserve to hear her. But, against my better judgment I'm gonna let you. So be nice. Come on up here and let 'em hear your pipes, Soph!"

I killed with my first song and, at the audience's request, followed up with four other numbers. At the end, I earned a big standing ovation and from that night on I was a Rathskeller regular.

After closing time, all of the ladies of the German Village decided to go back to the house to celebrate one bank moving on to bigger and better things and another one taking her place. I guess the party got a little out of hand when Delilah and the girls decided to honor me by singing some of my songs as loud as they possibly could. One of the neighbors must have had enough of the noise, because in the middle of the festivities we were raided by the police. They marched us all out onto the sidewalk and, though I know it sounds serious, we were all laughing so hard it was difficult to panic until the paddy wagons showed up. Luckily, Officer McDougal was driving one of the vans and quietly saved Delilah, his damsel in distress, and me, her portly sidekick.

Once my rathskeller money started rolling in I began sending fifty dollars home per week. I wish I could've been there to see Mama's face the first time she opened one of those envelopes. I was making at least a C-note per week even when business was slow, so I had money left over to buy a few stage costumes and a dress or two for my time off. I could see how a girl might get comfortable working in the rathskeller, but even when I was flush I forced myself down to Tin Pan Alley during the day. Durante and the others would let me have some of the best new songs in return for a nice necktie or a complimentary introduction to some of Delilah's comrades in arms (and legs, and other unmentionables). I think that's when Jimmy's nose grew to its full size.

It couldn't go on forever, though. Officer McDougal and some of the small-time politicians who came through the Village let us know that the winds were changing down in City Hall. The new mayor's office had its sights set on the beer hall district and, one way or another, they were going to turn it into a respectable neighborhood. I kept my eyes open for an escape route into Vaudeville, where I knew I belonged.

Just as I suspected, Delilah was destined for bigger things. After hearing that same scuttlebutt, she decided to open her own joint in a different neighborhood with the backing of a few of her richer clients. She became the madam of one of the most notoriously fun brothels on the East coast. For years, I'd stop in to see her and we'd split a sandwich and a beer in her lush office, laughing about how I knocked out the Chief of Police all those years ago.

It may not have been the most illustrious venue in the world, but I learned a lot at the German Village. Watch me on stage singing a bawdy song like my life depended on it even when I'm sick, tired, or feeling just plain old, and it's no surprise I perfected the art of performance amongst a pack of happy hookers.

Chapter 7

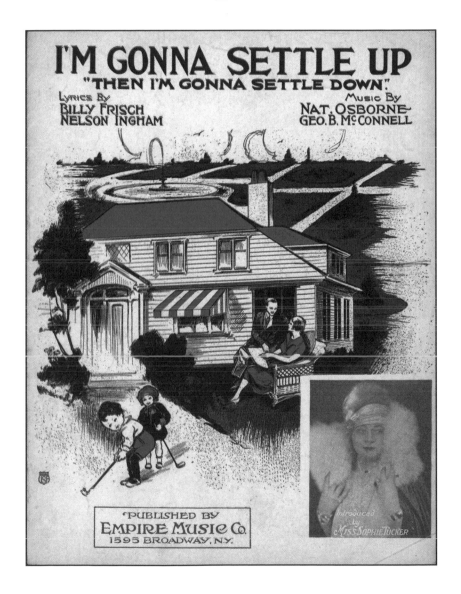

I'm Gonna Settle Up

I got a note the other day from my old friend Brian O'Connell, formerly the National Chairman of the Shriners. We met back in 1918 when he was looking for some saucy entertainment for his five thousand brothers at their national convention in Philadelphia. Brian heard about me through George LeMaire, a buddy from my earliest days in Vaudeville.

I used to conduct all my business meetings at Reuben's Deli over an original Reuben sandwich.

The day Brian met me I'd just come from a killer show at the Palace where the audience demanded six curtain calls. Surprisingly, his disposition was as cheery as mine. I liked him from the get-go. Brian had been authorized by the Shriners to offer me $5,000 for one night's entertainment. It was a good thing I'd inherited a decent poker face from Papa, because that was my salary for a week's worth of engagements at the time. Still, I knew not to accept an opening bid.

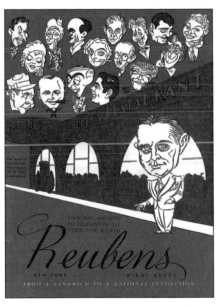

Sophie's caricature is in the top right-hand corner of the cover of Reuben's menu.

In 1918, Sophie Tucker was bigger than the Beatles are today. I often needed a police escort to get to my gigs. Magazines even wrote about my hairstyles—my up-do was the mop top of ragtime! Five grand was a great offer but I was a hot commodity and I wanted something no other woman had ever earned, even beauties like Nora Bayes.

I demanded to be installed as the first and only honorary Lady Shriner in the United States. Brian chuckled through his Reuben and extended a sauerkraut-covered hand. It was a deal.

It was a long road to that $5,000 Philadelphia payday from the German Village rathskeller and I couldn't have gotten there without George LeMaire. When I found out the beer hall era was winding to

an end, I put out feelers to every theater actor, producer, soft-shoer, juggler, piano player, and joke-teller I'd ever met. When George came into my rathskeller one night for a few pints and some tunes, I recognized him from around Tin Pan Alley and sent him drinks on the house, hoping for a lead that would land me on the circuit. LeMaire was well lubricated by the time my set was finished and I introduced myself. He was still a struggling comedian then, though at that moment he was mostly struggling to stay on his barstool.

Sophie and George LeMaire were in many shows together, including the Pepper Box Revue in 1923.

"Guess what, Sophie?" he slurred.

"You're drunk?"

"Besides that."

"I give up."

"There's going to be open auditions at a Vaudeville theater up on 108th Street and Broadway. They only pay twenty-five bucks a week, but it's the real deal," he said with a hiccup so forceful it nearly knocked him to the ground. I grabbed him up by his collar and kissed him right on his boozy lips.

I took the whole next day off to visit my pals in Tin Pan Alley and pick up three new songs, which I sang as quietly as I could on the subway up to 108th Street. It sounded like someone had muted a bullhorn, but I didn't mind the stares.

I'd spent months winning over drunks so surly they couldn't pay a hooker to be nice, but I'll admit walking into that theater made me shake right down to my bones. I jiggled like a Jello mold all the way down the aisle to sign up for my slot, but thankfully I heard a familiar voice as I was writing my name on the sheet.

"Hey, Chicken Fat Girl! How's our favorite waitress?" hollered Eugene Howard. The brothers enveloped me in a hug. It was no sour dill but it did the trick to help calm my nerves.

"Are you here to audition? We're booked here all week," said Willie, "I'm headlining. Eugene is just trying to break in his new dog act."

"He's right. I've replaced this *shmegegge*[1] on stage with a Great Dane. He smells better and never piddles on my shoes, like some people," answered Eugene. They swore up and down they'd put in a good word to the manager on my behalf.

"Thanks boys," I said. "Now, if you'll excuse me, I'm going to visit the powder room and lose my lunch."

"That'll be the first time a lunch ever got away from you!" Willie yelled after me.

It felt like there were a hundred acts auditioning that day and they were all over the theater pacing and reciting, sitting and singing, juggling pins over the heads of waltzing couples who were rehearsing their steps for the umpteenth time. The theater manager, Mr. Brown, stuck me at number forty-eight, so for the next four hours I watched every svelte girl on the island of Manhattan warble a little tune. They were lovely, but so indistinguishable it was like someone unfolded a string of paper dolls across the stage.

One of the few standouts of the afternoon was an acrobatic family act with a young boy so funny he made your sides hurt. He had a *punum*[2] you couldn't forget. In fact, no one ever did. Little Buster Keaton went on to be one of the most famous faces in the history of Hollywood.

---

1   *Scmegegge* – An annoying person full of hot air.

2   *Punum* – Face.

After a few more wispy girls singing weepy songs, a distinguished-looking gentleman set up an odd triangular contraption that looked like a staircase, with five steps on each side. He wiggled it a few times to make sure it was stable and then gave a nod to the piano player. What followed was a flurry of tap steps up and down those stairs that grew so fast by the end of his act you could hardly see his feet. Everyone in the audience forgot he was our competition and we all held our breath, equally entertained and terrified he was going to break his neck. We applauded wildly when he tapped off the stage, and for years to come audiences continued applauding Bill Robinson, also known as Bojangles. His pal Shirley Temple might've had the dimples, but he had the feet.

Buster Keaton, one of the biggest stars of silent film.

By eleven o'clock they'd made it through forty acts and there were still a few singers, a comedian who was close to tears with anxiety, and a handful of other performers before my turn. The poor *schmuck* on the audition sheet before me was a juggler so bad that people assumed he was actually a clown. As he broke egg after egg, though, we realized it wasn't an act. Selfishly, I was thrilled to be going on after anyone as long as it wasn't another beautiful nightingale.

"Okay, everybody, that's it for tonight," announced Brown. I jumped to my feet.

"What do you mean?" I screamed. "I'm next. I've been sitting here for four hours! I gave up twenty bucks in tips to be here tonight."

"Well, I'm tired and I want to go home. Come back in a month."

I stormed down the aisle and strode up onto the stage, fists clenched.

"Listen, I'm the girl the Howard Brothers told you about. I've waited eight years for this. Let me sing one song and I'll treat you to a cab and tuck you in." There was an uncomfortable silence while Mr. Brown weighed his options: one more song, or trying to move my ample derriere off the stage himself.

Reluctantly, he took his seat. I gave the piano player my music and stepped to the front of the stage. I may not have been pretty or thin, but after all of my performances at the German Village, I knew exactly what kind of a song would pep up a tired crowd.

The piano player jumped to life and I belted out the debut performance of Irving Berlin's "The International Rag" into the cheap seats and beyond. I'm pretty sure the girls down on 41st Street and even my family at home in Hartford could hear me loud and clear. There was a stunned silence after my last note rattled the chandeliers.

"Make sure the paint is still on the walls," Brown said to his assistant. "Then get this broad a contract."

"Thank you Mr. Brown!" I said, beaming. "You won't be sorry."

"What's your name?"

"Sophie Tuck, sir," I said quickly, still out of breath from my performance.

"Sophie Tucker?" repeated Brown. "Has a nice ring to it. But we're gonna have to black you up. You're so big and ugly I can't have you scaring the crowds."

Sophie in burnt cork and long black gloves
for her first Vaudeville job.

I kept my trap shut. If he liked Sophie Tucker, Sophie Tucker I would be, and Sophie Tucker didn't have a problem with covering her face in black (or any other shade of) grease paint in order to get on the circuit. Sophie Tuck, on the other hand, felt the sting. I'd been imagining myself as the next Nora Bayes when this Brown guy saw someone that belonged in the funny papers. It was hard to dwell on my hurt feelings when, at the same time, I was so thrilled to have finally made it into Vaudeville.

It was a different world back then. A man like Brown could make you paint your face and you'd do it because you needed the break and audiences ate it up. On the flip side, Bojangles was a headliner, but even a bottom-feeder like me got a better dressing room than he did simply because he was black.

After I got the job, George LeMaire taught me how to swap my Yiddish accent for a Southern one, and managed to hide a fat girl like me inside an even bigger cartoon. Under my breath, I swore to myself I wouldn't spend the rest of my life singing with shoe polish on my mug.

I was placed third on the bill on the five and ten cent New England circuit, where the headliner was a singer named Valeska Suratt, a former opera star who was well past her prime. Curtis, our manager, gave me only two instructions when I got to the Main Street Theater in Springfield, Massachusetts. First, I'd have six minutes on stage and not a second more. And second, I was never, ever to speak to Miss Suratt. Not a hello, not a thank you, not a glance in her direction.

It turned out Springfield was a great Vaudeville town with a faithful Monday audience, the folks who wanted to be the first to see the week's new acts. Monday's matinee was crucial to us troupers, because if we got a big reception the word of mouth would drive up the gate all week, which would result in a good report to the main office. I was raring to go and I can tell you this: no one slept through the third act that day. I'd been practicing for this since I was singing for penny candy from John Sudarsky's papa and sure enough, the crowd went wild for me. My six minutes were through, though, and I knew the rules so I stood in the wings and ate it up. All of a sudden Curtis was standing next to me, out of breath.

"Get out there and sing your last song again!"

"But I thought…"

"Just get out there before there's a riot!"

Curtis moved me to the fifth spot for the night show. On Tuesday I was the closing act before intermission. I opened the second half on Wednesday, and I got an official waiver for the encore rule. I couldn't believe how well things were going as I got ready for the Thursday matinee, when I turned around to find Valeska Suratt staring at me while I put on my makeup.

Valeska Suratt

"Are you the new girl everyone's raving about?" she rasped, her eyebrows arched.

My throat clenched shut.

"Did they tell you not to talk to me?" she asked. "What else did they say?"

"Not to look you in the eye, ma'am," I said, politely addressing her shoes. I had watched Suratt's act twice a day for three days, trying to learn all I could. She had an interesting way of moving her hands in time to her music that made the crowds hang on her every gesture. At the end of her songs, no matter what the reaction, she would take one bow and walk off like Cleopatra. Once in the wings, Suratt continued her regal strut all the way to her private dressing room. She never acknowledged anyone backstage.

"First of all, you can look at me. And second, call me Val," she said with a smile, and stuck out her hand.

"Okay, Val," I croaked. "Nice to meet you. You can call me Sophie."

My new pal Val turned out to be as sweet as a piece of pie from Landi's Bakery. I could hardly believe my luck when she even offered to watch my act and invited me back to her dressing room after the matinee for pointers. She greeted me in a silk robe that was finer than any piece of clothing I'd ever seen on a broad out in the street. The walls of her dressing room were decorated with exotic scarves. Sparkling beaded gowns dangled from a lacquered folding partition. Suddenly, my one ratty stage dress felt about as fine as a horse turd in the middle of Park Avenue.

"Don't worry, my dear. You'll have your own dressing room like this someday. You really have a singular talent," Valeska said, noticing my awe.

"You think so?"

"Yes, darling. There's just one thing you really need to work on, and that's your volume. I was sitting in the back row and I could hardly hear you!"

It was the first time in my life I'd ever been accused of being too quiet.

"This is a large theater with terrible acoustics. If you don't sing louder than usual it will swallow up your voice and the last ten rows won't hear a note."

That night, I really cranked up the volume. I kept my eyes on the back of the house and when I finished it seemed like even the last row were on their feet, applauding wildly. A little extra volume did the trick.

"That was better, dear," Val said backstage, giving me a pitying pat on the shoulder. "You'll get the hang of it someday."

I was crestfallen.

"The difference between a professional and an amateur is respect for the audience. Tonight I watched you from the last row of the balcony and I could hardly hear you. You have to dig deep down and scream those lyrics so every single seat gets its money's worth, Sophie. They paid to see you! Give them what they came for, or you'll never be a headliner!" she boomed dramatically.

On Friday, no one in the United States missed my performance. My ribs hurt from the lungfuls of air I had to take in and expel, like a human accordion. And Val was right; the crowds were delirious with joy. I was trying to think of a way to repay her for the kindness she'd shown me when I got word from Curtis that she'd moved on to St. Louis. It was rare for a headliner to leave before the customary week engagement was up, but the booking agency wanted Suratt on the Mississippi circuit by Monday. She'd left me a final parting gift, though, by suggesting to Curtis that I take her headlining spot on Saturday.

I couldn't believe I'd climbed from a number three act to closing in just six short days. Only me and God had accomplished so much in a single week. I was even allowed to use the headliner's private dressing room and, even though Valeska's decorations were gone, her perfume lingered in the air and I breathed it in, feeling just a little bit regal. While I was waiting to go on, I nervously passed the time in my dressing room playing solitaire and kvelling[3].

Curtis came shortly before the end of the show to escort me to the side of the stage, where the other acts had gathered to wish me luck. I was too nervous to respond but I gave everyone a quick hug, straightened my dress, and bounced out on stage. I waved to the audience and surveyed their smiling faces. The excitement was so electric throughout the whole theater Ben Franklin would've tried to fly a kite in the aisle. The orchestra vamped and I took a deep breath, my whole body winding up like a pitcher ready to hurl my song up to the balcony.

Nothing came out.

---

3   *Kvelling* – Feeling excessively proud.

The conductor sensed a problem and played my intro again, but I had completely lost my voice. I looked to the side of the stage hoping to see Val. I needed my coach to get me through every performer's worst nightmare. I didn't have a clue what to do. Curtis waved frantically from the wings and I walked off the stage and back to my dressing room in complete silence. I was humiliated.

"Bad luck, Soph," said Curtis, after he'd sent out the jugglers for one more performance in my spot. "That's not the least of it, either. Your contract says you have to give twelve full performances to get your week's pay. You only gave ten."

I put my head down on the make-up table.

"If it was up to me Soph, I'd pay you. But they'd can me in no time. I'm sorry," he said and turned to leave. "Oh, and I almost forgot. Miss Suratt wanted me to give you this envelope after your last show."

He left me alone and I allowed myself to hope that perhaps Val had saved me one last time, maybe giving me a small portion of her headlining share of the week's take for stepping in at the last minute. I opened the envelope and suddenly everything was clear as crystal. The piece of stationary only had six words on it.

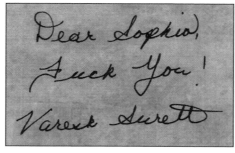

Suratt's message.

I had to give the old snake credit. Her plan was so subtle I'd been completely blind to it. She'd had it in for me since my first encore, kindly coaching me to sing louder and louder each night until I blew a gasket, even handing me the headlining spot to make my humiliation particularly painful.

I learned one of the most important show business lessons that day, which wasn't about projecting or stage presence or costuming or confidence or winning a crowd or any other tip of the trouper's trade. I finally understood the real value of an old chestnut: don't get mad, get even.

Years and years later, my buddy Brian O'Connell kept his word and I was inducted as the first honorary female Shriner in the whole United States at that big Philadelphia convention. Just like all of the other brothers, I learned the secret handshake, drank six successive beers, ate a smorgasbord of vile things, and took the Shriner oath. My favorite bit was the part where I had to promise not to cheat on my wife—instead, I asked for the telephone number of every handsome unattached Shriner who'd sworn the same thing. I earned my red Fez and gave my special "salaam" to the assembled brotherhood.

Once my initiation was complete, I was shown to my dressing room to warm up for my performance while the boys had their dinner. The bill that night included a slate of reports from the chairmen of various committees, a performance from an opening act, and then I would close out the night with a set of my bawdiest tunes. Because Brian had been so gracious about my lady Shriner induction, I offered to take care of the opening act for him and called my pal William Morris to make the arrangements.

By then I had been a headliner for five years but the thrill of the knock that announced I was needed in the wings still gave me goosebumps. I grabbed one of my beautiful purple scarves and went to wait for my introduction. When I got to my appointed spot, the opening act was winding down. There was a smattering of applause and she headed toward me.

"Lovely job," I cooed. "Really great stuff. You know, I'm doing some new tunes tonight. Would you mind listening to my act and telling me what you think?"

Valeska Suratt, a good deal older and not much wiser, looked at me blankly. She didn't have a clue who I was.

"It would be a pleasure," she said coldly.

With that, I went out and murdered the joint.

"How was that?" I asked her when I ran off the stage. The Shriners were applauding their hands off and stomping on the ground.

"They're still applauding. Go out and do another number," she advised.

"Do you think so?" I said, feigning surprise.

"Of course," she clipped.

This went on for six returns. When the Shriners had finally exhausted themselves and my catalog, I retired to my dressing room with Valeska in tow.

"That was something, wasn't it Val?"

"I should say so. I've never seen anyone earn six encores before."

"Thank God I asked your permission this time, right?" I said, clapping her on the back and hooting with laughter. Her face turned as red as a boiled beet.

"You rotten bitch!" she spat, pulling her spindly old arm back for a jab. She missed, but I didn't. I landed one of Mama's uppercuts square on her jaw.

"Take her to her dressing room, boys, and leave this on her lap for when she comes to," I said, handing a Shriner an envelope with her pay for the night, minus the twenty-five dollars she owed me for my first Vaudeville week. Inscribed on the outside of the envelope were five choice words of my own: "Don't get mad, get even."

I would've given anything to see her face when she woke up and found the note, but I had five thousand suitors waiting for me in the auditorium.

Chapter 8

You'd Never Know That Old Town of Mine

I've been snubbed by the best of them.

A few years back, I was invited to the opening night of my good friend Carol Channing's star turn in *Hello Dolly!* on Broadway.

Sophie and Carol Channing

We'd been pals since I saw her first act in Vegas, in which she did a spot-on impersonation of me. When I met her backstage she told me she wanted to grow up to be just like me. I told her she was doing just great as Carol Channing, but she should ax the Marlene Dietrich and Tallulah Bankhead impressions and do a few more minutes as yours truly. After that, whenever we played Vegas at the same time we would meet up in the El Rancho Hotel kitchen late at night, after our shows were over, to get the first crack at their freshly baked bread. I have no idea how Carol could eat a whole loaf and never gain an ounce. I guess I was gaining for two.

So, after Carol's opening performance of *Hello Dolly!* there was a party at a club called Arthur's filled with all of the A-list stars of the day. Elizabeth Taylor and Richard Burton were seated at the prime table and Burton

Elizabeth Taylor and Richard Burton

drank heavily all night. Every performer in the room got up to do a song in honor of Carol, and when it was my turn she insisted on hearing "Some of These Days." After I was done and the praise died down, Burton stood up.

"Ladies and gentlemen, up until now I thought my wife was in charge of butchering the English language, but I must admit I was wrong. Tonight I have witnessed the Empress of Butchery. Long live the Queen, Miss Sophie Tucker," he slurred. He was the only one laughing as he staggered back to his seat. I was a little miffed, but it was hard to be too offended by a man so drunk he couldn't appreciate that he was sitting next to the most beautiful woman in the world, Elizabeth Taylor, who shot me a quick look of apology. The next day, I received a telegram.

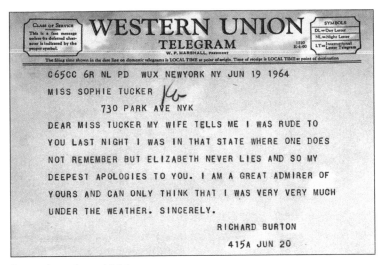

WESTERN UNION
TELEGRAM
W. P. MARSHALL, PRESIDENT

C65CC 6R NL PD WUX NEWYORK NY JUN 19 1964

MISS SOPHIE TUCKER

730 PARK AVE NYK

DEAR MISS TUCKER MY WIFE TELLS ME I WAS RUDE TO
YOU LAST NIGHT I WAS IN THAT STATE WHERE ONE DOES
NOT REMEMBER BUT ELIZABETH NEVER LIES AND SO MY
DEEPEST APOLOGIES TO YOU. I AM A GREAT ADMIRER OF
YOURS AND CAN ONLY THINK THAT I WAS VERY VERY MUCH
UNDER THE WEATHER. SINCERELY.

RICHARD BURTON

415A JUN 20

Burton's apology, 1964.

Like I said, I've been snubbed by the best.

I went to Los Angeles in 1918 hoping to break into silent films, even though my only claim to fame was my singing. Who knew what I was thinking? The best I could do was wrangle myself a couple of screen tests with some no-name directors, the last of whom suggested they bill me as the next Clara Bow-vine.

Even so, when an invitation came through from Mrs. Cecil B. DeMille, I thought I was on my way to the top. Her husband was one of the biggest movie producers and directors in the world. I figured if I got to their Beverly Hills mansion and turned on the old Tucker charm, I'd end up on the silver screen in no time.

When the big night came I wore a new gown, put on my

Silent film star Clara Bow.

best fur and rang the doorbell fashionably late at a quarter past ten. A butler answered the door, but I'd barely set my toe inside when Mrs. DeMille came tearing in from another room, yelling about my tardiness. I lied and said I'd had car trouble. It wasn't entirely false—getting a taxi in Los Angeles was never an easy task.

Mrs. DeMille instructed Clifford, the butler, to take my coat. However, she stopped me in my tracks as I made my way toward the sound of laughter and tinkling cocktail glasses.

"It's not time just yet, dear. Why don't you follow Clifford to the kitchen and fix yourself something to eat. I'll call you when we're ready for you to sing."

Even Clifford looked at me with pity when he realized I thought I was a guest, but was actually unpaid entertainment. I may not have been hobnobbing with royalty at this point in my life, but I'd been singing for the rich and famous in New York City and this just wasn't how things were done. Mrs. DeMille fluttered back into her party and I snatched my fur back from Clifford. He gave me a wink and opened the door.

"Mr. DeMille's gonna have to find someone else to sing for his supper," I joked, patting him on the arm. "I wouldn't be in one of his pictures now even if he cast me as Cleopatra. So do me a favor, Cliff, please tell old Cecil he can kiss my fat asp!"

I didn't give up on Hollywood after that, though. I was bound and determined to be snubbed by the biggest and the best in the industry. I ended up making a two-reeler in New York in 1919, but the brilliant director had me sing my hit "Everybody Shimmy Now." I guess he forgot silent films were really and truly silent. My soundless performance went over like a lead balloon.

Since I was still the biggest act in Vaudeville, I was approached again in 1923 by representatives of Dr. Lee DeForest, who claimed he had invented talking movies. Three years before Al Jolson introduced talkies to the world, Dr. DeForest offered me the chance to be the first. The only hitch was that everyone seemed to think he was a head case.

I turned down DeForest's invitation at first, but he hounded me for months. He was on a mission to start his own studio and sign a stable of stars. Finally, despite all the stories I'd heard from Hollywood about the mad scientist, my curiosity got the best of me and I went with a small group of friends to meet the lunatic himself. Imagine my surprise when I

found a warm, soft-spoken gentleman genius who played me an honest to
goodness talking film.

Dr. Lee DeForest on the left.

The Boss, William Morris, had a lot of meetings with DeForest
after that. We were on the verge of signing a deal when I ran into Jack
Warner—of the Hollywood Warner brothers, whom I'd met when

they were only running a Vaudeville
theater in Youngstown, Ohio—at
Club Morocco one night.

He pulled me aside and begged
me not to sign with DeForest for the
sake of my career. Turns out, DeForest
had shopped his technology around
to all of the major studios but no one
was willing to pay his unreasonable
leasing price to use it. Los Angeles was
now full of studio-financed scientists
trying to mimic DeForest's process
and Jack swore that they were close
to being able to sidestep him and

Jack Warner

debut their own talkies. Warner warned me that anyone who signed with DeForest would be blacklisted from the major studios for life.

My heart broke for the kind scientist. Despite my size, I've always felt like a little guy and fought for the underdog. But this time, the threat of being cut out of the motion picture industry was too scary, even for me. I backed out of my agreement and, I suppose you could say, snubbed someone else.

Six years later, what went around came around. Warner Brothers did come calling after Al Jolson made a splash in *The Jazz Singer* and they were after every famous singer in the country.

I went to Los Angeles with high hopes, with New York and Vaudeville in my rearview mirror. The week I got there, I arranged a special performance at the Rialto Theatre to showcase my talent to all the Warner executives. I sent out special invitations to Jack and his brothers and every Warner vice president, and reserved the first three rows of the theater for them. When the public found out about my one-night show, the rest of the tickets sold out in a matter of hours.

The day of the performance was electric. My accompanist Ted Shapiro and I planned a unique set of songs and we rehearsed harder than ever for the big event. I got over two hundred telegrams from all of my friends from New York to California. This was going to be the final curtain call for Sophie Tucker's Vaudeville career.

My intro music started, the crowd applauded wildly, and I bounced out onto the stage. As a tradition, I always waved to each section of the balcony first. Then I would wave to each section of the orchestra level from left to right. The gallery above waved back enthusiastically and so did the left bottom section. But when I turned to the center of the theater, I saw that the first three rows were completely empty.

It was the most colossal snubbing of my life. Not one of those *momsa*[1] Warner executives showed up. Luckily, my trusty poker face kicked in and the crowd never knew I was dying inside. Hollywood had invited me out as a nod to my fame, and for my loyalty when DeForest came knocking, but there was never going to be a big movie career. No one knew what to do with a middle-aged, fat singer when it seemed like there was a Mae West everywhere you looked. After one flop of a film, I generated about as much Hollywood buzz as a dead bumblebee.

1   *Momsa* – Literally "bastard," but slang for a contemptible person.

Thank God for Vaudeville. I spent a few days holed up with half a dozen cheesecakes and my foul mood, but by the following week I was back on stage and loving my life again.

Sure, I was snubbed by entertainment royalty, but I was also snubbed by some of the most powerful politicians in the world. When I was touring with the musical *Lemaire's Affairs* in 1923, my pal Ted Lewis and I were told that Calvin Coolidge had personally invited us to tour the White House. Ted Lewis is an entertainer who was hugely famous for his catch phrase "Is everybody happy?" Calvin Coolidge was the president of the United States and wound up being famous for diddly-squat.

Lewis and I did our best impressions of respectable socialites that day, trading our stage makeup for smart suits and getting to the White House promptly at nine. That meant we'd both gotten about three hours of sleep after the previous night's late show and weekly poker game. Meeting the President was a great honor but a Vaudeville poker game never, and I mean never, got canceled.

When we got to the Pennsylvania Avenue gate, Ted announced us to the guard and we were shown to the East Room where a crowd of a hundred men, women, and children had been parked to wait for their "private" audience with President Coolidge. We were instructed to be silent as we waited and, if he did arrive, we were by no means permitted to approach him in any way.

We stood like monks for the better part of an hour. Even the babies were afraid to cry. I can promise you, waiting in the White House was the longest I went without saying a word in my entire life.

The door finally swung open and a small entourage swept into the room, clearing a path for the President. He bustled by the small crowd without even turning his head. Ted and I had been

President Calvin "Silent Cal" Coolidge

positioned next to a second door, toward which he was clearly making a beeline. When I realized old Silent Cal was going to zoom right past us without so much as a glance, my tongue got the better of me.

"Hey Cal! How about a handshake for a loyal taxpayer?" I bellowed. The Secret Service stopped in their tracks. Silent Cal nearly wet his presidential pants.

We were whisked so quickly into another room I nearly lost my hat. A young man from Coolidge's entourage dragged Ted and me away from the East Room and out to the front of the building. I was convinced there would be a firing squad waiting for us on the lawn, but instead, the serious young man gave us a warm smile and turned into a pussycat.

"Miss Tucker, I just wanted to tell you that I'm a huge fan," he gushed. "I'll be at your show every night this week!"

"You mean you're not hauling us to jail?" said Ted.

"Are you kidding? The only thing that prick has done right since he got elected was appoint me the head of the Bureau."

"Which bureau, your mother's? You look like you're about twelve. What's your name, sonny?" I asked.

"J. Edgar Hoover, ma'am," he said, pumping my hand nearly off of my arm.

The future director of the F.B.I. J. Edgar Hoover.

"That's an awfully big name for such a young man. I think one name is plenty for a pipsqueak like you, Jedgar," I joked. "Listen, I'm going to put your name on my list so you can visit me backstage this week, okay? I figure I owe it to you for not charging us with treason."

He was overwhelmed and blubbered his thanks over and over. He took me up on my offer every night that week, though he spent most of his time backstage admiring my sequined gowns. Before we left the White House that day, I asked him to take a picture of Ted and me to prove to our friends that anyone, even two bigmouth degenerates, could get to meet the President if you had fans in the right places.

Sophie and Ted Lewis at the White House.

My royal snub is perhaps the crown jewel in my tiara of brush-offs.

I made three trips to England during the Twenties with the hope of winning over a new set of fans across the pond, but also because I thought it would be a gas to hobnob with the royals. Imagine me, the goulash waitress who used to sing for tips in a whorehouse, rubbing elbows with kings and queens? Sure enough, my first fan in the Windsor clan came to see the American everyone was talking about at one of my dates at London's Metropole Club.

"Soph, you'll never guess who just walked in," the Boss said, nearly tripping over his feet with excitement as he charged into my dressing room. "The Duke of York!"

King George VI, whom Sophie met when he was the Duke of York.

I'd met some bigwigs in my time, but in 1922 George, the Duke of York, was second in line to be King of England. Talk about a case of the nerves. I left my dressing room and stepped out onto the small set of stairs that led down to the stage. While trying to spot George, I tripped on the hem of my long gown and landed on my biggest asset smack in the middle of the stage.

"This is your fault, Mr. Duke of Yorkshire Pudding," I joked from the floor. "Everything was going fine until you showed up!"

Dukie and I actually went on to develop a very close friendship over the next decade. Other aristocrats were horrified that I called him "Dukie," but fun-loving George wouldn't have it any other way.

"Soph, you are one of the few pe-pe-people who treat me like an equal instead of the p-p-poor stuttering P-P-Prince. If you stop calling me D-D-Dukie, we will cease to be friends," he insisted.

Before he became King, Dukie had a little more leeway to

Sheet music for Follow a Star.

do things like disguise himself and meet me when I got off the boat at Southampton in 1931. He loved the theater. One time, I even snuck him in to watch my musical, *Follow a Star*, from the wings. Every once in a while I would glance over and sneak a wave and Dukie looked as happy as a pig in royal shit.

That first night we met, though, in 1922, George invited me to join him at his table when I was done with my act, despite my less than graceful introduction. He personally introduced me to his entire party, which included a beautiful young woman named Edwina, who was newly engaged to the prominent Lord Mountbatten. Our first meeting was nothing special. Everyone was fawning over the Duke of York, and Edwina hardly said a thing. She was shy back then since she was still so new to royal life. However, she would occasionally let slip a diabolical little laugh that let on she was more interesting than she seemed.

By 1924, Edwina had been married for two years and was a full-fledged party girl who knew she could get away with murder. When I returned to England that year I played two shows a night at the posh Kit

Kat Club and Edwina and her entourage were there for every performance, cheering me on. Afterward, she would kidnap me and we'd sneak off to various royal hideaway flats where the liquor flowed and little wisps of opium smoke wafted out through the keyholes. It seemed like everyone with a title had a secret den of iniquity, each more luxurious—and more outrageously sinful—than the last. Some of the things going on in those apartments could curl your eyebrows.

I was thirty-six and I thought I was indestructible, but a few weeks of cavorting around with Edwina left me with a diagnosis of severe physical exhaustion. At the end of that run I lost my voice and had a fever of 103°. I was ordered to a month of bed rest. And who was my nursemaid? Lady Edwina Mountbatten. Since she felt

Clara Barton, founder of the American Red Cross.

personally responsible for getting me sick, she visited me at my hotel suite morning, noon and night. If I was sleeping, she would just sit by me until I awoke. If I was hungry she would order soup and feed it to me. Somehow, there were never any doctor bills. Clara Barton had nothing on the Lady.

As close as we were back then, it was my 1928 transatlantic trip that bonded Edwina and me forever. She still showed up every night at the Kit Kat Club, but we only spent a couple of late nights each week at someone's digs. By then I was over forty and the Lady's ways were earning her bad publicity so we had to take our partying down just a bit. Even that didn't spare her a weekly royal scolding for her devil-may-care ways.

Toward the end of my trip, I got a telegram from Jack Warner finally offering me a contract to come to Hollywood to film a talkie. Jack didn't need me for a couple of months so I was in no hurry to get home from England, but a week or two later Edwina asked if I'd consider sailing back with her to the States. It seemed the Crown was trying to rein in their resident wild child by forcing her to do a diplomatic tour of America, under the strict supervision of the royal staff. She wanted me to come along as her partner in crime, someone to help her play hooky and have a little fun every now and then.

Sophie, Lord Sefton, Edwina Mountbatten, and someone named Peter Murphy.

That was easier said than done, because those Windsor handlers were attached to the Lady with everything but handcuffs. We still managed to sneak away here and there for a couple of wild pajama parties. Our favorite part of the voyage was hiding in my cabin and listening to the head of the diplomatic corps scream at his staff for losing track of Edwina. Oh, how we howled!

The press was waiting at the dock when we arrived in New York. Either of us would've been enough to cause a stir but this was like the Beatles at Kennedy Airport.

The Beatles press conference at JFK Airport in New York City 1964.

The Lady was permitted by her handlers to pose for pictures but under no circumstances was she supposed to speak. Thankfully, I had no such restrictions.

"How was England, Miss Tucker? How's the Queen?" shouted a reporter.

"Now boys, 'Queen' is so formal. You can still call me Soph," I retorted.

"What are your plans now that you're home in New York? Are you and Lady Mountbatten going to be seeing a lot of each other?" shouted a gossip columnist.

"I should think we'll be seeing tons of each other," I said with a wry smile. "When the Lady gets back from Newport she'll be staying with me in my suite at the St. Regis. We intend to paint the town red every night."

A photographer begged to get a picture of the two of us together, and I invited him to go ahead, provided he could get through Edwina's Beefeaters.

Before they could stop it, twenty newsmen were flashing away with their cameras. As Lady Mountbatten smiled her devilish smile she turned to whisper something in my ear.

"Sophie, when the King and Queen see this picture they're going to shit their royal pants."

With that, Edwina was whisked off to Rhode Island to start her diplomatic tour of the United States and her handlers did damage control by feeding quotes to the reporters denying our friendship. I knew that this snub wasn't coming from my

Sophie and Edwina on the dock in 1924. Note the royal handler's gloved hands entering from the left to break up this photo opportunity.

friend, so I decided to have a little bit of fun with it. When the papers denied that we even knew each other, I invited all of my reporter friends up to my suite at the St. Regis for a little press conference of my own.

"Sophie, are you feeling slighted by the English monarchy?" asked my pal from the Post.

"Not at all, Randy. If Lady Mountbatten had a change of plans, I'm sure it's because something much more important came up. Besides, whenever we're away from each other, I have this memento of our friendship to give me comfort," I said, gesturing over to a framed photo of Edwina. She'd inscribed it *To Sophie, I love you, Edwina.*

A week later, I got a private note from Edwina, which I made sure didn't make the papers:

> *Dearest Sophie,*
>
> *Sorry about the bad press. I hope you believe I had nothing to do with it. Somehow I will see you on your opening night at the Palace.*
>
> *Love,*
> *Edwina*

The night of my opening at the Palace Theater, I arranged for an aisle seat right up front in the orchestra section to be reserved for Edwina. The press had built up our "feud" to such a frenzied pitch I suspect most of the audience was there just to see if she'd show up. If the Lady turned up at my show she was a regular chum, a good egg amongst the royal chickens. If not, she was a two-faced princess who'd snubbed America's best pal, Sophie Tucker. I knew how much Edwina and I actually meant to each other, but even I was curious to see whether or not she'd come. It wasn't easy to ditch the British monarchy. The last time someone wanted to get out from under their thumb it took the Declaration of Independence, and you know how that turned out.

I waited a few extra minutes before I nodded to Teddy Shapiro to begin my intro, but Edwina's seat remained empty as the house lights dimmed. I took the stage and had just began waving to the balcony when the back doors of the theater flew open and, out of the light of the lobby, Edwina appeared in all of her elegant glory. The audience went cuckoo and I encouraged them into a standing ovation as Edwina took her seat in the front row.

"If this is what it feels like to be snubbed by the hoi polloi," I said when the crowd settled down, "I hope it happens to me every night for the rest of my life!"

I've been snubbed by royalty, politicians, and most of Hollywood, but hell hath no fury like a hometown scorned. Nothing compared to my first visit home to Hartford in 1907, about a year after I ran away to New York City. By then I'd been on the circuit for about six months and my salary was up to a whopping thirty-five dollars a week. It wasn't what I was making at the German Village, but I could still send money home to Annie for little Albert. I had promised myself I wouldn't stop in Hartford until I was headlining at Poli's Theater, but an engagement in Boston made me rethink that plan.

When we hit Boston, I made a point of letting my relatives know I was in town. Many of my mother's family had settled in Beantown and seeing some kin turned out to be a great remedy for a homesick twenty-year-old. Uncles and aunts and cousins galore came to my shows and, perhaps even more importantly, invited me back to their houses for the first home-cooked meals I'd had since I left Abuza's. Because of my warm welcome, I made plans to head home to Hartford as soon as I could. I had talked myself into believing my hometown would treat me even better than Boston had.

Boy, was I wrong. From the moment I stepped onto the empty platform at the Hartford station, the message was clear. No one wanted anything to do with me. I walked half a mile to my family's house and people I knew ignored my hellos. I'd been so singularly focused on headlining I'd forgotten that, back at home, I was still considered a hussy who left her husband and child to take off for the big city. Because of my cosmopolitan clothes and makeup, even my family had trouble remembering I was still the same old Sophie.

Sure, they welcomed me when I came through the front door, but there was no mistaking the chilly wind that blew through the Abuza household. Albert was now walking and talking a little, but every time

I'd reach out toward him he would go scurrying to Annie. What could I expect after he hadn't seen me in so long? My mother looked like she had aged a hundred years. Her hunchback, the result of chopping too many onions over a low counter for decades, was worse than ever.

The one person who hadn't changed a bit was Papa. He'd had years of practice ignoring Mama's wrath when he lost at the poker table, so it was easy for him to make believe my mother wasn't furious with me for leaving home. He gave me a big hug and kiss when I found him tinkering away upstairs. He needed a new doorbell after his last model failed miserably. The idea had come to him when he won his postman buddy's uniform right off his back at the poker table. Much to Mama's dismay, he purchased a parrot and spent months wearing the uniform and training the bird to alert the whole house when he saw a mailman coming.

He parked the parrot in the window and, like clockwork, when the mailman walked up the steps toward the door, the bird went berserk screeching, "Letters, you have got! Letters, you have got!" in a thick Yiddish accent.

Just like the cowbell door system, the parrot began to drive my mother bonkers. Papa had trained the bird by feeding it, and before long it acquired the insatiable Abuza appetite and began squawking its alert every time it wanted a snack. With the bird screaming about letters every hour of the day and night, it wasn't long before Mama suddenly developed a love for cats. Papa's dream of training a thousand feathered mailbox alarms was swallowed alive by a stray that *somehow* got into the house. Bye bye, birdie.

I got the latest news about the family from Annie, who was the only person besides Papa who was warm to me on that first visit home. I could always count on her to be on my side. She also filled me in on what was happening in Hartford and I learned that things weren't going so well at Abuza's Family Restaurant. My brother Phil had married a quiet girl named Leah and they were expecting a baby, so he'd left the restaurant for a more stable job sorting mail at the post office. To replace him, my parents had hired (and fired) a series of lazy, thieving employees. The money I sent home every week would've helped the situation but Mama was keeping all of it "in the bank," as she said, which meant it was stashed away in the toe of one of her old shoes. She was convinced that I'd need it when my show business dreams failed and I came crawling back home.

The night before I left, I sat down with Mama in her sewing room like old times. The Singer we bought her was humming as she repaired Annie's dresses and Papa's shirts. She didn't say much at first, but eventually let it slip that the year I'd been gone had been hardest on Annie. She quit school to watch Albert and work full time at the restaurant. Little Albert often stayed with Leah, but when Annie had a few hours off she gladly took him back. She'd take him to the park for a walk but all of the other women with children shunned her entirely. The whole synagogue wrote off the Abuzas the minute I left for New York City. Customers who'd come to the restaurant every week for years refused to eat even a crust of bread that came out of our kitchen.

Mama finally stopped her sewing and looked me in the eye for the first time since I left home.

"It's too late to change the past," she said with a cold stare. "You do whatever it is you're doing now but you better save up to give Annie a big wedding someday, you hear me? She has earned it. And you always provide for Albert, understand?"

"Yes, Mama."

With that, she silently turned back to her sewing.

I decided to walk myself to the station the next day, quietly slipping out of the house without causing myself any more sadness. Shortly before my train was scheduled to arrive, I heard a familiar voice say my name. The hair on the back of my neck stood up.

"What the hell do you want, Louis?" I asked my former husband without even glancing over at him.

"I heard you were in town and the least I could do is say hello. Thought you might be glad to see me again, spending all that time alone on the road. Seeing as how I was the only one in this town good enough to marry you, I figured you might have a few bucks of your big stage money to toss my way," he said, sliding down the bench until he was right next to me.

"Listen, you son of a bitch," I boomed. "I'm gonna give you five seconds to get out of my sight or you're gonna need an ambulance, you hear me? When I told you to beat it, I meant for good."

Louis put on one of his most evil smirks and walked away with a nasty chuckle. I hoped the back of his slick jacket and hat was the last glimpse I'd ever get of that asshole.

That was the last straw. I could give the cold shoulder as good as I'd gotten it from my hometown. I decided Hartford wasn't going to see me again until I'd made it as a full-fledged headliner, performing as myself. I was still stuck in the middle of the bill performing in blackface. Even if my own family and friends refused to recognize the old Sophie Tucker, the least I could do would be to make the whole damn country get to know the real me.

Chapter 9

He's a Good Man
to Have Around

Iknocked around New York City through the whole winter of 1907 doing twelve weeks in twelve different theaters and trying to figure out an angle to drop the blackface from my act. It wasn't until the spring of 1908 that I got lucky and met an agent named Joe Woods. Joe asked if I was familiar with burly-q. I told him we hadn't met, but I was good friends with his brother, barbeque. Joe rolled his eyes and explained that burlesque paid fifty bucks a week and would require some acting, so I lied through my teeth and told him I was practically a member of the Royal Shakespeare Company. For fifty bucks a week, I'd figure it out later.

Burlesque back then wasn't what it is today. The strippers didn't come on the scene until well into the Thirties, but it was still a night of good, raw fun. You might go to a burlesque show and come out feeling a little hot under the collar, but you'd never hear a single four-letter word. The beauty of the burly-q was its cleverness. Sure, every joke might've been about sex, but they were so veiled you'd have to puzzle them out like a dirty riddle.

I reported to my new job on the Wheel, burlesque's version of the Circuit, at the Bay Theater in Boston with instructions to find a man named Harry Emerson. He was the troupe leader and my first order of business was to convince him I would be better out of blackface, as myself. He insisted I continue painting on the burnt cork for at least a few months, but he did agree to put me in a little comedy skit he'd written.

"Woods told me you had a lot of acting experience," smiled Harry.

"I think you'll be pleasantly surprised," I assured him. Secretly I was praying we'd both be pleasantly surprised. At least Emerson had me slated to play his nagging wife, which seemed like an easy fit. Nagging a no-good husband was second nature for me.

I only had one line in the skit. To be more exact, I only had one word. For twenty-nine minutes and thirty seconds of a half-hour play, all of the actors in the scene feared my character's arrival. Then, just as the curtain was about to drop, I made my entrance and screamed my husband's name. I understood my role and why it was funny, but I was terrified I'd screw it up somehow. For all of the performing I'd done in my life up to that point, I'd never once had to act on stage. Sure, I painted my face and sang, but that wasn't the same thing. It was just Sophie in a funny accent. There was no one depending on me to get my lines right at the right time.

This might sound crazy, but I stayed up for hours that night rehearsing my one word, which was "Frederick." I tried it with two syllables. I tried it with three syllables. I shouted it into my pillow. I mimed it in the mirror. By rehearsal the next morning, I'd worked myself into a complete panic over my ability to land the stinking word. This was my "To be or not to be," and my future on the Wheel was the question.

"Did you read the script?" asked Harry Emerson, taking his place on stage.

"You bet I did," I assured him. "It's a riot."

"It's supposed to be a drama," he said, his face going cold.

"R-really?" I quavered.

"Kidding!" he said, and slapped me on the back. "That's what they call a zinger. Now let's see if you can do the same thing."

The actress I was replacing was nice enough to hang around for an extra rehearsal and Harry had the troop do the last five minutes of the play while I watched. Then, it was my turn. Everyone got back to their places and I stood behind the set door. When I heard my cue, I opened the door, stepped in and yelled my line. After a few seconds of silence, everyone applauded politely. Harry gave me an encouraging smile and had me do it again, but louder.

And again. And again. By take six, I was nearly in tears.

"You've got the volume," Harry coached.

"Maybe I should try it with three syllables?" I guessed.

"No, hon, it's the attitude that needs work. You've got to make your entrance, say that name, and make the audience believe you are the biggest bitch that ever walked God's green earth."

I thought I knew what he was getting at but I didn't get it right the next time, or any of the ten times after that. Harry had to dismiss the rest of the cast to get ready for the matinee and told me to take a break while he talked to his assistant. It wasn't hard to overhear him. The original actress had agreed to stay for the day's performances to give me a little more time to rehearse, but if I didn't get it right the next day I'd be out on my keister.

I got through my singing performances and went back to my hotel. Once again, I practiced all night until I collapsed in bed, hoarse from screaming. That night I dreamed I was being chased by an army of Cossacks named Frederick.

The next day I awoke early and snuck into the theater before any of the other performers arrived. I made my way to center stage and thought about the last two years I'd spent in makeup I didn't want to wear, singing songs I didn't want to sing, all to send money back to Mama who was convinced I was going to fail. I closed my eyes and pictured the sink at the restaurant full of dirty dishes. I saw Mama standing in a cloud of cabbage-smelling steam, yelling at me to hurry up and wash the pots so I could get home to Louis in time to cook him dinner. I pictured him grunting at me from behind his newspaper. Magically, I felt a thunderbolt of anger gather in my gut. I opened my eyes, took a deep breath, and let out my line in a bloodcurdling scream.

I had, as they say in the business, found my motivation.

At the matinee, I recreated my scream and Harry was so surprised he nearly fell over in his chair. It was the biggest laugh the scene had ever gotten and I was, officially, an actress. I went home that night and instead of practicing my screams into a pillow, I decided it was time to introduce myself to a Vaudeville bigwig.

Dear Mr. Ziegfeld,

My name is Sophie Tucker. I am a seasoned closing singer and very experienced actress with the Harry Emerson burlesque troupe. I read in the papers that you are putting together another Follies this summer. If you need a Southern singer, I would be delighted to join your company.

I have enclosed my upcoming schedule if you would like to come and see me. I would also be happy to come visit you when I am in New York to audition my vocal ability. Just be sure to hide all your glasses before I arrive, because I don't want to shatter what I am sure is very fine crystal.

Looking forward to hearing from you,
Sophie Tucker

For the next six months I soaked up all there was to learn from Harry Emerson about burlesque. Many of those classic bits Abbott and Costello made famous on the radio and in the movies were actually old burlesque chestnuts, like the Susquehanna hats, the blackboard arithmetic and the Niagara Falls routines. After half a year with Harry Emerson I'd memorized both parts of every two-man comedy classic.

I also made a lot of lifelong friends, some of whom ended up in high places in the entertainment world. One night after a show in Boston we burly-q troupers went to a local actor's hangout to blow off some steam and Harry, who had become my biggest booster, dragged me across the room to a table where a handsome woman was holding court.

Ethel Barrymore, 1908.

"Hello, Ethel," said Harry as we approached.

"Harry, you big blowhard!" shouted the woman. "How are things? Are you at the Bay Theater? We're over at the Majestic in the dullest drama I've ever been paid to sleepwalk through. Who's this young lady?" she asked, pointing her cigarette holder in my direction.

"Remember when you saw our show and you asked about the loud singer? This is her! Sophie Tucker, meet Ethel Barrymore," said Harry.

"Let me tell you," chuckled Ethel to the rest of her table. "This girl has got a set of pipes that won't quit. Now Harry, you know all these bums except for this one. He just hopped off the boat from England and you're going to want to know his name. Say hello to Charlie Chaplin."

Back then I was too green to know who I was talking to, but before I left town I made a point of going to see them both perform. I couldn't take my eyes off Ethel when she was on stage. She was a force of nature. And Charlie, he was performing in a vaudeville show across town at the Lexington and I was one of the first people in the country to see his unforgettable drunk act. He would start in one of the upper boxes on the left side of the theater and then stumble, fumble and tumble through the audience, creating havoc wherever he stepped. He was a brilliant acrobat who could make the most athletic twists and turns look like they were coming from the clumsiest man alive.

Sophie, Oona Chaplin, and Charlie Chaplin with friends.

No one was more delighted than me when Chaplin started to appear in films. It was a while before his true genius emerged, but the world was never the same after the Little Tramp took to the silver screen. I'm proud to say that he remained a fan of mine as well, and we kept in touch over the years to trade old dirty burlesque jokes.

Eight months later, even after all of the friends I'd made and things I'd learned, Harry was still only allowing me to sing in blackface. I was so angry every day it was no picnic to be around me. I just wanted to go out on stage as myself. I knew I could get a bigger reaction being the real Sophie than with a bland Southern routine that audiences could see in any third-rate theater in the country.

Then, one day, everything changed. We were coming back to Boston from Pittsburgh and our train arrived three hours late. That meant we had only ninety minutes to get ready for our first matinee. We hustled off the train the moment we pulled into the station, crammed into a couple of horse-drawn cabs and took off toward the theater. Our trunks, props, and scenery would follow in a big flatbed cart.

While I waited for the luggage to arrive, I gossiped with a young man I knew from the last few times I'd played at that theater. Lazar Meir was a ticket taker and glorified gopher who'd become a buddy because I'd always tip him a whole dollar to deliver my trunk to my dressing room.

When the cart finally arrived with the trunks, the show was due to start in just thirty minutes. The backstage ballet of actors and stagehands when they're under the gun is really something to see. It's what mesmerized me that first day Mr. Elliot snuck me into Poli's in Hartford. People move so quickly and so purposefully they look like an overwound cuckoo clock. We all darted into our dressing rooms and that's when I realized everyone had their trunk but me.

"Lazar!" I screamed from my doorway.

"It's not on the cart!" Meir hollered back from down the hall.

"I'm not on for forty-five minutes! Go back to the station and find my trunk," I yelled frantically. "My costume and makeup are in there!"

Harry overheard the commotion and began to sweat. He all but soaked his shirt through when Lazar came back forty minutes later and reported that my trunk was on its way to Portland, Maine.

"It must have had a craving for lobster," I joked.

"You'll have to go on in your street clothes," Harry said, fanning himself with his hat.

"And do what?" I asked.

"Wing it," said Harry, shoving me toward the stage.

"Wing it? What does that mean?"

"It's burlesque for 'Get the fuck out there, you're on!'"

The conductor had been vamping my intro throughout the chaos, but I held up my hands when I got to center stage and he cut the music. Then, I addressed the audience in my perfect stage Southern accent.

"Ladies and gentleman, don't look in your programs. I know y'all was expecting someone a hair darker than me." The audience chuckled, confused. "Well, sirs and madams, here's what happened. I'm Sophie Tucker, and they done lost my trunk. So I'm out here in my street clothes, without my make-up, and I'm in a pickle."

The audience laughed again. I knew I was winning them over, as odd as it was to see a chubby Jew with a Negro stage accent.

"Here's my dilemma, folks. Iffin I sing, you might not like me without my accoutrements. But iffin I don't sing, this Mama isn't gonna get her money. So can y'all do me a favor? I'm gonna sing, and when I do, please think dark thoughts. How 'bout that?"

My act got four encores that night, which was my biggest response so far on the Wheel. Lazar got word that my trunk wouldn't be back for two days and Harry gave me permission to do whatever I damn well pleased so long as the audiences went home happy.

I didn't want to go out in my street clothes again, so the hardest part was going to be finding a costume. The other girls in the troupe were at least three dress sizes smaller than me so there was no hope that I could squeeze into one of their beautiful gowns and keep it in one piece. At least I still had my music case. I never let it out of my sight because you can always sing naked, but not if the orchestra is playing the wrong notes.

In between shows I went with Lazar to my favorite Boston delicatessen to brainstorm over *blintzes*[1]. There had to be at least one pretty dress out there

Trixie Friganza

---

1   *Blintzes* – Eastern European pancakes usually filled with cottage cheese, folded, sautéed and served with sour cream.

for a heifer like me. I sent Lazar to fetch a paper so I could see if Trixie Friganza was in town. She was the other pleasingly plump singer on the Wheel, but it turned out she was clear across the country.

As luck would have it, there was one actress I knew in town who might be able to save me. I raced with Lazar across town in a horse-drawn cab to the theater where Ethel Barrymore was performing. Me and my famous pipes talked our way backstage and she took pity on me. Ethel loaned me one of her beautiful black gowns and a pair of her high heeled shoes to match. At least we were the same height, even if she was a size or two smaller in the waist.

Sophie in a slightly roomier stage dress.

We raced back to the Bay and I recruited a couple of the waifs lower on the bill to cram me into my dress. The thing buttoned, but I couldn't breathe, laugh, or bend any part of my body or the seams would explode from the stress of keeping me strapped in. The kicker was that this was the first time I'd ever worn high heels. The combined effect was like someone had stood a sausage on two four-inch toothpicks. I looked like a Hebrew National wiener in mourning but I was determined to make it work, come hell or high heels!

When it was time to take my place in the wings, I realized that the hem of my dress was so tight I couldn't move more than a few inches with each step. Getting to the stage at my speed would take longer than traveling the entire Oregon Trail, so Lazar wheeled me on his hand truck over to the boys in the Harry Emerson Quartet, who were standing just offstage. I'd arranged a musical number with the barbershop group earlier that day and thanked my lucky stars that they were all burly men.

The lights went out and it was time for Operation: Salami Drop.

The bass and baritone joined hands to create a seat. The tenor and lead hoisted me by my arms and, when the lights came up, we shuffled out together, me swinging ever so slightly in my human hammock. They set me down center stage, I straightened myself out, and the boys took their posts.

The orchestra started and everything was going fine until I hit the end of the first verse. Over those twenty-four bars I'd managed to waddle all the way to the left side of the stage, but now it was time for the Herculean act of turning around. To make things worse, Ethel's dress had an eighteen-inch train. When I spun to go in the opposite direction, the tenor didn't realize he was standing on my dress and I landed flat on my caboose.

The audience went wild. They thought it was all part of the act.

"What's so funny?" I said, as the orchestra vamped and the quartet struggled not to quar-wet themselves with laughter. "You try driving this dress in high heels!"

The four of them somehow got me up off the floor and pointed me toward the right side of the stage, and I shuffled slowly in that direction throughout my second verse. The baritone held my train and the alto scurried ahead of me just in case I took a nosedive. The audience? They were having the time of their lives waiting for me to fall on my ass again.

At the end of the song I'd made it back to the center of the stage. For dramatic effect I had planned five sharp turns for my big finish, and the boys, knowing what was coming, looked at each other and braced for impact like the offensive line of a football team. The fellas bounced me back up to standing after each turn, thereby inventing the first human ping-pong act. It seemed like we pulled everything off until the final flourish, a kick, which sent all of us tumbling into a quadruple-decker Tucker sandwich. The audience wouldn't stop applauding.

That was the end of blackface. It hadn't gone exactly as I hoped but it all worked out for the best; if Ethel had eaten a few more sandwiches over the years and given me a dress that fit, I might not have realized that I was meant to be a comedian. Harry encouraged me to keep the dress and shoes in the act and taught me to fall so I wouldn't end up covered in black and blues.

As for my missing trunk, the lovely Mr. Emerson gave me a $10 bonus to buy a new one because we sold out every show when word got around Boston that there was a girl with a falling act that was a riot. I gave five dollars of my windfall directly to little Lazar Meir. Right before we left for our next stop in New York City, Meir fetched my original trunk from his house, where we'd been hiding it the whole time. Stagehands are a dime a dozen, but it takes someone special to be an accomplice.

A couple of years later, Lazar changed his first name to Louie and his last from Meir to Mayer. He added a fancy middle initial when he took over MGM Studios. When I met Louie B. Mayer again in 1937 to sign my five-year movie contract in Hollywood, L.B. reminded the press about the fiver.

"During those years," Mayer said, "it was the biggest tip I ever got. But Sophie was such a doll, I would have done anything she wanted for free."

Sure, that's what he told the papers. But when he took me for $15,000 in a pinochle game a couple of weeks later, I demanded a five dollar refund.

Louis B. Mayer, formerly Lazar Meir.

Chapter 10

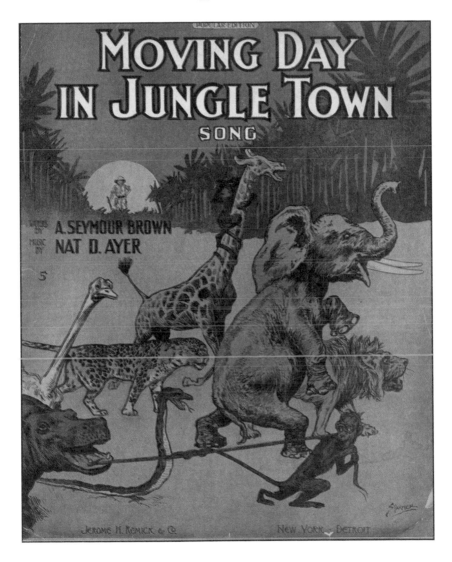

Moving Day
in Jungle Town

When I started in show business, the biggest headliners in the world were Eva Tanguay and Nora Bayes, who was touring with her hubby Jack Norworth.

That beautiful bitch changed men more often than she changed her stockings, but at that moment in time Jack and Nora were unstoppable. Jack's gone now but lives on during the seventh inning of every baseball game, having written "Take Me Out to the Ballgame." Nora and Eva mostly live on in my memory as the women who got me fired from the Ziegfeld Follies.

By 1909, I'd written a letter every other week for four months to Flo Ziegfeld, master of the best Vaudeville show on Earth. I'd had a great time touring with Harry Emerson's troupe, but now that I was getting laughs without the ridiculous makeup I refused to settle into burlesque for life. Being

Nora Bayes and her second of five husbands.

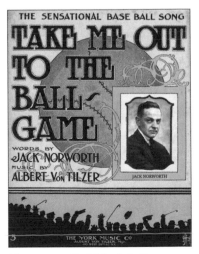

Sheet music for Take Me Out to the Ball Game.

125

a relentless pain in the ass paid off, because Ziggy finally sent me a telegram in May.

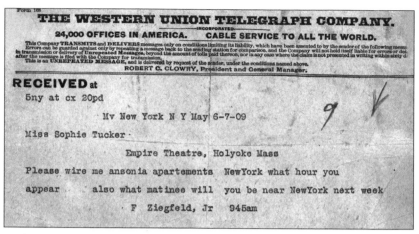

Sophie's telegram from Flo Ziegfeld.

Maybe Mr. Ziegfeld was interested, or maybe his secretary told him she'd quit if she had to open one more of my envelopes. Whatever it was, he must have quietly attended one of my shows because I received a contract in the mail to become a member of the Ziegfeld Follies at the rate of a hundred clams per week. Harry Emerson was less than thrilled about giving up his number one act, however, and sued me for $1,500.00 for breach of my burlesque contract. Eventually we settled for $150.00 over a couple of egg creams and we parted as friends. I didn't want any enemies out there who knew I had to use baby oil to squeeze into my gowns.

I was hired by the Follies to sing just a couple of songs during a big set change before the end of the first act, and for now, that was just fine with me. I would've hummed "The Star-Spangled Banner" while sweeping up after the animal acts as long as my name was in Ziegfeld's program.

I reported to the rehearsal hall in Atlantic City a few weeks later and I was instantly surrounded by so many gorgeous chorus girls I thought I'd stumbled into a mannequin factory. It was a big cast with at least forty luscious women, tons of scenery, and two big stars: Nora Bayes and Jack Norworth. I spotted Mr. Ziegfeld standing in the middle of all the chaos, marched right up to him, and stuck out my hand.

"Hello, Flo, I'm Sophie Tucker. What do you want me to do?"

People have asked me over the years whether or not I really called him Flo right to his rich old face, and I'm always perplexed by their question. What should I have called him? Irving? I was twenty-two and I'd never been big on formalities. Flo, on the other hand, looked at me like I was a fly in his soup and one of his army of stagehands whisked me backstage and parked me in a chair.

After four weeks of rehearsal I'd never been so well-rested in my life. I reported to my chair in the wings every day at nine in the morning and sat there until six in the evening when everyone broke for dinner. Between naps, I watched the intricate process of putting together a big production number. Three days out from the first show, I could tell you where every single chorus girl had to stand for the big finale but no one seemed to care that I was there.

Florenz Ziegfeld.

When I wasn't napping, I was palling around with a maid I'd met named Molly Elkins. I felt instantly close to her, but little did I know then that Molly would end up becoming one of my best bosom buddies. She took pity on me one day when I was going crazy with boredom and we got to chatting. She'd had something of a stage career herself, touring with one of the all-black review companies in her younger years. But the pay stunk and the gigs were rough, so she ended up taking a job dressing one of the stars on Ziegfeld's bill.

It was Molly who jiggled me awake when, two days before the show was scheduled to open, someone hollered my name a couple of times. It was finally my turn to report to the stage.

"Good morning," clipped Julian White, the stage manager. "I don't have a lot of time to talk you through this. We've got a big set change for the final number at the end of the first act, so we need you to sing three songs and sing 'em good and slow, because the boys have a lot to do back there. We'll run through whatever you're gonna sing at the dress rehearsal. The orchestra knows every song you've ever heard." With that, he rushed me back off the stage and brought on the dancers. I returned to my chair where Molly was now snoring.

As the chorus line kicked up their long legs, I overheard an argument between Ziegfeld and White about whether or not the show needed one more big number to close the Follies. Julian thought it was spectacular enough (and I thought he'd pull out what was left of his hair if he had to stage one more act) but Ziegfeld wanted to close things out with a bang, and he didn't earn his name on the marquee because he had bad instincts.

For the second time that day, Julian howled my name from the stage. Now I was to be the lead singer in a closing scene called "Moving Day in Jungle Town." Our recently retired president Teddy Roosevelt had just returned from one of his famed African safaris and Ziegfeld got it in his head that it'd be funny to close the show with me in a leopard skin suit singing atop an elephant—which was actually eight burly stagehands sweating inside an enormous costume. I'd wear whatever Flo asked, but I was pleased as punch that for once I wasn't going to be on stage *as* the elephant.

Sophie with Eleanor Roosevelt, Teddy's niece.

They fitted me for my new jungle attire and I tried it on the next day during dress rehearsal. It buttoned, but I looked like a leopard that had swallowed an entire antelope for lunch. The music wasn't ready yet, so all we could do was walk through the scene and hope to God the number would work out. I was about to take the stage in the Ziegfeld Follies without anyone having heard me sing so much as a note.

That was the Ziegfeld way: gigantic, chaotic, and lucky. He was so confident in himself and the performers that he'd invited a full audience down to Atlantic City for the preview performance. We'd be doing our show for the first time in front of a crowd that included all the bigwigs of Broadway, like Dillingham, Harris, and my old friend Irving Berlin. As usual, Irving had come through and had written me three new numbers especially for my spot before the end of Act One.

I was shaking in my boots all through the first act. Molly had to shove me out onto the stage when it was my turn to sing, but the miracle that happens whenever I hear my music happened again that night. Just like always, the footlights melted my nerves and I blew the roof off the joint. At the end of my third number, Julian frantically signaled for me to do another. Let me tell you, he didn't have to ask twice. I kept going for a fourth, fifth, and sixth song. The audience was standing, mad to hear one more. But the scenery was up for the first act finale and Julian motioned me off. Molly met me with open arms and we hugged and jumped up and down, silently celebrating how I'd wowed them when it counted.

There wasn't much time to gloat, however.

Nora Bayes was in a lather. She was outside her dressing room door screaming at Mr. Ziegfeld and pointing like a lunatic in my direction. Molly, who had been around divas her whole life, looked at me and mimed a noose. My goose wasn't just cooked; it was burnt to a crisp.

I returned to my shared dressing room backstage and waited for the other shoe to drop. Nora was a lamb onstage with an enormous group of loyal fans who turned out to see her every night, but offstage she was a snake. In all my years in show business, I've still never met a single soul who called her a friend. Molly patted me on the shoulder and tried to comfort me.

"Child, if Mr. Ziegfeld fires you, you thank him and smile. You're too young to burn any bridges," she said. In my head, I began writing a letter to Harry Emerson requesting his best fricassee recipe for all the crow I'd have to eat to get back on the Wheel.

Flo didn't fire me, thank God. He told me I wasn't going to be singing any numbers while they changed the scenery, but I was still going to close out the show on top of the elephant. I was so relieved I grabbed him by the lapels of his tuxedo and kissed him right on the lips. After that, Flo ran whenever he saw me coming. I guess even back then my kisses were deadly.

Nora had no interest in my silly little jungle number. She just didn't want any other singers sharing her spotlight and I was more than happy to oblige. I still had a job with the Follies and I still had my paycheck, which was now more important than ever because I was helping to put my brother Moe through law school at New York University.

Over the next few weeks of performances with the Follies in New York City, I learned not to take Nora's temper tantrum too personally. She blew up about everything and everyone. I grew to understand that to get to the top and stay there, you have to protect yourself. I resolved that when I became a headliner, I was going to be so unique it wouldn't matter who else was on the bill. There was no reason to intentionally hurt a newcomer's chances—unless they tried to show me up, in which case I had a few tricks up my sleeve just in case I needed to squash someone like a bug.

Sophie and the cast of the 1909 Ziegfeld Follies. Tucker is first on the left, holding a handbag.

By the third week, Nora had so many disagreements with Ziegfeld that she up and walked. Bayes left us high and dry during the dog days of August and it was hard for Flo to find a replacement. We were one of the only shows running through the unbearable heat. The only reason we could stay open at all was because our stage was on the roof of the Riviola Theater on Broadway and we performed outside. This was long before air conditioning and the outdoor stage was the only way to keep the chorus girls from dropping like flies.

Come September, though, we needed a headliner. Enter Eva Tanguay, the "I Don't Care Girl." If ever a billing was on the money, it was hers. Eva came out wearing three fig leaves and, for thirty-five minutes straight, she sang, danced, and defied the laws of gravity. If you look up sex in the dictionary, you'd see her picture.

Eva was the kind of headliner who'd worked her way up from the chorus, so she was a good deal friendlier than Nora. Too friendly, in fact. She'd take anyone for a ride: man, woman, or, as it turned out, elephant. One day I came in to find she wanted my spot in the finale and, after just eight weeks with the Follies, I was out of a job.

Eva Tanguay, the 'I Don't Care Girl'.

It turned out Eva did me a favor that day, however unintentionally. One of the bigwigs who'd come to our Atlantic City dress rehearsal was the up and coming William Morris, who was then the owner of ten theaters around New York City and Chicago. He came to the Follies on the lookout for new acts, so when he heard I was free he wired me to talk about coming to work for him.

Eva turned out to be an okay gal, too. Once I became a headliner I would see her here and there and she was always friendly. The press had an ongoing debate for years about who popularized the hit song "Mother," which we both sang and recorded. One night, decades after the Follies, I was playing the Palace and I got word that Eva was up in one of the V.I.P. boxes. She'd dropped in just to see me sing. In the middle of my act, I told the audience to give Eva a big hand and asked her to say a few words.

"Sophie, there are a few things I borrowed from you over the years without your permission. One was the song 'Mother,' and the other was an elephant. If you sing one, I'll return the other," she said with a smile.

We were fast friends from that day on. Sadly, as it so often happened, Eva was such a hard party-er that she ended up ill, alone, and broke in her later years. She'd blown all of her money on so-called friends who only hung around until her parties stopped. I got a few of us old-timers together to do some benefits in her honor, and we managed to find Eva some decent doctors and get her set up in a nice cottage in Hollywood for the rest of her life. She was a good old dame.

The same, however, cannot be said for Nora Bayes.

As the years went by, my star kept rising and Nora's naturally began to fall. She was forever a headliner, but she eventually toured as a nostalgia act. Whenever our paths would cross, she'd roll her eyes and always pretend to forget my name. It seemed to cause Nora pain to have to acknowledge my existence. Whenever she got the chance, she'd try to upstage me. The only time we actually performed together was at benefits and even then, even when it was for charity, she'd insist on bumping me down the roster so she could close the show. She did it so often she had some special material worked out exactly for that situation.

"Wasn't Sophie great?" she'd ooze. "Many of you may not know this, but Sophie Tucker used to demonstrate songs for me in Tin Pan Alley."

Nora loved inflating the one time I sang "Shine on Harvest Moon" for her into a story that made me sound like I'd been her personal servant.

After seven years of her mean-spirited digs, I got fed up. I had opened a nightclub in New York City in 1926 called Sophie Tucker's Playground. Around the same time, I got a call from Eddie Darling, the booker at the Palace, asking me to appear at the National Variety Artists benefit, which was one of the biggest shows of the year. He wanted me to close the show, but I'd heard that before.

"But Eddie, what about Nora? I really think *she* deserves to close the show," I said, sarcastically.

"No way," said Eddie. "She's been an even bigger pain in my ass than usual. The management here at the Palace voted her the Grand Poobah of the I.O.M.F."

"What's that?" I asked.

"The International Order of Motherfuckers," Eddie chuckled. With that, we arranged a scheme to sink Nora Bayes and her horrible attitude for good. Eddie leaked it to the press that I might not make the benefit that year because of all the urgent business I needed to attend to at my brand new nightclub. The papers reported that Eddie had promised me I could go on whenever I pleased, just as long as I showed up. All the while he was cooing in Nora's ear that she'd have her precious closing spot.

The night of the benefit, I had a packed house at the Playground. Per usual, a couple of my good friends popped in to join me on stage. That night my guests were Georgie Jessel and Eddie Cantor.

My two buddies barged on stage after I finished one of my big numbers.

"Sophie, you have to get to the Palace!" shouted Cantor. "The N.V.A. needs you!"

"I'm sorry, but my job is here, Eddie," I said, taking a deep bow and gesturing out into the audience. They were eating up the obvious theatrics, since the gossip pages had been trumpeting will-she-or-won't-she updates for days about my performing at the benefit.

"Don't worry Soph," said Georgie, elbowing me in the ribs. "I'll watch the place for you."

"Someone lock up the liquor!" I shouted back to the bartenders. "Ladies and gentlemen, do you mind if I step out for a moment? I have a little bit of business to attend to at the Palace."

With that, I hopped in the car I had waiting at the stage door and darted across town to the theater. When I got there, Eddie Darling took me by the arm and we strolled slowly to the stage in time to hear the emcee announce the final act, Nora Bayes. We watched Nora's stale material from the wings. She caught a glimpse of me as she took her first bow and walked off stage. True to form, the Grand Poobah had a few choice words for Eddie.

From left to right: William Morris, Eddie Cantor, Sophie, and Georgie Jessel.

"No fucking way, Eddie," she hissed. "If that blimp sings after me I'll never play this dump again!"

Eddie was cool as a cucumber. He took her by her bony old shoulders, spun her around, and booted her back out on stage to take her bows. I went on last that night and it was a huge success. And Nora? She never closed another major benefit or played the Palace again.

My revenge was somewhat bittersweet. She hung on playing second-tier houses for a few years until she got sick with cancer and decided to move up to her cabin on Lake George to live out her remaining days.

I've always been a sucker for someone on the circuit when they are approaching their real final bow. When I heard Nora was going to drive through the city one last time on her way up to her cabin, I called in a favor from Eddie and the Palace crew. I got her driver to agree to pass by the theater on Broadway, where she was greeted with a display of every one of her life-size cutouts propped up on the sidewalk outside the Palace and her name displayed proudly on the marquee one more time. I was told she blew a kiss out the window of her car.

Nora, though, was determined to get the last word. Four months later, my Warner Brothers debut film *Honky Tonk* was set to premiere in New York City. It was a big to-do with a red carpet, limousines, and a parade of starlets in their best furs.

This time everyone from Warner Brothers was in the audience, but I'd already seen the picture and I knew it was a real stinkeroo. *Variety* was going to tear me to pieces in the morning.

Opening night of Honky Tonk *in New York City.*

When I woke up the next day and unfolded the paper, however, what I saw made me laugh until I cried. The front page screamed the news that Nora Bayes had passed away during the night, which bumped the story about my crummy picture way off the front page. True to form, the head of the I.O.M.F. had managed to upstage me one last time from beyond the grave. It was the one and only time Nora, my showbiz nemesis, did me a favor.

Nora Bayes 1881-1929

Part II

A New Home

Chapter 11

She Knows Her Onions

The S.S. Anchoria

It was no easy task to become Sophie Tucker, Vaudeville headliner and international star, but Sophie Abuza, the Jewish immigrant with the Italian name, had an even more complicated journey.

To start with, nobody has a clue when I was born. The only thing everyone agrees on is that, true to form, I entered the world wailing at the top of my lungs. Most people think I was born January 13, 1884. However, if you went to Ellis Island today and found the boat manifest for the S.S. Anchoria, it says my mother, brother and I arrived in New York City from Glasgow on September 26, 1887. I'm listed as approximately half a year old. My actual date of birth was December 25, 1886, as best as anyone in my family can remember.

Manifest of the S.S. Anchoria, which lists Jacka (Jennie) Abuza, 30, Inna (Phillip) 3 years old, and Sonia (Sophia), ½ year old, traveling from Odessa to New York City.

Work papers Sophie filled out in 1937 to work for MGM Studios. Note that Sophie wrote that her birthday was 12/25/1887—admitting the correct month and day, but giving herself a second 49th year.

I had to fudge things a little in 1906 when I got to Manhattan since Tiny from the German Village told me I had to be at least twenty-one to work in a beer hall. The birthdate that has stuck, January 13, 1884, is the one I wrote on my first set of working papers in New York City. I chose that year because it made me older and I picked the month of January on a whim, but the number thirteen was a tribute to Papa's rotten luck.

Aside from my birthdate, my whole family history was always shrouded in a little bit of mystery. Papa loved to retell a few tales about when I was a baby, but whenever I asked Mama how we got to America she would order me to scour pots. It wasn't until the end of her life that I convinced her to finally spill the beans about how the Kalishes got to America and became the Abuzas along the way.

Here were the things I knew as a child: Mama was born around 1850 to the Lestz family in Tolchene, Russia. Her father had turned his back on his family's lucrative silver and diamond business to marry a farm girl and start a little country store that sold produce, dry goods, and jars of my grandmother's goulash. My life's an open book, but the one secret I'll take to the grave is my grandmother's goulash recipe.

My father, Zachary Kalish, was born in 1855 in a village near Tolchene to a family of horrible tailors and worse gamblers. If she were still alive today, Mama would brain me for revealing the fact that Papa was five years her junior, but I don't think there's anything wrong with a lady calling up a player or two from the minor leagues.

Papa insisted he ended up marrying Mama because their fathers were friendly in the old country and used to play cards in Grandpa Lestz's store. Papa swore that his father bet his only horse on a hand of cards and lost to Grandpa Lestz, who had no use for livestock but needed a husband for his oldest daughter. If you believe Papa, you could say that I owe my existence to Grandpa Lestz's winning pair of deuces. It never took much to beat a Kalish at cards.

However they met—and Mama rolled her eyes to the ceiling whenever Papa told that story—six years later, my brother Phillip was about two and I was on the way. Grandpa Lestz had closed the grocery by then and was living with Mama and Papa in their small house out in the country, where Papa spent most of his time hiding to avoid being conscripted into the Russian army. This became a valuable skill later on in Papa's life when he lost big at his own poker table on the second floor above the restaurant. He'd disappear like a ghost and Mama would be left to yell at the wind.

With each Cossack rampage, there was only one thing that saved my parents' house from being burned to the ground and that was the famous Lestz goulash. Word had gotten around amongst the Russian soldiers the Kalish house was off limits as long as there was enough bubbling goulash to go around. Still, one morning when my mother was out at the market, a brand new young Russian soldier came to the house looking for able-bodied men to enlist. Grandpa Lestz offered him a seat and promised that he'd have a lunch to write home about if he'd just wait for my Mama to return. The impatient young Cossack decided Grandpa's hospitality was a trap and shot him in the stomach, leaving him to bleed to death on the kitchen floor.

Mama returned from the market to find her father at death's door, sprawled out next to the big pot of goulash on the fire. She cradled his heavy head in her lap.

"Smells like you need to add more onions," croaked Grandpa Lestz.

Those were his final words. My father and all the other young men in the village came out of hiding the next day to bury Grandpa, believing that even the Cossacks would never stoop so low as to ambush a funeral. They were wrong. Papa and the others were in a prison camp by sunset.

Mama, having just lost her father and now her husband, had had enough of Mother Russia and her army. She loaded up our family's few valuables into our cart, hitched up the horse, dressed little Phillip in his warmest sweater and coat and drove off into the night toward the forest where she knew Papa was being kept. She'd even made sure to pack a kettle of goulash for the road.

It began to snow as Mama and my brother bumped down the dark dirt road. I must have had a craving for a hot bowl of goulash on such a cold winter night, because I kicked up a storm in Mama's belly all the way to the front gate of the prison camp. She told Phillip to creep into the back of the cart and not to make a sound, grabbed her kettle of goulash, and dug out Grandpa Lestz's old rifle from under a pile of blankets. She stashed the gun behind a tree on the way to the guard shack, where she knocked softly on the door.

"Igor, is that you in there?" she whispered, recognizing one of her farmhouse regulars through a crack in the planks of the door. "It's Mrs. Kalish. I've brought you and the other men dinner." She cracked the lid of the kettle and let the oniony aroma of her cooking work its magic.

The door flew open. Igor and a second guard stood in the doorway, equal parts hungry and terrified that Mama would get them killed by their Cossack captain. "Mrs. Kalish," Igor pleaded, "you have to get out of here."

"I just want to kiss my husband goodnight," Mama said, as the delicious fumes floated toward Igor's nose.

Igor's shivering body began to thaw in the cloud of steaming stew. He grabbed the pot from her and motioned for the second guard to unlock the big gate. When Igor ducked back into the shack to put down the heavy pot, Mama reached for her gun. The other guard turned his back to Mama and shouted Papa's name into the prison yard.

With one shot and a ruthless lunge of her bayonet, Mama liberated the whole camp. The men streamed out through the gate and took off for the woods. My mother found Papa and they ran for the cart. Just as Mama was about to slap the horse into motion, my father told her to wait a moment and took off running back toward the guard house.

When he returned, he was holding the kettle of goulash. I'm sure Mama must've been tempted to unload another bullet right into his behind, but I'm with Papa. Wasting good goulash is an unspeakable crime!

According to my father, after my pregnant mother liberated him from the Russian army in December 1886, my family headed west in our cart until I decided to make my big debut somewhere in the wilderness between Ukraine and Hungary. Papa kept the cart bumping along until Mama's hollering started to spook the horse. He tugged the old mare to a halt in front of the first farmhouse he saw and dragged my big

Jennie Abuza, formerly Jennie Kalish, née Jennie Lestz.

brother with him up to the door, but they were greeted by a farmer's shotgun barrel and what sounded to be a whole lot of cursing in a language they couldn't understand.

Thank heavens Mama had hauled herself out of the cart and waddled halfway up the path. The farmer's wife threw her husband out of the way, ran out to meet my mother and led her right into a bedroom in the little farmhouse. Papa and the farmer found a common language in cards and the universal appeal of Papa's terrible luck. A hair-curling *geshray*[1] signaled my entrance into the world and luckily kept Papa from losing his pocket watch.

After that, the next story Papa liked to tell took place a month later, when my parents had traveled from the little farmhouse all the way to Budapest. They found their way to the Jewish quarter by stopping stranger after stranger until they found one who spoke Yiddish. It was getting dark as they rattled down the crooked little streets looking for a safe place to park their cart for the night. As they rounded a bend, they found the lane up ahead was blocked by an angry woman. She was throwing rocks up at a man, clearly her husband, who was hanging out of a second story window and screaming that she'd been making eyes at someone named Lipschitz. The wife hollered back something not so nice about the husband's limp noodle.

The woman eventually got fed up and took off down the block. The husband continued hurling insults at her back until he noticed Mama and Papa sitting in the cart with their mouths open.

"What?" he yelled at Papa.

"We didn't mean to intrude, we were just looking for a place to sleep," shouted Papa.

"And I'm looking for a cook who doesn't *shtup*[2] all my customers!" said the man, gesturing down the block at his wife. "Looks like we're both out of luck."

"If you have a bed for us, I can cook," Mama chimed in. "And I've only got eyes for this *schmendrik*."

"Can she really cook?" the man asked Papa.

"Look at me! Does it seem like I've ever skipped one of her meals?" he laughed, opening his coat to reveal his belly.

The man came downstairs and introduced himself as Vladimir Rabinski. He was in quite a pickle. The rabbi's daughter was getting married the next day and the entire congregation expected a huge banquet in the hall that Vladimir owned and operated. His wife was supposed to cook all the food, but Vladimir wasn't looking forward to the idea of crawling on his hands and knees to his mother-in-law,

1   *Geshray* – A bloodcurdling scream.

2   *Shtup* – Have sex.

begging the witch to send her daughter home after their fight. To save face, he was more than willing to take a chance on Mama's cooking in exchange for letting my family snooze in the pantry that night. Papa said that I slept like a log on a mattress made entirely out of unpeeled potatoes.

Mama rose at dawn and sprang into action. She cooked so fast her hands were a blur. Papa helped Vladimir clean and drag all of the big banquet tables into place. I supervised the whole operation from my baby basket. In between raving about Mama's goulash and setting up chairs, Vladimir would sneak over to tickle my belly, which was already my most prominent feature.

The hall was picture perfect by sunset. Mama had cooked everything in the kitchen, down to the last green bean. Vladimir joked that Mama had cleaned out his cupboard so thoroughly in preparation for the wedding feast, she'd even thrown his boots into the chicken soup pot to give it some more flavor. Papa said it sounded like an oncoming freight train when the crowd of starving Hungarians tore down the street from the ceremony in the synagogue to the hall. After the dust cleared hours later, there wasn't a morsel left uneaten.

Vladimir was so happy with the Kalish family caterers he tried to convince Mama and Papa to stay on in Budapest and work with him as equal partners. My parents were determined to get to America, though, so even Vladimir's offer to split his business thirty-seventy wasn't enough to get them to stay. Vladimir loaded up our cart with food and handed them a wad of money to help make their journey a little more comfortable.

"Are you sure you don't want to come with us?" offered Papa.

"How could I leave all this? I'd miss my *farbissen*[3] wife too much, and it wouldn't feel like spring without a good beating from the soldiers. But if you get to America, send me a new pair of boots to replace the ones Jennie fed to the rabbi!" joked Vladimir.

In 1931, my third husband Al Lackey and I spent our honeymoon retracing the route my family took from Russia all the way to the United States. Al was a buffoon and I spent most of our relationship rolling my

3   *Farbissen* – Bitter, disagreeable.

eyes at his harebrained ideas, so it seemed fitting to honor Mama and Papa, the comedy duo who originated that particular routine.

I wanted to find out for myself if the places my father had described over and over again really existed, so when we arrived in Budapest I did just like Papa and inquired around until someone could point us to the Jewish quarter. My nose led me to a little bakery where I bought a few pastries and asked the old woman behind the counter if there was still a big hall where a wedding reception might take place.

"The old hall was just down the street, but it was demolished in the war," the little old lady said sadly.

As we talked—and I inhaled her baked goods— she revealed that she'd even eaten Mama's cooking at the rabbi's daughter's wedding back in 1887. I couldn't believe the story was true. Forty years later, her only complaint was that there hadn't been enough food.

We put up with as much of the village gossip about the rabbi's grandchildren and their husbands as we could stomach, and then we asked her to point us toward a good

Sophie revisits Budapest in 1931.

restaurant for lunch. She directed us toward an odd little café that used to be a stable back in the eighteenth century, the owner and sole waiter proudly explained. Al, always a joker, insisted we skip the meat unless we wanted to end up munching on a distant cousin of Man o' War, but I was hardly listening. The smell coming out of the kitchen was intoxicating.

Man o' War, a famous racehorse of the 1920s.

"What's cooking back there, Pops?" I asked the elderly owner.

"That's our world-famous goulash," he explained, gesturing to a little old woman in the kitchen who gave Al a big wink. "The recipe goes back decades."

When in Hungary, I decided, do as the Hungarians do, and I was awfully Hungary. The little old man took our order for two bowls and two beers and walked back into the kitchen, where we could hear him bickering with his wife.

"I saw that wink. Why don't you just go serve yourself to him on a platter, you old tramp?" hissed the man.

"I'm gonna serve my fist to your face if you don't leave me be," spat his wife.

We pretended not to have heard anything when the waiter came back with our food. The smell was so nostalgic it brought me right back to my parents' restaurant. So eerily familiar was the sensation of eating this particular goulash, I had to call back the old man.

"Your name wouldn't happen to be Vladimir Rabinski, would it?" I wagered.

"Yes. Should I know you?" he asked warily.

"I think my mother gave you the recipe for this goulash."

After a few seconds of thought the man broke into an enormous grin.

"Baby Sonia!" he said, pulling me into a hug.

Vlad sat with us for the rest of our meal and I filled him in on thirty years of family history. After we'd had coffee and dessert, Vlad proclaimed he'd saved the best for last and slammed his foot up on the table.

The bottom of his boot was stamped "Made in the U.S.A." Mama had kept her promise to send him a pair of new boots when she reached the United States, and had quietly sent him a new pair every year as a thank you for his kindness. That was my Yiddishe momme.

Chapter 12

Way Back When

After Al and I left Budapest, we headed toward Vienna to meet up with an old friend of mine. Vienna was the next stop from the stories Papa told while we were children, and this one was perhaps one of the tallest tales to emerge from that little fireplug of a man.

The Kalish family left Budapest and headed through the woods toward Vienna, Phillip snoozing in the back of the cart most of the way and Mama entertaining me with songs up front with Papa. Ten miles outside the city, a cart carrying a load of hay sped past us. The driver waved merrily and Mama and Papa waved back. Papa continued along until, just past a sharp bend in the road, he found that same hay cart overturned. He pulled back on the reins and hopped down from his perch.

"Be careful," whispered Mama. "Maybe this wasn't an accident. We haven't seen anyone for miles. There's no one to help us."

Papa armed himself with a fat fallen branch and began to walk slowly toward the wreck. He crept quietly to the driver's side of the cart and poked his branch into the mess of hay and broken planks.

"I'm in here! I was robbed!" croaked a voice from inside the mess.

Papa put down his branch and dug the injured driver out from under the cart. As he was propping him up on the side of the road against a bale of hay, he saw the man's eyes go wide with fear. Without hesitation, Papa grabbed his branch and spun around, swinging with all his might.

This was one of the few stories that Mama would join in on when Papa told it, and she always had a little smile on her face because of how truly proud of Papa it made her feel. Papa hardly remembered anything besides swinging and swinging and hearing Mama scream from the cart in fear. Mama, on the other hand, said three thugs sprung out of the woods and Papa managed to bean one right in the melon on his first shot and crack another in the kisser on his second. Terrified, the third took off running for the woods.

Papa ran after him. The thug grabbed a rock from the road and pitched it like a spitball right at Papa's skull, but Papa shouldered his branch like Joe DiMaggio and managed to hit the rock right back toward the thug's nose. His vicious line drive knocked the robber's lights right out.

Sophie and Joe DiMaggio.

Once it was clear that all of the thieves were out cold, Mama ran toward the hay cart with me in one hand and her rifle in the other. She and my brother stood guard—Phil hiding behind her skirts—while Papa went through their pockets and brought his haul back over to the injured driver so he could reclaim his belongings and money.

"Who are you, Samson?" cried the hay cart driver. "I've never seen anything like that! This is all the money I had in the world. My name is Johannes Pikus. I owe you my life—and all of my family's lives! What can I ever do to repay you?"

"As a matter of fact, we're looking for a place to stay," replied Papa, gleefully pocketing the rest of the robber's cash. "If you could somehow find us a bed for the night, we'll call it even."

"I'll tuck you in myself if you do me one more favor," said the driver.

Papa may have been short and stocky, but he was pure power when a good deal presented itself. Mama tended to the injured driver while Papa managed to flip the cart back over and load up the scattered bales of hay. He hitched the carts together and our little wagon train headed into Vienna. (Once again, I supervised the whole operation from my bassinet.)

The next morning, my family woke up in a big bed on the second floor of a Viennese farmhouse. We heard a commotion that sounded like a small army in a mess hall and went downstairs to find a big family yakking a mile a minute and enjoying their breakfast.

"Good morning from the entire Pikus family!" shouted Johannes, his head now lovingly bandaged and his mouth full of sausage. "This is my father, my mother, my wife Mary, and my children Christine, little Mary, and Junior. Please, sit and eat as much as you like."

Papa said the meal was one of the most delicious he'd ever had, but I suspect any breakfast seasoned with the hero treatment would be delectable.

"How did you get to be so handy with a tree branch?" questioned our host.

"I've had too much practice defending myself from the rotten Cossacks," Papa chuckled. "We're off to America to avoid them for good."

Coincidentally, the Pikus family's close friends and neighbors were entertaining some visitors from Ohio—a land so exotic, it sounded to us like Tahiti, or Shangri-La. Johannes offered to take us along with his family for a visit after breakfast so we could ask questions about the best way to get across to New York. Both families piled into our cart and rode through the countryside, me happily in the care of little Junior who, at three, already seemed to have a way with the ladies.

The visitors from America were part of the Mueller family, longtime neighbors of our host Johannes Pikus. He had grown up with Otto Mueller and his sister Nancy, who had moved to America and married

a handsome American named McKinzie Young. When my family and
the Pikuses arrived, McKinzie and Nancy and their four children were
out in front of the Mueller's house, tossing a ball back and forth with
big leather gloves while their grandparents watched, delighted. Otto
Mueller seemed confused.

Johannes introduced my family to the Youngs and the Muellers and
asked Otto what the children were up to.

"I'm not sure," he said. "McKinzie insists Americans are crazy for
this game. They toss the ball around and hit it with a stick, and then
sometimes they run in a big circle. It's Greek to me."

"It's easy," laughed McKinzie. "And men make big bucks playing
this in the States!"

"It's not so easy. My nephew Denton's been throwing that ball at me
all morning and I haven't hit it with that stick even once," laughed Otto.

"How about everything in my wallet against everything in yours
that my friend Zachary Kalish here could hit that ball," said Johannes.
He'd been suckering Otto, who could never resist a bet, since they were
both children.

"You're on," said Otto, shaking with Johannes.

I was up on the porch with Mama, Nancy, and Mrs. Mueller, the
matriarch of the family, all of whom were munching on candy and
watching the men make fools of themselves. Junior, ever the ladies' man,
popped a delicious Viennese sweet in my mouth and Mama said she
watched me fall in love with my first taste of chocolate. It's been my
longest love affair— long after I gave all three husbands the boot, me and
chocolate are still going strong!

Nancy told Mama that Denton was the star of his school's baseball
team and it would be a miracle if Papa managed to hit the ball, but Mama
just smiled and took another sweet. Denton's first pitch proved Nancy right.
Papa swung and missed by a mile. As Otto giggled with glee, Mama got up,
walked over to the back of our cart, grabbed the gnarled old tree branch she
had saved from the last night's ambush, and delivered it to Papa. He winked
and put down the Youngs' regulation baseball bat.

Denton fired another fastball to Papa and, to McKinzie and Otto's
amazement, Papa connected with his ridiculous bat and the ball soared
toward the house. It landed square in the middle of the plate of Austrian

chocolate. When Mama got back to the porch, she found me sitting in Junior's lap with my mouth all over the chocolate-covered ball.

"If you can't outpitch a man with a tree branch," said McKinzie, smacking the back of his son's head, "you're never going to make it in the big leagues!"

Johannes took the ball from me and asked Denton to autograph it. He handed it to Otto as a memento of yet another lousy bet he'd lost to Johannes over the course of their friendship.

I didn't run into my first boyfriend Junior Pikus again until 1919, when I was playing at Reisenweber's nightclub in New York City. This was before Al and I were married and Al brought Junior, then a no-name young pitcher for the New York Yankees, along to my show that night. I joined Al after my set and when he introduced me to Junior, the name clicked with Papa's old story.

"Junior, this might sound loony but—you wouldn't happen to have family outside Vienna, would you?" I said, taking a stab.

"Al, you said your lady was a singer, not a mind-reader!" laughed Junior. "Yeah, I grew up there but I came over when I was ten and stayed with some cousins here."

"You're not going to believe this," I gasped. "My father used to tell a story about staying with a Pikus family outside Vienna on our way to the States. This was maybe 1887."

"I would've been three then. How old were you?"

"Two months," I said. "Rumor has it we had quite a love affair." I told Junior the whole tale and we made a pact, then and there, to someday head back to Vienna together. That's the old friend Al and I were supposed to meet at the Vienna train station in 1931, on the second stop on our honeymoon tour of the Kalish family's history.

Unfortunately, Junior was late and the railroad had lost our trunks somewhere in the station. Angrily, Lackey hailed a taxi cab to take us toward the center of town so we could kill some time while waiting for our luggage to turn up. There was nothing more I wanted than to take a hot bath and relax, but all of a sudden in the car, Al was feeling horny. He did his very bad Valentino impression and I did my very good impression of the iceberg that sunk the Titanic.

I hopped out of the car in a particularly quaint little corner of town and Al followed along. We had stumbled into the Jewish Quarter of Vienna. A little stroll seemed like a good way to bring Al from a boil down to a simmer.

Eventually we came upon a little music shop and, when Al pointed out the record in the window, we decided to have a little fun. We greeted the man behind the counter and weren't surprised when he answered in Yiddish. My biggest hit at the time was still "My Yiddishe Momme," which was the record he had stacked high in the window display.

"Tell me about that record you've got in the window there," I asked.

"Oh, that one? Everyone's got that record. I can hardly keep it in stock! The only things you can count on finding in every single house in this part of town are salt, pepper, and 'My Yiddishe Momme,'" he said, handing me a copy.

"What if I told you I was Sophie Tucker?"

"Permit me to introduce myself. I'm Ludwig Van Beethoven."

"Why don't you put the record on, Ludwig?" I asked.

Imagine the look on his face when I began to sing along with my own record. He stared at the cover and back at me, cursed a blue streak, and ran out the door wildly screaming that Sophie Tucker was in his store. Before long I was surrounded by a throng of Yiddishe mommes, papas, children, grandmothers, and even a few Yiddishe cats and dogs. So much for a calm stroll!

"Hey Al!" someone yelled from the back of the crowd. Junior had finally turned up.

Pikus grabbed my hand, I grabbed Al's, and we made our escape through some of the

"My Yiddishe Momme" has sold over three million copies to date.

finer back alleys of Vienna. Eventually we ended up at the Grand Hotel and collapsed on a lobby couch.

"You still move okay for a washed up old pitcher," Al said, poking Junior in his gut. He went to go check us in. Even if our luggage was still lost, I could at least get my bath and catch a few winks before we went to see the Pikus family the next day. Junior popped a piece of Austrian chocolate in his mouth and offered me one. I'm sure my public would've thanked him for keeping me in classic Sophie Tucker shape.

Al came storming back through the lobby. "Well, the good news is that they found the trunks. They're in Bratislava," he said with a scowl.

"How's that the good news?" I asked.

"Because the bad news is that our reservation was wrong. They don't have us on the books until tomorrow and there isn't even a spare broom closet in this dump tonight," he said. I shoved another piece of chocolate in my mouth and sank back on the couch, getting ready to settle in for the night, but Junior suggested we really reenact the Kalish journey and stay with his family. He'd bought the big Mueller spread a few years back to give his family some extra space, so there was plenty of room for all of us. Besides, imposing on the Pikuses was practically a family tradition.

Later on that afternoon, I was once again parked on the same porch in the Austrian countryside, happily munching on chocolate. Instead of Papa and McKinzie Young out on the lawn it was Junior and Al, who reluctantly volunteered to be a catcher for Junior's mandatory daily workout. He was still an active Yankee and had to keep his arm limber.

Some things never change, though, and Johannes Pikus senior and Otto Mueller were seated near me on the porch. The two old friends had lived together since Junior bought the Mueller property. As usual, Otto had placed an extravagant and unwinnable bet on their chess game.

"You should take Al to the majors, Junior!" I heckled from the peanut gallery. My husband managed to communicate a rude hand gesture back to me, even while wearing his mitt.

"Why don't you let me try to hit a few?" Al asked Junior. "That'll put a cork in Sophie."

Junior lobbed a few slow pitches toward Al and he whiffed on every one. Johannes and Otto, still somewhat mystified by the allure of baseball, looked on and chuckled.

"Hey lover boy, can you swing the other way? The wind is giving me a chill," I yelled.

"You think you can do better, Babe Ruth?" Al hollered, tossing the bat in my direction.

I came down off the porch and picked up the bat. I'd played my fair share of baseball in Riverside Park when I was a young girl in Hartford, but that was more than thirty years earlier. I knew that baseball was something you didn't forget, like riding a bike, but batting against a Yankee was like remembering how to ride a bike blindfolded and with no hands.

Junior's first pitch was right down the middle and I took a swing and missed. Al cackled and tossed the ball back to Pikus triumphantly. I shot Lackey a glare and instructed the Yankee to throw a straight fastball. I purposely kept the bat on my shoulder and let the ball hit Al right in his crown jewels.

After that, he stopped laughing.

I don't know whether Junior just wanted me to shut Al up or whether the patron saint of baseball was also on holiday in the Austrian countryside that day, but on my third pitch I managed to knock the ball right toward the house and through a window on the second floor.

I looked up in horror.

"That's okay, Soph, that's my room. It gets a little stuffy in there sometimes. I could use a little bit of a breeze," joked Junior.

As we were standing on the lawn gawking at my home run, Otto ducked into the house and emerged with something in his hand.

"I think you earned this," he said, handing me a dirty old baseball. I looked down and, in childish writing, I saw Denton Young's name on the ball my Papa had knocked into the plate of chocolates all those years before. Otto had kept it as a reminder to be careful when he made bets with Johannes.

It's a shame Otto and Johannes didn't keep up with that odd American sport with the bat, since Denton Young did in fact make it to the majors. When he did, he had an arm so fierce his pitches earned him the nickname "Cyclone," which he shortened to Cy.

Cy Young's 1893 baseball card.

Chapter 13

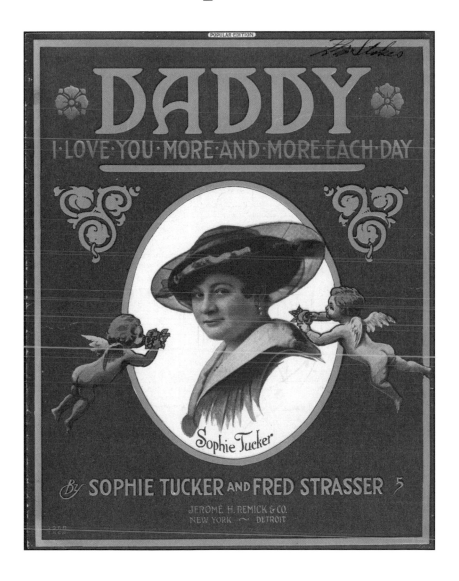

Daddy I Love You More and More Each Day

I know that there probably wasn't a lot of dancing and dining by candlelight in my parents' journey from Russia through Europe, but Al and I made sure we did twice as much of both to make up for Mama and Papa's hardships. After leaving Vienna, we took a detour into Italy to visit Milan and take in an opera at La Scala in honor of my father's story about his short-lived career as the world's foremost tin-eared composer.

The way he told it, my family left Austria heading for Hamburg, where we hoped we would find a boat to take us to America. I was growing fussier and fussier by the day, apparently more than happy to pass the time on the road learning the full range of my vocal ability. Papa would sing to soothe me, but I had a hard time falling asleep to Yiddish lullabies when Papa sounded like an out of tune bassoon. His voice nearly qualified as child abuse.

What's worse was that Mama noticed we were heading in the wrong direction and Papa wouldn't turn the cart around. It's nice to know that the age-old tradition of men refusing to ask for directions goes back to a time before we even had automobiles.

After a few days traveling toward Germany (according to Papa) or toward who knows where (according to Mama), we ran into three Italian soldiers who seemed to be looking for someone. They stopped our cart and searched through our belongings, but Papa and Mama kept quiet because they didn't understand the language and, more importantly, they'd noticed a man hiding fifty feet over their heads in a tree. The soldiers eventually gave up and continued searching further on down the road.

When they were out of sight, Papa waved up to the man in the tree and he dropped down in front of our horse.

"Thank you," said the man in Yiddish.

"How did you know we're Jewish?" said Papa.

"I recognized the old lullaby you were singing before the soldiers stopped you. It was my grandmother's favorite."

"Was your grandmother tone deaf too?" asked my mother.

The man smiled and stuck out his hand. "My name is Charles Abuza. I'm Italian, but my father was Jewish, so I learned Yiddish from him and my grandparents.

"What are Italian soldiers doing in Germany?" asked my father.

"Here's a better question. What is a nice Jewish family doing in Italy, thinking they're in Germany?" laughed Charles. My mother elbowed Papa so hard he nearly fell off the cart. She explained the situation while Papa massaged his bruised ribs, and Charles suggested that we continue on to the port in Genoa instead of backtracking two weeks to Hamburg. He had a cousin who lived there who could help us get on a boat, and he would be glad to make the introductions in exchange for a ride.

"Won't the army be looking for you?" asked Mama suspiciously.

"I doubt it," answered Charles. "Our unit isn't even issued bullets. I guess they're afraid we'll shoot ourselves in the foot. Anyway, I think those idiots were more interested in stealing my cigarettes than keeping me in the service."

Mama knew that without Charles, Papa would probably steer us all the way to China, so she let him hop on the back of the cart and Phillip helped hide him under some spare blankets. With that, they struck out toward their new destination. Whenever we passed soldiers, Mama would smile and wave and Phillip would sit on top of lumpy, blanket-covered Charles.

Somewhere in the beautiful countryside outside of Florence, Papa pulled the cart off the road for a picnic lunch and Charles filled them in on what he'd done before the army, besides hiding from them. His most recent job was counting toothpicks into boxes at a toothpick factory, which he said was as boring as watching paint dry. His family was filled with musicians and he thought maybe he could get into the family business once he got back to Genoa.

"What do you play?" asked Papa.

"Cards mostly, but I can also tune a piano. That's the plan so long as the army doesn't find me. I think I'm safe, though. The generals are still working on marching."

"Be careful when they get good at it," warned Papa. "The Cossacks learned to march on our heads. I'll always be looking over my shoulder."

Abuza took his identification documents from his pocket and handed them to Papa. His name had never brought him any luck, so he hoped maybe Papa would make a better go of it. Charles suggested Papa whip out his new papers the next time he met up with a Cossack and repeat the phrase "Vaffanculo[1]!"

Papa stashed the papers inside his coat, thinking maybe he could sell them for cash in an emergency. He didn't think he'd ever have any use for Abuza's documents, since it was unlikely our little Russian bear could convince anyone he was Italian.

"If you can say 'si' and 'no,' and 'parmigiano,' you know all of the Italian you'll ever need," said the man formerly known as Charles Abuza. "Now let's get going."

Just outside a little town called Torre del Lago, our guide asked how we planned to pay the passage to America. Mama grabbed a sack in the back of the cart and showed Abuza two heavy silver candlesticks, an heirloom from her mother that she intended to sell to buy our tickets. That was all the proof Charles needed to trust that our family wouldn't steal anything from him in the night. He led the family to a beautiful villa that had belonged to the Abuza family for ten generations, with big old windows that faced the Mediterranean Sea and, off in the distance to the north, the city of Genoa. It beat sleeping in the back of our cart, that's for sure.

Charles told my parents his cousin Giacomo was staying at the villa to get some work done, but no one expected that work to be composing a tune on the piano. Giacomo, it turned out, was a recent graduate of the conservatory in Milan.

"When you said your cousin was in the music business, I thought he also tuned pianos," laughed Papa.

1   *Vaffanculo* – Italian slang, commonly understood to mean "Fuck you!" or "Fuck off!"

"Giacomo is a serious composer," explained Charles. "That's a fancy word that means he writes music and makes no money."

Cousin Giacomo

Mama took Phillip upstairs to give him a much needed bath and Papa stayed downstairs, rocking me to Giacomo's beautiful playing and fretting about securing our passage to the States. Charles tried to assure him that with Mama's candlesticks we'd have enough to sail around the world twice, so Papa tried to relax and began humming his usual horrible, tuneless lullaby. On the other side of the room, Giacomo stopped playing to listen.

At this part of the story, Papa would always insist that Giacomo took down the notes of his horrible melody. He played it a few times on the keys and then they hummed it together. Since Mama was upstairs she couldn't confirm or deny any of this, but for her whole life, she would always stick her fingers in her ears when Papa sang his tune. If Giacomo wrote down Papa's melody at all, she insisted, it was to make sure he never used it.

In 1931, Al and I wanted to take a few days to travel around Italy and get in some of the more romantic stuff we could do in Europe on a honeymoon. After all, the Abuza family exodus wasn't exactly the stuff of love poems. We took in the sights via gondola in Venice, but Al just spent the whole time coming up with shitty business idea after shitty business idea while I shot them all down. An old Vaudevillian and a bad businessman might make a great couple, but boy, were we lousy at being lovebirds.

Sophie in Venice, visible on the far right of the boat.

First, Al thought maybe he would invest in a hotel and theater in the middle of the desert in some ghost town named Las Vegas. I told him he was seeing a mirage.

Then Al thought maybe he should open a bank. I suggested he take a cue from Black Tuesday and take a leap off a tall building.

Eventually I requested "O Solo Mio" from our gondolier and convinced Al to slide over and check my fillings—anything to keep his motor mouth from running.

Our next stop was in Verona to see Juliet's balcony. We found a small army of brokenhearted weepers sticking little notes into cracks in the side of the building where the family who inspired the Capulets supposedly once lived. It looked to me like any tenement on Delancey Street.

We sat on a low wall and stared up at the balcony for a while. Al concluded that there was no way anyone would pole vault up two stories for a flat-chested fourteen-year-old virgin, let alone commit suicide for love. I offered to test Shakespeare's theory, so long as he drank the poison first.

Juliet's balcony, Verona.

In Florence, we found ourselves sitting on a bench at L'Accademia in front of Michelangelo's David. We did everything we were supposed to do. We sat in silence. We read from our little guidebook. We admired the craftsmanship. And, eventually, we dissolved into chuckles because neither one of us could do anything but stare at his marble *schlong*[2].

"Well," said Al. "At least we know he was Jewish."

"Come on," I said. "I've got a sudden craving. Let's see if there's anywhere in this town where I can get a foot-long frankfurter."

In Pisa, we stood in front of the leaning tower

Michelangelo's David and the leaning tower of Pisa.

2   *Schlong* – From the Yiddish for "snake," also slang for penis.

and Al was disappointed that we couldn't climb up to the top floor for a little funny business. Thank God—after two weeks of eating pasta, if they had let me inside I would have toppled the whole thing over.

I read from our guidebook that Galileo was from Pisa and that he'd invented the thermometer and the telescope, which elicited a surprisingly sincere tip of the hat and moment of silence from Al. He explained that he owed the inventor a lot, since his friend Benny Rabinowitz owned a telescope when they were growing up and only charged him a penny to watch Irene Blatsky, their stacked neighbor, take a bath.

During our last stop in Milan, I dragged Al to La Scala to see Puccini's *Turandot*. I didn't know much about opera, and all Al knew was that he was not interested. He promptly fell asleep as soon as they dimmed the lights. I, on the other hand, was in love. I don't know whether I was more impressed with the golden building itself or the singers on stage, but I'd never experienced anything like it.

La Scala Opera House in Milan.

In Act Two, I recognized a melody during one of the big arias. It took me a minute to place it, but I was listening to Papa's terrible lullaby floating out of the mouth of one of the world's best tenors.

I had a hunch so I checked the program, and I was thunderstruck. Sure enough, Puccini's first name was Giacomo. Perhaps Charles Abuza really was related to Giacomo Puccini, and perhaps Papa's little melody had traveled from Russia to Italy and wound up in his opera. More likely, maybe Papa heard this record somewhere and strung together a story that made for a better tale. It's clear I didn't get my gift for song from Papa, so maybe, instead, he handed down my gift for inventing stories in the name of publicity.

I didn't really care either way. I was just happy that Papa was there with my snoring husband and me, his song echoing through La Scala instead of a steamy restaurant kitchen in Hartford.

Chapter 14

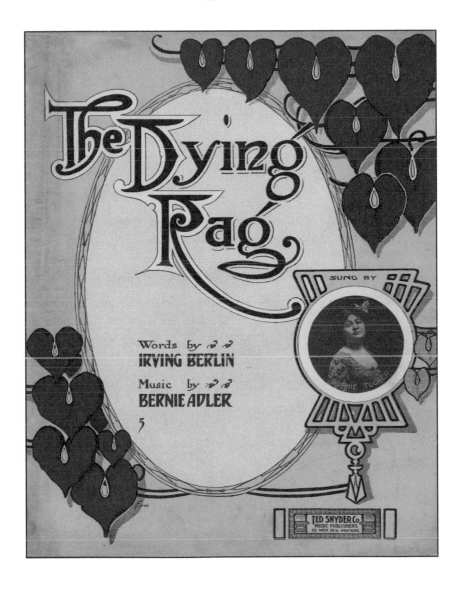

The Dying Rag

My father loved to describe the busy port of Genoa in detail, with cranes lifting cargo off of big boats and rugged longshoremen lugging crates onto ships bursting at the seams with goods and people. In April of 1887, Genoa was a huge center for shipping and Papa remembered seeing negotiations happening right out on the piers, the captains standing like statues while importers and exporters threw up their hands, begging for a better deal.

The port of Genoa circa 1887.

While Papa and Charles headed to the main office of the port to see about booking passage to America, Mama took us kids to a nearby open-air market to kill time. She stopped by a big produce stand to marvel over the foreign fruits and vegetables and wound up eavesdropping on a couple of women complaining in Yiddish that the price of beets had gone up right before Passover.

Mama was shocked. She'd been traveling for so long with such focus on getting to New York that she'd nearly forgotten one of the most important Jewish holidays of the year. She struck up a conversation with the owner of the stand, a kind woman named Milly Palumbo who handed Phillip a little bunch of grapes and waved away Mama's coins. When she found out we had no family in town, Milly scribbled her address on a piece of paper and offered to host us for Seder[1].

Mama smiled appreciatively, but she refused. She was sure we'd be setting sail for America in a matter of hours.

"I don't think there are any ships leaving for the United States today," Milly said, pressing the scrap of paper into Mama's hand. "If you're still here tonight, bring your little ones to our house and Philip can read the Four Questions[2]."

Back inside the main port office, Papa and Charles waited on a long line to ask about ships headed across the Atlantic. While Charles read his newspaper, Papa passed the time listening to couple of men sitting nearby, a captain and an exporter, working out the details for a business deal involving a large load of fruit. Eventually he tired of eavesdropping and noticed an illustration of a lady holding a torch on the front of Charles's paper.

"What is this?" Papa asked, pointing to the drawing.

"That's who's going to greet you in America. They're calling it the Statue of Liberty," said Charles.

After what seemed like forever, they made it up to the counter and found that Papa could book the family tickets for 75,000 lire on the next passenger ship. Unfortunately, that ship wouldn't depart Genoa for five weeks. Charles tried to comfort Papa by telling him that we could stay at the Abuza villa until then, and even promised that they would play cards for toothpicks instead of his remaining lire.

As expected, Mama was livid when she found out she'd have to wait another month in Genoa. She was sick of horning in on strangers and

1   Seder – Jewish feast that marks the beginning of the Passover holiday.

2   The Four Questions – The youngest child in attendance will ask four traditional questions as part of the Seder.

feeling so *fartoost*[3] that she'd forgotten about Passover. To calm her down, Charles took us to a nearby tavern for pizza. He was shocked my parents had never heard of it, but he forgot that we were from Russia, where the specialty was pestilence. Once Abuza convinced Mama that it was acceptable to pick up the pizza with her hands, she and my father ate and discussed with Charles the plan for heading back to Torre del Lago. Charles was afraid to travel by night on the outskirts of Genoa. In those days, thieves hid on the side of the road hoping to rob travelers with pockets full of cash from a big dockside deal. They agreed to find a place to stay in the city and head back in the morning.

Here is where the story changed depending on who I begged to tell it to me when I was a child. Both Papa and Mama agree that the tavern was full of soldiers and a few of them seemed to recognize Charles as a deserter. In Papa's version, he snatched a gun from an officer and kept one soldier at bay while another got up close and personal with Mama's fist. He insisted they fled the bar in a hail of gunfire.

Mama, on the other hand, would roll her eyes and explain that they simply snuck out of the tavern after paying the bill and set out to find the Palumbo household, taking the kind fruit lady up on her offer to host us at her Passover Seder. I know which version I'd rather see on the big screen, so I'd like to believe that Papa was telling the truth and Mama was being modest about her vicious uppercut.

The Palumbo house was all lit up when we arrived. Warmly welcoming smells floated out of the kitchen window. Mama believed that you could judge a person's character by their brisket, so she had no qualms about knocking on the door once she got a whiff of that heavenly aroma. Milly was delighted to find us on her stoop and we were kindly ushered inside. When Papa and Charles shook hands with her husband, they instantly recognized him as one of the men at the port office who they overheard trying to set up the fruit deal. William, as he introduced himself, seated the men around the table and poured them all a glass of wine. Milly asked Mama to help her with the food in the kitchen.

Mama always said that, of all the kindnesses she received along the way from Russia to America, the one that touched her most was Milly

3   *Fartoost* – Discombobulated, confused.

inviting her to help with the Seder preparations. For a woman who'd rescued her husband from a prison camp, given birth on the road, and bumped and jostled in a horse cart halfway across Europe, feeling like she had a home for the holiday made her eyes well up.

While dicing vegetables and manning various bubbling pots and pans in the kitchen, Mama explained to Milly that the next boat wouldn't leave for five weeks. Milly offered to let the family stay at her house at least for the night, since Mama reminded her so much of her own daughter who lived far away in Rome with her husband. It was nice to have some life in her house again.

Out at the table, Charles noticed a bowl of odd-looking fruit and picked one up to investigate it.

"It's a citron," explained William.

"I thought so!" exclaimed Papa. "We call that an *etrog*[4]."

"That's right, the Jews use them for religious purposes, but the rest of the world uses them for medicine. Go ahead and keep that one. I've got a hundred thousand extra on my hands that are going to rot in a warehouse down by the port," explained William glumly.

A citron.

William's business partner had been killed a few days earlier in a crane accident down by the docks. The partner was the one putting up the money to export the fruit, leaving William with an angry unpaid sea captain and a warehouse of fruit he couldn't afford to ship to New York.

"At least we are all here, safe and together," shouted Milly from the kitchen. "God may have taken our friend, but he delivered us the fastest onion chopper in Europe!"

We conducted our Seder and then ate until we were so full that Phillip fell asleep at the table with half of a roasted potato on the end of his fork. William, Charles, and Papa, who was rocking me in his arms, sat around the table rubbing their bloated bellies and trying to come up with something to do with the massive load of citrons. Papa suggested

4   *Etrog* – Citron, used by Jews during the harvest holiday of Sukkot.

they convince Genoa's finest ladies that diamonds were out of fashion and citron earrings were all the rage.

"Speaking of diamonds," said Mama seriously, taking a seat with the men at the table. "I have an offer for you. Could these pay to get your etrogs across the ocean?" Mama produced a small bag from her apron pocket and emptied several large diamonds onto the table. Papa looked up at her, shocked.

"My grandfather gave each of his grandchildren a gift like this when they were born. I think he would appreciate me investing mine instead of making a necklace out of them," she explained.

William was astounded. "Of course, these would more than pay for the shipping costs. But why would you go out of your way for us?"

"We'll do it for a five percent return on our investment," said Mama, relishing her role as the family dealmaker.

"It's a Passover miracle!" shouted William, overwhelmed. "All you want is five percent?"

"Not exactly," she said. "You also have to get our family on the boat with the shipment to New York City."

"But it's not a boat for passengers, Jennie," stammered Papa, still shocked by Mama's chutzpah. "The captain won't let us on board."

"My friends, with these in my hand, we can buy a captain who will," said William, grinning like a fool.

A couple of days later, Charles and the Palumbos stood with my family on the dock near the cargo ship that was, indeed, about to depart for New York with a heavy load of citrons, four Kalishes, and all of our possessions stuffed into one big trunk. Milly had loaded us up with a package of leftovers to get us by for at least a few days on board, after which we'd be at the mercy of the ship's galley for food.

"Now remember," said William for the hundredth time, "when you get off the boat in New York, look for a man holding a sign that says 'Pfizer.' He works for the medicine company buying all the fruit. He'll take care of everything and help get you on your way to Boston."

"And then in a month when you get paid, you'll wire the money to the Bank of Boston," parroted Papa. "The Pfizer man will give me the bank address and who to see. And you'll send a letter to Jennie's cousin Boris in Boston to let us know when the money is on the way."

"I'm going to miss teaching you Italian," Charles said as he shook Papa's hand.

"*Grazie*," smiled my father. "You should get out of here before one of these soldiers recognizes you again."

"Don't worry so much! They won't come near me if I'm standing next to your wife," Charles joked.

Our boat sounded its whistle and the captain gestured gruffly that it was time for us to get on board. Mama and Papa gave one last round of hugs and handshakes to our friends, climbed up the gangplank and took a spot on the top deck so Phillip could wave and watch us sail away from the port.

As the boat started to pull away from the pier, Papa and Mama saw a group of soldiers walking toward Charles. He didn't notice them coming because he was waving at us instead. They tried to gesture for him to run, but Charles just waved goodbye all the more enthusiastically. Before they could warn him, one of the soldiers tapped him on the shoulder and, realizing he'd been recognized again, he took off running down the pier toward the sea.

This time neither Mama's ingenuity nor one of Papa's tall tales could save our friend Charles Abuza. The soldiers took aim at his back, shot twice, and our Italian friend fell forward onto the dock. The last thing Mama and Papa saw as they pulled Phillip away from the gruesome site was Charles lifting his hand one more time to wave goodbye.

Al and I had been touring all over Europe for a month by the time we found ourselves in Berlin for the Passover of 1931. True to form, Al had managed to land us smack dab in the middle of Deutschland for this sacred Jewish holiday—perhaps the worst of Al's bad ideas.

I had managed to eat so many pastries, chocolates, and plates of schnitzel that I could no longer button my dresses, so I found a small seamstress shop in Berlin to have my whole wardrobe let out a few inches. Al, tickled pink that I'd eaten myself right out of my clothes, accused me of trying to smuggle all of Germany's Black Forest cake back to the U.S. before that new Adolf fellow cut off our supply.

Hilda, my seamstress, giggled nervously. By 1931, it was just starting to get tense for Jews in Germany and even in the company of two Americans, it could mean trouble making fun of Hitler.

Al and Sophie in Germany.

"Are you married, Hilda? Would your husband ever talk to you like this?" I asked, changing the subject with a wink.

"My Jerome is housebroken," she with a laugh. "Besides, he's too serious to joke around. He's a physicist."

"Good, because I'm gonna need some heavy duty physics to get the zipper on this dress up," I joked. "Where does your husband work?"

"Nowhere," said Hilda. "They let him go two months ago. He says it's just politics and things will get back to normal after the next election but..." she trailed off.

"Those bastards," muttered Al.

"Hilda, listen to me. Jerome could get a great position in the States. I know people, I promise. If you want to get out, let me know. I may seem like just a fat lady in a too small dress, but I've got connections," I said, seriously.

"Oh, I know who you are Frau Tucker. My yiddishe momme loves 'My Yiddishe Momme,' even if we can't play it loud enough for the neighbors to hear anymore," she said with a smile.

"Well, hear this loud and clear, Hilda: you need to get the hell out of here, and soon."

"Frau Tucker, does your husband ever listen to your advice?" she asked. "Jerome will never leave his country, and I'll never leave him. So that's that. But if you don't have plans yet for tonight's Seder, I know my mother would be thrilled if you'd come and join us."

I accepted her offer without a moment's thought, which is how we ended up in Hilda's house later that night. We were surrounded by twenty of her closest relatives, three of whom managed to tie me into one of Hilda's tiny little aprons to help out in the kitchen. Thankfully, all my years at Abuza's Restaurant came back to me. Before I knew it, I'd made a pound of chopped liver and tried to set up my teenage niece with Hilda's youngest son in a transatlantic arranged marriage.

Al Lackey

My brilliant husband, over at the table, was trying to figure out why a doctor of physics couldn't prescribe something for his high blood pressure. Jerome just laughed. Al took his good mood as an opportunity to try to talk up life in the States, but he would not be moved. He was surrounded by his family, all of whom would also have to be promised safe passage to America before he would even consider leaving. I was well-connected, but bringing over twenty people would be a tall order even for me. Still, I would find a way if only Jerome would relent. But I could tell by his face, as he looked around the table at everyone he loved, this proud man would never leave his homeland.

Good chopped liver will glue together more than just crackers. By the time Hilda and I had cooked together, said the blessings together, served our families together, and spent an evening eating until Hilda needed to reinforce everyone's seams, I knew she was firmly lodged in my heart.

"Jerome, there's no way I'll be able to get by without Hilda," I said. "She's a miracle worker. She can feed me until I'm ready to burst and magically, my dresses still fit. I'd love to bring her over to the States and have her help me out in the theater."

Jerome was quiet for a moment, and then chose his words carefully. "This will all blow over, like the zeppelins. Those big balloons are frightening when they're overhead but then they float away," he said, sighing and leaning back in his chair. "This is home."

"I have friends who can help you out. There's an organization that can bring over your whole family and help you get settled. I'm sure you'll be able to come back some day, but from what I've heard from people in high places in the U.S., this country's on the verge of a nervous breakdown. You've got to protect this precious bunch and get out of here as soon as possible. Please, just don't wait too long," I begged.

German youth with Nazi flags.

The last time I ever saw Hilda and her family was a week later, when they saw us off at the train station with a basket of leftovers, just like Milly and William Palumbo had given Mama and Papa. And, while the sight of Charles Abuza bleeding on the dock may have been more gruesome for Mama and Papa, the last thing Al and I saw as we pulled out of Berlin were a group of young boys in brown uniforms with Nazi armbands playing in a field. Thinking about that scene still chills me right down to my bones more than thirty years later.

Hilda and her family never made it out of Germany. They all died at Auschwitz with the exception of her youngest son, Noah, who somehow managed to get to Israel where he married a nice girl and has a few kids of his own. I send him a little something each year when Passover rolls around because, as Milly and Hilda proved, once you celebrate a Seder together, you're family.

Chapter 15

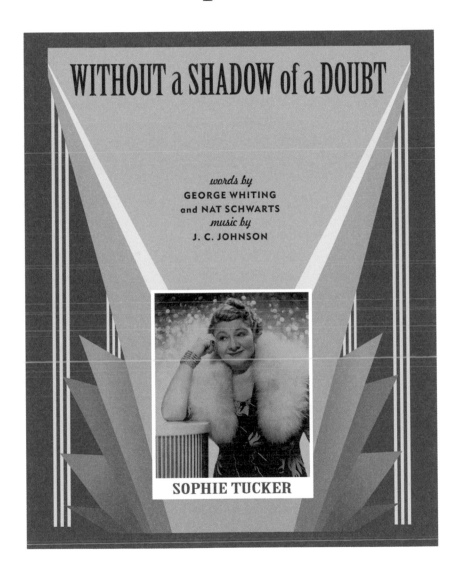

Without a Shadow
of a Doubt

Letter from Collie Knox

LONDON - The indestructible Sophie Tucker plans a trip to Scotland. She is in Australia at the moment. She is billed as "A Stone-Age Judy Garland", and is, so we hear, in tremendous voice. Miss Tucker is apparently anxious to pay a call on her aunt, Mrs. E. Hawkins, in Edinburgh, Scotland. Somehow one does not connect out Sophie with aunts. "She is an old lady", says Sophie, who is herself claimed to be 81, is unofficially reported to be 78, and admits to 74. "My aunt is nearly 90 now", says she, "but she came down to London to see me last time, when I couldn't get the time to go to Scotland". Sophie is due in Britan in October. "Retire?" she exclaims. "Don't mention that word to me. I've never missed a performance in 59 years on the stage, and I'm hotter than ever." We over here are very fond of this remarkable character.

Sophie visited her Aunt Tizzy in Edinburgh, Scotland several times over the course of her career.

My Papa was an open book, even if half the stories in it were fiction instead of history. But Mama could be as tight-lipped as a bear trap when she wanted to be. When I was a kid, I couldn't even get her to tell us what was for dinner. That's what drove me and Al to Scotland in 1931 to search for answers about the last leg of my family's journey to America. Thankfully, the one thing Mama always sang from the rooftops was gratitude, and she insisted that if I was ever in the U.K. I had to look up my Aunt Tizzy Hawkins. Obviously, I'm not actually related to anyone whose veins don't run with borscht, but Elizabeth "Tizzy" Hawkins earned her honorary aunt-hood through the kindness she showed my family back in 1887. She and my mother exchanged letters until the end of Mama's life, but it wasn't until Tizzy spilled the beans that I learned the crazy circumstances that had drawn them together.

Papa would only tell us some of this story when I was a young girl. I liked to request it anyway, because he would always pull off his fat gold wedding ring and let me play with it while he spun his yarn, as long as I promised to give it back to him as soon as the story was over. Otherwise he was never without the ring, even when he was working in the yard or fixing the pipes under the sink.

Sophie's Papa's wedding ring.

My parents arrived in Glasgow well after midnight in May of 1887. Luckily, the trip from Genoa only took a week. If it had been any longer my crying, which rivaled the boat's steam whistle, would've gotten us all thrown overboard. No one on the ship spoke Yiddish so Mama and Papa had tried to keep out of the way as much as possible. Through gestures and Papa's few words of Italian, he managed to piece together that the ship would be moored at the Kingston Dock for about a week to load and unload some cargo and pick up a final batch of coal for the long trip across the Atlantic.

William Palumbo had assured us our trunk of belongings would be safe on the ship with the citrons, so Mama and Papa packed a small bag and set out to find a place to stay while we waited to set sail.

Milly Palumbo had given Papa some English pounds and directions to the Jewish section of Glasgow, known as the Gorbals. We ended up at Green's Kosher Hotel, where fifteen-year-old Tizzy was then working as a housekeeper, giving each guest their single towel and set of sheets and cleaning up the rooms once they left. In the few months she'd worked there, she had managed to pick up enough Yiddish to be able to chat with my family when they checked in and, being a sucker for a fat baby like yours truly, she slipped Mama a few extra towels. Throughout that week she would find a spare moment here and there to sneak into my parents' room and play with me and Phillip.

At the end of the week, Papa took the family back down to the docks to board the boat for the final leg of their journey. With his lousy Italian, the thing he hadn't been able to grasp was that the old captain had turned the ship over in Glasgow to a new captain for the trip to New York. The new captain had no knowledge of the deal William struck with the old captain and had even less patience for Papa's yelling or his two hysterical children.

"Kalish! Citrons! New York!" Papa kept repeating, waving his arms frantically and gesturing toward the deckhands for help.

The new captain finally checked the manifest and found a listing for Kalish, but only for one passenger. It became clear that the new man in charge was a stickler for regulations, and would have sooner shipped a live tiger than allow women or children aboard his cargo vessel. One of the crew explained that we'd sailed with them from Genoa under an arrangement with the old captain, but there was nothing anyone could say to sway him. The boat was setting sail, and Papa either had to get on board to protect Mama's investment or stay on the dock with his family. He really had no choice.

There was hardly even time for Papa to hug us all goodbye before he had to run up the gangplank. Mama waved to the ship until she could no longer make out Papa's dark shape on the deck. She was alone in Glasgow and Papa was sailing on to New York. Standing on the deck in front of the Statue of Liberty a few weeks later, the sight wasn't as thrilling as he had hoped. Sure, Papa had made it all the way from Russia to New York City, but he was alone.

A view of the Statue of Liberty circa 1887.

When the ship finally docked, Papa walked down the gangplank with a tattered piece of paper he'd had in his pocket since he departed from Genoa. There were easily a hundred people on the pier, but way in the back of the crowd Papa noticed a young man waving a sign that said "Pfizer."

"*Redt Yiddish*[1]?" asked Papa, thrusting his piece of paper at the young man.

"Doesn't everyone? I'm Paul Weissman. Welcome to America! Where's your family?" responded the man in perfect Yiddish. Papa breathed a sigh of relief and quickly explained what had happened to Mama and us kids. As concerned as Paul was about our well-being, he had to hurry Papa forward to the immigration processing office since Pfizer had arranged for a friendly clerk to stamp Papa's papers.

1   *Redt Yiddish* – "Do you speak Yiddish?"

"Papers?" asked Papa. "What kind of papers?"

"Identification documents, from your country. Papers that explain who you are—a birth certificate, a marriage certificate, do you have anything like that?"

Papa reached into his coat and produced the only thing he had: Charles Abuza's military documents.

"This says you are Italian and weigh a hundred and thirty pounds," fretted Paul.

"I ate a lot on the boat," smiled Papa.

"Let's just pray they don't think you ate Charles Abuza on the boat," frowned Paul.

When Paul and Papa got up to the processing desk, Paul exchanged a few pleasantries with the clerk. Apparently Pfizer had sent him a case of grapefruit the week before, a luxury intended to grease the wheels for Papa and his shipment of citrons to enter the country.

"*Benvenuto*, Signore Abuza," said the clerk to Papa. "I notice that you seem to have gained quite a bit of weight on board the boat…"

"Si?" guessed Papa.

"You know Paul, I've had a real craving for my wife's upside-down cake, but she can't find those pineapples anywhere," he said, his approval stamp hovering over Papa's paperwork. Paul nodded.

"Welcome to America, Mr. Abuza," said the clerk.

"*Grazie parmigiano!*" responded Papa with a big smile.

With that, Zachary Kalish became Charles Abuza, a brand new American. Paul escorted him into Manhattan and onto a horse-drawn bus heading uptown to 82nd Street, where Paul's family owned a boarding house. Pfizer would pay for Papa to stay there while he waited for the rest of us to arrive, and Paul promised to send along a letter from Papa to let Mama know he was safe and sound. Paul also instructed the Pfizer office in Glasgow to wire him once the three of us were on our way to New York.

That's everything I knew from Papa. Mama told me we spent four unremarkable months in Glasgow until she got the money together to pay for our passage. Then we joined Papa in New York and moved on to Boston, where we stayed with Mama's family for a few years, and eventually settled down in Hartford.

Aunt Tizzy nearly fell out of her chair when she heard that Mama said we spent a quiet summer in Glasgow.

"Quiet? *Quiet?!* I don't know about you, but I wouldn't call being arrested for murder part of a particularly quiet summer," screeched Tizzy.

Al and I looked at each other and nearly spit our biscuits and tea across the room, we were laughing so hard. Tizzy looked at us in shock. She was as serious as a heart attack.

After Papa left, Tizzy explained, Mama took Phillip and me back to Green's Hotel and asked for a room for another couple of days. Unfortunately, the hotel was booked solid with guests fresh off a big steamship that had just arrived in the port. In fact, every hotel in the Gorbals was full to bursting. Mama lugged our suitcases over to a sofa in the lobby and slumped down, not quite sure what to do next.

Tizzy spotted Mama and came over to take me off of her hands for a few minutes, since juggling a cranky bowling ball isn't the best way to think. The next boat for New York would depart on Wednesday, in three days, but those ships booked up weeks in advance. Tizzy was pretty sure it was already full. The boat after that wouldn't leave for ten days. Tizzy had a suggestion, though, for a cheap place to stay. Mama had no better ideas so she waited in the lobby until the end of Tizzy's shift and then followed her through Glasgow, unsure where she was headed.

Eventually they reached a little house on a narrow side street where Tizzy unlocked the front door and showed us inside. In the sitting room sat her mother, who instantly recognized Mama, Phillip and me from Tizzy's stories. Though she couldn't speak any Yiddish, she took me from Mama's arms and her delight with my chubby little fingers and toes spoke volumes about how welcome we would be in the Hawkins home. There was an extra room, since Tizzy's older sister, Touie, had moved out recently to live with her new husband, Artie. He was the one who gave both sisters their funny nicknames. Elizabeth became Tizzy and Louisa became Touie; I guess if I'd ever met Artie, I'd be Tophie.

The problem, they learned early Monday morning at the docks, was that passage for all three of us on a ship leaving in ten days would cost fifty pounds. Unfortunately, Mama's silver candlesticks were still packed in the trunk with Papa, on their way to New York, and Mama had already exchanged all her grandfather's diamonds for the investment in the citron shipment. All that was left of the Palumbo's travel money was five measly pounds.

Together, the women figured out that if Tizzy could convince the hotel to let Mama pick up a few cleaning shifts and Mrs. Hawkins could get her some extra sewing piecework at night, we'd have enough money to get across to the States in a few months.

Later that morning, Tizzy snuck Mama in through the basement service entrance of the hotel and got her a uniform. There was a big commotion going on in the lobby which made a convenient cover for their lateness, though Tizzy was a little surprised to see five policemen milling around with Mr. McGregor, the hotel manager. Her plan was to put Mama to work immediately and show Mr. McGregor what a good job she could do. Hopefully, he would hire her on the spot.

Mama and Tizzy worked all morning on a towering pile of laundry in the basement. There was a full weekend's worth of sheets, towels, and staff uniforms to launder and Tizzy hardly had to demonstrate the job to Mama before she was scrubbing grease stains and coal out of all of the linens like an old hand. Mama was never one to shy away from difficult chores—particularly ones where she was encouraged to check pockets for loose change. Every shilling she found in a pair of work pants brought her an inch or two closer to New York City.

Working with Tizzy was a ball. Together they poked fun at all manner of stains the workmen managed to leave on their pants. No one in the hotel, it seemed, could eat dinner without it ending up in their laps.

"Look at these!" Tizzy laughed, holding up a giant white shirt and matching pants covered in rusty red stains. "These belong to Oscar, the chef. Saturday night was roast beef night."

"My god, it looks like he slaughtered the whole cow," said Mama, holding up a bunch of bloody towels wrapped in a bloodier sheet. She gathered up all of the stained white clothing and linens and dumped them in a big metal washtub filled with hot water.

"Damnation! We're all out of bleach," said Tizzy, checking through the shelves.

"What's bleach?" asked Mama.

"They don't have bleach in Russia? It helps get the white linen whiter."

"If it's anything that would have made life easier for the Jews, we didn't have it in Russia," said Mama. "Don't you worry about these whites."

Mama nearly scrubbed her fingers to the bone on the pile of stained sheets and towels and when she was done, they were so blindingly white you couldn't look at them without sunglasses. They left the wash drying on lines strung up behind the hotel and went upstairs to eat a late lunch and find out what the police had been doing in the lobby that morning.

Tizzy introduced Mama around to the other employees in the kitchen over leftover roast beef sandwiches. According to their gossip, a few Russians had been staying at the hotel and joined the staff's regular Saturday night card game. The big winner was found dead in the lounge that morning and it looked like someone had stolen all of his money.

"My God! Who saw him last?" asked Tizzy.

"Last time anyone saw him was Saturday after the game," explained Bernard, the boiler man.

"We all left after the dead one cleaned us out," lamented Ralph the janitor.

"He was counting my whole week's pay when I went home," added Oscar, the chef. "Then Kenny tried to clean the lounge this morning and there he was, dead."

"I'm guessing you mopped up the mess with all of those towels and sheets we just washed," said Tizzy. Mama couldn't quite follow along with all of the English, but she certainly recognized the scrubbing motions that Tizzy made to act out how they got rid of the mess.

"Yes, that's exactly what McGregor told us to do. You have to hand it to the boss. He had a dead Russian in his lounge and managed to get it cleaned up and call the police without losing his head," shrugged Oscar.

After Mama and Tizzy's shift, the two of them went up to Mr. McGregor's office to ask about hiring Mama as a temporary laundry girl for the next few months. The hotel had been short staffed since another girl left to have a baby, so all Tizzy had to do was flash a few of Mama's snow white towels and, just as planned, she got the job.

Over the next couple of days, they worked a few uneventful shifts together scrubbing the linens and checking the pockets for change. If Mama could've paid for our passage with lint and old hankies, we would've travelled first class. Things were becoming pleasantly routine until their work was interrupted by a visit from Inspector Boyd of the Glasgow police.

The detective was making the rounds of hotel employees asking about the dead Russian. As it turned out, there was another Russian man missing since the card game. Tizzy had to translate for Mama, since she didn't speak a word of English beyond "more soap." The Inspector asked to see the towels and uniform shirt that had been covered in blood. Unfortunately, Mama had scrubbed every bit of evidence out in the wash, and had folded the uniform and placed it on the shelf with the other kitchen uniforms.

The detective was just about to leave when he turned on his heel and asked if either Tizzy or Mama had found anything odd in the laundry since the murder. It was a last-ditch effort to drum up some evidence, so Boyd was shocked when Mama produced from her uniform pocket a handful of change and Papa's big gold wedding band. Tizzy was just as surprised, since Mama hadn't mentioned anything to her about finding the ring. Still, she translated for Boyd as Mama explained she discovered it amongst the pile of dirty linens under the laundry chute during her first shift at the hotel, one day after Papa had sailed off to America. Mama had rolled her eyes and said a prayer of thanks when she found the ring, but was too embarrassed to reveal another of Papa's classic foul-ups to her new friend Tizzy. She just quietly slipped the ring into her pocket and said nothing. Three days later, Mama was still mystified as to how that hunk of gold came off of her husband's finger and wound up in the laundry room.

"Why didn't she sail with her husband to New York?" asked Boyd, his eyebrows arched.

"They were all supposed to leave on a cargo ship last Sunday, but there was some kind of mix up with a new captain who would only let only her husband on board," explained Tizzy.

"Now, because that *schlemeil*² lost all of our extra money in a poker game the night before he left, I'm stuck here with two children and no money for passage to America. That's why I'm doing the wash," said Mama.

Tizzy translated everything for Inspector Boyd except for schlemeil, but once again, Mama had surprised her. She didn't understand why Mama hadn't mentioned at lunch that her husband was part of the Russians' poker game, until she remembered that Mama couldn't understand the conversation. It was all in English.

The detective said he needed to borrow Papa's ring for a day or two and left. Tizzy was concerned, but Mama refused to worry about the police. She was more determined than ever to get across to America, if only so she could smack Papa right on the back of the head for losing his ring. Neither woman gave the police much thought until they found Boyd waiting outside the hotel a few days later when they were leaving work. He took Mama by the shoulder.

"Translate for her," he commanded Tizzy. "Let her know she's under arrest for aiding and abetting the murder of Yaakov Simotz."

Two weeks passed before Tizzy, who had worked herself up into a state that rivaled her nickname, was permitted to see Mama at the police station and deliver a letter that had arrived from my father. When they finally led her into an empty little room where Mama sat at a table, shackled by her wrists and her ankles, Tizzy wept. Mama, however, was as cool as a cucumber—and as sour as a dill pickle, given her circumstances. She asked over and over again about me and Phillip, but had almost nothing to say about the very serious charges against her.

"These schmendricks think my husband killed the winner of that card game and then I helped him escape, but that's nonsense. If Zachary killed everyone who took his money at the card table there would be no one left on Earth," said Mama with a shrug of her shoulders.

"I talked to the police and they say there is going to be a trial in a month. We'll take good care of the babies until then, but you need a lawyer who speaks Yiddish. Otherwise we'll never be able to get you

2 *Schlemiel* – An inept person, a dope.

out of here," sniffled Tizzy. "What's in that letter from your husband? Anything that will help your case?"

Mama scanned the letter. "Apparently New York City is having lovely weather. He hopes I'm doing well," she said, rolling her eyes so hard her shackles rattled.

Tizzy arranged to bring Mama a pencil and paper so she could write an urgent letter to Papa in New York, and she also set up a visit with old Hymie Schwartz, one of the only Yiddish-speaking lawyers in Scotland. Hymie was a retired real estate lawyer and a soft-hearted family friend so he agreed to help Mama for free, but he'd never argued a criminal case in his entire life. He no longer had any connections at the courthouse and so his main purpose was merely to gather information about the case and translate it so Mama knew what was happening.

Hymie was able at least to piece together the prosecution's case. Bernard, Ralph, Oscar and Kenny, the regular card-playing hotel employees, claimed that Papa had lost all his cash and his ring to the other Russian, Yaakov Simotz, in the poker game. Kenny said after the game he went to get his coat and hat from his locker and saw Papa going back into the lounge, where he figured Yaakov, the winner, was counting his money.

The cops were going to make the case that the two Russians got into a scuffle over the wedding ring and, when Yaakov wouldn't return it, Papa ended up beating him to death. There were indentations of the ring all over the dead man's face. Plus, a few of the hotel guests heard Mama shouting at her husband up in their room after the game was over, which they said was proof she knew Papa had lost the ring. The cops believed Mama knew he killed Yaakov to get the ring back, and then helped to smuggle him on board the cargo ship the next day so he could avoid jail. The fact that Mama had the ring in her pocket when the police came around didn't help her case.

I guess it never occurred to any of those nincompoop detectives that my mother would definitely have hidden that big old ring if she or Papa had anything to do with the murder. I also know Mama never noticed Papa's wedding band was missing from his finger before he got on the cargo ship. If she had, there would have been a second murder that weekend.

If it wasn't for the fact that the courts were backed up that summer, Mama would probably still be doing hard labor. However, a delay of a few months allowed a letter to arrive from Papa, in which he explained what happened. He did lose his ring in the poker game. He'd bet everything he had on his four kings, but Yaakov cleaned him out with four aces. The witnesses did get one thing right: after Papa told Mama he lost all his money, there was a screaming match and she booted Papa out of our hotel room. He hadn't told her anything about the wedding ring since she would've booted him clear to the moon.

Exiled from bed, Papa decided to stroll by the lounge and take a stab at convincing Yaakov to give back his ring. Yaakov, it turned out, had a soft spot for a fellow Russian. He was headed to Philadelphia and agreed not to sell the ring if Papa promised to send money for it when we got settled in Boston. Papa figured that with the citron money he'd be able to buy it back in no time. They shook hands and Papa never saw him again.

Besides my father's letter, it was Tizzy's brother-in-law Artie that helped set Mama free. When Touie and Artie arrived at the Hawkins house that August for a visit, Tizzy had to explain the sudden appearance of an adorable little boy and a baby girl who could out-wail the bagpipes from the local Jewish Lads Brigade that practiced up the block.

Jewish Lads Brigade

Artie, a doctor by trade, was particularly interested in Mama's case. Back home in London, he loved following the newspaper accounts of all the latest murders and puzzling out "who done it". After listening to Tizzy's story, Artie felt strongly that things weren't adding up.

Thankfully, Artie still had a few connections around town from his university days. He took Tizzy along with him to meet his old chum Randolph, who now worked in the city prosecutor's office. Randolph took pity when he heard that Mama only had a washed up old real estate lawyer for her defense and arranged an introduction to MacGille, Mama's prosecutor, so Tizzy and Artie could take a look at the files he had put together.

Then Tizzy and Artie went to the morgue. Being a doctor came in handy when Artie went inside to examine the body of Yaakov Simotz, who had been kept on ice pending Mama's trial. Tizzy sat outside, breathing into a paper bag and trying not to think about all of the corpses on the other side of the door. Mama's new defense team then returned to the Hawkins house and spent all night at the table surrounded by their notes,

Tizzy's brother-in-law Artie, 1883

figuring out how they could prove Mama's innocence. Aunt Tizzy said I sat in her lap and helpfully drooled on all of the most important clues.

The sun came up the next day and Tizzy and Artie woke up bleary-eyed but cautiously optimistic. Tizzy ran to her shift at the hotel. Artie went to ask Inspector Boyd to arrange a meeting with MacGille, Mr. McGregor and the hotel employees from the card game so he and Tizzy could make the case for Mama's innocence.

That afternoon, they all gathered with the authorities at the scene of the crime: the hotel lounge. Bernard the boiler man, Oscar the chef, Ralph the janitor, and Kenny, his assistant, sat around the big card table while Tizzy quietly folded pillowcases in the corner, trying to listen in.

"Thank you so much for joining me here, gentlemen. And thank you for indulging me and my sister-in-law who, as you know, works with all of you here in this very hotel. We've grown quite fond of Mrs. Kalish and her children and want to make sure she receives only the fairest of trials here in Glasgow," explained Artie.

The first thing he did was ask Inspector Boyd to quickly summarize everything he discovered about the night of the murder. The Inspector restated that after the card game, Kenny went downstairs to get his coat and hat and when he came back up, he saw Papa entering the lounge, where Yaakov was still counting his winnings. After that, it took Kenny about ten minutes to walk home, where he went to bed. Oscar said that since there weren't any bars open after their late game of cards, he went directly home and fell asleep without even changing out of his chef's uniform.

Bernard and Ralph stated that they changed out of their work duds before they began playing poker. Right after the card game, they had a quick smoke in front of the hotel with Kenny and Oscar and then went straight home.

"Wait a minute, my good fellow," interrupted Artie, gently tapping Brody on the arm. "That doesn't quite make sense. If Kenny and Oscar went straight home, then how were they smoking outside with Bernard and Ralph?"

Boyd scratched his head.

"Don't fret too much about it, old chum. Perhaps these men just forgot to tell you. Before we proceed, I wonder if I could trouble this fine establishment for some lunch. I've been running myself ragged all day and I'm positively famished. Oscar, do you think I could have one of your famous roast beef sandwiches and maybe a cup of tea?"

"Why not bring a tray for all of us?" asked McGregor, the hotel manager.

"Inspector Boyd, why don't you go assist him?" Artie asked pointedly.

As the men left for the kitchen, Artie grabbed Boyd's arm and whispered something in his ear. Boyd nodded and hurried quickly out of the room.

While the employees and MacGille waited for the food, Artie asked Tizzy a few questions about how the laundry room worked in the hotel. She explained that she would wash, dry, then fold all of the towels in a particular way, in thirds, and then deliver them throughout the hotel. Sheets were folded in another special way and stored in the linen closet on each floor until they were needed. The men's uniforms were kept on a few shelves in the basement and organized by department, with shirts on one shelf and pants on the other. There were an assortment of sizes and they were all laundered every day, since McGregor was a stickler for tidiness.

Oscar returned with the tray of sandwiches, Boyd trailing behind with a big pot of tea. Everyone took a cup and a sandwich and tried to forget about the murder for a moment.

"What did I miss?" asked Oscar.

"Just the doctor boning up on the finer points of the hotel laundry," chuckled Bernard, shaking his head.

"You should see what we have to do to get Oscar's uniforms clean," remarked Tizzy as she distributed napkins to all of the men. "It's truly a bloody mess every day. Roast beef stains are no walk in the park."

"As a matter of fact, Tizzy mentioned that it took Mrs. Kalish forever to do your laundry after our poor Yaakov turned up deceased," Artie said, looking at Oscar. "Not only was your uniform covered in Saturday night's dinner, it seems that it was also used to help clean up the bloody lounge. Unfortunately, Mrs. Kalish did such a good job with the laundry she erased some helpful evidence."

While Artie was talking, Tizzy quietly tapped Boyd on the shoulder and together they slipped out of the room. They came back a few moments later with something hidden behind Tizzy's back. To distract the men from her disappearance, Artie directed the conversation toward Papa's big wedding ring. The men laughed when Artie mentioned it, since Papa had thrown it into the pot with such confidence. The funniest part, they said, was that Yaakov could fit two of his fingers inside the huge ring.

"Do you remember trying it on?" Artie asked Oscar. "You have pretty big hands. It seems like it would be a good fit for you."

"Nope, I don't remember anything like that," Oscar said quietly, and continued to chew his roast beef sandwich.

"Mr. Kalish remembers you trying it on," Artie added.

With a flourish, he produced the second letter Papa had written to Mama from New York. Tizzy had written out a translation for Artie during the previous night's detective work.

Words cannot express how sorry I am for losing my mind…and the wedding ring your grandfather made for me. I was so sure my cards were winners. I remember dreaming about all of the things I would buy for you in America as the men passed around my ring and tried it on.

Until that night, the ring had never been off my finger since the day we were married. As the other players laughed at its size, I realized how much it meant to me. It made me anxious to watch one man, the big heavy chef, slip it on and admire its perfect fit. The way he stared at it, I knew I would never get it back if I lost it to him.

After two more rounds of raises I thought the worst was over, because the chef had dropped out. Yet still, the unthinkable happened. At the end of the game I lost the ring to the other Russian.

I hope someday you will be able to forgive me. Please know, I made a deal to get the ring back as soon as I got our money from the citrons, and I believed Yaakov, the other Russian, when he promised me he would not sell it. I can only thank God my precious ring somehow found its way back to you. I pray every night that, in the same way, He will deliver you back to me and reunite our family here in America. I am so sorry, Jennie. Be strong. The truth will bring us back together. I look forward to the day when you slip my ring back on my finger. I promise you I will never remove it again.

The room was so silent, Tizzy could hear the tea getting cold.

"Now Oscar, my meticulous sister-in-law and I would like to prove that *you*, in fact, killed Yaakov," he said calmly. Oscar's face turned red with rage. Inspector Boyd and MacGille, the prosecutor, exchanged a confused glance.

Artie explained that just before Inspector Boyd accompanied Oscar into the kitchen to make the roast beef sandwiches, he'd asked Boyd to observe whether or not Oscar sliced the beef with his left hand. Boyd reported that, indeed, Oscar was left-handed.

"I investigated Yaakov's body this morning and deduced from the impressions on his face that he was beaten by a man who was left-handed. However, the marks left behind also revealed that his killer was wearing the ring on his right hand. Certainly, Mr. Kalish could be left-handed. But he would have been wearing the ring on his left hand, since it was his wedding band."

Artie stood up and began to pace calmly around the room. On the night of the murder, he explained, Oscar met Kenny and his poker buddies outside for a smoke after the card game. Kenny mentioned having seen Mr. Kalish going back in the lounge. But Papa had already cleared himself in his letter, when he wrote that he left Simotz alive after they shook hands on their deal to get the ring back. However, Artie theorized, after the four men went their separate ways, Oscar hid a few blocks from the hotel and then doubled back, hoping to find Yaakov still in possession of the ring.

Oscar returned to the lounge and spotted the golden prize still next to its new owner. The chef asked if he could try the band on one last time, and offered Yaakov all his money in exchange for the big hunk of gold, but Yaakov had already promised to keep the ring for Papa. Things became heated and Oscar, a burly brute of a man, boiled over and beat Yaakov to death. Now he had the ring, but he was covered in blood that no one would ever believe came from a roast beef dinner. He left the lounge and went to the kitchen to wash up and change out of the bloodied uniform. He stashed the uniform among some dirty towels and headed out as though nothing had happened. He figured Kenny would tell the police that he saw Papa go into the lounge last and no one would ever suspect him.

Artie pressed on, more urgently. Oscar came to work early Monday morning to deal with the evidence he'd left behind, but he quickly realized he couldn't destroy the bloody uniform since Tizzy would notice if it went missing. The solution to his problem presented itself when Kenny came running into the kitchen after discovering Yaakov's body in the lounge. Oscar ran down the hall with every towel and piece of cloth he could find, including his bloody uniform, and mopped up the mess. When everything looked as gruesome as his uniform, he sent it down the laundry chute. It seemed like the perfect plan. The most damning piece of evidence was going to be washed clean.

"However," said Artie to his suspect, "you forgot one thing. The ring. It slipped your mind that you had put it in your uniform pocket so you could wash your hands after the murder. That's why it turned up in Mrs. Kalish's pile of laundry. And *that's* what sunk you, Oscar. Tizzy, tell him why."

"We were out of bleach," Tizzy explained, "but Jennie still scrubbed that uniform until it was like new. That day, I also noticed something interesting. After Jennie washed your pants, she folded them slightly differently than I do and put them away on the *bottom* of the pile of clean uniforms. You see, I always put clean uniforms on the *top* of the pile, which means that these," she said, producing a pair of pants from behind her back, "are the pants that you were wearing the night of the murder. They're still folded Jennie's way and they have been sitting on the bottom of your stack of uniforms since then."

Artie took the pants from Tizzy and explained that while bleach erases stains entirely, soap would have only removed stains from the surface of the bloody uniform no matter how hard Mama scrubbed. If Oscar placed Papa's bloodied ring in one of the pockets of his white uniform pants, it's likely that there would still be some proof.

"I never had that ring!" sputtered Oscar.

"Then there's no harm in checking," said Tizzy, turning the pockets inside out. And there, in the left front pocket, Artie pointed to a faint spot of blood.

"If I'm not mistaken, Inspector Boyd and Mr. MacGille, you'll find that you can read a reverse impression of the engraving on Mr. Kalish's ring. Tizzy, would you be so kind as to translate this for me?" asked Artie.

"I think that's Yiddish for '*guilty*,'" said Tizzy, grinning as wide as she could.

After Oscar was taken into custody, things moved quickly for Mama. She was released in early September and she all but ran back to the Hawkins house to see Phillip and me. I greeted her with a new shriek I had perfected over the three months we'd been apart, and Mama was so happy to see me she didn't even mind the ringing in her ears.

When the newspapers got wind of her story, Mama made the front page of both the *Glasgow Herald* and the *Glasgow Times*. Aunt Tizzy insisted that for a brief moment in the summer of 1887, the Kalish family was more famous than the King of England. An officer of the Glasgow Pfizer office recognized Mama's name in the news and was finally able to answer the many telegrams that Paul Weissman, Papa's New York Pfizer connection, had been sending all summer. Every week, the office had received the same message:

> Please inform New York when Jennie Kalish and her two
> children leave Glasgow.

When the Glasgow office wired back the details of what had happened, Paul arranged for Pfizer to foot the bill for our passage to the United States and we were on a boat within the week.

When Al and I heard the entire story, we needed a jack to lift our jaws up off the ground. I knew Mama liked to keep things to herself, but I couldn't believe that she'd managed to keep her summer in a Scottish prison a secret for my entire life.

Tizzy even had a few old newspaper clippings that mentioned Mama's case and Artie, the doctor who liked to do detective work. Tizzy proudly pointed to the line where he mentioned her, which said: "We never could have solved this case without the invaluable assistance of Elizabeth "Tizzy" Hawkins."

Artie went on to write a few novels and he tried to name one of his characters after Tizzy, but the publishers made him change the character to a man.

"So, is Artie still doctoring?" asked Al.

"No, he gave it up after his first book got published," Tizzy answered.

"Write down his name for us," I requested. "I could use something to read on my boat ride home."

"There's one thing I always wanted to know," Tizzy asked as she wrote down the name. "What did the inscription on your father's ring mean? Your mother never told me."

I pulled a chain out from around my neck under my blouse to reveal my father's wedding ring.

"It says *Ani Le Dodi Ve Dodi Li*. It means 'I am my beloved's, and my beloved is mine.'"

Tizzy sighed and smiled.

Al and I were silent and astounded on our way back to our hotel that night. I didn't even think to look at the piece of paper Tizzy gave me until I was changing out of my dress to get ready for bed. I was lucky I was standing next to something soft, because I just about fell over when I realized who Tizzy had been talking about. It's a *shonda*[3] her literary namesake, Tizzy Watson, never made it to print.

Tizzy's brother-in-law.

<hr />

3 *Shonda* – Embarrassment, shame.

Chapter 16

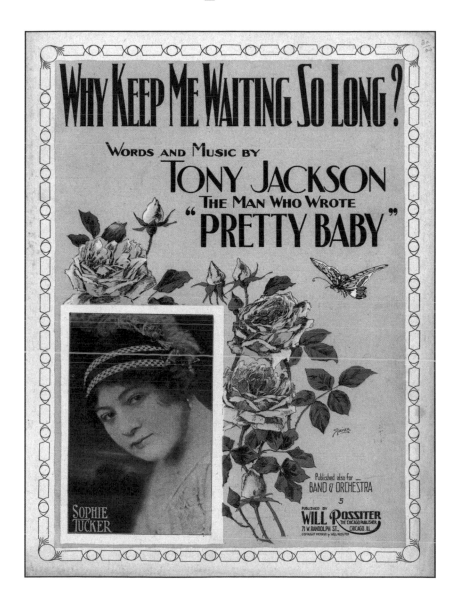

Why Keep Me
Waiting So Long?

Al and I headed back to the States after we visited Aunt Tizzy but, unwilling to end our honeymoon just yet, we spent a week at the beach in New London, Connecticut. I'd taken my mother there a few years earlier when her health started to fail so she could get some fresh air, some sun, and perhaps for the first time since she was a child, relax.

That was the trip when I finally got Mama to explain why my family moved to Hartford after living in Boston for eight years. This was a story even Papa wouldn't tell and I was too young when we picked up and moved to understand why we were leaving Mama's cousins behind. Mama was so unwilling to talk at first I had to fish the story out bit by bit, like boiled dumplings from a big pot of water.

Papa was anxiously waiting on the dock when our boat arrived from Glasgow. He was there with Paul Weissman from Pfizer, who wanted to apologize to Mama personally for all of the trouble she'd gone through to get to America.

Over our first American meal (I'm sure pastrami was involved), Paul said that he'd sent a telegram to the Palumbo family in Genoa and explained our entire situation—Mama's delay, Papa's new name, and where they could wire back the diamond money.

Sophie and her mother at the beach in New London, Connecticut, 1925.

Paul had the transfer all set up with an associate named Mr. Wainwright at the Bank of Boston. Everything finally settled, he showed us to Grand Central Depot and got us on a train heading north.

As we pulled out of the station, Mama said she couldn't hear the train whistle over my bawling. I was probably screaming because, even at the ripe old age of nine months, I already knew I belonged in New York City. Mama and Papa, on the other hand, fell in love with Hartford through the train's window when we briefly stopped there to let off passengers. They watched people bustling up and down Front Street and imagined opening a little grocery in a vacant storefront in the middle of the block. Mama said she wished that she could just hop off the train and start a new American life right then and there.

When we arrived in Boston, we were met by a welcoming committee of at least ten extended family members, some with their arms outstretched to hug us and others eager to hoist our trunk on their backs. Boris, Mama's first cousin, and his wife Celia invited the whole neighborhood to meet us at a party with enough food to feed the entire Russian army.

Mama admitted that the first day with her family was a little overwhelming. Phillip was happy to be running around with children his own age but she was afraid to take her eyes off of him. After bringing him halfway around the world and nearly losing him in Glasgow, she felt like a mother bear defending her cub. It didn't matter if the threat was merely a bunch of other little cubs. Besides that, Celia was an overbearing neatnik, and I was a whirlwind of crumbs and drool and sticky fingers. Mama could hardly move without Celia following behind her with a rag and a broom. She was grateful to her family but felt like she was imposing for the hundredth time. She wanted her own life in the United States.

Cousin Boris Klein

"What's your plan for the money once it arrives from Italy, Signore Abuza?" asked Boris, Celia's mild-mannered husband. He was a particularly kind man who'd always dreamed of being a scholar. Just like I imagined singing on a stage, Boris imagined himself behind a big wooden desk with his nose in a book.

"We were thinking about opening a little grocery," said Papa. "We learned a bit about the produce business coming over here from Genoa, and no one will be able to turn down Jennie's jars of goulash. My wife knows her onions."

As the party wound down, my parents presented Boris with a gift for allowing us to stay with his family. One of the things that Mama had managed to pack before leaving the *shtetl*[1] was her father's beautiful leather-bound edition of the Talmud[2].

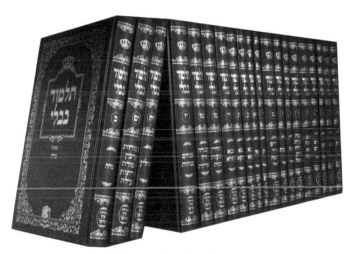

The twenty books of the Jewish Talmud.

Since he was a boy, Boris had kept a spot open on a bookshelf in his study for the Talmud he hoped to own one day. After opening the bundle they produced from their trunk, he nearly cried with joy and Celia, ever the housekeeper, was right there with a handkerchief to prevent even one tear from landing on his gift.

1   *Shtetl* – A small town with a large Jewish population; often used to refer to such towns in Central or Eastern Europe prior to the pogroms and the Holocaust.

2   *The Talmud* – The main guide texts of Judaism, second to the Torah, which total approximately 6,200 pages. They contain the opinions of thousands of rabbis on law, ethics, philosophy, customs, history, theology, lore among other topics.

The next day, Mama went downtown by herself to claim the money from the citron shipment. She didn't trust Papa to do it and come straight home with all of that cash burning a hole in his pocket.

Boston, late 1800s.

Mama found her way to the bank and showed a young clerk the paper Paul Weissman had given Papa explaining why she was there. The clerk read the instructions, showed Mama to the front door and directed her from the National Bank of Boston, where she had come by accident, to the Bank of Boston, which was just across the street. It was an easy mistake for a woman who knew only a handful of English words.

Mama made her way across the bustling road without getting killed by a speeding horse cart, but picked up the phrase "Fuck you!" from a driver who came within inches of running her over. She wrote it down phonetically in Yiddish in a little black notebook she kept in her pocket. She thought it might come in handy someday.

This time in the correct bank, she asked to speak to Mr. Wainwright and was shown to a hard wooden chair in front of a big desk. After a few moments, an older gentleman emerged from the depths of the bank and took a seat behind the desk and began talking. When he realized she had no idea what he was saying, he held up a finger.

"Rosenwaser!" he shouted.

Out came a young clerk who took one look at Mama and smiled. Mr. Wainwright jabbered to Rosenwaser for a moment and then looked at Mama expectantly.

"Hello, Mrs. Abuza," said Rosenwaser in Yiddish. "Please excuse Mr. Wainwright. His Yiddish is about as good as my Irish jig. He wants you to know that he understands that you are waiting for money from someone in Genoa. All international transfers first go to our branch in New York, so it's likely that the money is still tied up there. He suggests that you try back in a week. It should have arrived by then."

"Tell him that if my money's not here the next time I visit, I'll dance the Irish jig on his face," said Mama.

"Maybe I'll keep that between us," smiled Rosenwaser.

A month went by. Mama went downtown and met with Rosenwaser and Wainwright every week, sometimes twice a week, and each time they told her there was no money for her. Papa was beginning to lose hope in William and Milly Palumbo and worried perhaps that the new Abuzas had been taken to the cleaners. Mama didn't. She believed there must be some explanation for the delay.

Boris hardly minded our extended stay in his house. He was so busy with his beautiful new set of Talmud books he barely looked up when he got home from work. General Celia, on the other hand, was much less hospitable to the Abuza battalion. She waged war on our extra laundry and additional dirty dishes as though our dirt was an invading army.

One night when Mama and Papa were out for a walk, Boris and the family received a visit from Mendel Rubins, a neighbor who ran a little Kosher restaurant. Celia showed him to the study and went to make him some tea while Boris pried himself away from the first of his holy books. Mendel went to the special shelf and admired the whole set. He pulled out a thin volume toward the end of the series.

"What's this one about?" he asked, flipping through the pages.

"The rules governing divorce. It will probably take me ten years to get to that book, though," answered Boris.

"God forbid you should ever need it," he smiled, setting it down on the couch beside him. "I came to ask your opinion about something. So many of my my customers are complaining about Mrs. Fishbind, my cook! Her brisket is so tough, customers are losing teeth. The only one who likes her cooking is Shlomo, the dentist."

Celia returned with the tea and glared at the misplaced volume Mendel had dropped on her couch.

"What you need is a wife," laughed Boris. "The old widow Fishbind is no substitute for a partner who could help you with your business. Maybe you could even make a few little busboys."

"Well, until then, the gossip is that your cousin Jennie is quite the cook. Plus, I heard that she and her husband are still waiting for their money from their friends in Italy. And between you and me, there's no way that money's coming."

"We're all trying to stay positive."

"Positive won't put food on the table. Maybe she might want to cook a few nights a week for me? It's better than sitting here twiddling her thumbs."

"I'll ask her," said Boris. "It'll do my waistline good to get her out of here. My belts can only take so much more of her cooking before they surrender."

Boris walked his friend to the front door for a fifteen minute Jewish goodbye. By the time he got back, Celia had already tidied up the teacups and replaced the Talmud volume about divorce in its proper place on its proper shelf.

Tired of being chased around by Celia's dust rag, Mama agreed to take the job at Mendel's restaurant. The only condition was that he first let her travel to Brooklyn to visit the Pfizer office to find out what had happened to the citron money. Until our trip to New London all those years later, I never knew that my Mama, who I could hardly picture out of an apron, had gone all the way to New York City by herself to lay down the law with the head honcho of a huge company.

Once Mama made it to Brooklyn, she marched directly into the Pfizer office and demanded to see Mr. Pfizer himself. His secretary smirked and told her that Mr. Pfizer was on vacation and wouldn't be back until the end of the week. Mama said she would wait. She took a seat and sat there all day, and all day the next day. And all day the day after that. Occasionally she would nod off in her chair, but mostly she kept her eyes peeled for anyone who might be the man in charge.

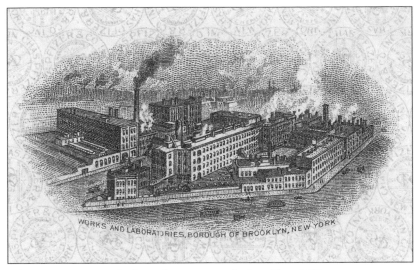

The main entrance of Pfizer Pharmaceuticals, Brooklyn, NY.

On the fourth day, Mr. Pfizer came tearing into the office like a tornado with two assistants spinning in his wake.

"Who is this?" he barked, pointing at Mama.

"I'm sorry, Mr. Pfizer. Her name Jennie Abuza. She insists on talking to you. She's been sitting here for four days. Should I have called the police?" asked the receptionist.

"No, no," tutted Mr. Pfizer. "What can I do for you, Mrs. Abuza?"

"Two minutes," asked Mama, in her heavily accented English.

"Two minutes? You waited four days for two minutes? I wish I had ten salesmen like you," laughed Mr. Pfizer, and he showed Mama into his office.

"Abuza," he said, stroking his bushy muttonchops. "I remember that name. Aren't you the woman who had all that trouble in Scotland? With the false arrest?"

Mama nodded. After she explained the money had never gotten to the Boston bank, Mr. Pfizer consulted a number of ledgers on his desk and frowned. The books showed they had paid the Palumbo family in full immediately upon receipt of the shipment of citrons. They were even slated to arrange a second shipment on the same terms, but the Palumbos hadn't responded to any of their subsequent telegrams. It was like they had dropped off the map entirely.

"I'm afraid that these people in Genoa may have been less than honest with you. I'm sorry I don't have better news for you, Mrs. Abuza. It seems like you've had quite a streak of bad luck."

"No," my mother disagreed. "The Palumbos are good people. There is a reason."

Mr. Pfizer came out from behind his desk and shook Mama's hand.

"I'm terribly sorry about your money. However, if you ever decide to move to New York, please come see me again. I could always use a persistent saleswoman."

Mama left New York no richer than when she came, but she refused to give up faith in William and Milly, her Italian Passover family.

Charles Pfizer, founder of Pfizer Pharmaceuticals.

Three years went by. Phil turned seven. I was four and a half and now singing my first hit song "Ta-Ra-Ra Boom-de-ay" as loud as possible. Moe was born and immediately put his fingers in his ears. And Boris had finished studying the first three volumes of the Talmud.

Mama and Papa managed to move to a little apartment in the same building as Boris and Celia. Because Mama routinely worked grueling sixteen hour shifts at Mendel's restaurant, she often had to leave Papa to take care of all three of us screaming kids. We got by on Papa's hash, and Papa got by on aspirin for his splitting headaches.

Over the prior three years, Mama's cooking had tripled the business at Mendel's restaurant. She asked for a raise at least once a month but Mendel always had an excuse. One month the butcher raised his prices, the next month the roof needed repairs, and so on and so on. With no hope of finding a better job, she continued to work for next to nothing. Papa managed to pick up a few shifts here and there as a bartender at a local tavern called Herman's, but neither one earned enough money to make any progress toward opening their own business. They were barely making enough to pay the rent.

I don't remember much from those years but I will never forget the five of us sitting on a blanket in a park one fourth of July. I watched the fireworks burst into dazzling color over the Boston harbor. Everything seemed perfect to me. Unfortunately, Mama mostly remembered the sadness of those years, when it seemed like all hope was lost.

The years kept slipping away and nothing changed. Boris finished another few volumes of the Talmud. Papa would pish away his meager earnings on card games with his friends and Mama worked harder than ever at the restaurant. She closed up when the last customer left, cleaned the kitchen by herself, and counted up all the receipts. Mendel had taken to stopping by late at night when she was doing the bookkeeping, after he'd had some drinks with his buddies down at Herman's tavern. My mother was uncomfortable being trapped in the dark restaurant alone with him.

As we sat on the beach in New London, Mama looked off at the ocean and stopped talking for a long time. I'm not sure what convinced her to tell me what happened, but I sat silently as she spoke.

She was scrubbing a sink full of pots one night when Mendel came into the kitchen and hovered nearby, flipping through his stack of bills.

"We had another good day," she said.

"We've had better," said Mendel. "If you're going to ask me for a raise, it's not a good time. They're gouging me left and right for the vegetables and I'm barely breaking even."

Mama knew Mendel was lying through his teeth. By now, she was the one who ordered the food, ran the register, and paid the bills, so she knew there was more than enough money coming in to pay her a little extra each week.

"My family needs more money. I've worked for you for seven years and I'm not asking for much," said Mama.

Mendel exploded. "Listen, you ungrateful bitch! This is my building, my stove, and my dishes! When that money of yours comes from Italy, you can give yourself a raise and buy your own restaurant. In the meantime, you should be grateful you have a job!" he yelled.

"Does Boris know what kind of a person you really are? You are a cruel man," Mama said softly.

"Maybe you're the cruel one, Jennie. Maybe you should be nicer to me and we could work something out," said Mendel, sidling up to her. He slid a hand up under Mama's apron.

She grabbed a butcher knife out of the sink, spun around, and held it to his throat.

"Listen, you *putz*. I built this restaurant. If you don't want to give me a raise, fine," Mama hissed. "I'll even keep working here because I need the money. But if you ever, and I mean ever, come near me again, I'll make soup out of that pathetic little *schmeckel*[3] of yours. Do you understand me?"

Mendel nodded his head very slowly. Mama put down the knife and the gutless bully ran out the door.

My parents' lives would've gone on forever in a sad parade of hellish work shifts if it wasn't for a little bit of divine intervention. A couple of years later, Mama and Papa were woken in the middle of the night by a frantic pounding on their door. Boris stood outside blabbering and gesturing so wildly neither one of my parents could understand him, but he insisted they wake us kids and follow him down to his apartment.

"It's the most unbelievable thing!" shouted Boris, leading them into his study.

"More unbelievable than a good night's sleep?" yawned Papa.

"Yes, this is a miracle. A real miracle. Jennie, do you remember when you were first living here with us and I told you Mendel wanted you to cook in his restaurant?"

"How could I forget? It was the happiest day of my life," answered Mama sarcastically.

"Just listen to me! That day, Mendel took down one of my Talmud volumes and left it out on the couch. I remember it because Celia gave

3   *Schmeckel* – A small penis.

me such a glare when she noticed Mendel was making a mess," he explained.

"Sure, fine, but what's the miracle?" asked Mama, eager to get back to bed.

"While I was talking to him, my little Adah heard the doorbell and answered it. It was the postman with a letter marked *Special Delivery*. She knew she wasn't allowed to interrupt my conversation with Mendel, so she waited until I walked him to the door to say goodbye before she came into my study to drop off the letter. She stuck it in the book she thought I was reading, but unfortunately, she put it in the Talmud book that Mendel left on the couch."

Mama and Papa looked at each other, puzzled.

"Enter my neatnik wife! As soon as she saw Mendel at the front door, getting ready to go, Celia went to straighten up the study. First she chased our daughter out of here and then, of course, she put the divorce book back on the shelf." explained Boris. "And tonight, after eight years of studying, I finally got to that volume. I'm sorry that this letter is so late, but I think it's for you," he said, handing over a yellowed old envelope.

The letter was postmarked Italy, October 1887. Mama held the letter to her heart and bowed her head to thank God before she opened it.

> *My dearest friend Jennie,*
>
> *Please forgive the lateness of this letter.*
> *I am sorry to tell you my beloved William succumbed to a heart attack three months ago. It has taken me this long to get over the shock of discovering him slumped over his desk. William wouldn't respond so I ran down the street to find the doctor, but it was already too late. There was nothing he could do.*
> *My daughter and her husband came to Genoa and were a great comfort to me. After the shiva[4] was over,*

---

4   *Shiva* – The Jewish mourning period observed by family of the deceased for seven days following the burial.

they convinced me stay with them in Rome so I wouldn't be alone. I can hardly even remember the few months I spent there. I know I must have slept and eaten each day only because I am here now, writing this letter. But I felt stronger little by little, and a few weeks ago I finally came to the decision it was time to get on with my life. I made my way back to our house in Genoa. This week I even opened the fruit stand again.

The only thing I couldn't do was go into William's study. It was just too painful. However, I forced myself to face my fears today and sat in William's old chair at his desk and cried. When I wiped my tears away, lo and behold, there on my husband's desk was the enclosed letter he had written to you. It must have been lying here since the night he died.

After reading it, I can only tell you how mortified I am that you still have not received your money. The last thing I wanted to do was cause you and your dear family three months of fear. Please accept my deepest apology.

Give my love to all of the Abuzas,
Milly

Mama thrust the letter at Papa's face so he could see that she'd been right, all these years. She put Milly's letter aside as she wiped away some tears. Then she read aloud William's letter of explanation from June 18, 1887.

Dear Mr. and Mrs. Kalish, or should I say Abuza?

Paul from Pfizer let us know you have a new Italian name. I hope you have all finally arrived safely in Boston after your delay in Glasgow.
Now, let us attend to the happy business of getting you your money. Although Pfizer was supposed to send payment to my bank in Genoa, the money was instead

*sent to another bank in Rome. I went all the way to Rome to sort things out and your money is on the way, but it will be waiting for you at the National Bank of Boston, **not** the Bank of Boston as we originally thought. The bank in Rome only does business with the former, not the latter.*

The money should arrive in two weeks. I know we agreed to a 5% interest rate but Milly insisted on sending an additional 5% as a gift to help get you started in America. Once again, we thank you both from the bottom of our hearts for trusting us in this business deal.

With much love,
William and Milly

I actually saw a few tears in Mama's eyes as she remembered how Papa picked her up and spun her around the room. After eight years in Boston, her new American life was finally about to begin.

The next morning, Mama strode proudly into the National Bank of Boston. This time, unlike her first trip downtown eight years prior, she spoke much better English and walked out with her money in a matter of minutes. Then she went to Mendel's restaurant where she was supposed to work a full lunch and dinner shift.

Mendel was seated at a table reading his newspaper when she arrived. She didn't say a word as she breezed into the kitchen, slammed around a few pots, and returned with a big kitchen knife in one hand. With the other, she plunked a bowl of soup down on the table in front of her vile employer. He lowered his paper to find two small dumplings floating in Mama's perfect chicken broth.

"My family and I are leaving Boston. You'll need to hire a new cook. And make sure it's a man. If I hear from my cousin that you hired a woman, I'll come back here and serve you a bowl of soup that looks just like this one, but *you'll* provide the dumplings. Do you understand me?" she asked, lowering the knife toward the front of his pants.

Mendel nodded his head.

She started to leave, but she stopped and pulled something out of her pocketbook. She rifled through her little black notebook, looked Mendel square in the eye, and delivered her farewell address.

"*Fuck…you!*"

After that, Mama and Papa gathered us up, thanked her cousins, and boarded the first train to Hartford, that little town they'd loved so much from the window of their train to Boston eight years earlier. What started out as a plan to open their own small grocery was about to blossom into Abuza's Family Restaurant, home of the world-famous Lestz goulash.

Part III

Coming Home

Chapter 17

Me and My Shadow

The day I got canned from the Follies, my new pal Molly Elkins walked out the door with me. She was tired of doing the dirty work for nasty headliners who thought they could push her around just because she was a Negro, when in fact Molly could out-sing and out-act half the performers up on stage. We made a good team and we figured she would come along with me, wherever I landed.

My release from the Follies made page three of *Variety*. William Morris, then still a theater owner and a stranger to me, sent me a letter right away requesting that I perform at a private benefit he was throwing at some fancy mansion out on Long Island.

The benefit wasn't going to take place for a few days, though, so Molly and I found ourselves with some unexpected time off. We were thrilled to finally do some of the fun stuff nine-to-fivers did every weekend.

First, we took a trip down to Coney Island to spend a day at Luna Park. We laughed ourselves silly, squeezing our extra-large bottoms onto the roller coasters and taking in several of the city's finest freak shows.

Molly Elkins

I remembered that my pal Jimmy Durante was working as a singing waiter at Feltman's, one of the restaurants on the boardwalk, so we strolled by to say hello. Molly spotted him before I did.

"Schnoz!" she yelled, and ran up to give him a hug.

"Molly! Soph! You two know each other?" he laughed.

Sometimes I forgot how long Molly had been in showbiz. She'd done tons of shows with Jimmy's performing partner Eddie Jackson in the Harlem reviews when she was younger, so the three of them had socialized quite a bit.

"Sorry to hear about the Follies, Soph," said Jimmy as he slipped us a few hot dogs. "I heard that you have something brewing with William Morris, though. He's the real deal, and a good fellow to boot. If you can get in with him, you'll be on your way."

"If you say he's good people, I'll believe it. I trust you, Jimmy," I said.

"Better not!" he howled, taking a big bite out my hot dog and sending us off down the boardwalk before he got caught.

Molly insisted we visit her favorite palm reader before we headed back into the city. I'd seen ads for fortune-tellers in the paper, but I always felt guilty wasting a quarter on some gypsy hogwash when I could send it home to help Annie and the kid. Molly, however, dragged me to the fortune-teller's table and thrust my palm into her hands.

"You're going to have some trouble. Two women, I see," she moaned.

"That's old news, honey. Bayes and Tanguay have already done their worst," I laughed. "I think you got yesterday's edition of my palm."

"Well…you'll be coming into some money," she said.

Molly sat down next and, strangely enough, after a failed bunch of guesses the swami told her she too would be coming into some cash. Unlike yours truly, Molly bought her act hook, line and sinker, and insisted that we spend the next day out on Long Island at Belmont Park to celebrate her forthcoming fortune. I didn't know Belmont Park from Central Park, so when Molly told me there would be lots of grass and a couple of nags, I thought we'd be having a picnic with some of her old friends.

The next day, we packed a lunch and took off for Long Island in Molly's Model T. I'd only been in an automobile a few times, so it still hadn't lost its thrill. Molly must've been able to see that I was eating it up because she pulled the car over just after we got across the Brooklyn

Bridge. She pointed out which pedal did what and, after my first and only driving lesson, she let me take the wheel. I zoomed down the highway as fast as a Model T could zoom—which was just slightly faster than we could walk—and my love affair with automobiles was born. I still can't get enough. I'd have given up any of my three husbands before I gave up my keys.

Hell, I'd have given them all up for free, but that's another story.

Imagine my surprise when Belmont turned out to be one of the most famous horse tracks in the country. Molly and I might've only been friends for a few months, but she could already see that I had "Sucker" written on my forehead, just like Papa. I was hooked from the first race.

Molly knew everyone at the track. She was friends with the jockeys, the owners, and most importantly, the touts who spied on the horse trainers and passed on inside information. Those were the fellas you really needed to snuggle up to. She introduced me to a handful of her most colorful touts, all nicknamed after the things she bought with the winnings from their tips: Wilbur Washing Machine, Jimmy the Icebox, Mr. Model T, and on and on.

Belmont Park, 1909

We got a hot tip and went to place our bets. While Molly was up at the window, I ran into an old Abuza's customer named Harry

Cooper. He was now a vaudeville accompanist and occasional emcee who, it turned out, would be hosting Mr. Morris's big shindig. He promised to make sure I got a good spot in the lineup in exchange for a free plate of chopped liver the next time he was in Hartford. Without my Follies paycheck and one measly benefit show lined up, it was all I had to offer.

The night before the big benefit, Molly and I were back in Manhattan and stopped in to see my old friend Delilah, who was off her back and working as the madam of her own high class establishment. After a short gossip session, Delilah told us one of her hoity-toity johns had given her two tickets for the Metropolitan Opera. She didn't want to go, so Molly and I took them off her hands.

"We gotta do this right," said Molly. "Are you game?"

She took me to Lady Symone's, a shop that rented secondhand society dresses for the night. Molly and I picked the gaudiest old gowns we could find and coiffed, powdered, and rouged ourselves until we looked like a couple of floozies crashing a debutante ball.

We hoped to dazzle the crowd when we walked into the Metropolitan Opera, but we were willing to settle for scandalizing an old lady or two. Instead, no one even looked at us twice.

New York City Metropolitan Opera House in 1909.

Somewhat discouraged, we fluttered our fans and walked to our seats, hoping at least to enjoy a good show. When the music started and the big soprano started to wail, we looked at each other in shock. It was the first opera for the both of us, and neither she nor I had realized it wasn't going to be in English.

"You know, where I come from we call this *drek*," I whispered to Molly when I couldn't take it anymore.

"Yeah, up in Harlem we have a name for this too. Horseshit!" giggled Molly.

An usher overheard our cackling and came to quiet us down.

"But we don't understand what anyone is saying!" I yelled.

"It's in German!" he hissed.

"What a dirty trick!" Molly exclaimed, wagging her finger at him.

"Ma'am, you must lower your voice!" he hissed.

"Somebody get the hook! This broad's a snore!" I exclaimed, pointing at the stage.

Before we knew it, the usher had grabbed me with one hand and Molly with the other and was dragging us up the aisle toward door. We made such a ruckus, even the fat lady on stage couldn't keep her eyes off of us.

"Not much of an entrance," hooted Molly, "but what an exit!"

That was our last night of freedom, so I was happy we didn't end up in jail. The next day we had to get down to business preparing for William Morris's big benefit show that evening. I needed a new song but didn't have the cash to buy anything fresh down on Tin Pan Alley, so Molly volunteered to teach me one of her old numbers from her days on stage. Even better, since we were the same size, she still had an assortment of costumes that fit me like a dream. I vowed to keep Molly around forever, if only for the spare outfits.

We picked a few gowns, packed up the Model T, and headed back out to Long Island. I told Molly I couldn't afford to pay her to be my dresser, but she just laughed me off.

"This one's on the house, girl. When you hit the big time, you can pay me back plenty."

I stuck out my hand. "That's a deal, Mrs. Elkins."

At the estate we were greeted by an honest to goodness butler, straight out of a murder mystery.

"Hey Jeeves," I said as he lead us through the mansion. "Have any of your butler friends ever done it?"

"Sorry to disappoint you, ma'am, but my name is Elwood. And have any of my friends every done *what?*"

"You know, in mysteries it seems like it's always the butler who did it. Have you ever done it, Ellie?"

"Not yet, madam."

We arrived in the back garden, where they'd set up a stage and a big tent behind it to serve as our dressing area. Just inside the tent I spotted Harry Cooper, the emcee, and he gave us the lowdown on the benefit. The extravaganza was sponsored by one of the Vanderbilts in order to raise money for an orphanage. William Morris was hired as a producer, for which he'd earn a hefty sum, and he called in acts to perform in exchange for promised future bookings at one of his theaters.

I was a little bit nervous when I looked out at the lawn and saw two hundred empty chairs sitting in front of the stage with the mansion towering behind it. It felt fancier than Poli's.

"Harry, do you really think this is gonna be right for me? This seems like a crowd that's used to pheasant under glass and all I'm serving is brisket."

"They're going to love you, just like every other audience does. Sing your guts out like you usually do and you'll be fine," he promised.

It was time to get dressed and Molly helped me into one of her beautiful gowns. Then, at the last moment, she surprised me by putting a real diamond necklace around my throat.

"If you're gonna be a headliner, you gotta know what the real stuff feels like," she said.

"Oh my God! Where did you get this?"

"From one of my Belmont pals. It pays to know Jerry Jewels!" she giggled.

Given my new accessory, I had second thoughts about which dress I wanted to wear. Molly put on one of the others so I could compare, but just as I decided I wanted to switch costumes I was called to the stage.

"And now ladies and gentlemen, I'm going to bring out one of the biggest voices in Vaudeville. Straight from the Ziegfeld's Follies, please welcome the incomparable Miss Sophie Tucker!" shouted Harry.

I got a big round of applause, but as soon as I hit my mark I could tell the crowd was confused. They were expecting one of those typical, slim Ziegfeld girls. Despite my wavering confidence, I did the only thing I knew how to do, and that's sing. I reeled them in with a couple of peppy tunes and by the end of the second song, they were mine. However, I also realized I'd forgotten to pin a fake rose to my dress, which I needed as a prop for my last number. I gestured at my right lapel to Molly on the side of the stage and she bolted for the tent.

"Thank you, ladies and gentlemen. You're such a wonderful audience!"

Thanking the audience was a sure bet to kill a few seconds with some applause, but when it died down there was no sign of Molly returning to the stage.

"What an honor to be invited to perform at such a beautiful place. You know, when I was a girl growing up in my parents' restaurant in Hartford, Connecticut, I could hardly have pictured that I'd end up here with all of you! If you should happen to pass through Hartford, say my name at Abuza's, the best kosher restaurant in town. That'll get you an extra matzoh ball in your soup, on the house."

Crickets. I was right—this wasn't the right crowd for my usual jokes. The Vanderbilts certainly didn't know from *kneidls*[1].

Thank God Molly came to my rescue. She sauntered out onto the stage with the rose and quickly made a bit out of trying to pin it on my dress. The conductor picked up on our ad-lib and gave her a drum beat as she moved the rose around my dress, trying to decide where it should go. To my relief, the audience loved it.

When she finally pinned the rose on my shoulder, though, she accidentally snagged the sleeve of her own flowing dress. I thanked her and, not realizing that we were pinned together, she began dragging me along with her as she turned to walk off stage.

1   *Kneidl* – A matzah ball.

Sophie, in a particularly elaborate costume.

"Molly! Molly!" I yelled, but she couldn't hear me over the audience's roars.

We tried to yank ourselves apart but the orchestra had already started the introduction to my final song, so we looked at each other, took a deep breath, and launched into a synchronized rendition of the old number Molly had taught me earlier that day. Fred and Ginger had nothing on us!

We were the hit of the benefit. By the time we got ourselves unhooked and changed into our street clothes, someone was waiting for me next to Molly's Model T.

"Hello, Miss Tucker," said William Morris, a short, balding man holding his straw hat in his hands. "I wanted to introduce myself and tell you how great I thought you were tonight. I think you've got real headliner potential. I'd love to talk with you, but unfortunately I have to be in Great Neck in forty-five minutes for another engagement."

I hadn't heard anything past the word "headliner."

"Molly, you're going to have to drive home by yourself tonight. I'll meet you in the city tomorrow. The Boss and I have to talk," I said.

"Boss?" asked Mr. Morris, confused.

"If you make me a headliner, I'm going to be calling you 'Boss' for the rest of your life."

"Okay then, Sophie, let's take a ride to Great Neck," he said, chuckling.

The next thing I knew, I was sitting in the front seat of William Morris's Reo, and the only thing speeding faster than the car was Morris's mouth. He talked a mile a minute about his ideas for my career, all the while munching on a knish. I would eventually come to find out that he always had a stash of knishes somewhere, but back then during our first meeting, I took it as a sign that Morris was the man to guide me to the big time. It was hard not to trust someone who loved a knish as much as I did.

He finally took a deep breath before he mentioned his only reservation.

"I heard there's a son," he said.

"How did you find that out?" I asked.

"We have a lot of mutual friends."

"Which one told you?

"Ten of them told me. They also told me you send money home every week to your parents and sister to take care of the baby, you're never late, you're loyal to the end, and everyone loves you except for Nora Bayes. Oh, and most of all, you love a good sour dill pickle."

William Morris's favorite food, the knish.

I was astounded. "Okay then, what's your story?" I asked.

"I would say that except for your pipes and your extra fifty pounds, you and I are the same person," he said with a laugh.

There is a hell of a lot of people I could take or leave, but I'm nice to everyone simply because it's easier to have friends out there than enemies. If you're lucky, though, once or twice in your life, you might find someone as special as William Morris. When you meet that person, you can instantly feel your whole life charging forward like a brand new automobile with the pedal floored. Just make sure you hold on tight, because they're about to take you on the ride of your life.

Chapter 18

Learning

The Boss had about a hundred and fifty ideas for my act before we were even halfway to Great Neck. He had a theory that my extra weight was my biggest asset, noting how Molly and I turned the audience from disappointment to uproarious laughter precisely because we were both the furthest thing from a Ziegfeld girl. I told him he could kiss my asset, but of course, Morris was right on the money. I just wasn't taking enough advantage of my girth. Being big could be very funny, and very funny won an audience far faster than very pretty.

His biggest problem with my act, though, was that there was no variety. I was ready to leap out of the speeding car if the Boss asked me to be the world's first singing fat lady juggler, but he was just talking about learning some slow songs. The audience needed a chance to breathe in between my funny novelty songs, and for that I'd need to master a schmaltzy[1] ballad or two.

"The Boss," William Morris.

"Don't worry, I'll send you some songs next week when you're in Rockaway," he offered.

"What's in Rockaway?"

"One of my American Theaters," he said with a wink.

"You've got theaters in other countries?"

"Not yet. But I'm going to make you a star in England too," he promised.

1   *Schmaltzy* – Excessively sentimental.

I couldn't believe it. I'd impressed him enough in the Vanderbilts' backyard that he thought he could make me a headliner on two continents. The catch was, I had to promise to eat, breathe, and sleep show business. It was the same advice Mr. Elliott gave me when I was a kid in Hartford.

"Okay, Boss, count me in. I'll eat show business, just as long as it tastes good with mustard," I said.

Indeed, for the next six weeks, I ate, slept, and breathed the Boss's American Theater circuit, cycling through show after show in all his locations around New York City. Uptown, midtown, downtown, Queens, Brooklyn, and Newark; with each performance, I was rounding out my skills as an entertainer and I watched my name creep up the bill. By October of 1909, after three years in showbiz, the Boss raised my salary to a hundred dollars a week and officially made me one of his headliners. I begged Molly to come to New Jersey and cry with me as we watched them install my name at the top of the Newark American Theater marquee.

A few weeks before Christmas, William Morris sent me to New Orleans with two goals in mind. First, he wanted me to experience a Southern audience and second, he thought it was high time I learned about a little thing he called "chariblicity." There was no one more creative than the Boss when it came to pulling off stunts to get free ink.

When I got to Louisiana I was instructed to comb the local newspaper to find a charitable event, volunteer to help raise money, and get all kinds of New Orleans press in the process. It didn't take long to find that the *Times-Picayune* was sponsoring an auction to raise money to buy Christmas toys for poor kids, so I marched myself down there before I had even unpacked my bag.

Freddie Harman was the reporter in charge of the auction and he was thrilled I wanted to be involved. I suspected we both had other motives besides a rubber chicken in every toy pot—he himself was something of a go-getter who would one day become the editor-in-chief of the paper. Regardless, neither of us wasted any time using our God-given talents in the name of Christmas.

I promised to rally a troop of entertainers to turn the auction into a real spectacle and Freddie promised to print an article every day covering my efforts. We got permission to hold the benefit in the middle of the busy business district during lunch and Harman made arrangements to borrow one of the paper's flatbed delivery trucks to serve as our stage.

On the big day, I was the Master of Ceremonies and an old comedian pal of mine named Bill served as the auctioneer. W.C. Fields, as he was better known, had them rolling on the floor, and had Freddie rolling in cash donations for his charity drive.

We caused a near riot when we auctioned off the last item, which was a kiss from yours truly. Back in 1909 it was rare to see a lady's ankle. For certain, no one had ever

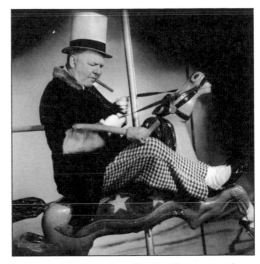

W.C. Fields started in Vaudeville as a juggler and ended as one of the biggest comedy movie stars of all time.

seen a woman willing to trade a wet one on the mouth in exchange for a donation. Scandal aside, I just wanted to make sure Harman had a good story with some funny quotes.

To everyone's surprise, including my own, a gentleman at the back of the crowd ponied up five whole dollars for a crack at the old Tucker pucker, which gave Freddie the perfect punchline for his piece.

When the winning bidder couldn't reach Miss Tucker, she gathered her skirts and hopped off the makeshift stage.

"Honey, for five dollars these lips will travel!" she said with a smile, and parted the raucous lunchtime crowd like the Red Sea to deliver her prize to the generous gentleman in the back.

New Orleans owes a great deal of gratitude to Miss Tucker and her talented friends for helping to provide needy children with a proper Christmas. Sophie will be performing all this week at the American Theater.

Sometimes stunts like that worked, but sometimes I got out-stunted. Take what happened in Dayton in January of 1910. The Boss sent me on a tour with Bill "Bojangles" Robinson around the Ohio Valley. We had some pretty good success because we came up with a novel idea to attract attention as soon as we arrived in a town.

At that time there was a new woman's fashion craze called the sheath skirt, which had a slit along the side that revealed a lady's leg right up to the knee. It was quite a sexy get-up compared to the ankle-grazing skirts women had worn for a century. The good people of the Midwest had never seen a dress that exposed a woman's knee or anything else, so to get the ball rolling in a new town, I'd put on my finest sheath skirt and Bill and I would walk a block or two in the city center. My calves never let us down. By the time we got to the town square, every breathing male who had spotted my leg was gathered around us with their mouths hanging wide open. Then Robinson would do a little dance, I would sing a little song, and the whole episode would get a nice write up in the local paper.

Sheath Skirt and Pretty Wearer Demoralized Business Today in the Business Part of the C

Miss Sophia Tucker, a pretty young woman, attired in one of the new Sheath skirts, was the sensation on Washington street today.

In the New Leslie, where she took dinner, the guests were so badly rattled that they forgot to order further than the soup course.

To Charles W. Nolan's show window where she gave a demonstration this afternoon, she drew a crowd that blocked the sidewalk and seriously interfered with traffic on the streets.

At The News office, where Miss Tucker came to let the boys see the skirt in order that they may write more intelligently of its fascinations, the whole force laid off long enough to make a respectfully distant inspection.

So far as known nobody fainted and the nerve shock was really not so great as many who had read of the Sheath skirt expected.

There is nothing shocking about it. It fact it might be rather characterized as "fascinating." Still, taking even that for granted, something might depend upon the charms of the wearer.

Miss Sophia Tucker wore the skirt so gracefully and withal so modestly, that there was really nothing about it which might offend the exquisite sensibilities of the most fastidious.

To begin with the skirt which Miss Tucker wore was black. It was a nicely cut, neat fitting garment and looked like any ordinary walking skirt from at least three sides. But it is the architecture of the fourth side that is responsible for the name —"sheath skirt."

SOPHIA TUCKER,

Actress who is making demonstrations in New Castle today of the Sheath skirt.

When Miss Tucker came into News office no suspicions were aroused for the "sheath" part was a fully buttoned down to the bottom. It was a closed skirt all around very tame looking affair, so the thought, who had been nothing furore in the fashion journals this dainty piece of wearing apparel.

Continued on Sixth Page

...it is explained, is that a woman can't jump far enough in case of danger. With the sheath skirt she could jump in the mill street gutters in the hardest rain without any fear of stumbling.

It is the advantage from a safety point of view that ought to commend the sheath skirt to every woman who does not feel like leaving her husband a widower.

Down in Charles W. Nolan's window Miss Tucker gave the same demonstration as in The News office, only to bigger crowds. It was the first appearance of the new fangled skirt and of course everybody, including the men, had to see it. In fact the men actually crowded the women back in their mad endeavors to get a glimpse of Miss Tucker—and the sheath skirt.

But coming back to the anatomy of the skirt, it might be added further it is considerably cooler than the ordinary skirt. Especially is this true when it is left unbuttoned.

Miss Tucker says she don't see any reason why any woman, unless she is bow legged or a cripple, should object to wearing one of the skirts.

That there are a great many women in New Castle who think the same is shown by the many applications Mr. Nolan had to his advertisement for a demonstrator.

The advertisement was published in The News only one time, yet there were 29 young women who applied for the job of "demonstrating." About 2,900 inquired and side-stepped. Mr. Nolan sidestepped many who were willing. Mr. Nolan selected Miss Tucker because the dress it her so well.

It will probably be the only demonstration that will be given in this city as it is expected that the skirts will become very popular within the next few weeks.

Miss Tucker does soon shouting stunts and sings songs at the park this week.

This newspaper got the "sheath skirt" story right but put in the wrong picture. That's not Sophie--but her shows still sold out.

By the time the troupe got to Dayton, we had our routine down to a science. After unpacking at the hotel, Bill met me in the lobby and we found the main thoroughfare to start our promenade. Something wasn't right, however. There were plenty of people walking in the street but instead of looking down at my legs, everyone was looking up to the sky. After we strolled onto our third block full of people with their heads in the clouds, I finally asked one of the pedestrians what, literally, was *up*.

One of the locals told us there was some kind of exhibition going on that day at the county fairgrounds and the newspaper said everyone should look up around noon for a surprise. Sensing an opportunity, Bo and I went searching for the crowd at the fairgrounds. If Mohammed wouldn't come to the mountain, this mountain would go to him.

When we got there we found thousands of people, so I thought we'd hit the jackpot. Suddenly, though, we heard a jarring mechanical growl. Bill and I couldn't get close enough to see where the noise was coming from.

The engine got even louder and we could see the crowd's heads following something from right to left. The crowd roared. All of a sudden, there it was: a man operating a winged contraption that was floating up to the sky.

After a show later that week, the operators of that same flying machine visited my dressing room.

"We loved your show tonight, Miss Tucker," said one of the wide-eyed boys.

"Thanks, fellas. Last Sunday, you two put quite a show on yourselves! I finally discovered something my legs can't compete with."

That's how I met Orville and Wilbur Wright.

After Ohio, the Boss sent me on to Chicago with instructions to see Jack Lait, who was in charge of public relations for the city's four American Theaters. I introduced myself to Mr. Lait as soon as I walked into the West Randolph Street theater. Lait was reading the racing results in the paper when I approached him.

"Tucker. Number four spot. Big voice, a little racy," he said without lifting his head.

"Does it also say I run good in the mud?"

That got his attention, forcing him to look up to check out his new smart-ass filly. Jack was shorter than me and always had a half-smoked cigar hanging out of his mouth. Come to think of it, I never saw Jack light a new cigar in all our time together. I'll bet that stingy bastard just chomped on the same butt for forty years.

Sophie, Jack Lait and his family in 1935.

When he got a load of me I could tell he had an instant crush, which I knew would come in handy someday. He was definitely flummoxed, so I filled the silence by neighing like a horse, and for the first of many, many times I heard Lait's signature high-pitched laugh. I stuck out my hand and squeezed his tiny mitt.

"So you're the guy that's gonna turn me into a star, right? I had a dream that a tall, dark, handsome man who giggles like a hyena would make me famous."

After Lait stopped his tittering, he agreed to watch my act during that first Monday matinee and tell me what he thought. After three years on stage I wasn't a babe in the woods anymore, but I was going to have to prove myself all over again in the Second

City. I needed to adapt my act for the locals and drum up some name recognition as fast as possible.

I gave it everything I had at the matinee and got two encores out of the enthusiastic audience. When the curtain fell I made way for that week's headliner, Consul the Great. He could dance, juggle, and balance things on his head while riding a unicycle, which wasn't too shabby when you took into account that he was a chimpanzee. While Consul pedaled around on stage, I looked for Jack. The stage manager told me he thought he'd seen him watching my act in the wings, but there was no sign of him anywhere. I waited an extra forty-five minutes before I gave up on him and went back to my hotel. I ate a light dinner and returned to the theater for the evening performance, but still, Jack was a ghost.

I was disappointed for misjudging his interest in me. I was sulking in the wings and waiting for the tap dancer before me on the bill to finish up his act when, suddenly, Jack appeared out of thin air.

"I was about to send a search party after you," I pouted.

"Sorry, something came up. I'll tell you what, though, I'll watch you from here and then we'll talk. Okay?"

I took the stage and wowed them again, Lait nodding his head and applauding like mad from the wings.

"That was perfect! Just like you did it this afternoon!" he said after my third encore.

"How would you know?"

Without answering, Jack took my hand and dragged me behind the back curtain to the other side of the stage. There, near the stage door, Lait introduced me to Amy Leslie and Ashton Stevens.

"Jackie thinks you have a big future," smiled Amy. "And based on what we saw tonight we're inclined to agree."

"I don't want to be rude, but who the hell are you two?" I asked.

Jack giggled and admitted that he had fibbed a little; he had actually watched my first matinee performance and loved it. As soon as it was over, he ran out of the theater to track down these two friends to convince them to come to the evening show.

"Don't forget you owe us both a steak dinner," threw in Leslie.

"I'll buy dessert if someone tells me what's going on!" I said.

It turned out that Ashton was the chief critic for the *Chicago Examiner* and Amy had the same job at the *Chicago Tribune*, the two biggest papers in town. Lait hadn't tipped me off for fear that I might get nervous and flub a potentially bang-up review. Ashton didn't disappoint:

Speaking of elephants and ladies, there is Sophie Tucker. If life were as large as Sophie Tucker, there would be room for all of us. I don't mind saying at once Sophie Tucker is my headliner, even if the American Theater management does employ other type and position for her. Most of her songs are red, white and blue, and some of them omit the red and white. Miss Tucker can move an audience or a piano with equal address. – Ashton Stevens

The next two weeks I took Jack's crash course in publicity, the most important part of which was learning how to spot an opportunity to stage a stunt. It took me years to perfect the art, but I couldn't ignore the potential press that presented itself when I moved from the Southside American Theater to one of the Northside locations.

While I was waiting to check in with the rest of our troupe at our Northside hotel, a commotion broke out at the front desk. One of the comedians told me the hotel had no reservation on the books for Consul the Great. His trainer loudly threatened legal action and then took his chimpanzee and stormed off. I did the same, right to the closest phone booth in order to call Jack and tell him my idea for a terrific stunt. He loved my plan and said to stand by while he made some arrangements.

Everything was in place an hour later. When I stepped up to the front desk to register, I loudly asked to see the manager.

"My name is Sophie Tucker and I understand you have no room for Consul the monkey," I boomed. I signaled to Consul's trainer and he came over, holding the chimp by the hand.

"If this sad fact is true, Mr. Manager, I would like to give up my suite so Consul has a place to sleep this week. Can you see to that, my good fellow?"

The next day, Consul and Sophie Tucker made the front pages of all the Chicago papers. Lait had tipped off three reporters and photographers who lived on the Northside. From the moment I stepped up to the registration desk, every word of my performance was recorded in triplicate. I made sure I handed Consul his room key with my good side facing the cameras.

Actress Who Came to Aid of Homeless Stage Chimpanzee

WOMAN SACRIFICES COMFORT FOR THAT OF CHIMPANZEE

Theatrical Star Gives Up Suite in Order to Provide Suitable Quarters for Consul the Great.

The pages of romance and history are replete with stories of woman's sacrifice for man. But where, in literature, is there a chronicle of a woman's submergence of self for a chimpanzee?

Miss Sophie Tucker has the distinction of setting this precedent, and Consul the Great, a hairy ape, is her debtor.

It appears that chimpanzees, no matter how popular for theatrical purposes, La Salle the theatrical man was also refused.

It began to look grave for Consul's comfort in Chicago. The man bethought himself of a comfortable and fashionable actors' boarding house near the Wabash avenue theater, and he applied there. Yes, Consul could come if they had room, but they were filled to the roof.

On the roster of the boarding house the theatrical representative saw the name of Miss Tucker. She is also one of his stars and was occupying a suite there.

A knock at the door, a brief conversation and Miss Tucker shook her shapely head in assent. The porter called and took out her trunks. Miss Tucker is a very beautiful woman and she is welcome at any hotel. So she moved to one of the fashionable hostelries, and Consul when he arrives tonight will occupy the luxurious quarters which Miss Tucker surrendered to him.

Sophie slept on Jack Lait's couch that night, though he perhaps would've preferred they share a bed.

I'd always heard the saying that no news is good news. Jack Lait, that brilliant little man, taught me that *all* news is good news. A headline is a headline, even when you're playing second banana to a monkey.

Chapter 19

Prohibition, You Have Lost Your Sting

After I made all the papers as the singer who took pity on a monkey, I was promoted to headliner at the Northside American theater. Consul the Great was a little miffed to lose his prime spot on the bill, but I was used to dealing with chimps after being married to one.

My shows sold out every night. I was such a big success, in fact, that when the headliner from one of the other American Theaters fell ill unexpectedly, the Boss offered to double my salary if I played both houses for the rest of that week. I owed so much to Morris, if he asked I would have done it for free—but I wasn't about to turn down the extra loot, either.

The problem was that the theaters were on opposite ends of the Northside, so the Boss came up with a plan to ping-pong me from one theater to the other. I'd start each afternoon at one theater and close before intermission, then hop in a waiting taxi and zoom over to the other theater and close the second half of the matinee. Then I'd grab a bite to eat and reverse the route for my evening performances. The Boss was so appreciative he even covered all my cab fares.

Pretending I had a chauffeured limousine was fun for a day or two, but I was so stingy I couldn't resist pocketing that extra ten dollars in taxi money. I met a cute kid named Sammy Morton who worked backstage at one of the theaters giving each act their five minute warning. He had a signature rat-a-tat he'd bang on your door and a little tune for belting out "You're next!" It was his only line, but he got to perform it eighteen times a show. Sammy seemed like a kindred spirit so I didn't think twice about asking to borrow the bike he used to get to the theater every day. Sammy said it would be no problem, since he could "borrow" another one for himself in no time.

The two American Theaters were about six miles apart. It took me about forty-five minutes to ride from one theater to the other, which was just enough time to make my curtains. By the end of that week, I could've anchored the Swiss cycling team. The press caught wind of my new bicycle routine—with a little help from yours truly—and ran a few photos in the papers of me pedaling from one end of Chicago to the other. Those

Sophie on a bicycle in Chicago, a few years later.

newspaper stories were particularly helpful one afternoon when I rolled up to an intersection halfway through my route that was completely blocked off by the fire brigade. I detoured over to the next street, but that one was being repaved with new cobblestones. The next street was too full of traffic for even a bike to sneak through. I finally found an open route but I was so late I was in a panic that I might miss my curtain.

Instead of running in through the stage door when I got to the theater, I pedaled right into the main lobby, through the back door, and straight down the main aisle to wild applause. Thanks to all the press my bicycle route had gotten, the audience thought they were in on the joke. The publicity was great, but from then on, I took a cab.

I didn't know it at the time, but I had invented "doubling." At one point, I was the only act in Vaudeville working sixty weeks a year. I even managed to triple once in London, with matinees and evening performances in two theaters, and then a third shift at a nightclub with eleven o'clock and two o'clock late night shows. Oh, to be young again!

I went to return Sammy's bicycle at his mother's luncheonette around noon on my day off. The bustling little establishment reminded me so much of Mama and Papa's restaurant, I almost strapped on an apron and started serving tables out of habit. Instead, I took a seat and ordered a plate of chicken, which was delivered to me by Sammy, who was sporting a big purple shiner and a bandage on his head.

"Does your mama swing a mean ladle, too?" I asked.

"Just some neighborhood stuff my friends and I had to take care of," he said, brushing it off.

I'd heard about a young Jewish girl who was attacked in a park and put the pieces together in my head. Sammy and his friends must've knocked out some teeth to make sure nothing like that ever happened again. I patted him on his hand and gave him a nod.

After my lunch, I asked Mama Morton if I had permission to take her extra waiter out for a walk in the park and an ice cream cone to thank him for letting me use his bicycle. There must have been a charm school in the old country where girls went to perfect their disapproval, because Sammy's mother pulled off an eye roll that would've made Jennie Abuza green with envy. She only agreed to cut him loose after I helped clear the lunch dishes, marched back to the kitchen to scrub off the schmaltz with some famous Abuza elbow grease, and set the tables for the dinner crowd.

We passed a quiet afternoon in Lincoln Park eating ice cream and gossiping about the theater folks in Chicago until suddenly Sammy's eyes lit up. He grabbed my hand and commanded me to come with him. We ran down a few small paths until he came to a halt at a dusty old stable.

"Horses? Is there a race track nearby?" I asked, already reaching for my purse.

"No, even better. These are for riding! My friend Arnie runs the stable on Sundays but usually I'm stuck at Mama's restaurant. C'mon Soph, once you take a ride you'll never want to stop," he said.

"You sound like one of my bad dates," I laughed as I followed him into the stable.

Before I knew it, I was up on top of a nice old horse named Bluebell. Arnie was demonstrating how to use the reins when Sammy went tearing past on a crazed young stallion named Thunderbolt. He did a few laps around the stable and came to a rearing halt in front of me and Bluebell, who was calmly chewing on a piece of hay.

"Ready?" he asked.

"Are you going for a ride or trying to get to the moon?" I asked, gesturing toward his wild horse.

He promised to go slow and by the end of the day I'd moved up to trotting. He was right, I truly loved riding. Over the years, whenever I was in Chicago, Sammy and I would make time to reunite with Bluebell and Thunderbolt and go for a ride through the park.

Sophie as an equestrian in "Follow a Star," in London, 1930.

In those early days, us Vaudevillians were a tight bunch. After the curtains dropped on our evening shows across the city, we'd all congregate downtown at the 350 Club and take over their piano. Since none of us were exactly shrinking violets, our nights were filled with some of the bawdiest, loudest, funniest numbers we'd never get away with singing in front of a paying crowd.

There was one young girl who really stood out from the bunch. I'm no Greta Garbo, but believe me, this babe's face was as goofy as a rubber mask. But lordy, what a talent! She had a voice that could shatter glass. She even put that *punim* of hers to use, accenting every funny line with a wacky look. She was a gem. When I went to introduce myself, she jumped out of her chair.

"Miss Tucker!" she said, sticking out her hand.

"You know me?" I asked.

"Sure, I saw you singing on top of an elephant at the Follies a few years ago. I just got my hearing back last Tuesday," she joked.

That was the beginning of a lifelong friendship with my partner in crime, Fanny Brice. I was based in New York at the time and Fanny was still living where she grew up on the Lower East Side, so we palled around the Big Apple whenever we were both in town. However, we were both playing so many shows in Chicago by the end of 1912 that we decided to set up a permanent residence at the Sherman Hotel. In no time, we were on a first name basis with the whole staff and the manager, Frank Behring.

Frank was no dummy. He ran a nice lounge off the hotel lobby and knew how to capitalize on the rumor that two of the hottest headliners in Vaudeville might turn up any night of the week to sing a song or two after their late show. He gave Fanny and me dirt cheap rates for some of the best suites in the hotel in exchange for doing a couple of songs each night to drive up his nightclub business.

Fanny and I would meet up in the lounge and perform a number or two, sure, but the real act was what followed. After we sang we'd sit at our table, nurse a drink, and play a slow game of gin rummy. The local boys couldn't resist trying to pick us up. If they were dressed to the nines and flashed a wad of cash, the game was on.

"Do you boys like cards?" I'd ask.

"Sure," they'd respond. Without fail, they'd suggest a game of poker.

"I've never heard of that. Is it hard to learn?" Fanny would ask, batting her enormous eyes.

Fanny Brice helps Sophie blowout the candles at a birthday party.

It was a nice side business. The boys kept us in drinks and we cleaned them out. Once in a blue moon we'd lose, which kept us humble, but most of the time we won and won big. We'd chat with the fellas as we played, learning where they worked, if they had families, or where they lived in town. Before they knew it, they were writing us IOUs that were as good as gold, since we knew enough about them to pay a visit to their jobs (or worse, their homes) to collect.

We should've known better the night we started playing cards in my suite with a couple of fellas who said they did "this and that" for work and lived "here and there." By the end of the evening we'd won about five hundred dollars in cash and IOUs for another five hundred. It was getting late. Fanny headed to the bar for one last drink and I yawned and told the boys it was time to call it a night.

"I think you're right, Soph," said one of them. He pulled a gun from his coat and pointed it at my forehead. "Fork over all your cash. And those jewels, too."

I laughed. "Congratulations! You're the new owner of a Woolworth colored glass necklace. I hope it looks good on you," I said, tossing it at his chest.

By then, Fanny had snuck up behind him. She hauled off and brained him with a whiskey bottle. He tumbled to the floor, dazed, while she bent down and picked up his gun. Fanny grinned with glee—that's how excited she was to debut her best gangster impression.

"Keep your hands where I can see 'em, wiseguy," croaked Brice, aiming the gun squarely at the second crook.

Sophie, with stage pistols.

"You've got one problem, Fanny. The gun isn't loaded," chuckled the thug.

"Lucky we brought this one with us too," I said, pulling a pistol from Fanny's purse. She never traveled without it. I aimed it right at the whiskey-covered thug now scrambling to his feet.

"Listen, punks," said Fanny. "If we ever see either of you again, were gonna pay a visit to our close personal friend, Police Chief O'Hara. I guarantee he will lock you up and throw away the key. Do you understand?" They nodded. "Now empty your pockets."

Fanny collected our money for the second time and found an extra six hundred dollars between the two of them. She handed them two dollars for cab fare and told them to scram. After the thugs left, she collapsed into giggles and I just plain collapsed. Another quiet night at Brice and Tucker Headquarters.

I got up close and personal with Chicago's real underbelly a few years later during Prohibition, this time without Fanny by my side. I was taking off my makeup in my dressing room after a show at the Oriental Theater one night when I got a knock at the door. I figured it was the stage manager wishing me goodnight so I hollered a big "Come in!" and was greeted by a couple of toughs I'd never seen before.

"Our boss wants to see you," said one.

"I'm doing two shows every day this week," I said. "If you give me his name, I'll leave four tickets for him at the box office."

"He wants to see you now," said the other.

"And what if I've got plans?" I asked.

They both drew back their jackets to reveal identical revolvers. I took one look at their stony faces and knew these punks were the real McCoy, so I quickly changed into my street clothes and followed them out to their car. We all piled into the back seat and I became the turkey in a gangster club sandwich.

"Where are we going?" I asked the driver, who responded by tossing me a blindfold and ordering me to put it on.

"I'll wear whatever you want, so long as you don't plan on wasting any bullets tonight," I said.

"Not as long as you keep quiet," said one of my new boyfriends.

"Say no more. I'm the Sphinx."

"Good move, Cleopatra," said the other.

We drove in silence for a little while until I felt the car come to a stop in a quiet area of town. They pulled me out of the car, still blindfolded, and walked me down a flight of stairs. When I was finally allowed to take off my blindfold, I looked around and quickly gathered that I was in one of the new speakeasies that were popping up all over Chicago. This one was still under construction, but they'd already finished building a small stage and had brought in an upright piano.

In filed ten beefy men in cheap double-breasted suits. They stood along the stage like bowling pins, until the last two parted into a seven-ten split so a heavy, round ball of a man could roll through. This last thug was obviously the boss.

A typical Chicago Prohibition speakeasy in the Roaring 20's.

"Nails Morton tells me you're a regular Joe," he said after giving me the once over. He must have been able to read the confusion on my face. "Nails Morton! You two ride horses together in Lincoln Park?" he elaborated.

I did the math, but came up with the wrong answer.

"Sammy is *Nails*? Look, if he's in trouble, I've got money," I said, reaching for my purse.

Everyone laughed, except for the boss.

"Nails is fine. He runs the Northside for me. He couldn't be here tonight, but he sends his regards," said the boss, flatly.

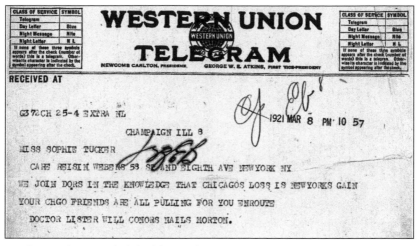

A telegram from Sophie's buddy, Nails Morton.

"Look, I've been feeling a little low, so I asked you here tonight to sing for me. I'm a big fan. I know all your songs. I'd love to hear that new one you do, 'Some of Those Days'."

"Can one of these palookas tickle the ivories?" I asked. Sure enough, one of the men took a seat at the piano before I could decide whether or not I should sing my song with the boss's incorrect lyric. As you may or may not know, my signature song is "Some of These (not *Those*) Days." I made an editorial decision to change the line and I launched into it, singing (perhaps literally) for my life. The boss man stopped me mid-song.

"Sophie, don't you know when someone's putting you on? I know the real words," he said, his face still a block of marble.

"Usually, but this is my first time performing in front of a firing squad, pal!"

From then on, though, it was smooth sailing. I sang that song from the top and the boss requested a few more. The other men hooted and howled and clapped after each tune, but the boss barely moved a muscle until he motioned me over to his table after my third number.

"Thanks, Soph, you've really cheered me up," he said, his face as unreadable and icy as before.

"This is you cheered up?" I asked. "You'd never know it. Maybe next time you could hold up a sign or something."

"You're a funny girl," he said in his monotone. "This is for you."

With a tiny twitch of his eyebrow, one of his flunkies produced a wad of cash and flung it onto the table in front of me. I tried to insist that he didn't have to pay me.

"Yes, I do," he said.

"Okay, have it your way," I relented.

"I always do."

His name was Al Capone, and he was right about almost always getting his way. A couple of years later, we ran into each other again at Nails Morton's funeral. I had heard it was "an accident" that did him in, and I assumed that was underworld lingo for a bullet to the brain. However, when I got to the memorial service, I found out from dear old Mrs. Morton it was actually Thunderbolt who'd whacked my good buddy. That crazy horse threw him off his back during a particularly wild ride through the park and Sammy never woke up.

Samuel "Nails" Morton.

Capone was sitting alone in a corner and, shockingly, I could see on his face how upset he was feeling.

"I'm as broken up as you about Nails," I said, sitting down next to him. "If it were up to me, I would've put Thunderbolt out to pasture years ago."

"Who's Thunderbolt?" boomed Al.

"The son of a bitch horse that broke Sammy's neck," I told him.

Capone's face turned bright red with fury. The next day, a strange murder in Lincoln Park made the front page of the Tribune. The photo showed a confused cop staring at Thunderbolt's severed head, which was perched atop a fence post near the stables.

Capone ended up living in the penthouse of the Sherman Hotel, so Al became my regular gin buddy on the nights when Fanny Brice wasn't in town. He even insisted I play fair and never throw a game, so I creamed him most of the time. Whenever I opened in Chicago, Al would always sit ringside and cheer me on, and he sent flowers in his place the few times he was away "on business" and couldn't make it. I'll never forget the telegram I got in 1931 on my opening night in Paris:

PARIS 19544 14 2C 18/50 !

THEY BETTER LIKE YOU TONIGHT OR ELSE !.+ AL CAPONE

People have said a lot of vicious things about Al Capone over the years and a whole lot of them are true, but Al always treated me like a pal. Even so, I must have been *meshuggah*[1] to put our friendship to the test in 1926, when he was at the height of his power. Al was the king of the underworld during Prohibition, when the illegal liquor trade was landing more and more of my friends in the big house. I'd get letters about how rotten life was on the inside, so on my

Sophie doing a show at San Quentin Prison tuberculosis ward in 1925.

1   *Meshuggah* – Crazy.

days off I'd try to arrange a show at San Quentin, Leavenworth, or some other prison. Let me tell you, there's no better audience than a bunch of inmates. They're so starved for entertainment they'll applaud a spider.

A couple of fans from one of my Joliet shows came to visit me one night after a double bill with Harry Houdini. I toured with him quite a bit back then. Our acts were so different it gave us both the opportunity to play for new crowds who might not otherwise come to see us. Harry was a wonderful performer, but a lousy friend—every night on stage I'd ask him if he could make my extra thirty pounds disappear. That lovable bastard was the best magician out there, but he said that some tricks were just impossible.

Anyway, I'd just started dating Al Lackey back then. One night, as I was receiving the usual crowd of well-wishers in my dressing room after a show, Al pointed out a couple of thugs he didn't recognize. He offered to go escort them out, but he was due to go pick up a case of hooch from one of Capone's guys for our after party that night at the Sherman Hotel. Al sheepishly turned out his pockets and found only a losing racing form, which meant the liquor was on me that night, as usual. The odds were long that he'd return with the booze but I gave my hapless Lackey a wad of bills anyway and he took off, leaving me to take care of the gruesome twosome myself.

"Hi boys," I said as I approached the two men in the corner of the room. "Hope you enjoyed the show. Have we met?"

"We loved the show, Soph. Not as much as the one in Joliet last year, but you still got it," said the one who introduced himself as Vic. His partner in crime (pun *completely* intended) was named Mick. Now that I looked at them, I actually did recall having a little chat with the pair after a prison show. It's hard to forget two grown men with rhyming names and identical mustaches. These two were the Tweedle-Dee and Tweedle-Dum of petty larceny.

"How long have you guys been out of the can?" I asked.

"Just a few days," Mick replied. "We figured we'd take in your show and then get back to work on a new job." Mick waggled his eyebrows and Vic winked. I was pretty sure they weren't talking about a new gig as altar boys.

"Well fellas, if I can't talk you onto the straight and narrow, you might as well come to my party tonight at the Sherman. We'll celebrate your brief vacation from the Graybar Hotel," I said.

The party was hopping a few hours later. Fanny and her hapless honey Nicky Arnstein showed up. Fanny and I might have been in command on stage, but when it came to picking men we were about as talented as a one-armed juggler. I have to say, Arnstein put Al Lackey and Louis Tuck to shame when it came to being a world-class deadbeat. Nicky was constantly in hot water.

Fanny and I barely had time to catch up before the party was busted up by a bunch of coppers. They didn't arrest anyone—they did much worse. They took our booze. I tried not to cry over spilled gin, though it did bring a tear to my eye to see so much expensive bootlegged liquor marching out the door. But it was Prohibition, and that was just how things worked. Vic and Mick, however, were spitting mad.

"Don't worry Sophie, we'll get your liquor back," Vic swore. "Just leave it to us. We've got a connection at the warehouse where the cops keep all the liquor from these raids. We planned on cleaning the place out in a couple of nights anyway."

"That's the worst idea I've heard since my boyfriend bet a C-note on a horse with three legs!" I shouted. I couldn't talk them out of it, though, and they left in a flurry of winks and promises to return my booze.

The next night, Fanny invited me to the opening of Nicky Arnstein's new spot right on Lake Michigan. I had to hand it to him; he and his partner Big Tim Murphy had done a bang-up job making

Fanny Brice and Nicky Arnstein

the Lakeside Casino look like it belonged in Monte Carlo. He gave Fanny and me a thousand dollars in chips apiece and let us go to town at the blackjack table. Everything was going swimmingly until the police came swarming into the joint blowing their whistles and waving batons. It figured. It was my second raid in two days, and this time I was up seven hundred dollars for the first time in my unlucky gambling career.

Fanny grabbed my hand and yanked me toward a back exit that led out onto the street, where Nicky Arnstein was hiding. His wheels were being watched by the cops, so we snuck over to Fanny's car to make our getaway.

"Didn't you pay off the cops?" I asked Arnstein.

"Fuck them!" he shouted, tearing down Lakeshore Drive.

"Nicky…please tell me you cleared this with Capone," Fanny pleaded.

"Fuck him too!" he yelled, making a squealing turn.

This was a problem. A big one. I went to Capone's clubs exclusively when I was in Chicago, and I was due to play cards with him the next night. The raid was clearly a message from Capone that Arnstein hadn't paid his proper tribute. I just prayed that my larger-than-life presence had escaped notice at the casino bust.

"He'll never know you were there," said Arnstein dismissively.

"That's very reassuring, you putz!" yelled Fanny. "I'm sure Sophie's gonna sleep like a baby tonight!"

I woke up the next morning to a knock on my door. It was a C.O.D. delivery that came to $66.66. I scrounged up the money from my purse and accepted the package, which was a small box so heavy I needed both hands to haul it to a table. Inside was an even smaller package wrapped in the early edition of the newspaper, which blared the headline, "SOPHIE TUCKER AT LAKESIDE CASINO BUST." I queasily unwrapped the paper to find a red construction brick and small card from Al Capone with just two words on it: "Not happy."

I immediately rang Fanny. "Well, that's good news," she said with a laugh. "He could have sent you some cement shoes and a one way ticket to the bottom of Lake Michigan."

As I was on the phone, I got another knock at my hotel door. This time it was Vic and Mick, with identical beads of sweat rolling down their brows. I hung up with Fanny and Mick explained that they'd overheard a couple of mooks at a diner hatching a plan to steal my diamonds in the hotel garage that night on my way to the theater. Mick and Vic ran over to let me know so I could arrange for some bodyguards. I tried to hire them to do the job, but those idiots were going to be busy robbing the cops' liquor warehouse blind.

I placed a call to Chief O'Hara and explained my stickup threat. He was more than happy to give me a police escort in exchange for twenty-five passes to my show at the Oriental. As promised, when I left the hotel lobby that night to get to the theater, there were four squad cars waiting for me and I saw neither hide nor hair of any two-bit thug.

Although the police were able to keep me safe on my way to and from the theater, there was nothing they could do when it was time for me to face the music of an angry Al Capone at our late night gin game. I was sweating bullets by the time I reached the door to his penthouse suite at the Sherman, which was protected by the usual ten gorillas. I hoped that some pressing criminal business might have popped up that would keep Capone from our game, but one of the apes opened the door and ushered me inside.

"He's waiting for you," he said. It sounded like a threat but, to my surprise, me and Al passed a few hours playing gin rummy with nothing more than idle chit-chat. We gabbed about my shows at the Oriental, the hotel manager, even the weather. When we got to the subject of horse racing, Al hinted that perhaps I might want to put some money on Running Bear in the first race at Arlington the next day.

"You know who's going to win?" I asked.

"Sure. I know lots of things. And besides, maybe you can win your $66.66 back," he said, hardly looking up from his cards. I thought I was going to lose my lunch all over Al's coffee table. Something told me he wouldn't appreciate me redecorating with a regurgitated Reuben, so I took a deep breath and tried to explain myself.

"I'm so sorry about that whole Nicky Arnstein fiasco. I had no idea he hadn't cleared his operation with you. I don't even like that rat bast—" I blubbered, but Al cut me off.

"I know you didn't know. But next time, check with me before you go to another club. Understand?" he asked, and I could almost make out a smile on his face.

"Cross my heart, Al. What's gonna happen to that asshole Nicky? I could care less, but Fanny would be pretty broken up if she had to wear a diving suit to her wedding," I asked.

"Nicky will learn his lesson, but he's not going for a swim just yet," said Al. "You and Fanny can have a drink to celebrate, as a matter of fact. I'll be getting your liquor back to you tomorrow. At the end of each month, Chief O'Hara lets my boys pick up all the liquor in his warehouse in exchange for a small donation to his retirement fund."

Forget about losing my Reuben—now I was worried I was going to lose consciousness entirely right in the middle of Capone's living room. Right that minute, Mick and Vic were pulling up to the police warehouse across town with five trucks. They paid off the guard with a fat stack of cash and their crew cleared out the whole joint in the blink of an eye. Then they drove back across town to another warehouse to stash their booty and toast each other with what would have been a bottle of Al Capone's finest champagne.

I'd just gotten back to my room when the phone rang. Thankfully, Mick and Vic were the type who liked to gloat.

"Mick," I said after he was through crowing about their perfect crime, "get in your trucks and put every last bottle back where you found it. That liquor belongs to Capone!"

"Holy shit, he's in with the cops?"

"It's Al Capone! He's in with the Pope!" I yelled.

"Sophie, we couldn't get back into the warehouse even if we wanted to! The guard we paid off to open Fort Knox is already on his way to Canada," said Mick. I could hear the panic in his voice.

"Look, you get your trucks back to the warehouse and I'll send help, okay? Just trust me."

I hung up the phone and ran down the hall to another room and pounded on the door until my sleepy friend opened up. Forget about making my flab disappear—I had a much easier trick for master lock-picker Harry Houdini to perform.

Magician and escape artist Harry Houdini.

As luck would have it, I didn't get to play cards with Capone again for years. I got a call the next day to fill in for a headliner in New York who came down with the flu. By the time I found my way back to Chicago for an extended run, Al had just started his own extended run on an island just off of San Francisco.

Our paths crossed again in 1945 when I was doing a few dates in Florida and Al was living in a mansion on Palm Island. I guess his associates had put aside a little retirement fund for their old boss. My first night there, I got a note after my show inviting me for a much delayed hand or two of gin. Even after eleven years in the slammer, you never said no to Al Capone.

I arrived at Capone's joint the next day with a little housewarming gift and nearly passed out from shock when Al greeted me with a big smile on his face. Retirement looked good on him.

We played a few rounds of cards and caught up on all of our old friends, most of whom were either retired or locked up. Eventually, my curiosity got the best of me and I had to bring up Mick and Vic's heist.

"Remember that deal you used to have with Chief O'Hara for all that booze? Did you know that the night after the raid on Nicky Arnstein's casino, while we were playing cards, a pair of two-bit crooks stole it right out from under your nose and me and Houdini got them to put it back?"

"Of course I knew," said Al, chuckling. "You think you're the only one who thought Houdini might be good at picking some profitable locks? The only reason I paid off Chief O'Hara was because Harry refused me—and then the son-of-a-bitch disappeared right before my eyes!"

After all these years, I'd forgotten that Al Capone knew almost everything.

"Well, my friend, I'm pooped. It's time for me to head back to my hotel. How much do I owe you?" I asked.

"By my count, $54.00," he said.

I handed him my housewarming gift, which he unwrapped to find the same red construction brick that'd cost me $66.66.

"Keep the change," I laughed.

A rare smile from Al Capone.

Chapter 20

Real Estate Papa

After my rotten visit to Hartford in 1908 I swore I wouldn't go back until I'd made it big, but by 1909 I was feeling homesick. I'd missed the last four of Albert's birthdays and, regardless of how many letters we wrote back and forth, I was dying to see Annie face to face.

I'd also kept in touch with my old schoolmate John Sudarsky over the years, sending him a letter every month or so with some of my press clippings. He was working at the *Hartford Courant* and managed to publish a story that said I was headlining the Ziegfeld Follies—a minor exaggeration, sure, but it turned me from a bum into a bit of a hometown hero. John also conveniently forgot to publish a follow-up report that I'd been canned. Annie told me the good press had taken the heat off of her and the family, so she thought the coast might be clear for me to come home for another visit.

She was right, for the most part. I didn't get any dirty looks at the train station or on my walk to the restaurant. That honor was reserved for Mama, who was still angry I left home, and Albert, who refused to say hello from behind Annie's skirt.

"Come here, Bert! I've got a gift for you," I said, holding out a box filled with candy and toys.

He inched toward me to snatch his present and I grabbed him into a hug, but he squirmed and cried until I let him go. Even while he was throwing a fit, Bert somehow managed to get away holding his gift. The kid was turning into a full-fledged brat. The little Duke of Wails screamed whenever he didn't get his way, particularly around Papa, who was Albert's easiest mark. He'd immediately fork over whatever Bert was blubbering for, whether that was a bar of chocolate before dinner or a toy he saw in a window downtown.

One of Bert's school photos. He's marked with an "x," just to the left of the teacher.

Mama was upstairs scrubbing some clothes in the washtub and muttering under her breath in Yiddish. I greeted her with a peck on the cheek, and she asked me to pass her a new bar of soap.

"Thank God I took an early train so I could be here to hand you the soap," I kidded.

"Come here," my mother said with a big smile.

Who could resist that? I leaned over and Mama smacked me right across the face.

"Welcome home," she said.

At least Phil, Moe and Annie were all smiles. They greeted me with hugs and kisses and all the recent neighborhood gossip. Phil also reintroduced me to his new wife, Leah, who was cowering behind him in the entryway. We'd grown up together and even been in a few of the same classes at school, but I don't think I'd ever heard her make a peep. It didn't look like that was going to change any time soon, either, as she silently stuck her hand out for a shake and then scurried off into the kitchen like a mouse.

Annie and Phil both agreed that Leah's biggest problem was she couldn't figure out how to get a word in when the loud Abuza clan got to yakking. She was afraid to interrupt, and she was even more afraid of saying something stupid. Every time she opened her mouth, she felt like she was being thrown to the lions. And then there was Mama—even though Leah was an excellent cook, Mama would never let her help out in the kitchen. Mama had no time for a wallflower who flinched every time she clanged a pot lid.

Phil asked if I would have a word with Mama about being kinder to his wife.

"Do I look suicidal?" I asked. "I'd rather talk a grizzly bear into being kinder to a salmon—at least we both like lox!"

I'd planned my visit to coordinate with Rosh Hashanah and Yom

Leah (fourth from the left) hides in the background at one of Sophie's public engagements in 1931.

Kippur, when I knew the restaurant would be closed. It was easier to catch up with my family when we didn't have to worry about whether table four had gotten their matzoh ball soup. Mama cooked us an enormous dinner every night and everyone enjoyed themselves, even though we had to talk over Bert's screaming and brace our coffee cups every time he kicked the table in a tantrum. Over dessert, I had a brilliant idea.

"A friend of mine in New York mentioned a wonderful school that might be Bert's ticket right into Harvard or Yale. It's called the Peekskill Military Academy," I said.

"They take six year olds in military academies?" said Annie, dodging one of Bert's fists as he grabbed a cookie off the plate in the middle of the table.

"Don't you think that's kinda rough for a little tyke?" asked Phil.

"Don't you think you should mind your own goddamn business?" I asked.

Mama was in the kitchen washing dishes, but when she heard me get mouthy with Phil she flew out to the table and smacked me across the face with one of her soapy hands. I'd been away for three years and had made my own way through show business, but I forgot that nothing had changed. Phil was still my older brother and in Mama's house, we were to respect the men—even though we all knew Mama ran the show. Besides that, she was *still* mad as hell that I'd left home in the first place. As far as she was concerned, I gave up

Bert at age six in his military academy uniform. Sophie won this argument.

my authority over Bert when I left him with Annie and got on the train to New York. The truth was that Sophie Tucker never gave up her authority to anyone, but I just bit my tongue. There was no arguing with Mama.

Thankfully, we were interrupted by the sound of a loud Chinese gong.

"Don't ask," said Moe without even looking up from his strudel. Papa, it seemed, hadn't given up on inventing the perfect doorbell. I ran to answer it, eager to leave the table.

"If it isn't the Queen of Broadway," said my dad's old pal T-bone, who was standing on our stoop with Sammy the Socket and Deaf Davey. "Is your father upstairs? I'm feeling lucky tonight."

"Sorry boys, no cards today. It's the Jewish holidays," I said.

The guys were disappointed, but they each gave me a hug and wished me well. Before they left, T-bone reminded me that if I needed anything at all while I was in town, I could give him a shout. Neither he nor I ever forgot that time the cheating butcher "fell" on his meat cleaver.

There was one errand I needed to take care of before I left town. Somehow, Louis Tuck had tracked me down in New York and sent me three threatening letters asking for cash in exchange for steering clear of Albert. Louis was no genius, but he had figured out that I would pay anything to keep him out of the picture. I had no choice but to drop in on Tuck during my last night in Hartford.

"Well, look who's here," said Louis when he answered the door. "I see in the funny papers you've made it to the big time."

"And I see in the obituaries you're not dead yet."

We stared at each other for a long moment like two dogs getting ready to fight. I swear, I almost growled. Instead, I threw five twenty-dollar bills at his head, which startled him so badly he tripped over one of the floorboards on the porch and fell flat on his back. He tried to turn his head to count the dough, but I pinned his throat with the sole of my shoe so he couldn't move.

"Maybe I didn't make myself clear the last time I saw you. So, let me repeat: no more letters, no more threats, nothing. If you so much as think about me or Albert, you are a *dead man*," I hissed. I pressed my foot down on his throat harder and harder until Tuck turned bright red and gasped for air.

"Do you understand?" I asked.

The bastard nodded. I released him and said goodbye with a swift kick to Little Louie. Hopefully, the ice he'd have to keep down his pants for the next couple of days would be a good reminder to keep his distance.

With that, I nearly gave up on the idea of ever coming home to Hartford again. Sure, I'd taken care of Louis, but each time I visited it pained me to see Mama and Papa still working their fingers to the bone. Earlier that week, I accidentally caught sight of them both struggling to pull down a big bag of flour from a high shelf. It struck me how old they were getting, and as long as Mama refused to spend the money I sent home there was no retirement in their future. The way she saw it, I'd given up a picture perfect family life in order to run around with gangsters and actors and whores—all of whom were lovely people, contrary to popular opinion—so there was no way she'd ever spend a dime of my money.

So, rather than kissing Hartford goodbye, I decided that I'd have to find an indisputable way to prove I was successful enough for them to sell the restaurant and take a load off.

First, though, I needed cash. I set my plan in motion in February of 1910, when I asked the Boss to meet me at Reuben's. When I told him I needed a quick thousand dollars he nearly spit his seltzer across the table. Once he realized I was serious, we put our heads together.

"If you go to New Jersey and record a couple of those new cylinders, I can get you two hundred bucks. Then, if they sell, I can get you eight more for another hundred each. How does that sound?" he asked.

"Great, but I need all the cash up front, Boss."

"It can't be done, Sophie. The guy won't even pay Caruso in advance and he's twice as big as you are."

"Maybe he'll pay me by the pound," I joked, picking a strand of sauerkraut off my dress. "Order me a dozen knishes and I'll have my grand in no time."

"Take it up with the head honcho at the record company, Sophie. If you can talk him into an advance, I'll eat my hat between two slices of pumpernickel."

Before a matinee in Newark a few days later, I enlisted Molly and her Model T to take me to West Orange to pay a visit to the record man himself, Thomas Edison. Our plan was to get to the Edison recording studio first thing in the morning so I could finalize the contract, sing my two songs, convince Mr. Edison to give me a thousand clams, and get to the theater with time left over for lunch.

Edison's studio in West Orange, New Jersey.

When we arrived at the studio, we were directed to a prim little man at a desk just outside Edison's office. His plaque read "Clyde Kuperman, General Manager, Edison Phonograph." It was polished to gleaming.

"Good morning," he greeted us. "How may I help you?"

"Hiya Clyde, I'm here to sing a couple of songs for Mr. Edison, but first I have to work out a few details about some money he owes me. Wanna go play matchmaker and introduce us?" I asked.

Clyde could not have been less entertained. He rifled through a stack of papers and slid my contract and his pen across the desk as distastefully as if he was offering a hanky to a tuberculosis patient. I signed and flung it back to him.

"So how about me seeing Mr. Edison, Kuppy?" I asked.

"You don't call him Tom?" he snipped. "I'd appreciate it if you would address me as Mr. Kuperman, if you don't mind."

"I do mind! How's that gonna sound in the morning? 'Don't forget to make the bed, *Mr. Kuperman?*'" I razzed.

"Madam, *please*," he sputtered. "Mr. Edison is engaged and will be all day. And he never talks to any of our recording artists."

"You hear that Molly? Kuppy thinks I'm an artist. How about I come back later and you, me, and Mr. Edison paint the town red?" I flirted.

"Miss Tucker, Mr. Edison is busy before any of us arrive in the morning and he's busy until well after we all leave. As a matter of fact, he'll be busy for the foreseeable future," he said, ignoring all my advances and escorting us to the recording studio. Molly just shook her head and laughed.

A studio was a hectic place back then because everything was in one room: the musicians, the singer, the recording equipment, all of the technicians, and the wax cylinders onto which we recorded. I was positioned in front of a giant metal horn and told to sing into the hole, which seemed simple enough.

Sophie in a recording studio.

The first number I was supposed to sing was an old tune called "That Lovin' Rag." When the technicians began recording and the orchestra played the introduction, I took a deep breath, stepped up to the horn and let 'er rip. All five technicians jumped out of their chairs yelling and waving their arms for me to stop.

"Miss Tucker, you just melted the wax off our cylinders. Could you take a few steps back and please sing a bit softer?" said one technician. "We'll try it again as soon as my ears stop ringing."

It took eight tries and I ended up on the opposite side of the room, but we finally got it. The only catch was that I had to do that same thing twenty-three more times. In those days, each master cylinder would wear out after pressing ten thousand copies of the final record. So, with two songs, I actually had to cut forty-eight cylinders that day, which was tiring even for my tonsils. Because it took us five hours, Molly had to fly all the way back to Newark so I could close out my matinee. After that, I took a three hour nap and barely made it through my evening performance.

However, I mustered just enough energy to hop into Molly's Model T and high-tail it back to West Orange, arriving just before midnight. The gates were open but the whole complex looked dark.

"If I'm not back in thirty minutes," I whispered to Molly, "meet me at the West Orange pokey!"

I took off toward Mr. Edison's office. I thought I heard someone stirring behind the giant oak door so I took a deep breath, knocked a few times, and then barged in.

I'll never forget how the room was lit up like a Broadway marquee. I wasn't used to seeing so many little electric light bulbs in one place. There were all kinds of gadgets on the majestic mahogany desk at the back of the room, but no Edison. I figured I might as well have a look around and then leave a note asking about my money, so I took my time investigating the contents of his shelves. There sat the first stock ticker, the first light bulb, the first cylinder player and several gizmos that were too scientific for me to identify. The walls were full of framed patent certificates, awards, and photographs of Edison posing with a slew of different big shots. I leaned in to examine a few smaller photographs.

"That's President Theodore Roosevelt," said a shrill voice behind me. "But I haven't got a clue who *you* are or what you are doing in my office."

"I'm sorry, I knocked but no one answered. I'm Sophie Tucker, sir. I work in Vaudeville? Maybe you heard me sing today?"

"Miss Tucker, everyone in New Jersey could hear you sing today," Edison said with a grimace. "What are you doing here after midnight? I thought I was the only one who worked this late."

"To be honest, my pal Clyde out there at your front desk tipped me off to your late hours. I wanted to talk to you about a business proposition, so I decided to take a chance and have my friend Molly drive me back here tonight after my second show in Newark."

Edison softened. He seemed at least a little bit impressed that I'd worked as many hours as he had that day. He insisted I invite Molly up from the freezing cold car and offered to make us some tea while we talked. I stuck my head out Edison's second-floor window, put two fingers in my mouth, and let out a long whistle.

"Hey Molly, come on up! Tom wants to meet you!"

Over tea, I laid the groundwork for my proposition, explaining that I wanted him to advance me the money for eight future records even if it wasn't his usual practice.

"I'd like to think I'm a good businessman—" started Edison.

"We heard you're a stingy bastard!" interrupted Molly. Thank god he laughed.

"Now wait a minute," replied the inventor, "one man's stingy bastard is another man's savvy investor. It just doesn't make sense for me to give out cash in advance when I can't be sure you'll sell anything. I only grant second recording sessions to artists whose first records sell 20,000 copies apiece."

"Well, what if a certain singer sells 15,000 copies of each of her first two records and promises to deliver you a bonafide living legend? One that you've never been able to record? If she did that, would you agree to advance her $800 in exchange for a meeting with..."

I paused for dramatic flair.

"Mark Twain?"

Edison's jaw nearly dropped to the floor. He shook my hand on the spot.

Unbeknownst to me at the time, I'd actually put my grand plan into motion a year before I met Edison, shortly before I was fired from the Follies. A whole lot of A-list stars streamed in and out of Flo's backstage dressing rooms, visiting him and his headliners. George M. Cohan, Helen Hayes, and Mary Pickford all came to visit Nora Bayes, and each time a celebrity came by I grabbed a chorus girl and we planted ourselves just outside her dressing room door. It looked like we were having very important conversation, but we were just stargazing.

One night, Ethel's handsome brother John Barrymore stopped by to say hello and suddenly every chorus girl in the Follies had the same idea. They were lined up outside Nora's door just to get a glimpse of the notorious dreamboat of the silver screen. I gave up and stood in in the back of the dressing area next to a white-haired gentleman. He seemed tickled by the spectacle and we got to talking. It turned out we were both from Connecticut and neither one of us had high expectations of taking John Barrymore home that evening.

The original Yankee Doodle Dandy, George M. Cohan.

Helen Hayes, one of just fourteen actors to win an Oscar, Tony, Emmy and Grammy Award.

"America's Sweetheart," silent film actress Mary Pickford.

John Barrymore

We ended up going out for a bite to eat to escape the chaos backstage. Sam, as he introduced himself, was in town to deal with his lawyers. It turned out that a crook had tried to make off with about $125,000 of his money.

"That's a lot of smackers!" I yelled. "What is it you do exactly, Sam?"

"You could say I profit off of my misspent youth, I suppose. I wrote a couple of books about it. And some others," he said, shrugging his shoulders.

"Sam, your last name doesn't happen to be Clemens, does it?" I said, lowering my sandwich from my mouth. He nodded, and I dropped my roast beef on rye so hard I spattered his white suit with splotches of Russian dressing.

"Please, Sophie, keep it down," he laughed, dabbing a napkin on his lapel. "The last thing I need is another lunatic to realize who am and dream up some cockamamie idea to steal even more of my money."

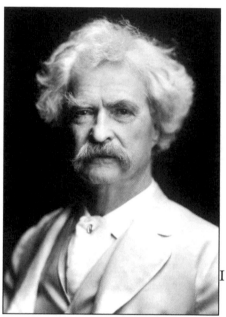

Sophie's new friend Sam.

Every day, he said, someone knocked on his door in Redding, Connecticut with some fly-by-night scheme. This was on top of the dozens of letters he'd received from the biggest thorn in his side, Thomas Edison, who wouldn't stop writing to ask if he would come make a movie at his studio.

"What do you think? Am I the next big matinee idol? Do I look like I belong on the silver screen with those swashbucklers?" he asked, miming some swordplay with his butter knife.

We had a few more fun dinners while he was in town and kept in touch over the next year while I traveled. I considered him a good friend and hoped desperately that he would now come through for his new pal Soph.

Sophie, reading, in 1937.

First, though, I had to fulfill my end of the bargain with Edison and sell 15,000 copies of each of my first two records. Just like Mama kept a little leather notebook of English phrases when she got to America, since 1906 I'd been keeping a notebook of names and addresses of every friend I made on the road. My list was up to 2,486 names by 1910. I printed up thousands of penny postcards and Molly and I addressed them to my buddies until our hands were so cramped we had to stick them in the icebox for relief.

> *Dear friend, good news! Edison Phonograph Records has decided to record and sell two of my hit songs. If you and your friends buy these new cylinders then I will get to make eight more. In return for your purchase, the next time I play your town there will be a free ticket waiting for you at the box office. Tell everyone you know the same deal applies for them. Thanks for your support. Love, Sophie Tucker.*

We sent them out and then all we could do was wait, and hope I had enough friends across the country to make my ridiculous plan work.

By March 31, 1910, my records had been out for a full month. The suspense was killing me, so I called Clyde for a sales report.

"What's the good news, Kuppy?"

"I told you, it's Mr. Kuperman, Miss Tucker. Let me take a look," he said, and he placed the phone down for a moment. I could hear him rustling papers on the other end. "All I have are the East Coast sales figures, and I'm seeing 16,283 copies sold."

I frowned. "Well, that's a good start. It's only been a month. I'm more than half way home, Clyde," I said with a sigh.

"No, Miss Tucker, you misunderstood me. That's just for the first record," said my favorite little stick in the mud. I think I could even hear a hint of excitement in his voice. "The other one's about the same. You've made your 30,000 copy sales goal. Actually, come to think of it, you've broken our sales record for most copies sold in the first month after release."

An early promotion for Sophie's records with Edison.

"Kuppy, I could kiss you right now!" I yelled into the phone.

"I'll take a raincheck on that, Miss Tucker," he said, and hung up.

The next crucial part of my plan involved throwing a big Sixtieth birthday party for my mother in May of 1910. I'd written Annie weeks before and asked her to convince Mama and Papa to close the restaurant for the day, and she managed to do it with a minimum of flying flatware. I came to town the Saturday before the party to work out a few final details.

When I arrived at the house, the birthday girl was in the kitchen peeling potatoes for dinner.

"Hello Mama. Happy birthday! I haven't gotten your present yet. What would you like?" I asked, giving her a peck on the cheek.

"You, home and married," she said.

"What's your second choice?" I asked.

"Core those apples," she said, gesturing to an enormous bowl on the table.

Sophie in the kitchen, 1945.

Mama was notoriously difficult to shop for. What do you buy the woman who wants nothing? Since the sewing machine, no present had even come close to making her smile. Just like the last time I visited Hartford, I was sitting at Mama's table and biting my tongue—this time, though, in anticipation.

Just before the big celebration dinner on Sunday, I asked Annie to set an extra place for a friend who would be stopping by to meet Mama and wish her a happy birthday. That sent Annie into a tizzy thinking she hadn't cooked enough food and she took off like a rocket toward the kitchen. I had to fight to get the apron out of her hands. I'd just convinced her to relax when, all of the sudden, the house was filled with the sound of a dozen cuckoo clocks. I looked at Moe.

"You guessed it," said Moe, eyes on his potatoes. "Papa's new doorbell."

I ran to answer the door and came back with Sam, looking dapper as ever in his trademark white suit. I introduced him as my friend, the writer, and then we dug into dinner. Sam even managed to keep up with us Abuzas in both appetite and chattiness. By dessert, we were all stuffed to the gills and nearly hoarse.

Before the cake, though, it was time for gifts. Annie gave Mama a beautiful white lace apron, which we knew she would never use for fear it would get dirty. Moe gave her a pretty brooch, which we knew she would never wear because it was too flashy. Mama's favorite color was black—navy blue if she really felt like living it up. Leah gave her a beautiful crocheted black blanket. The color was right, but Mama set it to the side without comment simply because it was from meek little Leah. Bert came the closest to making Mama smile because he gave her a wooden spoon, something she was sure to use.

My father presented with great fanfare a bracelet he'd won in a card game off Mr. Szycwick. Mama rolled her eyes and handed it back to him, telling him in Yiddish where he could stick his gambling winnings.

Before it was my turn, Sam got up and presented Mama with a small wrapped gift. She undid the paper to find a beautiful hardcover copy of *A Connecticut Yankee in King Arthur's Court*, inscribed inside to "Mrs. Abuza and her beautiful family." When Mama realized she'd been sitting all night with Mark Twain she spun in circles trying to decide between getting him more coffee and cake, or changing into a nicer dress, or shaking his hand. She clasped her heart and spoke a stream of quick Yiddish.

"What did she say?" asked Sam.

"She's wondering how you could know our family was so wonderful when you wrote your inscription," asked Annie.

"That's easy," explained Clemens. "I met Sophie for five minutes in New York City and I knew."

Mama's sweet moment was interrupted by the chorus of cuckoo clocks going berserk once again. I went to the front door to retrieve my second surprise guest. Finally, it was time for my gift.

"Papa, this is Mr. Thomas Edison. I told him all about your inventions and he insisted on coming here to meet you," I said.

Papa's legs turned to jelly in front of his idol. He wobbled over to Edison and shook his hand, weakly, for a full minute.

"I'm terribly sorry to interrupt your birthday party, Mrs. Abuza, but I come bearing a gift. Mr. Abuza, Sophie told me all about your one of a kind doorbell designs. Well, it just so happens that I'm expanding my company into manufacturing unique doorbells, and I'm here tonight to make you an offer. I'm prepared to pay you $800 for all your past designs, particularly the cuckoo model I just heard coming in. How does that sound? Do we have a deal?" he asked.

Papa nodded, his eyes as big as two bagels. He was so flummoxed, he didn't notice me gently elbow Tom's ribs.

"Oh, yes. There's one more thing. The only condition," Edison said gravely, "is that you must never make another doorbell. I can't have you competing against me. Do you understand, Mr. Abuza?"

He nodded once more, still in awe, and then I think Papa fell into a coma. Before they could shake to make it official, Mama walked over to Edison, grabbed him by the head, and planted a big kiss right on his lips. Papa may have thought she was happy about the money, but we all knew Mama was thrilled she was finally going to get some peace and quiet.

The next morning, I couldn't believe how well everything had gone. Edison and Clemens got to gabbing over dessert. They hit it off so well, in fact, that Sam invited Tom to visit his estate in Redding and shoot the silent film he'd been begging for, which meant I'd held up my end of the bargain.

I realized it was getting late and I was due to head back to New York, so I asked Mama and Papa to walk me to the train station. On the way, Papa wanted to know when I thought Mr. Edison might get him his money.

"Actually, Papa, Mr. Edison gave it to me already," I said. I had steered our walk toward Barker Street, where we stopped in front of a beautiful little house. I handed my father a key.

"Your doorbells bought you this house. Now you two can sell the restaurant and never have to work another day."

Papa took off his hat and threw it in the air. There weren't many successes in Papa's life, but for that one day he was the King of Hartford. As he picked up Mama and spun her around, she caught my eye. I knew I hadn't fooled her—she was onto me and Edison, but she winked and kept it to herself.

And, for once, she really smiled.

Edison and Twain.

Chapter 21

The Angle Worm Wiggle

In June of 1910, the Boss scheduled me for another run of shows in Chicago with one major goal: get arrested. It sounded crazy to me, but Morris was convinced that if I pushed the double entendres in my act just a little bit further, I could get some holier-than-thou son of a bitch to raise a stink. Push it a little further than that and he hoped the cops would haul me in for obscenity, which was the best publicity money couldn't buy. Everyone would pay triple at the gate just to hear the song that sent me to the slammer.

"You know what they call the little row boat attached to the back of a yacht?" the Boss asked with a smirk.

"My escape plan," I joked.

"It's called a dinghy. How do you think your audience will react if you sing a song called 'My Boyfriend Has the Biggest Dinghy in the Navy'?"

"They'll laugh their asses off. That's not double entendre; that's home run entendre. But that'll probably land me in the slammer for a year!" I protested.

"No one ever really goes to jail for obscenity," he said, waving off my concerns. "They'll just give you a slap on the wrist and you'll be out in a couple of hours. You won't even miss your evening curtain."

"Then go buy yourself a cookbook," I said. "If you're wrong, you better have a chocolate cake with a file in it waiting for me in my cell."

So, I arrived in Chicago an aspiring jailbird. Chi-town was in the middle of the hottest summer on record, with temperatures climbing higher than 110° some days, but the audiences were still coming out in droves. Maybe they thought it was a good deal. They'd hear some songs, laugh at some jokes, *schvitz*[1] for two hours and leave the theater five

1   *Schvitz* – Sweat

pounds lighter. I kept on doing my regular old act while I waited for newer, bluer numbers to arrive in the mail from the Boss.

One night, though, something else arrived in the middle of my set. Between songs, one of the comedians from the first half of the show pushed a piano right out on stage. He adjusted his stool and started to play a rag.

"Hey, hey, hey!" I yelled, truly clueless as to what was happening. "I'm in the middle of my act here. What's the big idea?"

"Sorry to interrupt, Miss Tucker. You and the audience might remember me from the first half of the show. My name's Frank Westphal and I've got a brand new song here for you, hot off the presses," said the comedian.

"And I suppose you want to play it now?" I asked, going along with his routine for the sake of the show.

"Here are the lyrics," he said, handing me the sheet music.

"I like the title, at least. Ladies and gentlemen, you're about to hear the debut performance of 'Give Me Back My Husband, You've Had Him Long Enough'."

I found out later that this Frank fellow stormed the stage on a dare from Lester Rose, our juggling act. I hadn't even noticed Frank had joined the troupe, but Frank had definitely noticed me, and Lester noticed Frank standing around in the wings each day, watching my act and looking moonstruck. When Lester got word that my new risqué song had arrived from the Boss, he bet Frank five dollars he wouldn't interrupt my act and deliver the song right then and there. That was all the encouragement Frank needed to break the ice.

Frank Westphal

Westphal was wild through and through. I got a new *high* school diploma when Frank introduced me to hashish, cocaine, and opium, all of which I had the good sense to use in moderation but goddamn, we had some crazy parties. I was young and stupid and Westphal was even younger and stupider. And, like all the other men I ever got serious about,

Frank was four inches shorter than me. I guess I liked to know that when push came to shove, I could push and shove my fellas right out the door.

Frank pointed out that I was a better entertainer when I had an accompanist who could double as my straight man. After Frank's first interruption we came up with a few other ways he could bust in on my act. Sometimes Westphal would break onto the stage with a fiddle and we'd do a little jig. Other times, he pretended to be a drunk looking for a bartender.

Even better, Frank taught me how to put over those new double-entendre-filled songs the Boss was sending my way by the dozen. At the time, there was a big hit by George M. Cohan called "My Wife's Gone to the Country." Westphal taught me how to knock 'em dead with "My Husband's in the City," to wild success.

The best of the bunch, though, was a sly little number called "The Angle Worm Wiggle." We rehearsed my wiggle both on and off stage—and under the stage, and in the alley behind the theater—so I was ready when I got a telegram from the Boss telling me I had a whole slew of dates on the West Coast. I should've been over the moon about touring out west for the first time, but all I could think about was Frank. My new beau wasn't part of the deal.

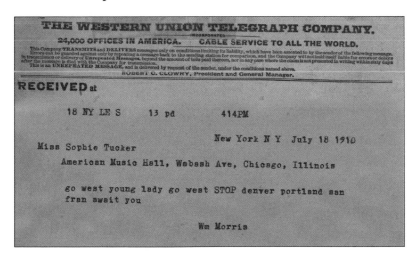

Westphal was so upset he proposed to me for the first of fifty times that week. Over the years we knew each other, Frank would go on to pop the question on stage, in restaurants, in parks, at the beach, on a sailboat, a roller coaster, on a Ferris wheel, on a bicycle built for two, on a seesaw and in the front, back, and rumble seat of a car. I turned down each proposal, but I always found a way to soothe his rejection. Maybe that's why he kept asking.

As far as I was concerned, there were two big reasons not to get married. The first was that we were Vaudeville performers on different circuits. We'd never see each other. The second was that I was still legally married to Louis Tuck. There were only a handful of people in show business who knew about my marriage and about Bert, and I decided to make Frank a member of that small club. I thought the truth might cool his engines, but the day I clued him in he proposed two more times—once over breakfast, and once while I was brushing my teeth before we went to bed. He got a particularly minty rejection that time.

At the last minute, I sent a telegram to the Boss and asked if he could also book Frank on my tour. The answer came in a telegram a week later.

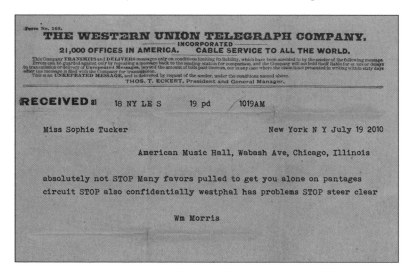

I knew Frank had bad habits, but I was shocked it'd reached the Boss's ears. For that to have happened, he must've caused trouble at a theater. The only thing I knew for sure was that Morris had my best interests at heart, so I took his advice. Nothing, not even a good love affair, was going to derail my career. I never told Frank about the telegram. Instead, I said my goodbyes and took off.

The West was mesmerizing. I managed to hit a few of the tourist spots on the way to my first date. I saw the view from the top of Pike's

Peak and I even rode down to the bottom of the Grand Canyon on a donkey. After bearing my load for eight hours, I'm sure they had to shoot that poor beast to put him out of his misery. It's a rare thing to get to kiss your own sorry ass goodbye.

Our country sure is beautiful. You've gotta see those crazy red rocks out in Utah, or Yellowstone Park. In my third grade class, Frankie Meyers held the record for being able to spit and hit a target six yards away, but that Old Faithful geyser had Frankie beat by two hundred feet!

My first stop on the Western Pantages Circuit was Portland, Oregon. The Boss had gotten me $350 a week for my whole tour, a fact he'd leaked to the local papers in order to boost ticket sales before anyone had even heard me sing a note. Just like in burlesque,

Sophie and her donkey are marked with an X.

my biggest responsibility was to astonish the audience at my first show. If I did, the customers would leave the theater on Monday afternoon excited to spread the good word, which would have audiences lined up down the block for the rest of the week.

I did not disappoint. The people of Oregon were the same as anywhere else, and everybody loved a suggestive song. Both the audience and the newspaper critics ate up every pound of me. Before you knew it, all my shows sold out. Even the mayor and the town judge invited me to dinner, but my favorite invitation came from Mr. and Mrs. Pence Egbert. They sent a note back stage which read:

*We don't want to intrude on your private time but it would
be our pleasure if you would join us for a home cooked
kosher meal.*

The Egberts turned out to be the most interesting people I would
meet in Portland. Pence was one of the leading lawyers in town,
a graduate of Harvard Law School, and the president of the local
synagogue. Estelle was just as smart and the leader of her local Ladies
Auxiliary corp.

"How many Jews live in Portland?" I asked.

"About three hundred. It's not easy when there's so few of us. Anti-
Semitism seems to be a thriving worldwide franchise," said Pence. "But
they usually leave me alone because word got out around town that I
win most of my cases. I guess the goyim figure when they get in trouble
with the law, having a Jewish friend isn't so bad."

I was happy to have at least one home-cooked meal at the Egberts',
because the next day I was off to the Chutes Theater in San Francisco.
That big earthquake had nearly leveled the city just a few years earlier
and there was construction going on downtown everywhere I looked.
The lumber yards were certainly making a killing.

So was I, as a matter of fact. When I met the manager of the
theater he had a puss on his face due to my high salary, courtesy
of William Morris. He might not have been happy at first, but
the crowds were with me and my reception at the Chutes was even
better than my reception in Portland. I think it helped that there
were a whole lot of rough and tumble construction workers looking
to unwind after a long day. I sold out all thousand seats twice a day
for two weeks. On Sunday, that same skeptical manager offered me
$500 extra to stay another week.

Let me tell you, it wouldn't have taken more than a buffalo
nickel to convince me to stay in a town with a nightlife district like
the Barbary Coast. A place that wild was too tempting for a girl
like me. I didn't mind a little dirt under my fingernails, but in the
Barbary Coast you could end up with blood on your hands. From
the moment I arrived in San Francisco, everyone from the clerk

behind the front desk at my hotel to the chorus girls in the opening number at the theater warned me not to go to the Coast.

"Sophie, you're taking your life into your hands if you go down there," said a stagehand. "I went there *once* and now I walk with a limp!"

In spite of his warning, I put a visit to the Barbary Coast at the top of my to-do list. First, I made friends with the toughest son of a bitch on the stage crew. Mike O'Toole was 6'6" and looked like he ate nails for breakfast. When I asked him if he'd be my tour guide, he shrugged and agreed—no one had ever given muscleman Mike a problem in the Coast, or anywhere else for that matter.

After Tuesday night's show, I got dressed and found Mike waiting for me near the stage door.

"There's just one thing to remember," he said as we headed down Pacific Street. "Don't look anyone straight in the eye. To a man, that means you're interested in a roll in the hay, and to a girl it means you're ready to fight. Take everything in, but don't make eye contact with nobody but me."

I did as Mike asked and barely looked up from my shoes until he steered me into a joint called the Golden Nugget. Mike ordered us a bottle of whiskey and headed off to take a quick leak. He wasn't gone five seconds when an angry redhead stormed up to the table demanding my name. I gave it to her without raising my eyes from the table, explaining I was just there with my friend Mike from the Chutes and I wasn't looking for any trouble.

"Bullshit, sister! The Chutes only has beauties. There's no way they'd hire a fat cow like you," she spat. With that, I stood up and looked the cheaply-dressed hooker directly in the eye.

"What's your problem, Big Bertha?" I asked.

"Michael O'Toole is mine, and I'll be damned if I let him carouse with a hippo like you," she yelled.

I don't remember who threw the first punch, but I do remember a policeman pulling me off an unconscious redhead and carrying me straight out the door. He deposited me on the sidewalk like a sack of potatoes.

"What were you doing in there, Miss Tucker? You could've gotten killed," he said.

"No one calls me a hippo," I said. "And how do you know my name?"

"I saw you a few nights ago at the Chutes. The missus and I loved it. I'm Officer O'Brien," he said, smiling, as he offered his hand to help me up off the sidewalk. "You know, that was *Mrs.* O'Toole you decked."

"I don't care if it was *Mrs.* First Lady of the goddamn United States! No one calls me a hippo and lives to tell the tale."

Officer O'Brien walked me all the way back to my hotel and, as a thank you, I gave him my Star of David necklace from around my neck. He handed me his St. Christopher medal in exchange.

"Just promise not to punch St. Chris if he gets on your bad side," he laughed.

By the time October 1910 rolled around, I thought I was

Officer O'Brien eventually went on to become the chief of the San Francisco police department and was buried wearing Sophie's Star of David.

done with the West and heading home. Little did I know that word had gotten back to the cities I'd already played that my new songs were all the rage. Audiences demanded that I return and sing "Casey Jones" and "The Grizzly Bear" and the tune that would go on to be my lifelong theme song, "Some of These Days." I agreed to reverse my trip as I made my way east, which put me back in Oregon for one of my final weeks in the Northwest.

I gave it my best in Portland again, but I got more than I bargained for. After doing all my new numbers at the first matinee, a fella in the third row pleaded to hear "My Husband's in the City" as an encore. As I was singing, I noticed a woman in the front row get out of her seat and walk out the back door of the orchestra section. The door opened again as I launched into the second verse and the same lady came back in, this time accompanied by two police officers. The applause was deafening when I finished my song, but out of the corner of my eye I could see the woman having a heated conversation with the two cops. Something was going on.

"'The Angle Worm Wiggle,'" shouted a gentleman in the balcony.

"The song? Or just the wiggle?" I asked.

"The whole song, wiggle and all," yelled someone downstairs.

"Well, all right. I guess we have a lot of wiggle fanciers."

This song also inspired a dance craze.

And that's when all my troubles began. Before I started singing "The Angle Worm Wiggle," there was a little routine I did to get everyone in the proper mood.

"Okay, everybody. I'm gonna need your help. Mr. Conductor, give me a little vamp while I get my equipment on."

I showed the audience how to clap along with the orchestra and I did a funny little hula as I took four big rings out of a pocket in my gown. Exaggerating every motion, I put one ring on each of my index fingers and thumbs.

"Are you ready for the wiggle?" I asked the crowd. As they hooted and hollered, I could see the woman in the back point at me and scream something to the police officers. I ignored the commotion and started to sing:

> When I hear that bouncy strain,
> I can't help but moan with glee.
> Bounce me around the room like a rubber ball please,

Do that angle worm wiggle with me!

The Wiggle was one of the numbers the Boss sent me when I was in Chicago. Frank Westphal helped me work out the dance, and over the last six months I got my little wiggle down cold. But honestly, the secret to the number wasn't the dance—it was actually the rings. They were nothing but cheap colored glass, but when I moved my fingers at just the right angle, the big stones sparkling from the reflection of the footlights helped accentuate the *interesting* parts of my body. The illusion of a more scandalous dance than I was actually performing never failed to get me a standing ovation.

That night, however, the two policemen came marching down the aisle just as I was supposed to start my second verse. The orchestra vamped again when they noticed the cops heading up into my spotlight.

"Ladies and gentlemen, the Portland Police! Gentlemen, what can I do for you? Are you selling tickets to the Policemen's Ball? I'll take two—I eat a lot!" I joked.

"Miss Tucker, can you come with us please?" one of the cops whispered in my ear.

"I'm a little busy right now, officer. How about dinner after the show?"

"No, Miss Tucker. There's no more show. You're under arrest for lewd and obscene behavior," the other cop whispered.

"I'm under arrest for obscene behavior?" I said loud and clear, doing another little wiggle. The crowd went wild thinking it was all part of the show, but off I went to the station house.

Morris had given me my new material hoping for exactly this sort of incident, but I thought I was in the clear after six months of positive receptions. Still, there I was in jail. Since all the press had shown up at that Monday matinee to give me a review, there was no shortage of headlines and eye-witness accounts for the morning papers.

SINGER ARRESTED FOR SEXUAL DANCE
MUSCLE DANCER GETS JURY TRIAL
VAUDEVILLE STAR WIGGLES TO JAIL

THE MORNING OREGONIAN. MONDAY, NOVEMBER 7, 1910.

SINGER PREVENTED FROM APPEARING ON STAGE WILL FIGHT CASE IN COURT.

MISS SOPHIE TUCKER, WHO DENIES SHE SOUGHT TO RIDICULE MRS. BALDWIN.

MUSCLE DANCER GETS JURY TRIAL

Intends to Repeat Her Performance for Benefit of Twelve Men.

When the case of Miss Sophie Tucker, charged with giving an objectionable performance at Pantages Theater, was called in the Police Court this morning, her attorneys demanded a jury trial. Judge Tazwell entered the order for a trial by jury Wednesday at 2 P. M. It is said that Miss Tucker will repeat the performance which caused vigorous action by Mrs. Lola G. Baldwin, superintendent of the Department of Public Safety for Women, for the benefit of the jury, declaring that her songs are copyrighted and are sung the country over.

Mrs. Baldwin immediately placed two warrants for Miss Tucker's arrest on state charges in the hands of the police, the amount of bail in each case being fixed at $250. When District Attorney Cameron learned of this action he said it was done without his knowledge or consent, and he feared would have an unfavorable effect as regards the jury trial. Deputy District Attorney Hennessy, in view of the fact that Miss Tucker is already under a bond on the charge, indorsed on the state complaints an order releasing her on her own recognizance. She was taken to police headquarters by her attorney and surrendered into custody, being immediately given her release until the date of preliminary examination.

Miss Tucker has been deserted by the management of Pantages Theater in her trouble, and is left not only friendless, but penniless. Manager Walker, she says, refused to pay her for more than three days' services at the theater, despite her contract, and the fact that she was willing to give any kind of performance required.

"This is not the first time Pantages has sinned in this respect," said Mrs. Baldwin. "There have been other objectionable performances there previously."

Miss Tucker and her lawyer had a conference with Mayor Simon and Mrs. Baldwin Saturday afternoon, at which time the girl offered to allow the authorities to select the songs she should sing and to appear on the stage in street costume, if desired, instead of her dress with the long train. Mrs. Baldwin protested against her performing at all, and said that if she went on the stage in any kind of act the state warrants would be filed. The Mayor thereupon said that her appearance at the theater would be entirely forbidden.

"I think that when we stopped the objectionable performances and made it necessary for this actress to appear in court to defend herself, her engagement having ended, we went far enough," said District Attorney Cameron. "The Pantages people have deserted her in her plight, and won't pay her according to

SINGER'S IRE IS UP

Sophie Tucker to Fight Charges in Court.

ACT NOT BAD, SHE SAYS

VAUDEVILLE SINGER WILL BE PROSECUTED

Prosecution of Sophie Tucker, singer at a local theater, will not be dropped, although the actress was removed from the bill yesterday. Mrs. Lola G. Baldwin, of the department of public safety for women, declares she will be in court Monday with her witnesses to testify in the disorderly conduct charge against Miss Tucker. The second warrant, charging her with

The police allowed a couple of reporters to interview me in my jail cell and a fellow from the Oregon Gazette gave me the lowdown on the woman who had the officers arrest me. Lola G. Baldwin had been making waves for a few months, trying to close all of the city's Vaudeville houses for what she considered to be indecent entertainment. I was her first successful arrest.

"All that's fine and dandy, but which one of you mugs called me a muscle dancer?" I asked.

"That was direct from the horse's mouth," answered the reporter, smiling.

"I think you were talking to the other end of the horse. Take this down, boys: Never in my four years on stage have I been so humiliated. I demand a jury trial and I intend to sue the Portland Police Department and Miss Lola G. (as in *grump*) Baldwin for $100,000 each. They have soiled my good name and now they are both going to pay for it. You got that?"

They got it and so did every paper in the United States. Next thing you know, I got a wire right to my jail cell from the Boss.

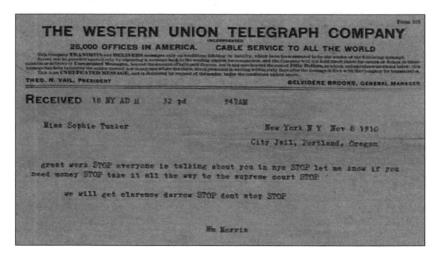

I sent a message to my new lawyer friend Pence Egbert, who immediately reached out to the local district attorney and we were all assembled in the courtroom the next day.

"Your Honor, my client, Miss Tucker, is willing to drop her two $100,000 lawsuits if she gets a public apology from the City and Miss Baldwin," declared my attorney.

"Judge, as the District Attorney of this city, I have been authorized by the Mayor and the entire City Council to sincerely apologize for any harm caused and will reimburse Miss Tucker for any salary lost," replied the city attorney. Everyone turned toward the Grump.

"I'll apologize to that woman when hell freezes over," she spat. I started to get out of my chair but Pence grabbed my arm.

"Lola, we are all reasonable people here," the judge said, trying to soothe her. "I understand you had a particular problem with just one of Sophie's songs. Is that true?"

"The whole act was questionable, Judge. But one was outrageously vile."

"And which song was it?"

"'The Angle Worm Wiggle'," replied Baldwin.

"I saw her do that one in July. I still chuckle when I think about it. Who else here has seen 'The Angle Worm Wiggle'?"

Everyone in the courtroom raised their hand.

"Did anyone here besides Lola find this song vile?"

No one said a word.

"Your Honor," Lola steamed, "it wasn't just the song. It was her wiggle dance. It had heavy lewd overtones."

"I object to the word heavy!" I yelled. Everyone bit their tongues trying not to laugh.

"Now, Mrs. Baldwin," continued the judge, "I saw this act and I don't recall a dance at all, let alone an obscene one. Sophie, in the interest of fairness, would you mind demonstrating your wiggle dance for me now so I can make a fair ruling?"

I conferred with my lawyer, and then I stood up and approached the bench.

Lola G. Baldwin

"Your honor, first I reach in my pocket and pull out one ring at a time and put them on my fingers." I took out my props and put them on my hands without any dramatics.

"Then I show the audience the rings."

I turned around and lifted up my hands to the people in the courtroom. This time though, there were no footlights to make them shimmer.

"And then, I do a little dance with the rings on."

As mildly as I could, I shook one hip.

"Your honor, I object!" screamed Lola. "That was nothing at all like the dance she did on stage!"

"Who was there last night?" asked the judge, and nearly everyone in the court raised their hands.

"Is Sophie telling the truth? Is this what she did yesterday afternoon?

All fifty people nodded at the same time.

"Hogwash," blurted Lola.

"Judge," interrupted Egbert. "Maybe Miss Baldwin would like to show us the parts of the dance we all seemed to miss."

"I'd be glad to, your Honor."

Baldwin got out of her chair and walked up in front of the judge, and proceeded to swivel and shake like nothing I had ever seen before. She looked like a witch on a runaway broom. She looked like a bag of sticks in an earthquake. I thought the judge was going to burst, that's how hard he was trying not to laugh. After a minute or two of bizarre gyrations, Baldwin huffed and puffed her way back to her seat.

"Mrs. Baldwin," began the stunned judge, "if Miss Tucker did what you just showed us, you would have grounds for arrest. I'm also quite confident that she wouldn't be making a living on the stage."

I consulted with my attorney and he stood up.

"Your honor, my client has just informed me that, due to the extraordinary display of dancing we all just witnessed, if Mrs. Baldwin drops her charges, no public apology will be necessary."

With a defeated nod from Lola, the judge banged his gavel and dismissed all lawsuits with regard to my wiggle or lack thereof.

When I arrived in Sacramento the next week, they were lined up around the block for every performance to see the girl whose wiggling put her in jail. The Boss had hit the nail right on the head. Get yourself arrested and become a star.

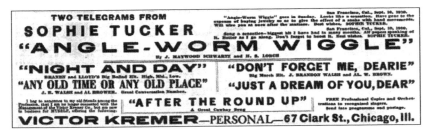

That wasn't the last time I got arrested, however. In 1960, New York City's Mayor Wagner was trying to crack down on the mafia-run nightclub business. He pushed the city council to pass a new law requiring everyone working in the café industry to be fingerprinted and carry a city-issued cabaret identification card. I thought it was ridiculous to lump the entertainers with all the regular café employees, so I saw this as another opportunity to drum up a little bit of publicity from behind bars. When I got my notice to come in for fingerprinting, I called my columnist buddy Earl Wilson and told him to print that the cops would have to come down to the club and drag me in kicking and screaming if they wanted my ink marks.

At first everyone thought it was a joke, but then some of Wagner's opposition took my side to embarrass the Mayor. Even Bob Hope got in in the action, telling the Daily News, "I can't be seen associating with the dangerous Sophie Tucker."

Queen Elizabeth, Ted Shapiro, Sophie and Bob Hope.

Right before my show a few nights later in the International Room at the Waldorf Astoria, two embarrassed rookie policemen came to get me. I asked them if it would be all right if we went after I finished my show and they agreed. I guess they didn't consider me a high flight risk. In return, I got the boys in blue ringside seats.

"Ladies and gentlemen, I have some exciting news. After the show tonight, I've just been told I'm going to a special singing engagement up the river. Is that right boys?"

I had the spotlight shine right on my new boyfriends in blue.

"I'm sorry ladies and gentlemen. The officers just informed me I got it wrong. I'm not going to sing. I'm going to Sing-Sing."

After the show was over the cops escorted me to their squad car and I insisted on being handcuffed just like any other prisoner. It made for a much better photo opportunity when they lead me into the police station, which was conveniently surrounded by journalists when I arrived. *Someone* may have tipped them off while I was backstage changing out of my performing gown.

"Welcome to showbiz, officers!" I laughed.

The next morning my mission was accomplished. In every paper across the country, there was 76-year-old Sophie Tucker's newly issued café card with my smiling mug shot on one side and my thumb print on the other.

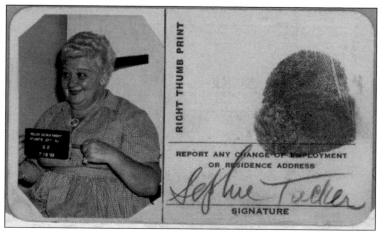

Sophie's cabaret license.

Chapter 22

Tell Me You're Sorry

Dear Mr. Albee,

My name is Sophie Tucker. Maybe you saw me in the Ziegfeld Follies of 1909. Or maybe you have heard one of the ten records I did for my good friend Thomas Edison. After being in show business for five years, I would very much love to work on the Keith circuit.

Enclosed find a dozen notices I have received in the past year. I am ready to work hard and fill your theaters every night. I would like to schedule an appointment at your earliest convenience to start talking about our future together.

Best wishes,
Sophie Tucker

By 1911, only the guys who built Big Ben had worked as hard as me to make the big time. Even though I was thrilled with everything the Boss had done for me, I took it upon myself to contact E.F. Albee, who ran the prestigious Keith circuit. It was the highest level you could reach in Vaudeville, but if you wanted to work for Albee you had to follow his very strict set of rules. None of his acts were allowed to use foul language or innuendo, women's costumes had to be tasteful, and he didn't tolerate any sort of political humor.

E.F. Albee

While I thought I could just recast myself into the Albee model, the Boss was far more skeptical. Albee was successful because he recruited only the most conservative, tried and true talent from smaller circuits, which meant that he was always behind the times. Despite that, he sold expensive seats that attracted snobby crowds who were willing to pay for a watered down taste of Vaudeville—minus all of the racy parts that made it exciting.

"You're saying I'm not wholesome enough?" I asked Morris.

"Honey, I love you like my daughter, so I mean it tenderly when I say your act is so unwholesome you'd give Albee syphilis. You're ready for the big time but the big time isn't ready for you. Albee wouldn't know what to do with you! Maybe in a few years."

"Years?" I sputtered. "I could be dead by then!"

"Then put it in your will. I, Sophie Tucker, being of sound mind and body, ask that my ashes be scattered along the Keith Circuit," the Boss joked.

Instead of sending me to Albee, Morris got me a role in a musical called *Louisiana Lou*. I knew I was in over my head from the first moment I set foot on stage in the practice hall. We only had two weeks to rehearse before opening night and every day the director took away one of my lines. He loved the way I did my songs but I was still not much of an actress. Even the star of the show, Alexander Carr, stayed late and ran lines with me. I promised the director I would get my act together when the curtain went up, but secretly, I was worried.

On opening night I still had my two songs but only five measly lines. With thirty minutes until curtain I was as nervous as I'd ever been, but I was all made up and ready to put on my big taffeta costume. However, after looking everywhere in the women's dressing room, it was nowhere to be found. A stagehand ran to the rehearsal hall a few blocks away and, thankfully, returned with my dress just seconds before I was due to make my entrance. Two dressers shoved my arms into my gown and pushed me out on stage. At least the commotion made me forget my butterflies.

"Why Miss Amelia," said Carr, "you look so beautiful. Turn around so we can see all of you."

As I twirled in a circle the audience roared with laughter. You know me; if I get a laugh on stage, I milk it. This time I had no idea why everyone was laughing, but I twirled around that stage six or seven times until the crowd was in hysterics. It wasn't until I got back into the wings that I learned my dressers, in their hurry to get me out on stage, hadn't done up the back of my dress and my 100% Hebrew National *tuchus* was flapping in the breeze.

Between scenes, the dressers closed my trapdoor and I managed to give some pretty good performances from there on out. I grew more comfortable week by week, and even threw in an ad-libbed line here and there. I came up with a real corker when Alexander got a little too fresh during one of our love scenes. I was wearing a beautiful forest green dress, so when he squeezed me much tighter than necessary, I turned to the audience and said, "Mr. Beauregard. Will you please get off my pool table? You're starting to scratch."

Alexander and Sophie in a promotional shot for Louisiana Lou.

As the months flew by and I got all of my original lines back (and then some!), everyone was surprised to see Alexander, a seasoned performer, become our production's problem child. The rest of the cast had become one big happy family, but Alexander was jealous that I was getting most of the laughs and encores from the audience and also the lion's share of the press. What started as a star vehicle for him ended up being a hit show because of me. He got downright nasty for a while, until I suggested we do a few comedy duets in place of my solo encores. A little more stage time seemed to do the trick and we were friends again by the end of our eighteen-month run.

We played our final shows in Boston. A chorus boy named Joey Trinity was a local and his mother, herself a retired hoofer, offered to host the whole cast for a family clambake. Boy, did we get more than we bargained for. On a beautiful day at the end of June, we had ourselves one hell of a party at the Trinity beach house. There was enough food for all fifty of us to have three lobsters, four dozen steamers and six ears of corn apiece. The cast got good and blitzed on several kegs of beer and I even spotted Alexander doing the backstroke in the Atlantic in his full suit and hat.

Suffice it to say, the final matinee the next day was not an award-winning performance.

I have a lot of wonderful memories of *Louisiana Lou*, but my favorite involved my five-year-old co-star Hazel Robinson. She had all of one job in the show, which was to bring me a basket of roses on stage. She was an itty bitty thing with a big scar on her face from a dog bite she got as an infant. Even worse, she had a nagging cough anyone could've identified as the beginning stages of tuberculosis. I used to let Hazel play in my dressing room and I'd slip her candies to soothe her throat, but eventually she got too ill to continue on with us and dropped out of the production.

Some thirty years later I was performing at a nightclub in Pittsburgh. At the end of each show I made a habit of getting off the stage, walking up the aisle and shaking as many hands as I could in thanks. During one of these evening exits I caught sight of a familiar face.

"Hazel, it that you?" I screamed. Little Hazel's scar had faded, but I would recognize her punim anywhere. She had beaten the tuberculosis and grown up to marry a salesman who'd chosen my show to entertain a bunch of his clients and their wives, all of whom seemed pretty scandalized by my blue jokes. Hazel didn't give a rat's ass, though, and greeted me with a big hug and kiss as soon as I came by her seat.

I received a beautiful letter from Hazel's daughter not too long ago. In it, she said that night led to some fireworks at home, but her mother said it was a small price to pay for one of her favorite memories.

Maybe it was the old dog bite scar but somehow you remembered her. Aside from the birth of my brother and me, she always said that was one of the high moments of her life.

Father was furious. He felt a disreputable past had just been publicly exposed and he had a few words with mother at bedtime. She didn't give one goddamn. The salesmen's wives could drop dead. Sophie Tucker had remembered her!

God bless you for those candies you pushed in a little girl's mouth about half a century ago. Stay young, Sophie.......the world needs you.

An excerpt from Hazel's daughter's letter.

When the play closed in the fall of 1912, I sat down once again at Reuben's with the Boss and he decided it was time to send me back to Vaudeville. I thought he'd heard from Albee and, at long last, I was being called up to the majors. Instead, Morris insisted that I take in all of the current shows around New York to see how Vaudeville had changed over the previous year and a half. I knew I'd have to work up a new act, but we reasoned that with a few tweaks to my old material I could slide right back into headlining.

I sat through ten bills over the next five days and watched nearly all of the acts that were on the circuit with me back in 1910. There were a few new ones here and there, but even those were carbon copies of the same old thing. When I found myself yawning through another dusty routine, I understood what the Boss was getting at. Nothing had changed and the audiences knew it. Even Nora Bayes and Eva Tanguay couldn't pack a house anymore.

"So?" asked Morris a week later, wiggling his eyebrows over a knish at Reuben's.

"Vaudeville needs to be shaken up worse than flat seltzer!" I exclaimed. Morris nodded in agreement.

"Even E.F. Albee's shows are slumping. His whole chain has been sleepwalking for the last two years. What he needs is something original. Whoever comes up with the next big thing is going to win all the marbles."

"I'm shaped like a marble," I said, taking a bite of a pastrami sandwich.

"You, my dear, are my big, beautiful shooter. Together we are going to conquer Broadway."

First, though, I needed to get my feet wet again. I was too rusty after being part of a large cast to be a top-billed solo act on stage, so I decided to play some small-fry venues to work out the kinks and oil up my joints. The Boss put me on a bill and I began to feel at home after a week or so, but I hadn't counted on a round of hazing from my veteran trouper friends. The Vaudeville old guard didn't look too kindly on those who crossed over to the legitimate stage and then came back. Luckily, it was mostly in good fun. I'd stayed in touch with everyone while I was touring with *Louisiana Lou* so there weren't any real sour grapes, but they still had some tricks up their sleeves that would make even a magician do a double take.

It began one night when I heard someone out front snoring during one of my big sentimental ballads. I ignored it until it got so loud I could hardly hear myself sing, and I motioned to the orchestra to stop playing.

"Ladies and gentlemen, I'm sorry for the interruption but someone out there seems to have turned in early tonight. Does anyone see our Sleeping Beauty?" I asked.

The entire audience pointed to the stage right upper box.

"Folks, drastic times call for drastic measures. Instead of singing, which seems impossible at the present time, I would like to demonstrate my range of major league pitches, okay? Usually I would use a regular old baseball, but tonight I have something else in mind. Molly? Can you go to my dressing room and bring back all my shoes?"

The audience laughed and applauded while I waited for Molly, who deposited a huge pile of heels in the middle of the stage with a little curtsey. The chainsaw in the balcony continued to buzz away.

"Pitching, my friends, is a fine art. Sometimes you want to start with a strike right down the middle," I announced, and hurled a pump right up toward the balcony. "Missed by a foot," I said, winking at my pun. The audience groaned.

"I forgot my windup," I said, flinging one of my two-tones with tassels as high as I could and knocking off the sleeper's stevedore. Still, he continued to saw away.

"No more fooling around!" I yelled, grabbing a high heel. "This ought to leave a mark. How about a countdown? Three, two…"

With that, my old friend Jack Rose woke up, waved to me, stood up, and bolted from the balcony. Too bad my missile had already been fired in his direction. Jack had that bump on the back of his head for a month.

Another night, in the middle of the same tender ballad, I was suddenly joined on stage by a midget dressed in a top hat and tails. I stopped the music and looked down at the dapper little man.

"Yes?" I asked, braced for what was sure to be a ridiculous explanation.

"Please don't forget to bring some cat food home tonight, my dear."

"Cat food?" I asked, trying to follow his lead.

"Yes, cat food," he said, nodding his head. "For our little pussycat, Mr. Whiskers. I'm afraid if we don't feed him, he'll confuse me for a mouse." The audience laughed hysterically.

"Ladies and gentlemen, please forgive me. I'm being rude," I said, playing along. "This is my new husband Big Bob. In an effort to support President Taft and his new austerity budget, I have decided to cut back on the size of my men…but in *height only*."

Big Bob turned to the audience and wiggled his eyebrows up and down. The crowd hooted and hollered so hard I thought they'd bring down the roof. At least my fellow actors had the decency to prank my act with good bits.

From then on, everything went along quietly until the week I played at Hammerstein's. By then, I had almost convinced myself that my old trouper friends had welcomed me back into their fold. But I should've known something kooky would happen at a theater that was famous for nut acts. Over the years, I'd played at Hammerstein's with a diver who leapt from a thirty-foot platform into a two-foot bucket of water and a high wire act who walked a tightrope strung from the balcony to the stage, over the audience, without a net. There was an old story about a fellow who pitched an act to Mr. Hammerstein. His big finish would be shooting himself in the head. The only reason Hammerstein passed was because the wannabe headliner didn't have an encore.

The trouble started the first night when I sang a peppy song called "Let's Go Up in Your Tree House and Leave the Rest to Me." There was a high note in the chorus and every time I hit it, someone backstage gave me a loud raspberry.

By the third night it was still going on. High note, then raspberry. I was starting to get a little hot under the collar about it. A good comic knew when to quit, or at least when to show himself. I couldn't see the culprit from the stage and I'd had enough.

On the fifth night, I was determined to nail the bastard. I saved "Tree House" for last and made sure I was close to the wings so I could dart offstage and catch the joker red-handed. Before I even got to the high note the raspberries started coming fast and furious. Not just one, but a whole series of rude noises that repeated like a slow machine gun.

I came through the side curtain ready to kill, but there was no one to murder except the pony from the dog and pony act. It seemed his ears were sensitive to my singing and he expressed his displeasure by nickering through his lips just like a human blowing a raspberry. I couldn't believe I'd managed to let a pony get the better of me. To show I was a good sport, I grabbed his reins and we did a duet encore of "Camptown Races." The pony did the "doo-dahs" and we both got a standing ovation.

Sophie and another horse.

Dear Mr. Albee,

After six letters, may I now call you E. F.? As I told you in my last several notes, things went spectacularly with my musical "Louisiana Lou." But like all good things, this too came to an end and I have proudly returned to the Vaudeville stage.

I have learned so much that performing seems second nature to me, but I realize I still have more lessons to soak up. Of course, I know I cannot possibly reach the pinnacle of success until I play in your theaters. Now that my musical has closed, maybe this would be the perfect time for us to get together. Time's a-wasting. I'm no spring chicken, and I'll never see twenty-six again. I'm ready whenever you are, E.F.!

Best wishes,
Sophie Tucker

After six weeks on the circuit, I had a whole new act and I was back at the top of my game. When the Boss called me to meet him at his real office, not Reuben's, I was convinced that all my letter writing had finally paid off and I was going to get my shot at the Keith Circuit. Instead, I found Morris looking like someone had died. I quietly took a seat.

"I'm being blackballed by Albee," he said with a sigh. "He won't book any of my acts in his theaters. He stopped talking to me a couple of months ago when I sold my American Theater chain to the Fritz brothers instead of him, and now it looks like he's taking it out on my acts."

"How do you know?" I asked.

"Well, one by one, my headliners have been leaving me. And then in today's *Variety* there was a press release from E. F. saying, from now on, Max Hart would be his exclusive booker for the Keith Chain. I've got no acts working for him anymore."

"And this guy Hart won't play ball?"

"Would you? If Albee found out he booked any of my acts, he would can Max on the spot."

I was heartbroken. I'd worked for nearly two years to get on Albee's bill, but I would rather eat dirt than work for someone who'd been such a bastard to the Boss. I'd do anything—another musical, more acts in other theaters, whatever it took to put William Morris back on top. The Boss, however, had other ideas.

"Soph, I appreciate your loyalty, but that's not how we're going to play this. You're going to sign with Max Hart. The big time is finally ready for you. Go and bad mouth me, or do whatever you have to do so Hart takes a shine to you. It won't bother me a bit. I know we're still pals. Before long, I'll come back bigger than ever."

I was stunned into silence for a few moments, but eventually I stood up and gave the Boss a big hug. "Us good ones gotta stick together, right?" I reminded him.

"Forever," said my mentor, giving me a squeeze.

That day I wrote Hart a letter from the deli, over one of the saddest tongue sandwiches I'd ever eaten. The tongue was still delicious, of course, but it just didn't taste the same without the Boss chattering nonstop across the table and putting away his third knish. When I didn't get a response from Hart—or from Albee, to any of my ten previous letters—I asked all my friends on Max's roster to recommend me. You would think that the combined swinging power of Eddie Cantor, Jimmy Durante, Irving Berlin and a dozen other headliners would knock old Soph a homerun, but I struck out. I didn't hear a peep from Hart.

So, I began going to his office every day. Unlike Edison who burned the midnight oil, Hart arrived to work before I was awake and left shortly after I had to report to the theater for my evening shows. His office door remained firmly closed whenever I was in his lobby.

After a weekend of serious brainstorming, I knew that if I was going to get anywhere with Hart I needed to go undercover. I took a week's leave from the stage and, that Monday, I got up at five in the morning to stake out the front door of Hart's office building. I knew what he looked like from his pictures in *Variety*, so it was easy to spot him when he showed up at eight o'clock sharp wearing a distinctive straw boater with a bright red band. Detective Tucker deduced two important things: first, that Max would be easy to spot with that hat, and second, that I could sleep two extra hours each morning for the rest of the week.

After that, I waited. Hart emerged around lunch time and I followed the boater with the red band all the way to the hat rack at Bernie's Grill. He ate a corned beef on rye with a cup of coffee while reading the New York Tribune, alone. After lunch, he went back to the office until six o'clock, sharp. Then he walked briskly home. In fact, he walked briskly everywhere, which was surprising for a man who looked to be at least sixty.

I stayed back a safe distance from his brownstone on West 24th Street. It was obviously a well-to-do, stuffy neighborhood and I would stick out like a sore thumb in my trendy dress, particularly if anyone spotted me creeping around suspiciously behind a mailbox. I found a dark alley across the street and waited. I was thinking about calling it a night, but my patience was rewarded when out popped Mr. and Mrs. Hart. They walked a block to Broadway and hailed a taxi. I shoved aside a guy getting into nearby cab and hopped in the back.

"Hey lady, my aunt is dying in a hospital!" he screamed.

"Don't worry. I die once a week on stage! There's nothing to it," I said as I waved goodbye.

Then, for the first and only time in my life, I got to say that immortal phrase of the silver screen.

"Follow that cab!"

By the end of the week I knew every one of Max's lunch spots, where Mrs. Hart shopped and got her hair done, and all the couple's favorite restaurants and night clubs. With a little help from some friends who were playing those same clubs, I put my master plan in motion.

First up, I had to get to Mrs. Hart. After all of my detective work I knew exactly where Gertrude was headed whenever she left her house, so my number one order of business Monday morning was to idle around Gialetti's Curio Shop. That's where Mrs. Hart always began her week, picking up some high-class *tchotchkes*[1] for her house.

Once I saw her step into the store, I waited a few moments and then made my big entrance. I strode up to the shop owner and projected like I was trying to sell my story to the cheap seats.

---

1   *Tchotchkes* – Knickknacks.

"How do you do? My name is Sophie Tucker. I just moved into the neighborhood and I was looking for some new items for my apartment," I announced.

"Nice to meet you, Miss Tucker. Please, take a look around. I would be happy to show you any of our merchandise. Welcome to 25th Street," said the woman behind the counter.

Since the shop was the size of a shoebox, there was no way Mrs. Hart could've missed the conversation. She investigated a set of silver candlesticks while I investigated her from behind a beautiful armoire, and eventually she left and went on with her shopping down the street.

I didn't want to be too obvious, so I sat tight for the rest of the morning, and then headed uptown to close my matinee at the 108th Street Theater. I made it back downtown in time to beat Gertrude to a lovely little flower shop called The Daffodil Place, a spot she visited every evening before dinner. I hustled into the shop, did my little routine about being new in the neighborhood, and told the florist exactly what sort of bouquet I was looking for. Gertrude entered while the florist was gathering my bunch of flowers.

"Here we go Miss Tucker," said the florist, handing me an enormous arrangement of irises and black-eyed susans.

"Oh please, call me Sophie. We're gonna be old friends!" I said, handing him a dollar and stepping to the side to allow Mrs. Hart to approach the counter. I pretended to rummage through my purse.

"I have your usual Monday order ready to go, Mrs. Hart. Irises, carnations, and black—isn't that funny! It's almost the same order as Miss Tucker. What do you think of that?"

"I think you have two customers with very good taste in flowers," smiled Mrs. Hart.

I took the next day off, but was right back to work the following day for an operation that required me to be quick on my feet. I knew that Gertrude liked to go clothes shopping on Wednesdays, but I wasn't sure which store she would go to first. I followed her from her house to the corner of 7th Avenue, where she made a right. That meant she had to be going to Aberdeen's. I sprinted three blocks north on the opposite side of the street and managed to make it inside the store and into the fitting room before Gertrude arrived.

"Hello Mrs. Hart, how are you today?" asked Marian, the shop girl. "We have a whole rack of new dresses that you might like."

"Thank you very much," Gertrude replied kindly.

I seized the moment and burst out of the dressing room.

"Oh, Miss Tucker! That dress looks divine," said Marian.

"I do like it, but I think it makes me look fat. What do you think, sis?" I asked Gertrude. "I think Marian here works on commission. I need someone who'll tell me the truth."

"I think it's stunning," answered Gertrude. "That's why I bought the same one last week."

"You did?" I exclaimed, playing dumb. "Well, I bet it looks beautiful on you. You're a pencil. It's a little harder to find something that suits us redwoods."

With that, I returned to the fitting room and put on my original dress. When I came out, I thanked Gertrude for her advice and handed the dress back to Marian.

"Why don't you keep this on hold for me until I lose a hundred pounds?" I asked. I could hear both women chuckling as I walked out the door.

I put my gumshoe routine on ice until the weekend, when it was time for my next big play. I needed an accomplice for this one, so I bribed James Bennett, a new tapper low on the bill at the theater, to play along as my date to one of the Hart's after hours clubs. He whined about how tired he was until I promised to buy him no less than four Old Fashioneds, which put a sudden spring in his step. We were going out.

Jimmy and I got to the Cotillion Club around eleven and the maître d' sat us in the cheap seats. Since Jimmy was about to clean me out paying for his booze, there was no way I could afford to grease the wheels for a better spot. Besides, tonight wasn't about seeing the show from the front row. I urged Jimmy to drain his drink so we could get on the dance floor and casually waltz past Mr. and Mrs. Hart, who were seated ringside. We slowly made our way to the front row of tables. Jimmy swirled me around and I pretended to see Gertie for the first time. I waved hello, got a wave back and motioned for her to join us on the dance floor.

"What's the big idea?" asked Jimmy, longingly eyeing his second Old Fashioned being served at our distant table. This kid could have hired himself out as a telescope.

"The big idea is getting me on the Keith circuit. That woman is the power behind the throne," I said.

Sure enough, Gertie coaxed Max out of his chair for the next song. I knew Max wasn't much of a dancer from the other times I'd followed them to a club, but he would usually take Gertie for at least one spin around the dance floor each night. I knew that this was likely the only chance I'd have to make my move, so I told Jimmy it was time to earn his booze. We two-stepped over toward the Harts and purposefully bumped right into them.

"Excuse us!" I apologized. "James is teaching me this new dance. Hello again! It seems like I'm bumping into you a lot lately."

Mrs. Hart smiled and asked me how I was settling into my new apartment, proving that she had been listening to me, the human megaphone, during all those planned run-ins. She introduced me to her husband just as the conductor of the orchestra was calling for a partner swap. I shoved Jimmy toward Gertrude and grabbed Max, and off we spun around the dance floor. I wasn't just getting my face-to-face time with him—we were practically cheek to cheek. I couldn't have planned it better myself.

"I thought you said you were just learning this dance," said Max, after it became clear that I knew the steps after all.

"Oh, you know how boys can be. They always like to think they're teaching us girls something or other. You seem like a man who likes a straight shooter though, Rex. What's your business? Are you a cop?"

"It's Max," he said. "And no, that's not what I do."

"Are you a barber? No, that's not it. I'll bet you shine shoes in Grand Central."

"You're way off," he said with a smile. I was winning him over. "I'm in show business."

"I thought you looked familiar!" I exclaimed. "You're Ernesto the knife thrower! I didn't recognize you without your turban. Is Gertie your assistant?"

"Not even close. I'm a booking agent."

"You're a bookie?" I hissed in a stage whisper. "Then keep your voice down! No respectable girl wants to be seen dancing with a criminal."

"Not a bookie, a booking agent!" he laughed. "I'm Max Hart. I'm the fellow who decides which acts go on the Keith Theater stages."

When the song ended, I grabbed Gertie and Jimmy and we all returned to the Harts' table. This time, I did slip a few bucks to the waiter for an extra couple of chairs, which appeared like magic. Jimmy looked at me like he was a puppy and I was eating a steak dinner, so I quickly ordered him another Old Fashioned.

"Gertie," I said when we were all settled. "I just found out you're married to Max Hart, the great booking agent."

"He's not so great," laughed Gertie, playfully slapping his arm.

"Even though you aren't a bookie, Max, I'd like to make you a friendly wager. No money, just a favor if I win. Gert, what's your favorite song?"

"I don't know…'You Made Me Love You'?" she answered.

"I like that one too. Okay, here's the bet, Maxie. I'm gonna go up there to the bandstand and sing your wife's favorite song. Gertie, you're going to be the judge. If you think I'm good enough to work for a week at one of your husband's theaters, all you have to do is say so. If not, I'll buy us all a round of champagne."

"I like the sound of that," smiled Mrs. Hart.

"What if the band doesn't know the tune?" asked Max.

"Want to make it two weeks on your stage if I win?" I wisecracked.

"Never mind, just go sing the damn song," he said with a smirk.

I got up and sang the sweetest rendition of "You Made Me Love You" anyone had ever heard, making sure not to deviate too much from the record in order to keep Gertie happy. Of course, it didn't hurt that I happened to hear her mention to a shop owner that this particular ditty was her favorite. Nor did it hurt that the conductor was the brother of a tap dancer I played with in Elmira, New York in 1907. It also didn't hurt that I'd gotten this conductor the musical arrangement from the sheet music company courtesy of Irving Berlin, as well as three other night spots the Harts frequented just in case they'd gone elsewhere that evening. I also thought about giving all two hundred people in the club a ten-spot each, but that turned out not to be necessary. When I finished, I got a standing ovation.

"Max, if you don't hire this girl you're an idiot," insisted my new benefactor Gertie as soon as I got back to the table.

"Sure, sure, but I think I've been snookered. Now I remember where I've heard your name before," frowned Max. "Aren't you the girl that's been sitting outside my office for a month?"

"Well, I'll be! Aren't you that guy I've been trying to see for a month?" I exclaimed, acting surprised.

"Be in my office at eleven tomorrow," directed Hart, shaking his head. "I don't know how you did it, but you did. I'll put you on my schedule. Just promise me you won't be appearing out of thin air anywhere else we go, okay?"

"Mr. Hart, I only appear out of *fat* air," I said. "But you don't have to worry. I'll make myself disappear until tomorrow morning."

The next day, I rematerialized in Max Hart's office. While he seemed game enough the night before, once he was behind his desk he was all business. Overnight, he did some detective work of his own, and thankfully all of my pals in the business said I was a good egg. I joked that I was also shaped like one, but Max's stony face made it clear that he was no William Morris. I instantly missed the Boss's wiggling eyebrows.

"Listen, Mr. Hart," I said, trying to level with him. "I'm going to make Mr. Albee a lot of money. Nobody works harder than me. I'll play in any spot—I'll even sing in a chorus. And I promise, if you book me next week anywhere on the Keith Chain, I will be your top headliner in a matter of months."

"Are you finished?" Max asked. I nodded. "I've got some things to say, and I don't like being interrupted. You're here because I want to stay married, and that's about it. Do you understand me?" he asked.

I nodded. Suddenly, I wondered what I'd gotten myself into.

"First of all, I don't care where you've worked before because you've never worked an audience like a Keith audience. These people aren't a bunch of bums, like the crowd at the American Theaters. The Keith clientele pays top dollar to see classy shows. I'm sure you've heard all about E.F. Albee and his strict rules, so we won't have to go over that. But you can bet your bottom dollar on this: if you decide to test the waters with some blue material just once, you'll be banned to the hinterlands forever. You won't even be able to get a job singing for nickels on the corner. Am I making myself clear?"

I nodded yes, again.

"Repeat it back to me."

"The Keith audience shits strawberry ice cream, and I better not fuck around with E.F," I summarized.

"You won't last a week," he said, rubbing his temples.

After my meeting with Mr. Hart, I went directly to Reuben's for a sandwich. Eugene and Willie Howard were at the restaurant and, once they understood that I'd just come from a meeting with the infamous Max Hart, they showered me with kisses and offered up their remaining sour dills. The Howard brothers had long been on the Keith circuit and were excited that perhaps we'd finally share a bill. However, their faces turned paler than their china plates when I told them Max had assigned me to the Keith Theater in Flatbush, Brooklyn.

After Willie finished choking on his sandwich, he took a deep breath and grabbed my hand. He patted it gently.

"Here's my advice to you, Soph. Get yourself a suit of armor and two six-shooters with extra ammo. That theater didn't earn the nickname 'Dante's Inferno' for nothing."

I thought they were pulling my leg. After the Barbary Coast in San Francisco I thought I'd seen everything, but Willie and Eugene swore they'd rather play the Coast for a week wearing tutus than set foot on the Flatbush Keith stage ever again. The entire audience was controlled by a clique of thugs who sat up in the balcony and ate new acts for lunch. The leader was a huge bruiser named Benny the Brute, who would command his cronies with a thumbs down or thumbs up after each act. Most got the thumbs down, which was the signal for the balcony to rain pennies and fruit down on the stage. Eugene insisted he'd once watched Benny make a magician disappear with a flying watermelon. Worse yet, the theater was half empty because no one in their right mind would sit in the orchestra level for fear they might wind up covered in the balcony's off-target tomatoes.

"Boys," I said. "Don't worry about me. I'm gonna be the first rookie act to make it in Flatbush. You'll see. If I managed to get into Hart's office, I can win over some sons of bitches in a stinking Brooklyn theater. It's gonna be great."

"What is? Your eulogy?" cried Willie. The Howards shook their heads and raised their seltzer glasses.

"To Sophie Tucker," intoned Eugene gravely. "She was a fine performer, felled tragically in a freak hailstorm of pennies. May she rest in one cent pieces."

I had just a handful of days to prepare for my Flatbush debut, so I quickly decided on my songs and gathered my charts for the orchestra. Then I came up with some snappy new entrances to spice up my old routine, and arranged a special rental agreement with a dress shop so I'd have easy access to fourteen different gowns, one for each performance.

I wasn't set to debut until Monday, but I arrived at the Flatbush Keith early Saturday afternoon and bought a gallery ticket for twenty-five cents. That was the biggest hint that Max Hart had screwed me; all the other Albee theaters charged fifty cents for their balcony seats, so this was truly the bottom of the barrel of the elite Keith circuit. Since the show didn't start until 2:30, I had my pick of the seats and I set myself up in the highest row. I wanted to be as invisible as possible.

An hour later, the clique started to file into the gallery's center section. Even though it was a nice sunny day they were all wearing long wool overcoats, which I soon found out were hiding enough fruits and vegetables to feed China. Then, five minutes before the curtain, the king arrived. There was no mistaking him. Benny the Brute greeted his fellow hecklers like a general addressing his troops.

As the lights dimmed, Benny stood up.

"Are we ready?" yelled the Brute. His buddies hooted and stomped their feet. "Then let the games begin!"

The first act's name card was placed on an easel off to the right of the stage, but I didn't even have time to read it before it was knocked down by a flying McIntosh. The hecklers cheered as the act, a brother dance team, took the stage. They weren't bad, but after a minute or so of decent soft-shoe, the Brute stood. Up went his fist. Down went his thumb. I could see the two boys on stage wince just before they were pelted by so many pennies it looked like the plague of locusts had arrived. They sprinted off the stage.

It didn't go much better for any of the performers who followed, though I noticed that older singers seemed to get the worst of it. An elderly baritone took the stage and only managed to boom out his first note before the audience turned him into a tossed salad. An older soprano was hit by so many grapes I'm pretty sure she could've opened her own winery and retired. At least that proved Benny had a heart—if he'd called for cantaloupes, they would've had to carry old Brünnhilde off the stage on a stretcher.

Brünnhilde appears in Richard Wagner's opera cycle Der Ring des Nibelungen.

There was only one act the Brute deemed worthy of respect. Benny raised both arms and signaled for silence the moment The Smith Sisters' easel card was placed on stage. Regardless of what the card said, though, I knew the moment they glided out from behind the curtain that it was actually Rosie and Jenny, the Dolly Sisters. I'd met them at a few big benefits around town and, while they were very elegant on stage, the minute the curtain dropped they were wild women who were game for anything. They'd recently been signed to Ziegfeld's 1913 Follies so I assumed they were breaking in a new act under an alias at the worst

shithouse of a theater they could find. If they could make it in Dante's
Inferno, the Follies would be a slice of heaven.

Benny was obviously a thug, but at least he was a thug with good
taste. If the Brute was only going to the cut-rate Flatbush Keith, he
had no idea that the Dolly Sisters were one of the biggest and best
acts in the country. Still, he knew they had something special.
Maybe there was hope after all.

The Dolly Sisters

At the end of the matinee, I followed Benny and his boys to a
neighborhood joint called Mike's, all of their now empty winter coats
slung over their shoulders. The fifty of them piled into the little bar
and, after a few deep breaths, I squared up my shoulders and strode
into the lion's den. Once I got inside, though, I found the bar to be
empty. I stood staring at the bartender, who I presumed to be Mike,

the owner. A faint commotion was coming up from a rickety staircase in the corner that led down to the basement. It seemed like Benny was using that spot as his little clubhouse. I made for the stairs, but the bartender dove out from behind the bar to stop me.

"You can't go down there, sister. That's a men's club. Get it?" he said, turning me around and pushing me back toward the bar.

"Yeah, I read you loud and clear. Men's club—hearts, darts, and farts."

"Hey, that's no way for a lady to talk!" he winced.

"You want me to sing it? Listen bub, I'm not just any lady," I said, thinking on my toes. "I'm Benny's cousin from Rochester. I just got in. He told me to meet him here, at Mike's, 328 Mercy Street, down in the basement."

"Pardon me, toots, but you're full of shit. There's never been a broad down in that club and I'm not about to break the Brute's rules," he said.

Mike seemed serious so I grabbed him by his collar and held my fist an inch from his face.

"Look, Mike. Either you break the Brute's rules or I break your jaw. Which is it gonna be?"

The barkeep must have recognized the family resemblance, because a few moments later I was heading down the stairs toward Benny's private club. The moment my bare ankle and high heel descended into view, everybody went entirely silent, like someone had ripped the needle off a record. *To hell with it*, I thought, and kept going. Maybe they wouldn't like the rest of my hefty package, but there was no turning back now. I walked my ample girth and girdle right into the middle of the room, which was filled with smoke and poker tables, around which were seated some of the most flabbergasted thugs you'd ever see.

"Which one of you boys is Benny the Brute?" I yelled.

"Who wants to know?" responded an equally loud voice in the back of the room.

"Sophie the Shark," I answered. "I'm looking for some high-stakes poker and I heard you run a clean game."

"No broads allowed, hon. Why don't you scram?" answered the voice.

"I'm no broad. I told you, I'm a shark," I answered. "And I can't swim with this purse full of cash weighing me down."

Out from the back of the room strode a behemoth of a man with a mop of bright red hair. Even though I'd seen him in the balcony, it was hard to appreciate that each of the Brute's legs were the size of a tree trunk until they were marching toward me.

"When you walk around town, Benny, do you need to carry a building permit?" I asked. A few of his henchmen chuckled, so I kept going. "Mind if I feel your muscle?"

Benny blushed ever so slightly and flexed one of his biceps into the classic muscle man pose.

"I wasn't talking about your arm, honey," I laughed as I reached down and grabbed Benny's giblets. The giant stared at me like I was Jack and I'd just crawled up his beanstalk.

"Mr. Brute, are you gonna glare at me all night, or are we gonna play poker?" I asked.

"D-Deal," stammered the Brute.

I took the invitation and sat myself down at the table. Benny seated himself directly across from me and the rest of his crew gathered around.

"I'll tell you what Mr. Brute, let's start easy and just get to know each other. Nickel, dime, quarter, three raise max, all right?"

The great heavyweight champ Max Baer was Benny the Brute's little brother.

He nodded and watched me suspiciously as I dealt the cards.

"I really came here today to introduce myself. My name is Sophie Tucker. I'm a Vaudeville singer and I've been beating the bushes all over the whole U.S. of A. for seven years now, and I'll be honest with you. I was up in your gallery today. I've been to Boston, to New Orleans, out to the

Barbary Coast and everywhere in between, and I thought I'd seen every variety of asshole this country has to offer. I gotta hand it to you Brutesy, and I say this with all due respect, you guys are the nastiest of the nasty. You and your boys are the number one meanest group of motherfuckers I've ever met."

I turned over my last card, revealing an ace, which gave me three bullets to win the small pot. I pulled in the coins, stacked them nice and neat and then looked up to see if steam was coming out of the Brute's ears.

Benny pushed back his chair, stood up, slammed his left hand on the table and pointed at me with an index finger the size of a bratwurst. I just about pished my pants until he broke into a big grin.

"Sophie Tucker? I like you!"

The rest of his merry men broke into a loud cheer of approval. I was now an official member of the Flatbush Gallery of the Gods.

I completed my initiation that night at the evening performance. Benny had me sit right next to him and I'm not proud to admit that I even chucked a few cabbages. We headed back to Mike's for a few late night rounds and I worked out the final details of my deal to make Benny's wildest dream come true, and in return, he promised to keep his crew in check for the next week. We sealed our friendship with two quick pokes from his pocketknife on our thumbs and a handshake. We were blood brothers for life. Or should I say Brute brothers?

On Monday, I arrived in my dressing room at eight in the morning to find that Molly had already arranged my gowns and accessories the way I liked. I met with the orchestra leader and we went over all the music breaks and cues until I was satisfied we were on the same page. After seven years, I didn't want to leave anything to chance, so I slipped the maestro an extra twenty dollars to make sure nothing went wrong during my set—which seemed to do the trick, since I received with a big kiss on the cheek and an earful of good wishes before each of my performances.

Dear E. F.,

This is the letter I've been looking forward to sending you for years. So much has happened since my last note, I hardly know where to begin.

A couple of weeks ago I happened to run into Max Hart at the Cotillion Club with his lovely wife Gertrude. The next thing you know, Max insisted I sing a song with the orchestra. He was so impressed he asked when I could start working the Keith circuit.

Although I was booked solid for the following six weeks, I decided to rearrange things and make myself available. Max wanted me to get cracking on the prime route, but I insisted on doing a week out of the spotlight first, to get my feet wet at your Flatbush Theater.

Though the gallery in this particular theater has a reputation for being a little choosy, I've found everyone to be rather lovely so far. Every soul, from the orchestra section all the way up to the last row of the gallery, have been perfect ladies and gentlemen. Not only that, the audiences these first four days and nights have also been kind enough to give me several standing ovations. I have been averaging five encores each show.

Thankfully, the results are showing up in the box office. Your manager here, Mr. Felix Leominster, informed me this is the first week in the history of the Flatbush Theater that there have been eight sellouts in a row. Of course, my goal is for all fourteen shows to be standing room only, since it is my fondest hope that I will be your biggest moneymaker for the foreseeable future.

On Sunday night, after the evening performance, I will be throwing a small celebration of my first successful run for you and the Keith family. Needless to say, it would be my greatest honor if you would join us for my Sunday night performance and the party afterwards, at Mike's House of Fine Spirits at 328 Mercy Street in Brooklyn.

Thanks, again, for this wonderful opportunity. I will never let you down.

Love,
Sophie

P.S. Maybe I can help you in a couple of weeks when you open The Palace, your new flagship theater on Broadway in New York.

My letter to E.F. painted a beautiful picture, but I neglected to mention a few bumps in the road that came at the beginning of my successful week. I peeked out of the curtain ten minutes before the start of the Monday matinee to make sure Benny had lived up to his end of our arrangement. Sure enough, the house was packed to the rafters just like he promised. I learned later that many of those theatergoers were strong-armed through the turnstiles fearing for their lives. Nothing like some good old fashioned diplomacy. When the lights came down, the entire house erupted into applause and I knew it was going to be a good show.

I stepped out of the wings to an over the top welcome. I'd asked the stage manager to do away with the easel for the evening so I could act as the emcee, and he was more than happy to oblige me since he was sick to death of having all his easel cards stained with tomato pulp.

"Thank you ladies and gentlemen. Before we start our show, I wanted to introduce a very special dignitary in our audience. No, it's not the Mayor or the Governor or even the President. To me, he's more important than all those guys. As a matter of fact, he's the reason you're all here today. Ladies and gentlemen, the Honorable Benjamin Brutowsky."

As the crowd roared, I had a spotlight shine on Benny in his usual seat. He stood up and took an awkward bow.

"Some of you might not know this, but Mr. Brutowsky has promised that this week's shows at the Flatbush Keith will be free of any flying objects. To prove his sincerity about your safety, sitting right in front of me in the first row, where she will be every show this week, is Benny's lovely mother, Mrs. Brutowsky. Give Mrs. B a big hand. How are you doing tonight, Mrs. B?"

"Call me Mama," she answered me from her seat.

"All right, Mama. Your little boy isn't gonna let anyone throw anything today, is he?"

"If he does, I'll kick his sorry ass!"

"Well, that settles it," I announced with a laugh. "We're gonna have a great week here in Brooklyn. I'm your host Sophie Tucker and here's our first act: The Eisen Brothers!"

Even though I was introducing all the acts, I wanted my own entrance to be special each time. For the first two days, the band played a fanfare and I was driven onto the stage in Irving Berlin's brand-new chauffeured Alco touring car. One of the Eisen Brothers opened the back door and I stepped out to reveal a flowing light blue chiffon gown. I knew I had hit on something special when the whole audience gasped in awe.

Irving Berlin's weekend car, a 1913 Alco touring sedan.

On Wednesday, I switched things up. I donned a long blonde wig and a flesh-toned bodysuit that covered me from head to toe (making sure not to disobey Albee's strict dress code) and rode out onstage astride a beautiful black stallion, doing my best impersonation of a very chubby Lady Godiva. The matinee entrance went off without a hitch, but the evening entrance really took the cake when I had trouble sliding down off the horse. There's nothing like watching five guys trying to get my fat ass down to safety. The horse, sensing I was upstaging him, took the opportunity to make a big deposit in the middle of the stage. As I held my nose and the stagehands approached with a shovel and a broom, I saw Mama B. laughing so hard I thought she might have a heart attack.

On Thursday and Friday, I asked the stage manager to dig up the crummiest jalopy he could find. I was chauffeured onto the stage in an ancient Model T that was covered in dents, backfiring and interrupting me at will. Each time it did I'd give it a glare and a kick and restart my song. The audience was in hysterics.

Even with that reception, I saved the best for the weekend shows. One of the stagehands loaned me his motorcycle and another did some quick mechanical alterations before my matinee. Just before my curtain, I slipped back into my nude-colored bodysuit and a stagehand drove the motorcycle onstage with me scrubbing my back in its new bathtub sidecar. To tumultuous applause, the Eisen Brothers came out with a big towel stretched between them to give me privacy while I got out of my tub. Then the boys "accidentally" dropped the towel, revealing my wet *tush*[2] to the crowd. That entrance went down in the annals of Vaudeville history. It's a shame it was before television.

On the other hand, though, maybe not.

Sophie pictured in a standard stationary bathtub.

2   *Tush* – Rear end.

Though I thought I had arranged every detail of my run at the Flatbush Keith, I was livid when someone dressed as a clown rolled an upright piano out onto the stage during my first performance on Monday afternoon. Since Frank Westphal pulled that little stunt back in Chicago, everyone under the sun was using his entrance as a bit in the middle of their otherwise ordinary acts. This time, though, I was furious. I had left explicit instructions that no one was to interrupt my act in any way. Still, there I was with a clown sharing my spotlight and I had to play along.

"Can I help you?" I asked.

The clown held up a finger, pantomiming that I should wait just a moment. Then, to the audience's delight, he took off four overcoats, six suit jackets, three pairs of pants and eight shirts, leaving him standing there in his red long johns. An assistant came out with a formal suit, and the clown changed into a sharp set of tails and shiny black shoes. He removed his hat and orange wig, and finally buried his painted face in a towel. After a lot of rubbing, he handed the towel to his assistant and took his place on the piano stool once again.

When he spun around to wave to the applauding audience, I realized that I was looking at none other than Frank Westphal, in the flesh. I couldn't believe my eyes.

Even though William Morris and numerous other troupers had advised me to drop Frank like a hot potato, we'd been writing each other love letters ever since I left Chicago to head out West. We'd only crossed paths a few times during the three intervening years. When I was in New York, he was in Omaha. When I was in Omaha, he was in New York. True to form, each of Frank's hundreds of letters contained a passionate proposal of marriage and each of my responses went back with a polite refusal. Yet somehow, here he was.

I found out later that a couple of our mutual friends on Tin Pan Alley told Westphal the good news about my upcoming first Keith engagement. He was in Pittsburgh at the time and near enough to make it to Brooklyn by Sunday night, just before I started my run. He secretly met with my conductor and used some of my love notes to prove that we knew each other. From that show on, we performed together. I couldn't believe we were in the same place at last.

After my Friday matinee at the Flatbush, I got an unexpected visit from Max Hart. He was waiting in my dressing room, pacing back and forth, fanning himself with his red-banded boater hat.

"I'm here with a message directly from Albee," he sputtered. "He says to tell you that he got all twenty-five of your letters. Are you out of your fucking mind? No one writes to E.F. Albee!"

"Am I in trouble?" I asked with trepidation.

"No. The son of a bitch loves them," said the bewildered Max. "He says to keep writing, they cheer him up!"

I just chuckled and sat down at my mirror to remove my pancake makeup. Hart explained that when he was summoned to Albee's office to talk about me, he assumed he was getting the boot.

"I figured it was the firing squad for me for sure," continued Max. "But then E.F. says to me, 'Congratulations on Sophie Tucker.' And I'm thinking, *what the fuck did she do?* But then he showed me the box office receipts and my eyes almost popped out of my head. They're off the charts! Do you have a lot of family in Brooklyn?"

"I do now," I chuckled.

"Well, I don't know how the hell you did it and, to tell the truth, I don't give a shit. If E.F. is happy, I'm happy. I haven't seen him in such a good mood since Nora Bayes came on the scene. Albee's so thrilled he's gonna come to your last show on Sunday and wants to meet you at Mike's afterward. Who the hell is Mike?"

There was just one hitch. Albee had done a little research and found out my old flame had been accompanying me on stage the last couple of days and his staff had turned up all the same dirt on Westphal that Morris had warned me about. Frank was trouble. Albee told Hart that as long as he got rid of the Frank problem, he was willing to offer me a contract for $1,500 per week. I tried to bargain with him, but Max relayed E.F.'s ultimatum. Westphal was a deal breaker.

The best Hart could do was to give me permission for Frank to stay on in the pit, not the stage, with a salary of $150 per week which was to be secretly deducted from my own salary.

When I broke the news to Frank, I lied through my teeth. He cruised in just thirty minutes before the curtain was supposed to go up on our

Friday night performance, holding his head in his hands and wearing yesterday's suit.

"You're not going to believe the news I got, Frank." I said as he collapsed onto a chaise in my dressing room.

"Tell me softly. I overdid it this afternoon with that Brute guy. He's an okay fella, but boy oh boy, can he drink."

"Instead of getting blitzed with Benny, why weren't you with me? We might only have a couple of more nights together," I said, hurrying to fix my hair. I'd been running behind schedule waiting for Frank to show up.

"Me and Bennie came up with a great plan so you and me can be together every night. Just ask that Hart guy to add me to your contract as your accompanist," he said with a yawn. "No Keith accompanist makes less than $300 a week. Hell, they like you so much you might even be able to talk them up to $500."

"I already asked and I don't know if you're gonna take what they're offering. Max would only agree to $150 per, and you have to play down in the pit."

"The pit?" he spat. That sobered him up.

Albee has a rule," I lied. "No accompanist is allowed on stage with a Keith headliner."

Particularly an accompanist famous for weeklong benders, I thought to myself.

"Jeez, Soph. Did you also negotiate me a bowl of dog food and a leash?"

"As soon as I get to the big Keith theaters, I'll fix everything," I promised. "I'll be bringing in so much money for Albee he won't be able to refuse me anything."

"Ruff ruff," barked Frank. He pulled his hat down and left.

Frank wouldn't so much as look at me that Friday night from his new place below the stage, but I had to admit that E.F. had been right. My act got better. I felt like 150 pounds had been lifted off my back. I used to feel more comfortable with Frank on stage because I could lean on him for jokes, but I had long since moved past that. The less I had to worry about Frank, the more I interacted with the audience.

The result was a much more personal experience for everyone—except Frank, that is.

To punish me, Frank would disappear to some bar after each performance and I wouldn't see him again until the next day. Despite it all, I still loved him. I've always been a bit of a brat and I thought I deserved everything—love, fame, and money—but the tricky part was figuring out how to have all three at the same time. Fame always brought me money, but the higher I climbed, the harder it became to find love. After Albee laid down the law about Westphal though, one thing became crystal clear. When Frank threatened my shot to headline the whole Keith circuit, I knew love belonged in last place. Somehow, I'd fix the romance thing later.

By Sunday night in Flatbush, I erased every thought of Frank from my mind and I pulled on my bodysuit one last time. I took my place in the bathtub sidecar, ready to perform the most important show of my life for Mr. E.F. Albee. Once again, Benny had come through with a full house and his Mama was still sitting front and center to make sure the skies were clear. The lack of falling pocket change meant the other acts were performing with newfound gusto and, believe it or not, most of them were asked to do an encore or two. However, nothing could compare to the standing ovation they gave my dripping caboose as I climbed out of the tub.

I waved to the crowd and put on my first gown. Everything was going better than I had hoped, until the entire stage began to rumble. Out from the wings came an upright piano pushed unsteadily by Frank, who was obviously drunk as a skunk. He must've had another liquid dinner at Mike's between shows. He was wearing yesterday's smelly street clothes and his squashed fedora. I had to think fast.

"Can I help you?" I asked, still smiling for the benefit of the audience but shooting poison darts at Frank with my eyeballs.

"I came to say hello to the great E.F. Albee," slurred Frank.

He began to diddle tunelessly on the keys. "Say, did you ever wonder what the E.F. stands for?"

I started to push the piano back off the stage, but Frank refused to follow. Even when I managed to get the keys out from under him, he just sat on his stool, spinning idly and pretending to play the air. At least the audience was enjoying themselves. They thought they were seeing the best drunk act since Charlie Chaplin.

"I'm pretty sure the 'E' stands for Edward," Westphal slurred as he rotated. A violent hiccup knocked off his hat.

I grabbed Frank's arm and stopped his spinning.

"Hiya, Soph! When did you get here? Ladies and gentlemen, Miss Sophie Tucker!"

The audience laughed and applauded wildly. I began to push Frank's stool toward the wings as well, but he kept wriggling out of my grasp and wheeling back out into the spotlight.

"What about the F? Is it Freddy? Or Francis?" he mumbled. "Oh, I know! The E.F. stands for Edward Fuck—"

The audience definitely heard the beginning of Frank's punchline, but I finished it with one of Mama's uppercuts. His whole limp, drunk body flew up in the air and came down like a ton of bricks. The conductor, bless him, had the smarts to play a rousing ta-da and some exit music as two stagehands dragged Frank's carcass off the stage.

"Wasn't he funny? Frank Westphal! Now where were we?"

Unfortunately, I knew exactly where I was. In ten quick minutes I was elected the mayor of Shitsville. Somewhere out in the audience sat one steaming Edward Fucking Albee, if he hadn't stormed out of the theater entirely. I was so sure that all of my work was shot to hell that I don't even remember the rest of my performance that night.

The next thing I do recall was being at Mike's and accepting everyone's congratulations. I was told that I got my usual ovations and did seven encores, and the audience went wild for the drunk guy in my act. Naturally, Frank was nowhere to be found. My career was in the toilet, and that's probably where my boyfriend's head was too.

Benny the Brute snapped me out of my funk. It was time for me to pay up on my half of our deal, so I took him by his catcher's mitt of a hand and lead him over to a booth in the back corner.

"Mr. Benjamin Brutowsky, I'd like you to meet your dates for the evening. This is Rosie and Jenny… *Smith*."

The Dolly sisters eyed him up and down.

"Well hello, big boy. Sophie told us about your clubhouse," said Rosie.

"And your muscle!" giggled Jenny.

I was told that Benny couldn't stop smiling for a month after that night. By the end of my week in Brooklyn, I had convinced the Brute that the future good behavior of his clique would guarantee more decent acts. He agreed to never let so much as a single raisin fly from the balcony at the Flatbush Keith ever again.

I escaped downstairs to the clubhouse and found a chair in a quiet corner to sit and sulk. I was so close. Why did Frank have to ruin it? I sat there sipping my suds and thinking about how ten little minutes could change someone's life. If I didn't sing that ten minute song at Riverside Park in Hartford all those years ago, I'd probably still be slinging schmaltz at Abuza's. If I hadn't stood outside Poli's stage door handing out restaurant leaflets for ten minutes, I never would have met Willie and Eugene Howard. And if Frank hadn't come out on stage that night during those first ten minutes, I would have been on my way to the classiest vaudeville circuit in the world.

I was crying into my beer when I heard someone come down the stairs.

"Hello Sophie. I'm E.F. Albee."

"Listen buddy, I'm not in the mood for a razzing tonight," I shot back. "Can you just leave me be?"

I slowly lifted my head and found myself staring at a distinguished looking gentleman, elegant from his curled moustache all the way down to his shiny shoes. It *was* Edward Fucking Albee.

"Sir!" I yelped and scrambled to my feet. "I didn't think that—after the rough beginning…"

"I'll admit, I took offense at first that some no-name singer had the gall to write me a letter. But after the fifth or sixth one I actually began to look forward to your notes," he said with a smile. "Soph—can I call you Soph?"

"You can call me anything you like, sir, after tonight's fiasco."

"That's what I wanted to speak to you about. When E.F. Albee tells someone he will be somewhere at a certain time, he is never late. I broke my own rule tonight."

"Water under the bridge, sir," I muttered sadly. "This party will go until dawn."

"No Sophie, I'm talking about your act. There was an accident on the Brooklyn Bridge and I was late to the show tonight. It's a shame, because I really wanted to see your entrance in that bathtub I've been hearing so much about.

My legs gave out and I fell back into my chair, stunned. I couldn't believe my dumb luck. Albee had totally missed the Frank debacle. *I'll be goddammed*, I thought to myself, *you still have a job*.

"Well, E.F.," I said, fanning myself so I didn't faint. "Can I call you E.F.?

"Sure Soph, if you accept my apology for missing your act."

"Forgot it. These things happen! Don't beat yourself up."

"I think we're going to make quite a team. I can promise you a great future in this business, kid," he said, sticking out his hand for me to shake.

"As a matter of fact, E.F., I just thought of a way you can make it up to me," I said, taking his hand. "My apartment's kinda small. I'd really like to move into something a little roomier. Maybe you can set me up in your new Palace?"

Chapter 23

That Naughty Melody

No one but Houdini could've made such a death-defying escape from unemployment. Albee made up for missing my performance by scheduling me directly into the brand new Palace Theater instead of an intermediate joint a rung or two up the ladder from Flatbush. I paid Max Hart a visit the following Monday to sign my contract and make everything official.

Max was on the phone when I walked into his office. He was rubbing his forehead in frustration assuring Gertie, who I'd learned over the last few weeks had a vicious jealous streak, that he wasn't making eyes at his newest chorus girl.

"Nothing's fishy, Gertie," he sighed. "Teresa is just another dancer. You're the only one for me. I swear on the Bible."

I decided to have a little fun. I plopped myself down on his lap and cooed directly into the telephone.

"That's my little Maxie Waxie!" I giggled.

"It's nobody, dear," Max said, trying to throw me off his lap like a bucking bronco.

"That's not what you said last night!" I cried even louder. "Why don't you tell her the truth and put her out of her misery. You know we're madly in love with each other!"

"It's just a prank, honey! It's Sophie, the girl from the Cotillion Club, Sophie Tucker!"

I motioned for Max to hand me the phone.

"Ya vol," I said in a thick German accent. "Who ist this Sophie Tucker? Who am I? Who are you? Maxie's wife! Maxie, you didn't tell me you were married. Listen fraulein, he's all yours…Hello?…Hello?… She hung up. It must have been something I said."

Max threw his phone across the room and I returned to my usual seat.

"Calm down, Christy Mathewson. No need to pitch a no-hitter with your hello statue."

"What in God's name is a hello statue?" asked the seething Hart.

"You know, you pick it up and say, *Hello, 'stat you?'*"

As usual, I got no laugh from Maxie.

Hall of Fame baseball pitcher Christy Mathewson.

"Don't worry, I'm having lunch with Gertie in an hour and I'll explain everything," I swore.

Max glared at me and slid my contract across his desk. As promised, I would be making $1,500 per, starting at the Palace in three weeks. Hart explained that E.F. had forgotten that my old friend Nora Bayes was already booked at the new theater, so I was to spend a week in Baltimore and a week in Philadelphia cutting my teeth in some of Albee's fancier joints. As expected, Max was more than a little concerned that my act was too much for the older, sophisticated crowds who came to those theaters. I suggested he have a doctor take everyone's blood pressure as my chaser act.

"Stop fooling, Sophie. This is serious. A single morals violation, just one, and you are done. Don't let the nice guy bit from E.F. fool you, either. If you break any one of his rules he'll chew you up and spit you out like a stick of Wrigley's gum. Promise me you won't work blue, will you?"

I agreed. Actually, I think my exact words were, "Maxie, you haven't got a single fucking thing to worry about." Secretly, though, I figured that if I sold out two shows a day for fourteen days in a row in Albee's biggest theaters, he wouldn't care if I did my whole act naked but for a pair of pasties.

The next day I was on a train to Baltimore, playing gin with Molly and trying not to wake Frank. He was snoring off another bad hangover and I preferred his chain-sawing to his belly-aching about his crappy salary.

"When are you gonna wise up and get rid of this shithead?" whispered Molly.

"I should have listened to you three years ago," I lamented.

"Well, what's done is done. But that doesn't mean you have to keep doing it," my friend said.

Molly insisted Frank was like a boil on my nose: lance it, and immediately everything would look and smell better. I knew she was right and, truly, I intended to ditch him as soon as I got to the Palace. My problem was that I didn't have time to stop by Tin Pan Alley before leaving for Baltimore and Philadelphia and Frank, despite his drawbacks, was an excellent writer. That made him my only option to put a new shine on some old material.

Even though I still saw red when I thought about how he nearly sunk me in Flatbush, I convinced myself that the only reason he got so drunk was because he was angry with me. Miraculously, everything had worked out in the end. I hoped that as long as I didn't let him get anywhere near the stage when he was three sheets to the wind, it wouldn't be too dangerous to keep him around for a little bit longer.

Frank and I wound up working out a new take on a recent hit called "I Wonder Where My Easy Rider's Gone" for me to debut during my first Baltimore show.

It was a jokey little tune about a woman who bet all of her money on a jockey who ran away with her dough. It ended with the lines:

I'd put all my junk in pawn,
To bet on any horse that jockey's on.

Frank rejiggered the lyrics to make it a little racier. It really wasn't hard to turn a tune from nice to naughty. In this particular case, all we had to do was rewrite the final two lines and add a few shimmies:

If he comes back, I know we'll win,
'Cause I'll be the saddle [shimmy, shimmy] *that he'll get in.*

When I debuted the new version for Molly in her hotel room, she didn't say a word. Instead, she silently began packing her bags. Her vote was clear as to whether or not I should test Mr. Albee's watertight contract for leaks. The audience went wild for my saucy new ending during my first show that night, but Molly wasn't entirely wrong.

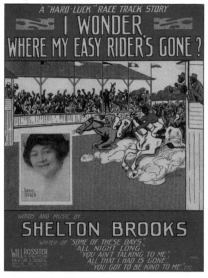

Stanley, the theater manager, was waiting for me in the wings as soon as I got offstage.

Thinking quickly, I lied. I insisted that Mr. Albee had

Sheet music from I Wonder Where My Easy Rider's Gone.

approved my songs in New York, when he was at my party at Mike's. Stanley was dumbfounded that Albee even knew what a party was, let alone attended one that I had thrown. I guess my story was convincing though, because he bought that E.F. and I were pals and agreed to let me continue to sing my songs with the racy lyrics. Even better, I convinced him that Albee didn't need to see a midweek report, either. Once E.F. saw my box office totals, I figured that I'd be bulletproof.

Frank was waiting for me in my dressing room, having fled the orchestra pit in record time so he could have his scotch on the rocks in peace. He was the only pit player on the circuit who sipped his drinks on the headliner's couch, and he liked to soak up the only perk he had left.

"The saddle line killed," said Frank.

"How about my hips? Don't they get any credit?"

"Were those your hips? It's been so long since I've seen them shake I wasn't sure."

"And whose fault is that?"

"I said I was sorry five times, Sophie. I'm sorry about Flatbush! I was a horse's ass. Besides, haven't I been a good boy since?" he said, clasping his hands together like a little choirboy.

"Good? Good, he says! You still come home every night lit up like a candle!" I yelled, angrily changing into my street clothes. I threw my heavy gown right at his melon and it knocked off his hat with a satisfying clatter of beads and sequins.

"Well, give this candle some money so he can go light up a dark bar somewhere," he said, sticking out his palm. I grabbed my purse, smashed some bills into his hand and Frank took off. I was so sick of his *shtick*[1] that I no longer even worried he might be out chasing skirts. His dream girl was one who would fork over money and never nag; my dream man was one who'd already been weaned from the bottle. Neither of us was going to get what we wanted.

So while Frank was getting sloshed in downtown Baltimore, I got busy. That night I treated every theater critic in town to a lavish dinner and rounds upon rounds of drinks. The next morning, I stopped by the newspaper office and made friends with a couple of photographers. For a mere sawbuck and some introductions to a few of the prettiest chorus girls, my little shutterbugs got my mug in the paper every day.

I even worked out a little routine to pitch to my Monday audiences, knowing that you could never underestimate word of mouth. After my last encore, I motioned for the crowd to stop applauding and take their seats.

"Ladies and gentlemen, you've been a marvelous audience today. Since you were willing to take a chance on me, a new headliner, I was hoping you might also be game enough to help me win a bet against a friend of mine in New York. You might know him. His name is Eddie Cantor," I said.

The audience applauded like mad. Eddie was one of the biggest comedians in the country.

"Sure, I like him too, but every once in a while he likes to bust my chops. Now, I'm in favor of women getting the vote. Eddie, he doesn't care so much, but he begged me to get his wife Ida involved in the movement. She's been nagging him for a summer home and a new car,

---

1   *Shtick* – Gimmick, comic routine.

and he thinks if I get Ida on the picket lines, she'll forget what she wants and it'll save him thousands!"

George Burns, Gracie Allen, Eddie Cantor, Sophie and Ida Cantor.

Again the audience applauded, though I think there were husbands and wives secretly appreciating different sides of that joke.

"So, Eddie, he thinks he can outdraw me any day. Well, I love a good challenge! I made a bet that I would have more box office than him this week, and you can help me win. If I do, he promised that he'll go to one of those Suffragette rallies in New York wearing one of my dresses! And if he wins, I have to wear one of his.

If you had a good time this afternoon will you do me a personal favor? Tell everyone you know to visit me in the next six days. I'll have different costumes and new songs for each of my fourteen shows here in Baltimore, so I can promise you won't be disappointed. Will you tell your friends and family? And if I sing you one more, just to say thanks, will you come back again this week?"

Sure enough, that was the last show that wasn't completely sold out. I played that whole first week to standing room only crowds for every matinee and every evening show, regardless of the blue lyrics I slipped in here and there. Everything was rolling along smoothly until

Sunday evening, when Stanley motioned me off the stage after my second encore and brought up the house lights, cutting my show short.

"I just got a wire from E.F. Albee himself!" he yelled. I looked over to Molly, who once again began packing up her purse and putting on her coat.

"I can explain about the song," I started.

"What song? Forget the song! You open at the Palace on Tuesday afternoon."

It seemed that there had been a disagreement with Nora Bayes and she, as usual, walked out intending to leave Albee high and dry, having no idea that I was waiting in the wings. I was supposed to bypass Philadelphia altogether and head straight to New York.

I had done it! After seven years of hard work, I had finally reached the pinnacle of Vaudeville: headlining at the Keith's best theater. Frank produced a bottle of champagne out of thin air and we toasted to the Palace, my latest and greatest conquest. From the first show I saw from the balcony at Poli's, I had no doubt that I was going to make it to this very moment.

My body did all the right choreography as I hugged and

The brand new Palace Theater in 1913.

danced with Molly and Frank, but, oddly, I was feeling a little glum. For the first time in my life, I didn't have a big goal. It was like someone had ripped out my gas pedal and I was just an engine, humming and chugging and burning its gasoline with nowhere to go. If I didn't come up with a new target to aim for, I knew that I would shrivel up and die at the ripe old age of twenty-seven. It didn't matter if I was the latest darling of Albee's theaters if all I had to look forward to was some newer act coming along to take my place.

On the train back to New York, I leaned my head against the window and did a great job of feeling sorry for myself. Molly and Frank assumed I was just tired from all the excitement and, thankfully, let me be. When I got sick of the New Jersey countryside I half-heartedly thumbed through the latest *Variety* and, as if put there by the hand of God, I found my next goal plastered across the top of page four:

NORA BAYES VOTED #1 BY KEITH AUDIENCES

There was no better way to start my new mission to oust Nora Bayes as the public's favorite entertainer than to replace her at the Palace Theater. Albee was nice enough to find a substitute for the Monday shows, which gave me a day off to get myself together and Frank enough time to juice up the lyrics of another new song.

I got settled into my suite at the St. Regis and then, figuring the best way to get rid of the knots in my stomach was to fill it with steak, I headed out for lunch at Delmonico's. That restaurant was the capital of the entertainment industry, where headliners went to schmooze and be seen. Even on a Monday at two o'clock, you could usually expect to see at least a few famous faces. I arrived to a smattering of polite applause from the other diners, as was the custom, but noticed that there was one lone clapper who just wouldn't quit. It turned out to be my old friend Al Jolson, who came over to my table to catch up.

"I never expected to see you here!" I said, giving him a hug. "You're as big a workhorse as me."

"Broadway's dark on Mondays, my dear. Just like God, I get one day of rest per week. It's not easy being the male Sophie Tucker!" he said.

"If you want that title, you're gonna have to pluck your eyebrows and put on fifty pounds," I joked.

Even with Jolie's nearly nonstop schedule, he'd heard that I was taking Nora's place at the Palace and was thrilled that I'd finally gotten my big break. Neither one of us could believe that E.F. had taken Bayes back so many times—and that he would probably take her back again—but it was hard to argue with any performer who put fannies in the seats.

I looked at Jolson, and suddenly I had an idea for my own show.

"Hey Al, can I ask a favor? I'm wild about the new number you're doing, the one about Mrs. Rip Van Winkle. Would you mind if I did it at the Palace?"

"It would be my pleasure," he said, bowing formally.

"Are you sure? It's such a hit for you."

"Don't worry, Soph. By the time you're done with it, nobody will recognize it as the same song. Just don't get down on one knee like I do—you'll need a team of he-men to get you back up!"

Al Jolson, the biggest star of early film, made a name for himself performing in blackface.

Frank and I stayed up late that night until we were satisfied with our new version of Al's song. I practiced until my hips were sore from shimmying and I'd practically pulled my winking muscle.

"Are you sure you want to go through with this?" asked Westphal as we settled into bed.

"Are you turning yellow on me?"

"I just don't want you to lose everything you've worked so hard for."

"If I don't do something to set myself apart from all the Nora Bayeses out there, I won't be around long enough to lose anything. You and the Boss gave me a great gift. Because of you two, I am the only fat sexpot in the world. And audiences eat it up with a spoon! I'm gonna play the outrageous Sophie Tucker as long as the crowds are buying tickets, and if that means doing bawdy lyrics like this, I'm gonna do them till I croak."

"Still, Soph. It's your first night. Maybe you should play it safe for a few shows at least?"

"Safe gets me back to Hartford washing dishes," I said, and turned out the light.

I intended to get to the Palace before everyone else that Tuesday so I could settle in quietly, but Albee was waiting for me as soon as I arrived. He kept a close watch over his beautiful new theater from eight in the morning until after the final curtain fell. I offered him a peek at my sheet music so he could make sure he didn't find anything objectionable, but he waved it away.

"Max has assured me you understand our rules. I trust you, Sophie. I know you're going to give us a nice, wholesome show."

"You heard all of my songs in Flatbush anyway, with the exception of one new one. I got permission from Al Jolson to do his big hit for my finale. Is that one okay with you?" I asked, giving him ample opportunity to put the kibosh on my plan.

"Who Paid the Rent for Mrs. Rip Van Winkle? I saw Al do that on his opening night. It was very funny. That's a great choice for your last number. I approve," he laughed, patting me on the back. "Just don't forget: think *wholesome*."

Sheet music for "Who Paid the Rent for Mrs. Rip Van Winkle?"

As he walked to his office on the top floor of the Palace, I crossed my heart and blew him a kiss.

Time flies when you're having heart palpitations. Before I knew it, I was once again in Irving Berlin's borrowed Alco touring car and making my grand entrance on the Palace stage. Because I was in New York, the whole theater was stocked with friendly faces. In the front five rows alone I spotted Irving Berlin, Jimmy Durante, George LeMaire, Eddie Cantor and even William Morris. I bet E.F. charged him double just to get in, but no feud was going to keep the Boss away today.

What a thrill it was! My act got all the right responses at all the right times. The thousands of performance hours were paying off. The tricks and nuances I had learned from the veterans had turned me into a world-class entertainer. I didn't have to think anymore. It all came out naturally. After half an hour, the only thing left to sing was my new finale.

"Ladies, gentlemen, friends, it's been a long road, but here I am!

I just wanted all of you to know something very important, especially the press—I know you're out there too! Here's your headline for the morning papers: Sophie Tucker is here to stay!"

The crowd broke into wild applause. Jimmy's schnoz turned pink with delight.

"My last song is on loan from my good pal, Mr. Al Jolson. Hit it, maestro!"

Who paid the rent for Mrs. Rip Van Winkle when Rip Van Winkle went away?
She had no friends, in that place
No one she had, to embrace,
But the landlord always left her with a smile on his face.
OH! Who paid the rent for Mrs. Rip Van Winkle when Rip Van Winkle went away?
C'mon and tell me,

Who paid the rent for Mrs. Rip Van Winkle when Rip Van Winkle went away?
She never married once again,
*She was so lonesome, **but then,***
You'll always find a rooster lookin' 'round for a hen.
Who paid the rent for Mrs. Rip Van Winkle when Rip Van Winkle went away?

My altered lyrics hit the bull's-eye. They had that little Sophie Tucker touch everyone had come to expect: taking perfectly innocent words and twisting them ever so slightly to make them naughty. Needless to say, this was a big deal in 1913, just like "The Angle Worm Wiggle" had been a few years earlier. The difference was that I'd just painted the pure white Keith stage with its first big splotch of blue. Now it was time to see if the Emperor of Vaudeville was going to let me get away with it.

As expected, the second my last friend offered their congratulations and left my dressing room, a page informed me I was wanted in Mr. Albee's office. I took a seat in front of his big desk and E.F. sat behind it in a plush leather chair, a slight smile on his face. I felt like I was back at school in Hartford catching hell for singing "Hello My Baby" in the middle of the Christmas chorus recital. Luckily, this time there were no paddles in sight.

"You know Sophie, my dear, I've reserved this spot for you," he said as he pointed to an open space on a wall filled with photographs of his many beautiful headliners. "My plan is to make you as famous as the other faces you see up there. But how can I make that happen if you refuse to cooperate with me?" He sighed like a disappointed father.

"I'm sorry about tonight, E.F. and I promise I'll cooperate from now on. By the way," I said slyly, "I meant to ask you. How was the box office last week in Baltimore?"

"Record-breaking, but that's not the point. You've got to be a wholesome, respectable entertainer!"

"You're right, of course E.F. Must've slipped my mind between all of my encores. How many did I have, anyway? Did someone count?"

"Ten," he frowned. "Eighteen minutes of encores. But you're still missing the point, Sophie."

"Wholesome! I know, wholesome!" I repeated. "Just like Nora Bayes. And, I'm sorry, I'm just so forgetful today. Remind me again, how much did the great Nora bring in last week?

"That's not the po—" he repeated again, until I cut him off.

"That's exactly the point, Mr. Albee. I doubled Nora's gate last week in Baltimore and even the week before when I was playing out in that Flatbush hellhole of yours. The fact is, the crowds can't wait to see what I'll do next! I'm exciting! You'll have to pardon me for saying it, sir, but lately Nora Bayes is boring them to fucking death."

Albee's face went so white all I could see was his moustache. He looked like the ghost of a walrus.

"Sophie, I'd appreciate it if you would please mind your language."

"I'm sorry Mr. Albee. Let me rephrase that. What I meant to say is that lately Miss Bayes is boring the audience to their fucking *demise*."

"What am I going to do with you?" he said, throwing his hands up in the air.

"Here's what you're gonna do with me. You're gonna send me on tour to every one of your theaters. Why? Because every time I open my mouth, people will line up to give you their money. I know you don't believe it yet, but I guarantee that I'm the next gold rush and you own the mother lode for the measly sum of $1,500 a week. You, Mr. Albee, are gonna usher in the next big *blue* wave of Vaudeville!"

I stood up.

"Now if you'll excuse me, I think we both have things to do. I have to go downstairs to get you a picture, and you have to go shopping for a gold frame so you can hang my big beautiful face right there!"

I slammed the door behind me and found myself in the empty corridor outside his office. I stood there for ten seconds, catching my breath and panicking. This time I thought I had really cooked my goose but good.

And then I heard it.

E.F. Albee was laughing.

Epilogue

Could I?
I Certainly Could

As a kid, I always threw a fit whenever I was asked to wash dishes at the family restaurant, so it serves me right that as an adult the only place where I can think straight is in front of a sink. I'm nearly seventy-nine and fading fast, so I'm mostly stuck in a wheelchair these days, but at night when I can't sleep I still wheel myself over to the sink and scrub a few glasses until they sparkle. Writing down all these stories has kept me up more than a few nights. To ease my nerves, I've even taken clean plates out of the cabinet and washed them again just for the calming ritual of suds, rinse, and dry.

Sophie, communing with dishes.

Of everything I've done, the little lies here and there, leaving my family behind, constantly touring for most of my life, I only have three real regrets. Their names are Al Lackey, Frank Westphal, and Louis Tuck. If I had one of those H.G. Wells time machines, I'd run from the altar so fast the newspapers would report a small buffalo stampede. Otherwise, by and large, I'm pretty sure I wouldn't change any of my other of decisions.

Especially when it came to Tuck, who just couldn't seem to resist being a pain in my ass.

The most important batch of dishes I ever washed were in Mama and Papa's kitchen sink back on October 26, 1913, during my biggest return to Hartford. It had been seven years since I'd left home, and that particular night was so gut-wrenching it required an extra-large stack of shmutz-filled dishes to calm my frayed nerves. I'd just made the most important decision of my life—bigger than leaving home, or ditching Frank to head out West, or pushing Albee's buttons—and, though I know I was right, I haven't told a soul what I did until now. I think about it to this day while I'm standing at the sink.

I survived my little spat with Albee and he did in fact book me on a national tour of the entire Keith chain. Better yet, at my request, I got to start at the Keith's newest acquisition: Poli's Theater in Hartford Connecticut. When it was confirmed, I once again enlisted my old pal John Sudarsky. John was climbing the ranks at the *Hartford Courant* and he promised that there would be front page articles about yours truly every day leading up to my arrival at the train station. John suggested that he also hang a banner from every streetlight saying "I Told You So!" but I vetoed that idea. I was pretty sure I'd make that point with the parade he'd organized, which would lead me from the train station, up Main Street, and to the theater.

Esther Williams

Now, I've had a lot of spectacular welcomes in my time. When I agreed to be one of the first headliners to play gangster Bugsy Siegel's brand new Flamingo Hotel in Las Vegas, he arranged for fifty fire trucks to line the route to his casino, each spraying an arc of water over my limousine as it drove down the strip. Talk about extravagance! It was better than being in an Esther Williams movie.

There we were in the middle of the Nevada desert, where water was more precious than gold, and Siegel was spritzing the streets just to impress me and the people of Vegas. They say the Syndicate bumped him off for his out of control spending. I just hope that my personal

Niagara Falls wasn't the straw that broke the camel's back—or Bugsy's neck.

Even with welcomes like that, nothing ever beat my parade in Hartford. I couldn't believe my eyes when I pulled into the station. There must have been over five hundred people waiting for me and waving signs. A band was playing "For She's A Jolly Good Fellow" and everywhere I looked I found a banner blazing a message of love. "Welcome Home Soph!" "Brown School Loves You!" "I Got a Pucker for Tucker!" And perhaps the most ridiculous of all, "You Were a Sure Thing!"

"Sure thing, my ass," I said under my breath. As sure as seven years of clawing, scratching, starving and making my own lucky breaks.

I spotted a grinning John Sudarsky on the train platform and gave him a big hug and kiss. He'd arranged the articles and the parade, but the crowd and the banners came from real, true fans. He had nothing to do with that part. I made my way through hundreds of handshakes and back slaps to a big car which took me downtown to a hastily built stage that could easily double as a gallows if the crowd didn't like my act. My family, a dozen or so town notables, and the mayor himself were seated on the big platform.

"Mama looks thrilled," I whispered into Annie's ear as I hugged her hello. My mother was either irritated down to the tips of her sensible black shoes by such a silly display, or she had a serious case of constipation. Little Bert, now eight, was busy greeting the crowd with his peashooter. At least Papa and my brothers were all smiles, and even mousy little Leah threw her arms around me when I greeted her. I'm sure she was happy just to be included.

"Ladies and gentlemen, we are here on this beautiful October day to welcome home one of the biggest headliners in all of Vaudeville, Hartford's own, Sophie Abuza Tucker!" announced the mayor. "Most of you know Sophie started her career right over there in Riverside Park. She went on to become Hartford's most famous—and only—singing waitress."

"The chopped liver's on me tonight, folks!" I yelled.

"And now after seven years of hard work and playing the brand new Palace Theater in New York City, Sophie Tucker returns to where her dream began, Poli's Theater. Soph, on behalf of Hartford, I want to welcome you home and present you with this golden key to the city."

"I only have one question Mr. Mayor," I said, when the applause died down. "Does this key open the front door to the Chipanic's ice cream parlor?"

"There's more, Sophie," chuckled the mayor.

"What? It opens Mrs. Landi's bakery too?" I said, grabbing my chest as though I was having a heart attack.

"We'll get you as many doughnuts as you like, Sophie, but in honor of your return, you can eat them in your complimentary Presidential Suite at the Hartford Hotel."

This was my cue to crank up the old Sophie Tucker charm. John and I had worked out this little routine before I arrived to make sure the crowds knew I was still the same old Sophie that used to clear their tables and sing for their pocket change.

"Thank you very much, Your Honor. And thanks to my friends, family, and all the rest of you for this unbelievably warm welcome home. I will never forget it as long as I live. I hope I'll be seeing all of you again this coming week at Poli's. I can promise you this. If you come, you also will have an experience you will never forget as long as *you* live.

I would also like to thank the management of The Hartford Hotel for their generous offer of their Presidential Suite. Unfortunately, I must graciously decline. After seven years on the road, my greatest wish is to go home and eat my mama's cooking. What could be better than that?"

The crowd burst into applause. Luckily, they didn't notice a patented Jennie Abuza eye-roll that would go down in the record books.

"But Mr. Mayor," I continued, "can you do me a favor? Please tell the manager at the hotel to hold my room just in case? If my mother asks me to peel any potatoes, I'm a-comin'!"

As the crowd burst into one final round of applause and John hopped down off the stage to pull his car around, I noticed a lone man standing across the street, away from the crowd. He was wearing a white shirt, white pants, and even a pair of gleaming white shoes. The guy was impossible to ignore, especially because he was waving both arms trying to get my attention. He took off his white hat and smiled. I couldn't make out his face, but that shit-eating grin could only belong to my biggest mistake, Louis Tuck.

Here we go again, I thought.

As soon as we were safe inside the two-year-old Barker Street house, everyone flopped down on the new sofas and chairs. Mama had finally begun to tap into the money I'd been sending home all those years and was warming to the idea of my success. At last, she'd begun to believe I wouldn't be crawling back home any time soon to wait tables.

With no restaurant to worry about, my mother's pace had slowed to a crawl. Annie had used a few of my more recent money orders (fat from my new Albee salary) to buy my mother a whole new wardrobe—entirely black, of course. This meant Mama had nothing to mend at night on her Singer. And, since Mama was only cooking for three, she was at the stove a mere hour per day, even if she still insisted on making everything by hand.

While all the leisure time gave Mama *schpilkas*[1], Papa relished his retirement. No more hours standing at the register or squabbling over the price of onions. With Bert living at his military academy for most of the year, Papa had all the time in the world to nap, and read, and play cards with the extra money that I slyly sent him on the side. The only thing he wanted from me was my Keith contract, so he could have it framed and hang it on the living room wall. To him, it was more impressive than a Harvard diploma.

I arranged for Molly and Frank to stay in a small hotel close to Poli's, explaining that Jennie Abuza had a heart of gold and a poison tongue. To Mama, either you were Jewish or you were out of the club. I could only imagine the bigoted Yiddish slang my Mama would let loose if I brought Molly, a black woman, to her house for dinner. There was no way I would subject my best friend to treatment like that. Mama's mouth was also a good excuse to get rid of Frank for a few days. I still hadn't gotten around to dumping him and he was still angry that he was making a measly $150 per week.

1 *Schpilkas* – Nervousness.

"Don't worry," I assured him as I gave him his weekly allowance. "It's like you're getting a raise. The liquor is cheaper outside New York City."

"Why didn't you just drop me off at the Hartford dog pound, Soph," he said, looking around his small hotel room.

"What happened to the lovable fella I met in Chicago?" I asked, throwing up my hands. "We used to have so much fun."

"You threw him out like the trash! No, come to think of it, your garbage has it better. You have to take it out once in a while," he said, slamming the door.

This couldn't go on much longer. I was on the verge of calling it quits with Westphal, at least for a while, because I understood his problem. My boyfriend really did have some talent. When we met he already had an act that could make him a nice living as a second banana in Vaudeville or burlesque. But he would never be a headliner. He just didn't have the magic. Even if we could get spots on the same bill, because of our huge salary difference there was no chance we'd live happily ever after. Most importantly, I was hard at work even in my dreams. Frank, on the other hand, dreamed solely about whiskey. We were doomed.

When I got to Poli's Monday morning, for old times' sake I walked down the same alley where I used to hand out flyers for our restaurant. The same old stage door was still open a crack. I took a big breath and opened it to find, to my surprise, the entire stage crew and cast of that week's bill was there to welcome me. As if that wasn't enough to make me blubber like a baby, the group parted to reveal the Howard Brothers. I was never so happy to see those two *nudniks*[2] in my life.

"Flatbush was booked this week," said Eugene.

"So we got stuck coming here," finished Willie.

"Well, their loss is my gain. Just what I need – more dead weight." I joked.

"Is that how you explain those extra pounds?" asked Willie.

"Be nice to the girl. She's a headliner," said Eugene.

2   *Nudnik* – A pest, nag.

"You mean she can get us run out of the business now?" gasped Willie.

"Maybe, but you're doing a nice job of that all by yourself," laughed Eugene.

The Howard brothers had rearranged their whole schedule to join me in Hartford for the week, though they nearly turned around and headed back to the Midwest Circuit when they heard that Abuza's Family Restaurant had closed.

"Is it true?" Willie asked. I nodded, and he faked a swoon.

"Bite your tongue!" shouted Eugene.

"That's the only tongue you're gonna bite around here," said Willie from the floor.

"Have no fear. Mama Abuza always cooks for the Howard Brothers!" I said, picking him back up. "She's so bored without the restaurant, she'd probably fill your luggage with Kasha varnishkes[3] if you asked."

Willie sprang up from the ground and gave me a big hug.

I took a quick detour through the lobby before I went to my dressing room. It looked exactly the same as I remembered, when I used to stand there as a kid and dream of this very day. The only difference was an easel smack in the middle of the room, holding one of the biggest, gaudiest gold frames I had ever seen. Papa had pulled a fast one on me when he asked for my contract. It would be impossible for anyone entering the theater not to see how much I was making.

I knew this week was going to be perfect.

Unsurprisingly, all my shows at Poli's got a huge response. As always, my entrances and costumes were unique to each performance, but more importantly, everything was polished from the very first note until the curtain fell. At the last second I decided to revive my old rose number so I could perform with Molly. Just like the old days, she came out from the wings and pinned the flower (and her sleeve) to me, exactly like she did four years earlier so we could do our synchronized routine. My heart

---

3   *Kasha varnishkes* – A Eastern European Jewish dish of kasha (buckwheat groats), noodles (usually bow-tie pasta), often with onions.

swelled knowing my old friends and family were enjoying my new life, and new friends.

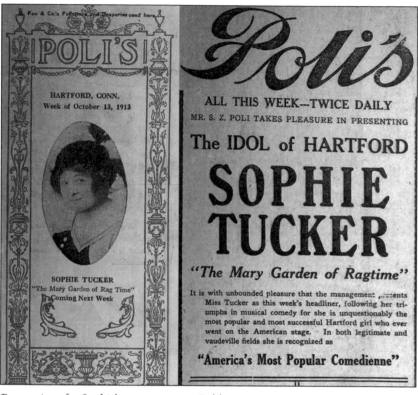

Promotions for Sophie's appearance at Poli's.

My favorite audience of the week didn't show up until Thursday night, when my mother's synagogue sisterhood took up the first eight rows of the orchestra section. When I got going with some of my loudest songs, those *altacockers*[4] stuck their fingers in their ears and screwed their faces up in pain like I was torturing them.

"You're telling me these people pay you $1,500 a week to stand up there for forty-five minutes and scream at the top of your lungs?" clucked Mrs. Frankel when the ladies visited me backstage after the show. "Are you sure this Mr. Albee knows you're hurting people's ear drums? If this ringing in my head doesn't stop, he'll be hearing from my son, the *lawyer.*"

4   *Altacockers* – Yiddish pejorative slang for an old person.

"Oh, why don't you just go see Mrs. Goldberg's eldest?" shot back Mama. "You know, her son, the *psychiatrist.*"

SOPHIE TUCKER MEETS OLD FRIENDS

Crowds Greet Hartford Girl At Poli's Theater.

SINGER OF RAGTIME HEARD AT HER BEST

Others Assist In a Bill of Great Merit.

Immense audiences gathered at Poli's Theater yesterday to greet Sophie Tucker on her first appearance in this, her native city. And a right royal welcome it was that was extended to her. Her many old friends and acquaintances took advantage of every opportunity to make her feel that they were glad to see and hear her in the profession in which she has made such a splendid name for herself. Her first appearance on the

Miss Tucker has made her reputation as a singer of ragtime melodies, of which she has made a special study. She has her own ideas as to how this kind of song should be sung, all of which make them sound a good deal better than the ordinary ragtime. Being the possessor of a powerful singing voice she can bring out the lines she wishes to emphasize with good effect, while her inimitable use of the pauses in the music form a delightful contrast to the other parts of her songs. Quite a little of her success can be attributed to the fine piano-playing of Frank C. Westphal, her accompanist. This young man is as much an artist in his particular line as Miss Tucker is in hers, his music being in perfect accord with the singer at all times. As was to be expected Miss Tucker was the recipient of some beautiful flowers, two large bunches being handed up to her after the final encore. In response to the hearty applause she made a pretty little speech of thanks, or rather, she tried to but the spontaneousness of the greeting apparently overcame her and all that was heard was her heartfelt "thank you."

Charles Reisner and Henrietta Gores kept their hearers in good humor every minute they were on the stage. They have nothing but a lot of nonsense in their act but it is so genuinely funny that it is a continual laugh from start to finish. The sketch of the week is presented by William Hawtry and company. It tells a humorous story of how a struggling actor appropriates a chicken that has been left at his house by mistake and of the ludicrous situations that crop up when the real owner of the fowl shows

A review of Sophie's show in the Hartford Courant.

My last shows on Sunday were sure to be a headache, with Molly and me packing up between the matinee and the evening performance in order to make the late train to Boston for my next engagement. That meant that my last chance for one more of Mama's meals was between my Saturday shows. I put away bowls of her goulash like I was a squirrel hiding it for winter.

"Mama, why don't you come with me on tour?" I said, ladling more on my plate.

"What would I do? Be a dance tapper?"

"I think Mama would do better with soft shoe," added Annie.

"What's this soft shoe?" asked my mother.

"There's no clickity-clicks in soft shoes," explained my father. "You just dance soft. Let me show you." Papa got up, grabbed Mama and did a waltz around the table that would rival Fred and Ginger.

"I'll stick to tapping-dancing," deadpanned Mama as Papa returned her to her chair. "And only as a solo act."

I went straight to my dressing room from my parents' house and was surprised to find Frank, not Molly, sitting in one of my chairs. He had been writing something on a piece of paper but when he saw me, he crumpled it up and tossed it in the garbage. That's when I noticed his suitcase was next to him.

"Where are you going?" I asked.

"I was writing you a note," he explained. "I was hoping I'd be gone before you got here.

Jennie Abuza, circa 1913.

I'm heading to St. Louis. I can't sit around forever playing second fiddle. Or, second piano, I guess," he chuckled.

"But I don't want you to go!" I said, surprising even myself with the truth of that statement. I didn't want him to leave. He may have been a complainer and a boozehound and a magnet for trouble, but deep down I still loved him. He was *my* mistake.

"Listen Soph, it's time we stopped kidding ourselves. The way we're going, if we spend five more minutes together we're going to ruin any chance for a happy future."

"You really think we have a future?" I whimpered.

"No doubt about it," said Frank, "I've got a surefire plan. I have a lot of great new bits I'm going to polish. I'm going to be bigger than Eddie Cantor, you hear me? Then, after I become a headliner at the Palace, we'll get back together and tour the world. How does that sound?"

"Great," I blubbered.

"I'm not kidding, Soph. The partnership of Westphal and Tucker is to be continued. You can count on it for life. I'm going to go now."

I grabbed him and held him tight.

"But before I go, I only have one more question," said Westphal. "Will you marry me?"

"Write and ask me tomorrow," I looked up and smiled. "Who knows?"

And with that, Frank was gone. When I look back at that biography they churned out in the Forties, I know that it's mostly filled with bunk and a whole lot of sloppy sentiment. But there was one thing they managed to get right:

Sophie and Frank (standing).

"Once you start carrying your own suitcase, paying your own bills, running your own show, you've done something to yourself that makes you one of those women men like to call 'a pal' and 'a good sport,' the kind of

woman they tell their troubles to. But you've cut yourself off from the orchids and the diamond bracelets, except those you buy yourself."

Frank was the closest I came in my life to real romance, but he kept a few mistresses besides me—his career, his resentment of my success, and booze, to name a few.

I'd like to believe that things are changing for women, that I've made it a little bit easier for a big lady with a bigger paycheck and an enormous mouth to have a little bit of love in her life. But the truth is, I just don't know. Men can be real schmucks when it comes to matters of the heart.

Molly joined me in the dressing room a few minutes later and when she figured out what had happened insisted we take a walk to calm me down. Mostly we just ambled along in silence. Words weren't really necessary. Molly knew me better than I knew myself. I showed her Riverside Park and the little stage where it all started. Then we sat on the bench where Annie and I used to sell Coca-Cola. Molly tried to assure me that Mr. Right would be coming soon, and I told her she was probably right. He might have been on his way right that very moment. The problem was, by the time he got there, I'd be in Boston.

Sophie and Molly Elkins, center.

Molly dropped me back off at the theater and left to take care of an "errand," which is what she called placing a bet with my old pal Tommy T-bone. She had a hot tip for the sixth race at Belmont. No matter where we were, Molly had an uncanny knack for finding the local bookie before she even found the hotel.

The show had already started by the time I got back to my dressing room, but that meant I still had a good ninety minutes to collect myself and get ready to take the stage. I took off my coat and hung it in the closet, then sat down at my makeup table to clean the mess I'd made of my face with all my tears.

"Hiya Soph," came a voice from behind me that startled me so badly, I drew my lipstick sheer across my cheek. I whirled around and sure enough, sitting in the back of the room was a man in white pants and white shoes, holding a newspaper that covered his face. I grabbed a towel, wiped the lipstick off my face, and pitched it straight through his paper.

"I thought we had an understanding," I hissed.

"No *Hello Tuck? You're looking good, Tuck?*"

"How about *What the fuck are you doing here Tuck?*" I spit back.

"I just wanted to come by and congratulate you on your big success, Soph," oozed Louis. His charm was so oily I'm surprised his fingers didn't turn his newspaper see-through.

"You've got one second to get out of here, you son of a bitch!" I screamed, picking up a jar of cold cream and aiming it at his melon.

"Calm down, I was just leaving. But, before I go, I was thinking maybe you could spot me a few bucks for old time's sake."

"Why would I give your sorry ass another penny?"

"I thought you might change your mind after I showed you this," he said, producing a folded piece of paper from his pocket. He started to pass it to me and I snatched it out of his hand.

Instantly, I recognized Albert's birth certificate.

That single piece of paper held two dark secrets, only one of which Mama and I had been in on all these years. The first was that the birth record listed Bert's mother as Annie Abuza, age thirteen. That much we had known, and that much I had been willing to keep hidden. I'll never forget the day when Annie came home sobbing from school, so wracked with tears that Mama and I could hardly understand her when she told us she was pregnant.

We never asked who knocked her up. Instead, over the next nine months, Annie's friends thought she was only gaining weight, while I stuffed my dress with pillows pretending with all my heart that I was pregnant. It was my first real acting job and I nailed it. To this day, I've never lied when I said Annie kept me company in the hospital room on the day of Albert's birth. I just never told anyone that it was Annie doing the pushing.

"So all this time you knew Bert wasn't ours?" I whispered to Tuck, slamming shut the door to my dressing room.

"How could it be?" he smiled. "You cut me off a year before he was born."

"Wait a minute. How did you manage to get this from the hospital?"

"You missed something, Soph. Read it again," he said, as cool as a cucumber.

I stared down at the paper and finally realized what he was hinting at. It didn't just say *Albert Tuck*, it said *Father: Louis Tuck*. I looked up. Louis was smiling a grin so big I thought his cheeks might bleed.

"Annie never told you, did she? Guess she didn't like to kiss and tell," he said with a smirk.

With all of the willpower I could muster, I icily asked Tuck how much he wanted to keep his mouth shut and get lost, this time forever. The sleaze promised he'd keep mum for ten thousand dollars, and as a final insult he demanded I deliver the cash to him that evening in my empty Presidential Suite at the Hartford Hotel. I knew I could take the money from the stash at my mother's house and wire it back in a couple of weeks, so I agreed. What else could I do?

"As long as you have the room, maybe we'll have a go at it for old time's sake," he suggested.

I shoved him violently out the door just in time for him to pass Annie, Mama, Papa, and Bert coming down the hall to wish me luck on my performance. Tuck didn't even look at them. He was probably daydreaming about how he'd blow my money. I asked Papa to take Bert to his seat and pulled Mama and Annie into my dressing room and closed the door.

Bert, age eight, 1913.

"What did he want?" whispered Annie, white as a ghost.

Annie began to shake and I fought back my own tears.

"All these years," I managed to choke out, "I thought it was some boy from school! But it was my husband? I know that scum is handsome, but still, how could you? You're my sister!" I cried.

Mama looked confused until Annie nodded her head, shamefully. They both went to the sofa and sat down. Mama was stiff and angry, and Annie was slumped over the arm, sobbing into her sleeve.

"I had no choice," she whispered in a strangled, hiccupping voice. "That night I was alone with Louis—when you gave me that fancy leftover steak—he—he forced me. After you were gone—he took the steak knife out of the drawer, put it to my throat and raped me."

The power of Annie's revelation nearly knocked me to my knees.

"That fucking bastard!" I exploded. Mama was so red I thought she might burst. I'd never seen her so angry.

"No matter who the father was, I won't go on lying!" sobbed Annie. "For eight years I've had to listen to everyone say what a horrible wife and mother you were, abandoning your family. And all for what? Because I was so stupid. I should never have stayed alone with Tuck in the first place! I'm sorry, Soph, I'm so sorry."

I ran over to Annie and swooped her up into a big hug.

"Go ahead, kid," I said. "Cry for the last time and then forget it. There's nothing for you to be sorry about. It wasn't your fault. Listen, I'm going to fix this. The day you were born, Mama told me you were the only baby sister I would ever have and it was my job to take care of you. That's what I did, and that's what I'm always gonna do. Someday you're going to find your Prince Charming and get married and live happily ever after. This secret will never leave this room. It'll go to our graves, okay?"

"But what about Tuck?" she sputtered.

"Him?" I laughed. "As long as they keep printing two dollar bills, I can keep him quiet. Now go find Papa and the kid and get ready for my act."

Annie gave me one last hug and left me with my mother.

Annie Abuza.

Mama got up slowly from the couch, smoothed out her dress, and cleaned off her little round spectacles. She walked toward the door and, just before she left, turned around and stared directly into my eyes.

"Break more than a leg, Sonya. Do you understand me?" she said coldly, and left.

Sophie and her mother

I barely remember doing the show that night, and soon I found myself backstage with Molly, once again getting out of my costume and wiping off my makeup. My pal hadn't noticed how preoccupied I was because her hot tip on the horse had paid off big and T-bone was on the way to deliver her winnings. I *futzed*[5] around, packing up whatever I would need for one more night at my parent's house, until T-bone arrived.

"Well if it isn't my favorite star and her lucky assistant," crowed Tommy as he walked into the dressing room and gave Molly a wad of cash. She giggled with delight and gave us both a big hug.

"Let's go to Charlie's! I'm buying," Molly offered.

"You go ahead. I want to catch up with my old friend for a few minutes," I smiled. As soon as I heard Molly's footsteps skip joyfully to the end of the hall, I closed the door. T-bone and I caught up with all the local gossip for a bit, until finally I had the guts to bring up what was really on my mind.

"Hey, Tommy. Remember that old favor you owe me?"

"Name it," he said, his eyes narrowing to icy little slits.

Like I said, the most important pots I ever scrubbed were the ones I cleaned when I got home from the theater that night. I was so on edge I filled the sink with suds and washed every plate, bowl, and serving platter I could find. Still uneasy, I took Mama's delicate good china down from the sideboard and washed that too. By the time I'd dried and replaced the last saucer, I knew T-bone had completed the favor I'd asked. I doubt he had nearly as much trouble sleeping that night, or any other, as I still do to this day. That's why I find myself washing plates almost every night since, wondering where T-bone dumped the body of Louis Tuck and whether it would ever come back to haunt me.

Maybe I'll stop worrying about it some of these days. Until then, pass the dish soap.

5 *Futzed* – Dawdled, wasted time.

Jennie, Sophie, and Annie Abuza

Authors' Note

"**W**ould you like to hear some dirty, filthy stories? I have some nasty, nasty ones," Bette Midler asked the crowd during a show at Ithaca College, back in 1973. "These jokes are from the files of the late and great Miss Sophie Tucker. She's dead, but not forgotten."

That was our first date. Over forty years later, we've seen dozens of the Divine Miss M.'s shows and heard as many bawdy jokes. We decided to find out about the woman who inspired such a showbiz legend, so in 2006 we tracked down a copy of Sophie's autobiography on eBay and read it cover to cover. Still curious, we sought out two more obscure biographies printed decades ago. One of these books mentioned that the New York Public Library housed a collection of Sophie's scrapbooks and listed all of the other far flung archives with Tucker memorabilia.

Using that list as our guide, over the last eight years we have managed to read more than four hundred of Sophie's scrapbooks, visit fourteen archives, and look at more than ten thousand pictures. We interviewed scores of Sophie's family members and friends, historians, and stars influenced by her singular talent. We've traveled to sixteen states, Canada, England, Scotland, Ireland and France in pursuit of Sophie.

In the process of becoming the world's foremost Sophie experts--and fans!--we discovered that Sophie was friends with everybody who was anybody during the first half of the twentieth century. She counted presidents, royalty, gangsters, and stars of stage, screen, and radio among her pals. Her scrapbooks contained Christmas cards from Elvis, thank you notes from a teenage Barbara Walters, and letters from Tony Bennett, Jerry Lewis, Carol Channing, and thousands more. We lovingly refer to her as the Forrest Gump of Show Business, for the depth and breadth of her influence from 1886-1966.

It became our mission to remind the world about Sophie Tucker. We began with a documentary film, then wrote this, our first fictional memoir, and are in the process of expanding her story into a Broadway musical, a movie musical, and a television show. The magic of Sophie's life is that there's plenty of eye-popping material than can be believed.

This book would not have been possible without the help of our late, great mentor, Phil Ramone. Without his advice and council, Sophie's legend might still be languishing in dusty archives around the world.

We also want to thank our editor, Kathy Cacace. If Tucker had Kathy, they would've already made an Oscar-winning movie out of Sophie's life.

Our assistant editors Elena Radutzky, Tad Asaro, Joe Yakacki, Mary Myers, Jim Stettler, Lydia Ecker and Dahlia Paloma have been equally integral to our vision. We couldn't have done it without them.

Last but not least, our graphic designers, Garik Barseghyan and Ari Ecker, who made all that you are now reading look like a million bucks, and Diego Lopez, who made all the black and white photos into gorgeous living color. You are all real artists of the highest order.

All the best,
Sue and Lloyd Ecker

About the Authors

In 1973, Ithaca College students Susan Denner and Lloyd Ecker went on their first date to see an up-and-coming new singer named Bette Midler. Over the course of the evening, the couple fell in love with the Divine Miss M., her Sophie Tucker jokes, and each other.

Over the last forty years, the Eckers got married and had three children, and developed Babytobee.com. The sale of that business in 2006 allowed Sue and Lloyd to pursue their passion for bringing Sophie Tucker's life to the page, stage, and screen.

With this book, the first in a trilogy about Sophie's life, and a documentary already under their belts, the Eckers now intend to take Sophie's story to Broadway with a musical, to Hollywood with a film version of that musical, and to the small screen in a long running television drama based on her unbelievable sixty-year showbiz career. Stay tuned to sophietucker.com for these—and other!—exciting developments.

If you're interested in the sights and sounds of Sophie Tucker's life, the enhanced online version of this book includes more than sixty audio and video recordings of performances by the stars mentioned throughout the story. To view them, visit www.sophietucker.com and click on Book Extras.

If you have any Sophie Tucker stories you would like to share, we would love to hear from you. Please write us at sueandlloyd@sophietucker.com.

To keep up with the latest news, sign up for our newsletter at www.sophietucker.com. You can also follow Sophie on Twitter by following @sophietucker. Sophie even has Tumblr account, http://sophietucker. tumblr.com/. It's updated daily with highlights from her hundreds of scrapbooks and memorabilia.

Susan and Lloyd Ecker are available for speaking engagements. For more information and inquiries, please contact us at sueandlloyd@sophietucker.com.